TIME AND MOTION

MATT HAYES

This book is a work of fiction. Any resemblance to actual events or persons, living or dead, is entirely coincidental.

"Time and Motion," by Matt Hayes. ISBN 978-1-60264-550-9.

Published 2010 by Virtualbookworm.com Publishing Inc., P.O. Box 9949, College Station, TX 77842, US. ©2010, Matt Hayes. All rights reserved. No part of this publication may be reproduced, stored in a retrieval system, or transmitted in any form or by any means, electronic, mechanical, recording or otherwise, without the prior written permission of Matt Hayes.

Published in the United States of America.

Acknowledgements

I would like to thank Janice Hayes, Edna Galer and Mark Evans
for critical reading of the preliminary manuscript;
Nicholas Linsdell my sense guru and Matt Smith for style guruing.
Special thanks as ever to Roger.

Cover: Matt 'Shimuzu' Smith from an original drawing by
the author of the remarkable futurist masterpiece
Unique Forms of Continuity in Space, Umberto Boccioni 1913 (cast 1972).

PART ONE
THE LUMPEN

ONE

'Take time to smell the roses.' The thought flashed across Michael's mind, dragging behind it the urge to break into song. For a moment he even felt tempted to sing, why not? Surely there was time for one last song? Surely no-one would mind? Unfortunately there were no words for how he felt today. Perhaps people in this state of mind never wrote songs. Perhaps people in this state of mind were too tired to search within and drag the lyrics out. Perhaps they just could not be bothered. The sun broke free through the leaden clouds but Michael felt no warmth on his face; perhaps the sun was simply peering through a region of thin cloud. He could not bring himself to look.

The light was flat, slightly surreal; he liked that. It was strange how light played tricks with reality, filling its colours with lustful attraction then fading the most beautiful of scenes into dour greys. Perhaps his life was the same, in a way. He was sure there must have been highlights; bright moments of joy and happiness, full surround sound Technicolor amongst the fog. For some reason he couldn't think of any now.

This was the problem. It had been the problem for so long. He couldn't really see why he hadn't realized it before. He had no past, or at least his past had ceased to exist for him; when he tried to summon it up, all that appeared was swirling nebulous nothingness.

For a moment a shaft of light did pass across the street. The beam illuminated a single yellow rose, beautiful and Redouté perfect but lit from within in a way that only living things are. Michael stopped, looked around to make sure he was alone and bent down to smell it. The day was cold and the poor blossom sat upon a nearly naked stalk, but he could still detect the heady scent. Dew dappled his nose and he wiped it away.

There, he had done it, smelt his rose and given reality a chance. He reached into the deep pockets of his jacket and withdrew a collection of pills. Popping them into his mouth like sweets, he swallowed them down with a draught from his hip flask. The flask felt good in his hand; it was silver in a leather pouch, hallmarked and engraved. The liquor warmed his throat and stomach. Strange how cold he felt, or was it numb? Perhaps the pills were beginning to work or perhaps he had always felt numb; he couldn't quite remember if he had ever felt any different. How had he allowed himself to become so very cold?

At last he reached the bleak waterfront. The mudflats were dark and, today, strangely beckoning. Michael's eyes followed the line of the bay, the steel of the sky, reflected like a blade in the distant water of the river. His artist's eye converted line to fluid movement across a page. The brush stroke dragged itself into virtual existence in his mind; the dilute paint coruscated through the fibres of the paper, chromatographic separation of dyes producing a muddy spectrum that no artist could create alone. He allowed himself a moment's satisfaction, but what was the point. It had taken him a lifetime to gain the skills to draw a few lines, to capture a few facets of the madness of reality, and this was simply not good enough. 'Prolific': how he hated that word with its loaded implication of superhuman effort and boundless enthusiasm. Who were these remarkable prolifics and where did their inspiration come from? He had worked, hadn't he, day after day, struggling with the everyday distractions thrown up by a life, a job, a girlfriend? Yes, a girlfriend. He had to stop, take a swig of whiskey, had to think. What would she do? How would she cope? He knew she would. She always did. She was a prolific, the superhuman effort required to deal with the suicide of your boyfriend of how many years: ten, twelve, fifteen? It would all add to her bottomless pit of inspiration, her boundless expanse of self knowledge and development.

It would make her stronger, more rounded, more balanced and understanding and bloody perfect.

He had loved her. Of course he had. Everyone loved her. She was magnificent, magnetic, drew men and women to her. Not a great beauty in a classical sense, but her inner beauty shone through. She was like a beacon, a light; why was living for her not enough? The thought hit him hard; it was the first time it had occurred to him. Perhaps that could be enough. He couldn't be her slave, live for her whim, it wasn't his way. He liked to be strong, physically and mentally. Was it a crime to want to retain a vestige of masculinity in this world? He felt fortified by the thought, but then withdrew from it. He was strong, wasn't he? And yet he was walking towards his death. He would take his own life; was that the action of a man with a strong mind? He knew the answer was yes. He knew this was the hardest thing he had ever done. That was why he needed the pills and the booze. True, they were the poisons that would perform the magic, transform the animate to the inanimate, and allow his spirit to breathe out and away from his body. They were so much more than that, though. He needed them to give him the strength to do this one last thing. He could not do this alone.

TWO

Edward Spinks sat opposite his boss. The man was enormous, a hideous comical sweating caricature of everything that modern bosses are. It wasn't that he hated the man. It was difficult not to like him. There was just something, an annoying, niggling creeping malaise that tapped on the back of Edward's mind and reminded him to be wary, wary, distant and prepared.

'I think you might find this interesting.' Edward's boss withdrew a folder from his top drawer and passed it across the table.

'It's in French. Will that be a problem for you?' There was no sneer attached to the comment, no self-aggrandisement, just a fairly cheerful question asked in an inoffensive manner. For a fleeting second images of slaughter passed across Edward's mind.

'No, that's fine,' he said, not meaning it. Tonight he'd have to spend his precious few hours of freedom with his old French dictionary and this doubtlessly dull as dishwater document. 'Thank you, Bill. I'll get on with things straight away.' He got up to leave, attempting to make light conversation as he left the office: a throwaway line, something about the weekend, something about the family. He couldn't remember what. There was no need; by the time he had opened the door and turned back to the room, Bill was totally immersed in another document.

Edward closed the door gently and walked back to his desk. How did he do it? This man, this annoying self publicist, was his boss. How had he allowed this state of affairs to arise? Everything seemed suddenly so unfair. There he was, thirty years in the business, someone who had worked up through the company, part-time Saturday boy, holidays from university, his first job, his last job. He had done most jobs in the building. Yet still the very top jobs eluded him. It wasn't fair. It wasn't right.

How did a man like his boss become so successful, like some bizarre solvent assimilating everything: languages, technologies, skills, political allies? There was no question that the man worked. He worked hard, produced reams of work, not all good, but quantity had a quality all of its own. He seemed to be at every meeting, every conference, gliding from office to shop floor on silent wings: a vulture, picking over the carcass of one project and flying off to the next before the hyenas had even smelt the fresh blood.

He had watched Bill carefully for months; desperate to find out what that special ingredient was, that special something that he himself lacked. At first he had called it privilege, later arrogance; the realization that it could just be old-fashioned talent made him feel physically ill. Surely this wasn't his missing element? He was talented, wasn't he? At school Edward had been called a protégé, a renaissance man, an ideal pupil, but that was the past, that was simply not good enough anymore.

The door to the office opened and Bill put his head round. 'I've reformatted what you gave me, and made a few changes. I've called the manufacturers and they'll be ready for process in two to three weeks. I've had a few ideas about where we could go next. I've sent them to your email. Perhaps you could get back to me when you've had a look.' Bill smiled, withdrew into his office and closed the door.

Edward's teeth ground together for the second time that day. Perhaps he was just getting old. Perhaps people like Bill Morris were the future. He opened his email and waited for what seemed an interminably long 'moment' whilst the email uploaded to his desktop. True enough, there was the documentation, six pages of dense technical script. He recognized his own work amongst that of his boss. Surely this wasn't possible. The bastard must have prepared so much of this before. He must have no life, just a vacuous

11

existence filled with work and thoughts of work. From his boss' office came Bill's raised voice. He was shouting amicably to a supplier, in perfect Italian.

THREE

Michael stood alone now on the shoreline. The wind was rising, hurrying the water towards him in a quiver of silver ripples, sending him that fraction of a second closer to his death. It wasn't that he had been bullied as a child. His parents had only the most reasonable expectations of him: a steady job, enough conformity, a smattering of pleasures. They had not expected him to become a great artist; in fact they were not too happy about art at all, they were 'realists'. For several years he had wondered if the so called 'realists' were an artistic movement he had somehow missed in his studies. In a way it was true. The realists were a group that just never got round to producing any art, because, after all, what was the point and shouldn't you get a proper job? Their lack of ambition had not entirely stifled his creativity, but it had made him realise that truly talented people were rare: one in a million. He was unlikely to be that one. Still, he had a job. It might be in advertising, he might not be totally happy with the copy, the endless rounds of vacuous discussions on the merits of lowest common denominator game show styling, but at least it paid and he could draw his landscapes in his own time.

Perhaps it was the landscapes that had depressed him. The wide open spaces that he had found he needed to explore, the big skies, uncluttered with buildings, with people, with her. Such places could get you down. The enormous skies could be oppressive under scudding clouds. The weight of those skies could crush a man.

No, that wasn't it. It was her. There was something about her, something that had made him feel less than a man.

13

He stepped into the soft, dark, cold mud.

It wasn't the sex, so often the downfall of the weaker-willed male. They had enjoyed that time together. No funny games, no dressing up. Just simple, passionate, intensity when the heat of their desire had worked them into the blinding white animal frenzy that was the only thing to quell that ancient ache. It wasn't good all the time, of course, how could it be? Maybe there had been other men. It didn't matter, he could deal with that. He knew how driven she was, how great her needs. He could share that, spread the labour of love. Besides, in this particular field he had been quite prolific himself. Perhaps there were no other men.

The water, seeping into his boots, percolating through his socks revived him to his senses.

Michael reached into his pocket and withdrew another handful of pills. The heat of the whisky and the cold of the river water formed a gradient across his body. He only had so much whisky; the cold edged higher as he stepped in further and sank in deeper.

FOUR

Bill Morris closed his eyes and lay back in his less-than-imposing executive's chair. He thought for a moment what a shame it was that equality in the work place meant he could not now cuddle up into an enormous bat-winged, leather fauteuil and have a comfortable forty winks. It was a sad day when the chief executive of a firm not only had to be seen to work, unable to hide behind an enormous desk, but actually had to do most of the work. In fact, these days, he felt like he did nearly everything. Perhaps he was a useless employer: a distasteful thought, but a possibility none the less. Maybe he had no interviewing skills. These people always looked alright on paper; they just never seemed to do anything when they actually arrived. They were always there, typing, tippety-tap, but where was the work? Where were the ideas?

Motivation, the problem had to be motivation. His mind drifted to his childhood. How had he been motivated as a kid? Long summers spent in the canning factory sitting on the production line turning over the tins that had fallen out of the machine the wrong way up. What had motivated him to do that? Need for money, he supposed, but it had given him the drive to do something better, more worthwhile, to prove to the world that he would make it at whatever cost. You could put up with any demoralizing job if it was just a stepping stone, one of many, to your final goal: world domination or perhaps just a comfortable seat on a fairly successful company. He thought of his mother: warm, kind, thoughtful, incredibly intelligent, and dead at thirty. He curled up, foetal, drawing his legs up to his chest and hugged himself. His mother had been taken away in a

15

moment; a car crash, a fool on a giant 1980s mobile phone. He shook himself awake. He must have fallen asleep because numerous messages were flashing on his PC.

He stretched his arms, curled his hands into fists and yawned deeply, breathing out the maudlin thoughts like tobacco smoke. No, he was definitely working too hard. Perhaps he needed to rethink his company strategies. He'd get in a consultant, why not? One of these time-and-motion people, find out where the slack was. He didn't want to sack anyone, but he had to know. Perhaps just pointing out to the offenders where the problems lay would be enough. It could be a positive exercise. Wouldn't he want to know if he wasn't pulling his weight? Maybe not, but it could inspire you to greater effort. A few people might resign. That was as maybe; there were other jobs for them to go to, no one would starve. He could employ others, try and get things right this time, send himself on a 'How to spot a spot-on employee' course or something. He was open to self-criticism. That meant he was a good boss, didn't it? He opened a few files, tinkered with the contents, wrote a letter to his doctor asking for another appointment to have his blood pressure checked out (he didn't like his secretary knowing about the state of his health), played a quick game of chess with his father who had momentarily logged on in Florida, and then, having agreed to a draw, checked his email. There was nothing from Edward Spinks.

That man was so slow. It was intolerable. His work was always of the highest quality, there was no doubt about that, but he needed to know things now, not tomorrow.

Spinks had better watch out. He might be for the chop. An idea dawned, yes: Edward could manage the time-and-motion study. He'd get him to deal with the consultants. That alone might smarten him up; give him the kick that he seemed to require. It would also give him a fair chance; he liked Edward, he was alright. He'd see to it immediately.

FIVE

Mary pulled her pink and green woollen hat tight over her ears, tucked her coat into the gap between her legs and the seat of the chair, checked her mittens were on properly and manoeuvred the electric chair down the wooden ramp and on to the street. She waved to her smiling yet suitably concerned looking husband who peered over the top of a pile of washing-up from the kitchen window. It was a bit nippy and sitting in the chair did not give you the same opportunities to get warm afforded by a bit of vigorous walking. She would have loved to be walking today. The Surrey countryside always afforded a good walk, even if the day was overcast, there would always be something: the steam off a dog, fungi piled up like a futuristic city in the hollow of a damp log, a flock of long-tailed tits excitedly ransacking a hedgerow. The chair of course only gave her a taste of the freedom she had taken for granted when she was younger, and suburban life with its parades of handy shops with graffiti-strewn walls didn't fill her with the same joys as the little villages she had imagined herself retiring to. Unfortunately the countryside didn't have the easy access buses, the post offices or the hospitals which, alas, she had occasionally to take advantage of.

Today she could not allow herself to dwell on what might have been. Today she had to think of others: more specifically, of poor Lilly. Lilly Anterton was on her last legs. She had been poorly a long time, too long. Mary's thoughts drifted to Lilly in her prime, a remarkable woman if ever there was one, a dancer, a linguist, a party girl in a time when there were remarkable parties to be had. Mary never knew exactly what it was that Lilly had done in the fifties.

17

It was something to do with the secret service, something she couldn't speak about. Mary had tried to find out; she had wanted to know so badly. How many times had they been drunk together? How many times had Mary secretly given Lilly the extra few shots of vodka, in the vain hope that she might spill the beans, share her secret life, which Mary imagined to be like some girl's annual adventure? She never told. It did not seem to matter how falling-down drunk they got together, how giggly and wobbly they became, how close and intimate they were, conspiring together on the night bus.

In a way Mary had been envious of that part of Lilly's life. Her own life had been eventful, running a busy pharmacy with all that it demanded, and dealing with the public was never dull; annoying, frustrating, infuriating, sometimes pleasant, never dull. Dealing with doctors and periodically scoring a point or two off the more arrogant ones was always a pleasure and probably made the job bearable, if not exciting. The excitement was the rub. Lilly's job smelt of excitement, even though she brushed such things off with a laugh. She always maintained that the vast bulk of her work was 'dish water dull', but she said it with a spark in her eye that left Mary aching to know more.

Lilly herself was never dull; boredom was anathema to her. Anyone who ever said they were bored wasn't worth knowing, there was no such thing as a bored person, only a boring person. Was that harsh? Mary wasn't sure. She considered herself somewhat boring, but Lilly had apparently not thought so. They had stayed friends for fifty years. Perhaps Mary was the stability in Lilly's life, a regular friend on whom she could rely in the maelstrom of her life, the jobs, the men, the inevitable lows after the highs. Not that there had been so many lows. Lilly's life seemed to be punctuated more with short periods of disappointment with the world. The world was full of minor irritations, predominantly because the rest of it seemed to have trouble keeping up with her.

18

Mary stopped at a road junction; looked left up the road, but found her view blocked by the local 'community mobility bus' parked up outside the driver's home. The irony of the moment slipped her by as she tried to navigate the less than perfect ramps off the pavement and edged her way across the junction. The wheelchair was a gift, a wonderful liberator and she did not know how she would have coped without it. She would have pined to death for want of fresh air. The only annoyance was that it was rather slow and every now and then you wanted a turn of speed. Mary's hearing wasn't what it was and she relied rather heavily on her less than perfect eyesight.

A car careered over the slight brow of the hill. If she was doing thirty, the driver could have braked gently and, smiling, ushered Mary cross the road in her own time. As it was the driver was somewhat harried by small children in the back, was doing forty-five, was late for a yoga class and wasn't expecting an elderly lady to be in the middle of the road. The four-by-four swerved like a drunken hippo narrowly avoiding Mary's outstretched legs. It climbed the pavement opposite, lurched back into the road a hundred yards further down and drove off at speed.

A full two minutes later the car stopped. The children were silent, little hands clutching the warm leatherette. Their mother sank over the steering wheel, deflating as if punctured. The preceding moments flashed through her head in fearful clarity. She had let out an involuntary gasp when she had first seen the wheelchair in the road, now it echoed around her head, each strangled syllable dilated into a roar. The clawing of her hands on the steering-wheel, the knuckles white against her pink, slender hands, tendons working, kneading and flexing, like shark's teeth set in their pink maw. A moment, a second, a blink of an eye had separated her from the worst day of her life. She hadn't braked; the ABS hadn't had a chance to work its voodoo. She had swerved blindly and wildly as the blood had drained from her heavy limbs to the pit of her stomach. Anything could have happened in those few seconds. What if a cyclist had been coming the other way, another car, a school bus? A wave of nausea passed over her, and her hands began to sweat and shake. She looked back at the children reflected in the rear-view mirror. Big, round, nervous eyes stared back at her. She got out of the car, pulled the children off the back seat and, shakily started walking them home. The big, black four-by-four remained, forlornly, jauntily parked, unlocked and abandoned on the pavement.

Mary steered the wheelchair into the grounds of the retirement home. Its little motors hummed with the exertion of climbing the hill leading to the entrance. She avoided the main door, whizzing to the left and momentarily going 'off road' across a flowerbed covered with ornamental bark. She felt a frisson of excitement as the chair bumped over the rough terrain and wheeled her round to a small clump of trees that were just outside Lilly's window. There was always a danger that the chair could get bogged down and she would need to be rescued. It was alright if a member of the public came to her aid, she could deal with that. The problem was if one of the staff found her first; the thought sent a cold shiver down her spine. Mary reached under her seat and withdrew an assortment of cakes made of wild bird seed and fat. Reaching up into the low boughs she distributed them and removed a few of the spent remains from her previous visits. The owner of the home had asked her not to keep 'hanging those things about for the rats and the squirrels'; apparently 'them birds make a mess and someone got to clean it up.' Mary had told the woman what she thought about that in no uncertain terms and it was remarkable how good the woman's memory seemed to be. Mary had hoped that Lilly hadn't suffered the woman's wrath in her stead. She had visited twice the next week just to be sure. It appeared no serious harm had been done.

Her work complete, Mary performed a neat pirouette with the wheelchair and trundled back to the front of the building and the dreaded reception. God knew she tried to be nice to the staff, and some of the new ones would smile back, nice as you liked. There were, however, a few sour-faced ones it was best to avoid. Occasionally she would see the owner glowering at her as if to say 'I'll get you yet, just wait until your batteries run out on your chair and your husband dies. You won't get away then'. It was not a future possibility Mary cared to think about.

Today everyone was smiles and she motored along the wide corridors to Lilly's little room. She never organized a particular time; the home had its timetables and regulations, enough regimentation for Lilly's poor trapped mind. Besides, it didn't do to be too regular, just in case she was delayed or indeed run over by some silly woman in a tank like she nearly was today; she didn't want Lilly to worry.

SIX

Michael swallowed another handful of pills. They were really beginning to take effect now. His eyelids were heavy and he could not feel his legs, in fact he could not feel very much at all. He was close now to the water and for a second it was illuminated by a shaft of sunlight. It glistened and sparkled, reflections danced and played. Michael watched all this as if in a dream. The light pierced him as if illuminating the very inside of his mind and for a moment he felt drawn to it. He tried to reach out to it, to walk towards it, but the mud slurped and sucked around him. It was so beautiful, the dancing lights. He wanted to cry. Perhaps he was crying. A cloud passed in front of the sun and the lights were gone. A chill gust of wind reached him from across the water; the sheer bitterness of it revived him and he looked at the stinking grey mud that stretched all around. Behind, a trail of waterlogged footprints was already being claimed by the perfidious river. He was sinking deeper now, up to his thighs; who knew what lay beneath the surface? He could be dragged down by nymphs and eaten alive by creatures unknown to science. He was suddenly seized by panic and tried to pull himself from the mud, to turn round, to get back to shore. In his frenzy he lost his shoes, his socks, his hip flask. The water began to pool round his legs, cold, clammy. His skin recoiled from it, but there was nowhere to go. He made two steps and his strength failed him. No, no, he mustn't fight it. He hadn't come here to fight. He'd come here to die. He sank down, down, into the mud, falling into it as he had fallen into her bed, giving himself to her completely.

The water woke him from his reverie. Cold and perfunctory, it swept past him, each little wave pushing it toward the shore. The sun was now low in the sky, sleeping behind billowing clouds, all colours curdled to a strange, purple hue. In the distance Michael could make out the Lowry silhouettes of a pair of herons on the waterline. His eyes dimmed and their image faded to grey. His head splashed back into the water, cold on cold. The first wave passed over his face. He shook it away, pulling fresh salty air into his body; it was just like being born, just like the first breath. The second wave flooded his ears and nose. He gasped and twisted; his every fibre yearned to turn away, to escape. The water came over his head. He was rocked by a wave, then another, perhaps wash from a large ship coming up to the docks. He swallowed a mouthful of gritty brine, then another, gulping it down, inviting death into him. His body rebelled, retching, and coughing, only to draw down more water as he choked and gasped. Somewhere there was a screaming voice, a wailing, but it was far off, distant, another country, a world away. Her face appeared before his mind's eye again, smiling. It had been at a party, a gallery evening, nice wine, she had looked particularly gorgeous. He breathed out his last gasp of air, a bubble that floated up and away, taking her face with it, leaving him completely and suddenly alone. He was cradled now by the water, cold in cold, rocking to sleep, falling, falling, falling.

SEVEN

'One hundred and twenty six. One hundred and twenty seven. One hundred and twenty eight.' Mary stopped outside the door to Lilly's room. Bizarre, how she always counted, always had to be sure, never wanting to walk into someone else's loneliness; to see a face, looking up from a bed, to see the eyes seeking company, to see the dread realization that you weren't the hoped-for son/daughter/niece. No, there were people of course who could give their love to strangers, remarkable people who would visit the lonely, those without family, with no-one of their own. Such people were marvellous, warm, and different to the rest of us. They oppressed some deep part of our psyche which demanded that we expend the bulk of our affections on our own kith and kin.

Mary was not one of those people. It upset her to think so; perhaps, if there was no-one for her to care for, she might be able to transfer that affection, harness her surplus of empathy. She knocked on the door.

There was silence. She knocked again and heard a faint voice from within. Gently opening the door she entered Lilly's room, the air was thick with Lilly of the Valley. They had joked that if Lilly had been Welsh, it would have been named after her. The perfume made Mary somewhat light-headed; perhaps it was the airlessness of the room, perhaps it was the flood of memories that that scent always evoked.

Lilly lay on the bed, thin as a bird, china-white features visibly hanging on her bones. Her hair was still quite thick, grey now, and arrayed around her head on the pillow. Someone had brushed it into a broad halo, it was a kind thing to do, but Mary felt it looked as if Lilly was being prepared for the grave.

The motors of the wheelchair seemed too loud in that place, inappropriate somehow for the gravitas of the situation. Mary tried to shrug off the thought. It was not a mortuary, it was not a church. She was just visiting her friend.

'Hello dear, how are you?' It took a moment for Lilly to recognize her lifelong pal. These days the residue of sleep seemed to take longer and longer to dissipate; perhaps it was preparation for the day when it wouldn't clear at all.

Lilly's face arranged itself into a broad smile.

'Mary, dear, it's so kind of you to come. How are you? How is Peter? And look, you have fed the birds. That is so sweet of you. I had a goldfinch outside my window for an hour yesterday. I've never seen one so fat, and a chaffinch, its colours, purples and greys; it looked like it had been made that very day, from the sky. The colours were so perfect.' Lilly smiled again. 'I'm rambling dear! Too much tea, not enough wine. Could you possibly bring me a bottle of wine next time you come? I'm desperate for something nice. I couldn't open it myself; you'd have to do it. I suppose we'd then have to drink all of it! Could you get yourself home after half a bottle of wine, do you suppose?' Lilly laughed and coughed and laughed again. 'Why must they give us wretched pills which do not let one drink, it is impossible. Do they think you don't want a drink when you are ill? God damn it, you need a drink when you're ill, more than ever!' She dissolved into laughs and coughs. 'Pass me a glass of water would you dear, I'll have to imagine it's Chateau Lafitte, not that I can taste bugger-all with these tablets.' Her exertions had exhausted her and she fell back into the pillow.

Mary fetched a glass of water, her motors whirring; feeling like some sort of robot.

When she returned to the bed Lilly was smiling but sad.

'Mary, you've never been to Paris have you? You must get Peter to take you, whilst you still can. I still dream about Paris you know. I wish I could be stuffed and mounted and hung on the wall in some seedy Parisian bar, just so I could smell the smoke and watch the sordid goings on! I'm sure it's still wonderful, and the Louvre dear, the Louvre, sod the paintings, sod the Mona Lisa, sod the tourists, just throw them out onto the streets, look at the building dear, you just have to see the building.' The coughing had returned and she had to rest again. Mary loved to see the passion, the number of times the staff had warned her not to excite Lilly so, to get her too worked up. It was always the same, the passion was always there, she rarely had to say anything; it just boiled out as soon as there was someone there to see it.

A blue tit preened itself on a twig outside the window; fluffing itself up into a yellow ball of down as it was ruffled by the wind. Its little blue head explored outstretched wings, left side, right side then rotating impossibly far back to peck at its back. Waves of ruffling ran from its head to its tail before it started all over again. Another bird flew close by, sparking it into flight; they flitted acrobatically from branch to twig, twirling round the tree in frantic arcs.

'They have such busy lives, so quick, their little hearts; how fast they must beat, how incredibly fast? Do you know Mary; I've lain here, on this bed, for nearly three years. That is longer than most of those little birds live. If they saw me they would think I was a monument, some unchanging thing, like the Louvre. They must think I'm impossibly old!'

Mary spoke for the first time. 'I feel impossibly old, dear!'

'But we aren't, are we? Can you imagine if we lived our lives like those birds, frantic, day after day, what could we achieve? Anything, everything, we'd live a life in one day.'

Mary thought for a moment before answering. She was the fulcrum, it was always like this, the conversations could fall one way or the other, and somehow, ultimately it always fell to her to navigate their course.

'Surely we would burn out, dear, twice as bright, half as long. We would be the same as the little birds, the little mice in the fields. I'd rather be an elephant, but Peter would rather I was a gazelle!' They held each other's hands and laughed and talked until the tea came round. Mary loved tea. It was an elixir to her, subtle yet powerful, but there was something about those strange institutional cups that could only make you think of the hundreds of mouths that had drunk from them before. For this reason, she always bought a flask. She told the staff (and Lilly) that she was lactose intolerant and had to have her special brew. It was a lie and she hated saying it every single time (and they always asked), but there was no polite alternative.

They talked some more until Mary glanced at the clock. It was remarkable where the time went, around Lilly it flew. It would be dark in half an hour and she really had to go. She left an audio book. It was strange how Lilly's vision was so good for distance but was useless for reading; she'd never understood how eyes really worked, even after the theory and the pharmacy. People's eyes just did not behave like they did in the books; it was almost as if they gave up in their own spiteful ways, to be as annoying as possible for their poor owners. Lilly for example could see freedom beyond her institutional prison, but couldn't escape into a good novel. She made her goodbyes and promised to return soon, somehow managed to navigate the inwardly opening door and escaped into the corridor. She waved her goodbyes to Lilly, who could only smile back.

Mary went as fast as she could past the door to the owner's office. She saw the woman's severe hair above the frosted glass, but, although it stiffened somewhat as she whizzed past, the dragon was insufficiently roused to appear. 'She is ignoring me,' thought Mary, relieved.

In a moment she was back into the street. It was cold and she pulled her hat down, pulled her mittens up and tucked her coat behind her legs. She would have to get back fairly pronto or Peter would be worried. She might have to get a light for her bobble hat. Maybe with one of those on her head there would be less chance of being killed by a truck.

EIGHT

It was unlike Michael not to call. He was a lot of things: frustrating, clumsy, forgetful, infuriating, sexy, but never thoughtless. Tonight was a big night (wasn't every night at the moment); there were charities to organize, dignitaries to coax, egos to pamper, even a few junior ministers to chat up. Launches of galleries were complex events and if things went pear-shaped (as they so easily could) that would mean saying goodbye to a lot of good publicity. Michael always said that no-one noticed the behind-the-scenes people anyway, and that every wine and cheese hobnobbing dinner was like every other (pretty pointless), but Suzi Rothermann knew better than that. The media were the lubrication of society; greasing the right wheels made things run the way you wanted them to. Michael would have dismissed this as self-delusional aggrandizement of a morally indefensible and corrupt system (he was full of such phrases). Suzi preferred to think of it as the personification of business, its smile, its heart and soul. Whatever it was, it entailed a lot of busy, busy people and a lot of face to face time with individuals who were often significantly less bright than her, yet who wielded rather more tangible power. The concept of power was something that Suzi had spent a great deal of time thinking about of late. Power itself had to be harnessed and directed, when she knew what she wanted to do with the power she would inevitably acquire, then and only then would she take it. At this stage in her career she was more interested in perfecting the necessary requisitioning skills. There were enormous reserves of power in the room at the moment, and very few people there had any idea what to do with it.

Collectively they could achieve great things. She would organise that collective; but not today. Today she would smile at people, make encouraging remarks and pretend to introduce them to their peers for their own benefit.

One of her many mobile phones started to vibrate in her bag. It had got to a stage now where she had had to buy phones with different frequencies of vibration. This was a slow, slightly annoying and throbbing kind of vibration. It was Michael's private line.

'Michael, where in God's name have you been? I've been trying to call you all day, you knew tonight was...'

'Suzi, darling; it's Margaret here.' Michael's mother's voice was measured, calm, but barely in control. She was holding herself together with sheer force of will, a will that could buckle at any moment. 'Please don't be alarmed. You need to come home straight away, something has happened, or at least... I've found a note... Please, dear, just come home immediately.' There was something in her voice that made Suzi's blood run cold. 'A note?' What could she mean?

'Margaret, please put Michael on the line. I'm sorry, but you have no idea how busy I am here today, everyone...'

'Suzi, Michael isn't here. I don't know where he has gone. He has left a suicide note...' At this point her voice broke off. There was a pause, the line became crackly. 'He left a suicide note... and the bathroom cabinet has been emptied. There is a bottle of ... whisky... on the kitchen table and... a note.' For a moment Suzi's mind spun, the room lost focus and form. If the sky fell to the floor she would not have been in the least surprised. Tears welled to her eyes and heat rose to her cheeks. Through the haze she saw the room full of people, cold in cold, lips moving, slowly, slowly. Smiles formed as muscles tightened, reflex, contraction, lips drawn, teeth bared. The smiles reached the eyes too late, far too late. The delay was long, longer than she had ever seen it, terrible, cold eyes in cold faces. Wine poured from a crystal decanter to a glass. It rolled through the intervening space like linen unwinding, splashing up the sides of the glass like a peony blossom opening, petals rolling back and coalescing as the glass filled. Voices came to her, strangely distorted, the words drawn into tortuous strings. Then, for a moment everything simply stopped.

A dull ache began to nag at the back of Suzi's mind; she tried to move, to call out to someone, to anyone. The ache became a pain, throbbing, persistent. She pulled the phone from her ear, every movement was accompanied by searing pain, yet she had to carry on for fear that if she stopped moving then all time itself would stop. In the corner of her eyes she saw her hands moving through space, the air around them shimmered and shook as if in a heat haze. The pain was incredible; perhaps she was dying, and this was the prelude to eternity. In those moments she thought of Michael. If he was dead, perhaps she would see him now. To her left she saw her assistant, frozen like everything else: mouth open, crumbs of finger-food forming an explosive cloud around her face, eyes looking up at the ceiling. Suzi reached for the girl's shoulder, the pain was almost unbearable, the air boiled and hissed around her. She reached out, fingers extending through resistive air. They touched. Immediately the world roared into movement again. The absolute silence was shattered by a million inconsequential noises, a million tiny frictions, a billion vibrations.

The girl before her gave out a high-pitched scream, a piercing cry that caused Suzi to recoil in terror. The girl spun on her heels; crumbs, crackers and arms flew outwards, her head flopped up and back and she rose up onto her toes as if an electrical current had torn through her. As she fell, time slowed again, but Suzi was too stunned to move. The girl's body lifted up and back and crashed to the floor, a dead weight, lying at Suzi's feet. Time ran as normal, the body flinched, shook and then was still. A plate crashed to the floor, the room became still and all heads turned towards her.

NINE

The message that flashed up onto Edward's computer filled him with the penetrating kind of sinking feeling that only a 'special meeting' can. Heads had rolled in the department at the same time the previous year, and although this year had, supposedly, been better, there was always the chance that those stalks uncut by the reaper in the last harvest could fall to the scythe in the new one.

The meeting itself lived up to Edward's worst case scenario-no, it was worse than that. He was going to have to organize a time-and-motion study. He was going to be the focus of every bile-filled whisper in every nook and cranny of the building. He would doubtless be the last sacrificial lamb/goat- he wasn't sure which- who would get the chop afterwards. Fire the fool that finds the fools to fire. He tried to think rationally about the situation. Surely, his was the safest position. He would hold the numbers; he could, perhaps, with a little bit of creative accounting, come out smelling of roses. It was just a case of finding a suitable company for the job. Not too clever, not too professional. The word 'malleable' came to mind.

He wasn't sure. The hard-nosed types that ran corporate services were doubtless well versed in the secret arts of corruption and bribery. He didn't know if he had either the stomach or the wallet for it. How on earth would these industrial parasites measure 'productivity' anyway? What sort of hackneyed, worn-out business cliché was that? At least Bill could have come up with some nouvelle-corporate jargon to sweeten the pill.

'Edward, could I see you for a moment?' Bill's head appeared round the door.

If it couldn't get any worse it was certainly trying. Bill had a company in mind, run by someone he'd known at college. They were computer whizzes with doctorates on how to make everyone else feel inadequate. 'Indisputable Industry Indices', I-cubed. Edward resisted his urges to bawl and tear his hair, to throw the aspidistra onto the floor and throw himself over the stainless steel balcony and into the vacuous space of the glass-walled 'togetherness' atrium. Instead he nodded gravely and offered to do some study on the subject. He walked out of the office feeling somewhat weak and dirty. Was this how the Stasi had felt?

TEN

Lilly sat in the darkness. She was clean and comfortable and tea had been bearable, if a bit stodgy. It rarely got much better than that these days. She had seen Mary and they had had a laugh together. She was so sweet, so very kind. So many of the old dears in the home moaned about their visitors; constant, whinging moans: to their faces, to their backs as they walked out of the building, to the rest of their families, friends, to the nurses, anyone who would listen. They moaned and moaned until no-one came to give them anything to moan about. Then they'd pause, reflect, maybe have a cry and then start moaning to your visitors and about your visitors and on and on it went. God knows Lilly hadn't been one to visit the elderly members of her own family. By rights she should never see a soul; as it was, she saw someone every other day or so. She was always thankful, even the people she didn't like very much sometimes brought things that could be bartered for treats or favours. A bottle of Lucozade was a horror to her, but could be swapped for crystallized ginger if another inmate didn't have the teeth for it. Hello! Magazine was good for twenty minutes of the TV remote and therefore a snatch of Taggart. A bag of chocolate éclairs bought you smiles from the day nurse for a whole week. It was like prison, only the drugs were folksier.

The nurse had popped in to wish her goodnight on her rounds, and Lilly had asked her to turn on the audio book, her own hands being too enfeebled to operate the clunky mechanism. The colour and build of the machine reminded her very much of radios she had used in the early fifties. She could still remember the call-signs. The story would run to the end of the tape now; however good, bad or indifferent she would have to hear it out. It didn't really matter what it was like. The sing-song of the voice was balm-enough in the darkness.

'The Unbearable Lightness of Being, by Milan Kundera'. The tape whirred into life, the introduction unfolding its description of light and weight, forces in opposition. Thoughts immediately began to crowd into Lilly's head, floating on the gentle waves of words, buoyant on this sea of ideas. Nietzsche, Robespierre, Africa, to place the three words together on the same page sent the mind into a whorl, and then to evoke an idea of 'eternal returns' time looping and repeating ad infinitum, 'nailed to eternity as Jesus Christ was nailed to the cross', was too much. Lilly began to wonder what she was listening to, nailed to eternity, living in this moment absorbing the ideas of people long dead, narrated by a man she would never meet. She wondered what it was that possessed people to examine these imponderables, to devote such time to analysis of questions which surely must have no answer. A million, million minds, wracked in the darkness had tried to unwrap these mysteries to no avail, why should anyone believe they could answer the questions alone, what could you add to the enormous pile of human suffering and thought?

It was no good, the storyline slipped away from her. She needed to stop the tape, needed time to think, to absorb, to rewind. The words tumbled out in procession. With the focus of her mind shifted; they contained little meaning. How many hours had she lain like this in the darkness? How many years would she have to endure the imprisonment imposed by her own body? She looked up at the clock on the wall, its second hand measuring the moments, sweeping time from the face and sending it into the past. Words from the tape drifted in and out of her consciousness: 'nailed to eternity, nailed to eternity, eternal returns, endless returns, eternal returns, lives lived in endless repetition.' Was this how it was going to be for her, for everyone, how many times would she see the clock face illuminated in the darkness, how many times would she watch the second hand pass between the numbers one and two, five discrete ticks, five discrete tocks, atomizing continuous time into conceivable moments. The tape droned on. Lilly could hear the ticking in the machine, little imperfections in the mechanism, wheels caressing wheels, phasing in and out with the seconds of the ticking clock, words on the tape phasing in and out with thoughts in her head. How long, how many times, an eternity of repeats, the second hand ticking, ticking, sweeping time, uncurling the future into the present, a future of repeats of night after night in this bed, of endless insipid cups of tea. Why hadn't she listened more carefully to the tape? Why had she let the narrative escape her? She wanted to escape now, into the story, lose herself in another's thoughts, live another life, if only for the duration of this cassette. She didn't want to have to suffer another repeat of this interminable scene, the floral wallpaper, the Victorian folly pictures, saccharine sweet, the dust gently settling on the picture frames. The clock, ticking, ticking, her life ebbing; sand slipping through her hands, until the last grains were gone and an eternity of peace replaced them. The clock stopped. The tape stopped. Everything stopped.

Initially Lilly thought she was dreaming. The mind in dreams made sense of the complexity of the day, juggling the experiences like the barrel of a fruit machine, throwing in scenes from the past, longings and ideas, turning the handle and clunking through the permutations. For Lilly, as the past slid away, the repetitions of her current life took up more and more of her mind's store of possibilities, an eternity of repeats. Soon it would be a fruit machine with only lemons; turning the handle more and more desperately would lead to fewer and fewer happy combinations. Surely this was what was happening now; she had fallen asleep and created a dreamscape that was a frame from a typical night, any night. The clock, the tape, the curtains, every pleat frozen, carelessly pulled together, asymmetrical forever.

No, this was different. The pain in her chest was still

there, throbbing as it always did, but tonight another pain was superimposed upon it; a pressing weight that resisted each breath, each rise and fall of her bird-like chest. This must be death, the grim reaper himself astride her breast, crushing the air from her, holding time captive until she relinquished her grasp on life. She did not know whether to fight or to cry out, to give up or try to shake him off. Perhaps she had already accepted her fate. Was the realisation that life was endlessly replayed, to accept the inconsequence of our fleeting moments of existence, the final lesson? A lifetime taught you this and then, once the lesson was fully accepted, in all its depressing realism, you were ready for oblivion. It didn't seem entirely fair. Lilly's eyes fell on the clock. The second hand, frozen between the numbers one and two, the Sword of Damocles suspended in space. Time of death was recorded at eight minutes past twelve, they would say. No, how foolish, how would they know? Time would continue uninterrupted for them, they would see the passing of another day, they would endure another repetition. Only for her would time stop forever.

The transition was smooth. Reality rushed into existence again. The roar of a peaceful suburban evening crashed into the room. The tape continued from where it had stopped, mid-phrase, mid-word, mid-whirr of the wheels. The pain subsided in Lilly's chest and she realised she could now follow the storyline. The plot was plain, crystallized from the solution of words. The shock of this realization nearly made her lose her train of thought a second time, but the associated joy drew her back to the smooth voice on the tape. Tonight would not be the same as every other night. The grim reaper had passed over her. The pain in her chest only served to throw life into sharper contrast. Tonight she and Milan Kundera would mingle in thought.

ELEVEN

Suzi was shaking as she fumbled with the electric key that operated the gates to her home. The red light flashed stubbornly as she tried it a third time, each time more angrily, each time faster. The three second delay as the million, million combinations and permutations were checked and compared and double checked and cross referenced via a computer server in Switzerland were unbearable. Her tears began to blur her sight and desperately she swiped the card again, more slowly this time, sobbing as she did so, hands barely steady enough to grip the thin plastic sliver. An interminable three seconds passed, and then the tiny diode flashed green, there was a whir of servos and the gates rattled and began to swing open. Suzi crashed the BMW into gear and roared up the long, pebbly drive. As the car skidded to a halt, she thought of how Michael had hated this house. The mock Tudor frontage, the curving drive, the neat, well-kept shrubs trained into manicured clouds. He had said it was a cliché, a comfortable upper middle-class prison of conformity, soulless and sterile. She'd almost had to drag him from his garret. The promise of converting the 'Victorian' conservatory into a studio which had clinched the move had left him sulky; he had 'prostituted himself for flat, north-facing light'. He could be unbearable. They couldn't entertain the elite of international media in digs overlooking the shunting yard, with a coke house in the basement and his easel taking up three-quarters of the scullery, the only room with natural light.

Crunching and wobbling across the drive she saw the white and drawn face of her mother-in-law at the open door. Michael had insisted she had a key, insisted she could pop round when she liked. Suzi had not been impressed. No normal person lived like that, it wasn't natural. She had a right to her privacy, a right to defend it from the gaze of an interfering woman. The matter had been yet another stipulation on their moving in together. For a man with almost nothing with which to barter, Michael had struck a remarkably tough deal. This was his life; it wasn't complicated or sophisticated, but if you wanted to be a part of it, you had to take the whole thing, mother included. In the event Michael's mother had been no trouble at all, thoughtful, helpful, painstakingly not interfering, tidying a cupboard here, buying the odd grocery there, leaving a pecan pie or dealing with minor problems with the gardener. They got on well and she never overstayed her welcome. In many ways Suzi got on with her rather better than she did with her own mother, an altogether more demanding woman, a woman who didn't have time for making pecan pies.

Michael's mother pulled Suzi into her arms as soon as she crossed the threshold.

She was shaking; silent sobs rocked her tiny frame. Suzi knew that there was no doubt in her mind that Michael was dead. Perhaps a mother had a special intuition, but sometimes a mother could be wrong. She hugged her tightly; the type of punctuation hug that implies you should stop and move on to something else. It was the only type of hug her own mother seemed to know. Perhaps this was the problem. Her mother's body language was solely composed of syntax. A blighted childhood could have been saved with a smattering of physical vocabulary.

She extricated herself from the older woman's grip.

'Show me the note Margaret, please. Maybe there is still time, we don't know that he has gone.' Michael's mother looked up at her.

'I'm sorry Suzi, but he is gone, I know. I knew two hours ago, it was why I phoned, it was why I came.' Her eyes were puffed with tears, but she had quickly regained some control. She took Suzi by the hand and led her into the

38

kitchen. On the table sat two empty whisky bottles and a note, written in Michael's artistic hand on a torn piece of fine art paper. Suzi slowly slid the note towards her on the table; the words swam before her eyes as tears rose to meet them.

The handwriting was steady; she heard Michael's voice in every phrase. He wasn't drunk when he had started to write this. Though he was clearly drinking towards the end. He must have sipped his whisky, staring at it in front of him, pondering the weight of the words, wondering if he had caught his feelings appropriately. He had obviously decided that he had. This was to be his last message to her, but on its fine art paper, reminiscent of the deeds to the house, it was to be his last message to the world.

Michael's mother walked over to the sink in silence, washed some mugs and put the kettle on as Suzi read. The letter spoke of love and sadness, an internal conflict of which Suzi was only dimly aware. He had chosen his words sparingly; a hopeless romantic in his art, he was careful with his prose, selecting words the same way he might have mixed colours. Suzi read the letter three times, each more slowly than the last, before Margaret placed the tea down on the table in front of her: strong, milky and sweet. She never drunk tea like that normally, but at this moment it was very welcome.

'How do you know he has gone through with it, Margaret? How can you be so sure? We should call the police.' Margaret took her hand.

'I just know. I've called the police already. They have sent a man to the river. They said they would send someone here, or call as soon as they found...' Her voice trailed into silence.

Suzi's mind was racing; how could he do this to her? Put her and his mother through this misery? He had repeated several times that it 'wasn't her fault'; the inadequacy he had felt in his own life was independent of the strengths inherent in hers. She could no more be less of a person than he could be more; it was their nature, their essence. His life was gone; his most creative period spent throwing

39

himself against the world's intransigence. He felt too tired to create anything, and besides there was no time left to create anything else, he was his art, and his art was spent. He told her that she had all the time in the world, she shouldn't mourn him, but move on, not waste the gifts she had been given.

Suzi was furious. Surely this was some kind of cry for help, a side to Michael's artistic temperament she had not yet seen. It was ridiculous, crazy to suggest his most creative period was past; he had a lifetime of work before him. He had all the time in the world. Every word he had written telling her not to blame herself wounded her deeply. He had no power to admonish her of guilt, his words merely indicated she was to blame, and what had she done? What were these 'gifts' she had been blessed with? He was the gifted one, an artist, a thinker, talented and beautiful. She had always worked for everything she had, worked every moment, struggled over the obstacles. How could she be held responsible for the twists of fate that had allowed her to thrive; the intrigues she had plotted were her way of playing a system that had not blessed her with luck. She had made her chances, and Michael was blaming her for that. Tears filled her eyes and she threw the paper from her. Her emotions were boiling. She felt dizzy and cold. The trees outside the kitchen window, swayed by the unseen hand of the wind, began to slow and blur. It was happening again, the pain was coming, and she felt it rushing towards her. No! She wouldn't let it happen again. She felt the hand of her mother-in-law upon her shoulder. 'Are you alright dear?' The words were beginning to fragment and run together. No! It mustn't happen. Her secretary could not be revived at the scene of the party; an ambulance had been called. She was cold, her breath shallow, her pulse barely detectable. They had taken her away to hospital and Suzi had had to extricate herself from the confused crowd. She had glimpsed the young woman's ashen face as the stretcher was lifted into the back of the ambulance, eyes closed. There had been no visible sign that she was still alive. Had she had seen suspicion in some eyes then? No one had really seen anything: a movement, a transient touch? Had she tried to support her colleague as she fell? Or had something more sinister happened, something inhuman.

Suzi pulled her thoughts together, focusing on Margaret's face. The pain was beginning to recede; she could hear her pulse in her ear, the dizziness subsiding. She took a long sip of tea. It was as cold as the grave. She looked, uncomprehending, at Margaret, but before she could ask what was going on; the sound of the doorbell interrupted her thoughts. She placed the cup on the table, noticing the steam coming from Margaret's own cup as she did so, and ran to the door.

Through the door panels she saw the unmistakable form of policemen in uniform, the fluorescent strips of their jackets repeated a thousand times in the frosted glass.

TWELVE

The 'time and motion' meeting was not as totally horrendous as Edward had expected; in fact things had conspired to put a very positive shine on the whole experience. The managing director, a Kevin Masters, was friendly and frighteningly reassuring in an extremely good silver suit. The man had spent a period in California and there were elements to his voice which grated on Edward's latent American-specific racism. It was difficult for him to pinpoint the source of this flaw in his otherwise generous non-prejudicial personality. He blamed the 'common language' and the brightly coloured, hair-swishing, suntan flashing, brain numbing American adverts for cosmetics that peppered his weekend television. He wanted to slap those 'little scrubbers' and 'smiling with confidence' brunettes into the last century. He liked flowing hair and a nice smile as much as the next man, but the venereal insincerity that flowed from these überbitches filled him with cold revulsion.

Kevin Master's personal assistant Agneta Sibilski was no überbitch. As soon as Edward met her he realized he was in deep trouble. Agneta was remarkable, a vision in sensible shoes, blond, affable, intense and wearing a pleasant and seemingly genuine smile. When she spoke to Edward she spoke directly to his face; when she listened, she did so with her full attention. She didn't hang on his words or nod inappropriately or with too much vigour. She genuinely knew how to listen and for a single man with a penchant for blonds with exotic accents, that was almost painfully erotic.

Edward caught himself catching glimpses of her in

reflective surfaces in the meeting room: a well-turned calf in a chrome-plated chair leg, a glimpse of the nape of her neck in a stainless steel lamp fitting. She wore a pillar-box red jacket which made finding her reflection in the many polished surfaces of the room a facile pleasure. After the hour and a half in the meeting, Edward felt he had thoroughly examined the company from all angles. He was in no doubt that the intimate investigation of his workings by Ms Sibilski would be of benefit to all concerned. When they shook hands on leaving, Edward had allowed himself to touch her, just a moment too long, to hold her gaze for that split second longer than was entirely polite. She had held his gaze too, exactly as he had expected, professional, polite, effortlessly beautiful and perhaps, just perhaps, responsive. He was thinking of trying the 'as we shall be working together over the next few months, would you like to go for a drink' routine, but it was too early in the play; that would come later. He escorted the visitors to the foyer when it was time for them to leave, a pointedly unnecessary gesture in an entirely open plan office, but it allowed him to watch Agneta's gentle curves for a few moments longer. Her reflection leaped from chromium fixture to fixture, ballooning and collapsing in the curved glass panels that formed the portico. He thought for a moment that he caught her glance back at him as she and her boss had stepped into the flow of people on the street. It could have been wishful thinking; strange how the mind played tricks in such moments. One image, stored for reference in the mind, superimposed upon another situation, desire fusing the two together and some aspect of light, colour or form allowing the realities to align themselves into this satisfying whole.

'What did you think?' Bill motioned Edward into his office as he climbed the stairs (two at a time). He checked himself from saying how wonderful he thought Agneta was, though the temptation to do so was almost unbearable. There was nothing like the garbled admiration of one man about a woman to spark the interest in her by another. Edward had always found Bill rather sexless. He knew the man was married with kids (one of each, typically perfect), but suddenly he felt protective of his new quarry. Instead he made small talk about the benefits of the wonderfully objective Indisputable Industry Indices.

The journey to the morgue took the police car through some of the less salubrious parts of town. Suzi imagined that this route was not entirely necessary; the police just using this opportunity to glide past the empty shops and shambling youths and drunks that inhabited their recesses. Why did under-employed youth find succour in such miserable places? If your life was miserable, why steep yourself in more misery? It was a question she hoped she would never have to ask herself. Michael had intimated that she would survive, carry on with her meteoric rise. She hoped at this juncture he was right. The car stopped at traffic lights beside a suspect-looking pet shop. Little furry things pushed damp wood-shavings around in a cage in the window. There was nothing that could be done for them and nothing that could be done for Michael. A drunk leered into the window, slicking out his tongue and putting two fingers up at the police drivers. He staggered into the road and as the car pulled away from the lights it missed him by the slenderest of margins. He stumbled to the ground and Suzi heard a torrent of abuse until they turned a corner. The police car slowed interminably as they passed a miserable looking estate. In front of one house they slowed to a crawl, a sheet blocked out the large crumbling downstairs window and a chink of light illuminated the rubbish strewn over the front lawn; a brand-new tricycle, a pedal car and between them, embedded in the ground at a curious angle, a microwave oven. The vignette looked like a surreal children's road accident.

Suzi had seen enough. 'For God's sake stop touring us like circus animals around the estates of south London and let me identify my boyfriend's body!' Michael's mother squeezed her hand. The police drivers sat up rigid in their seats and the car picked up speed. Street lights ticked off the passing of time, garish plastic shop fronts in various stages of decline seemed to have taken over the rest of the world whilst Suzi had been busy in business meetings. When alien archaeologists dig up our decimated society they will conclude we were a species with no collective aesthete. In her mind's eye Suzi swept the world away with the arc of her hands. There had to be a better way to build towns and cities, people just couldn't be trusted to get on with the job themselves. They had too little taste. What was she thinking? Her boyfriend was lying cold on a slab and she was worrying about town planning. She thought of Michael. He would see some tragic beauty in a boarded up dole office, or a squalid tobacconists; he could see beauty everywhere. So why had he decided to take his life? Surely you took your life when you were blind to the beauty, refractory to the wonders of life. If anyone had a right to be depressed it was her, she saw corruption and misery in everything; her day to day existence was just one long march of manipulation and deception. Michael had always brought beauty into the world, he was a creator of beauty and a thing of beauty, and she had thought that, by supporting him, both emotionally and financially, she was contributing to that beauty in her own way. She knew he wasn't happy in his job, but then who ever was? At least he had opportunities to paint, to disappear off to his soulful open spaces and escape the drudgery of mediocrity. She could not stop herself feeling angry with him. She wasn't ready for tears and she wasn't ready to accept his explanations.

Michael's mother sat in silence. She saw nothing from the windows of the car, all around was just an enormous, all encompassing darkness. The feeling of Suzi's warm hand was the only thing that told her she was still alive. At the moment of Michael's death, she had known that he had gone. How she knew she would never be able to explain, but the thought had come into her head not as a question or reminder of a mother's recurrent fear, rather it had come as a certainty. Michael's father had also taken his own life. The echo of the pain and darkness she had experienced then flooded back to Margaret. She had found his body, there in the darkness, curtains wide open, windows open to the elements. The warm day had cooled to a cold night and the body of Michael's father had lain there, insensitive to the transition. He had rolled up his tracksuit jacket to support his head, had lain back, smiling no doubt as he emptied the drug into the vein. Had he known it was a fatal dose of heroin? Was it purer than he had taken before? More concentrated? Who knew? It did not matter. She had begged him, begged him, babe in arms, to stop, to get help, but when he 'had his need' he did not want to know. She had known it would be the death of him, one way or another, either because of the gun in the bedside cabinet, or due to the valuables in the cupboard under the stairs. It wasn't right; it would all end in tears, her tears.

She had never really told Michael about his father. The tissue of lies she had spun was thin, but not so far from the truth. How well had she known him? Had she known the man at all? It was true to say he had run away; he had run away from life, from responsibilities, from both of them. It was true that there were other women. Heroin was expensive; he had had to subsidise his job as a legal secretary with some moonlighting as an escort. When you are suave and beautiful and the colour of rich old oak, women would pay for your company. It was also true that he had gone to the West Indies, but she had neglected to say that he had returned, smiling broadly and disappearing into their bathroom for long periods whilst she was banging on the door with her misery and morning sickness.

When he was old enough he had asked more and more about him, so she had spun more complex lies to put him off the scent. Michael was bright, creative and beautiful like his father, but he did not have the organised mind necessary to make an effective search, and Margaret had never given him the clues he would need to do so. There had been other men, of course, some had even threatened to be a father to the boy, but men seemed to lie easily to Margaret. Hers had been a hard life, but she had pulled through; she had never been alone really, friends and family, even in the dark times. It had been difficult to survive, to make a living with a small child. But she had provided, when providence, social services and charity had faltered. On reflection she had been prepared for this last tragedy in her life. When she first met Michael's father she thought she was the luckiest woman alive; there had been no wedding, no vows, only private promises in the dark. She had lost her own parents quite early in life, victims to cancer. They had told her that they loved her, that they would always love her, but death had taken them and their words seemed hollow comfort now. She had had to grow up quickly to be a mother to her younger sisters. Michael's father was from a big, successful family; they had taken her in like a daughter and their stability and love had been a pillar in her life when she had needed it most. This semblance of order had allowed her to keep both herself and the remnants of their family together. The death of Michael's father had brought that crashing down. They had been utterly destroyed by it, unable to look her in the face.

Somehow they had blamed her for his death. He had died in her custody so she had to be the one at fault. Their love had turned to a casual racism as they retreated from her. She had forgiven them this a long time ago, but they could never forgive her the loss of their boy. She had seen him sliding away from her, this she realised was the difference. Michael's grandparents had never seen their son's decline, the moments of self abusive ecstasy; they hadn't had to drag him to bed or place blankets over his inert body, eyes wide in the dark, praying that he would wake up again. They had not had to argue with weaselly, strange men on their doorstep when they came asking for money. For them, Michael's father had come to her perfect and whole, in his Sunday best and smelling of flowers. He had left her in a box. She hadn't fed him right (hadn't he become thin?) She had trapped him with a child (they hadn't wanted to know about Michael, born as he was to be out of wedlock). Their Christian charity died the same day their son did.

Michael was different. He had become more distant, too

thoughtful, too concerned that she would be secure should anything happen to him. The time had passed so quickly since he had met Suzi. She had dominated his life from the outset, given him every opportunity, sorting out a job for him, when he had had nothing for so long. He had seemed so happy, at least at first. She squeezed Suzi's hand a second time. This woman was not to blame for Michael's death. There had been insufficient time for her to help him; insufficient opportunity for her to see the signs. They had been together eight years, she tried to think, maybe more, but what was that to a lifetime? Their time had passed so quickly, there had been no terrible fights, no drugs, no poverty. Michael had not really known suffering; she had protected him from it. He had no right to take his life and she would not blame Suzi for Michael's bad seed placed in him by his father. Neither she nor Suzi had been responsible for that bad blood. She would mourn her loss and cry her tears; but she would not turn this woman away as she had been turned away herself thirty five years before.

THIRTEEN

Bill Morris would have described himself as a family man. A wife who liked cooking and a regimen of long office hours, long commutes, long Scotches and very short walks between the sofa and the car had made him comfy, but contented. He had always felt in some strange way that he was blessed, success had come naturally to him. The first few businesses had wobbled a bit, but that was way of the world. Venture capital had not fled at his initial failures and instead had given him the benefit of the doubt. He had a good line in spin and the business world seemed to be desperate for comforting voices. This he guessed was his forte, people tended to believe him. His wide-open, slightly child-like features engendered trust. Trust had bought him time when his company had needed it, and careful people management, good timing and the confidence to browbeat most people around him in a calm voice had floated him to the top of the pile and kept him there. Perhaps it wasn't that he was particularly gifted, it was the remarkable ineptitude of everyone around him that made him look good. The inadequacies of most people came as a constant surprise to him. Incompetence, tempers held together by the most fragile of egos, impatience, intolerance, lack of concentration, inability to think a problem through to its inevitable outcome and cogently argue a point. Skills that he took for granted were obviously not within everyone's capability. If they were, life would have worked out rather harder for him. He had probably never had an original thought in his life (something he tended to confess in hushed tones to his landlord after the ninth whisky and ginger) but you didn't need to have your own ideas if you could use the ideas of others. Genuine creativity was as common as muck. It was entrepreneurs that the world was short of; people with the vision to make things happen, not just talk about it. He was someone that made things happen, and people believed that he wanted it to happen for them.

The bar was full of the usual mix of post-work, casual, hormonally-charged thirty-somethings. Bill wasn't totally sure why he felt the need to immerse himself in this vacuous culture. He had no great desire to perpetuate his youth or ingratiate himself to these self-proclaimed inheritors of the Earth, he just liked a drink. The media haircuts and the office bimbettes that frequented these bars liked a drink too. He enjoyed an occasional glance at a bit of exposed thigh, there was no denying it. He was a wealthy married man, and he found it somehow reassuring that the attractive young women still found the time to talk to him. He wasn't deluding himself; he knew that their attention had to be bought, especially at these city prices. He'd stand them a drink; make a measured comment regarding how attractive/mature/interesting they were. This of course depended very much on how unattractive/insecure/boring they were, but, remarkably, it worked every time. He got the chat (maybe it was the attention he craved) and the chance to show off. Maturity and success must be an aphrodisiac, because it certainly wasn't his body they wanted. Perversely this excited him. The credit cards in his wallet were equivalent to being ten years younger with a six-pack. He could never buy back the years, he had given those to his wife and they could never be recouped.

He rarely, if ever, took his attentions further. They might whisper in his ear that their boyfriend was away, or ask him if he knew a nice hotel, perhaps with a bar, perhaps with a jacuzzi, perhaps with a whirl-pool-bath. It wasn't that he desired their lithe bodies, their smooth, tanned legs. It was just that wide-eyed look of someone who was more attractive, younger and sexier, but who was envious of him, who wanted something that he had achieved, that

50

they themselves thought was beyond them.

Bill was happy with his marriage, happy with his wife and loved his wonderful, perfect children. Margo somehow understood his weakness. Margo was uncomplicated, undemanding and sweet. Bill sensed that she knew she was no match for him, intellectually, physically, in any way really. There had been times in his relationship that he had abused this inadequacy, games they had played in bed and out of it, things he wasn't entirely proud of. Consenting role play had become a feature of their love life and there had been times when he had difficulty becoming aroused without it. Their relationship had matured now beyond the sexual realm. As he had grown heavier, sex excited him less and less. It had become a folly, a childish indulgence, and family life was more than sufficient consolation. He knew enough psychology to rationalise away his intellectual concerns about his sexual attractiveness and the moments of pure, unadulterated parent-craft spent with his children admonished him of the guilt that he associated with his wife. Perhaps his mental promiscuity (so rarely expressed as physical love) was another expression of his oppression of his wife. Thinking about it too hard never seemed to help. It was better just to buy another round, smooth another fragile ego and make another polite exit.

He said good evening to the doormen, something he always did. He liked to think he was acknowledging their power, predator recognising predator. In reality he appreciated that they could not possibly appreciate his powers, his gift. Some nights, when he was particularly drunk, he had felt compelled to demonstrate his gift to them, his word craft, his spontaneous wit. Fortunately the door staff seemed to have a short turn around and he had never strained their patience too far.

A glance at his watch confirmed that it he had reached his favoured 'slightly squiffy' stage rather earlier in the evening than usual. This was the point at which he usually took his leave. Another few drinks and he might go that fatal stage further, do the dirty and have to pay the piper. Today he'd had too many meetings, too many coffees and not enough food. The liquor had done the business and there were still tube trains running. He could have caught a cab, the money was no object, but there was something about the slightly tired know-it-all familiarity of the cabbies that riled him: their presumption that he cared about what they thought, their presumption that he read the Daily Mail.

The subway was just a short walk away. There was a smattering of interesting flotsam and jetsam roaming the streets, and the last tube train home always had the frisson of sexual possibilities with its cargo of after-work party-addled office juniors. There was never a shortage of young things to look at.

He made his way somewhat precariously around the piles of rubbish bags strewn across the pavement, weaving past a few late night lovers whose enthusiastic attentions seemed to take up all their navigational skills. He smiled back at them, for a moment losing his lecherous mind's eye, just enjoying their unselfconscious pleasure. He suddenly thought of his wife; the journey home would take him at least forty minutes by the time he had wandered through the park and relieved himself against an old London plane tree (something he found strange pleasure in, marking his territory like a lone lion) Perhaps tonight he wouldn't let her worry about him, would reassure her that he was on his way back to her. He paused at the top of the subway, wobbled a little on the threshold, placed his briefcase on the ground between his legs and withdrew his mobile phone from his coat pocket. He flicked it open and its cold, comforting light illuminated his face.

He didn't see where the man appeared from. There were narrow little alleys leading off the main street; he must have been standing in the shadows, breathing gently, waiting to strike. Bill felt a strange point of cold pressure on his back, (a knife? A gun?), smelt the man's cigarette breath and recoiled from the greased intimacy of a thin beard on the side of his face.

'Give m' phone an ya wallet.' The voice was deep, the speech slightly slurred, sodden with street inflection, menacing. Bill Morris felt the blood freeze in his veins. The heat from the whisky left him and the night air seemed suddenly colder against his skin. He must have stopped breathing, because when his chest started to rise, drawing in the moist air, the sound of its flux through his nostrils roared in his ears. As if in response to the life-giving breath he felt his blood stirring, felt the very pressure of his heart, felt its slow contraction, felt the walls of his congested aorta flexing in response. The blood was roaring in his ears now, a terrible crashing thud of Atlantic waves pounding cliffs; the footsteps of a giant measuring with each forty-league stride the passing of his life. Strangely, incredibly, in this moment when his life could be stolen from him in a careless instant he felt more alive than he had ever done before. He heard a car passing down a side street, its tires on the wet city tarmac squeezing black water aside. He could have sworn he heard each mark of the tire track contacting the road, the rhythmic drum of the pattern, endlessly repeating. In the distance a bell tolled, and he knew it tolled for him because he heard it like no other man had ever heard a bell before. He detected the Doppler shift as its motion took it away and towards him, swinging in its belfry; he could see it in his mind's eye, the individual oscillations of the metal, subtle vibrations, compressions and rarefactions of the air reaching him in train. It was wonderful. He saw a pigeon, startled from its niche, passing overhead; he saw the wings in graceful arcs collide at the extremes of their travel, rolling together, and peeling apart, individual feathers flexing and twisting, as turbulent air boiled off into the night.

He could not die now. Not when the world was so rich in wonder, not when his eyes had been opened for the first time. He began to turn, to face his assailant, but as he moved he felt a strange resistance, a viscosity to the air that he had never noticed before. He felt the transfer of angular momentum from the core of his body to his limbs and his loosely hanging clothes; his ample flesh resisting

53

his movements, sliding against cotton, pulling it tight and dragging it taut. He could feel the very flesh straining against his bones, his jaw twisting from his skull, the sinews of his face pulling it back into line, tooth grinding against tooth. He felt his cervical bones, fissile and chalky, rasping together, atlas over axis. In this moment they sounded like two great neolithic sentinels, crashing together, lintel and sarsen.

The face of his attacker slid into his peripheral vision. His eyes adjusting focus, slowly finding features, exploring the details of the face: a wide blue eye; wide blue eye; a thin, broken nose; soft lips, parted; the nose again; the eye; the eye, the nose; the lips; a long sloping brow hidden by a baseball cap; a blue hood with three white stripes; the eye; the eye; the lips.

Bill had never been so completely aware of a face before, had never really studied the lines, the proportion, the excrescences of flesh blossoming into features, the voluptuous rolling of muscles under smooth, milky skin. The muscles of this particular face were kneading the flesh from one conformation to another: a turbulent sea, a look of shock (or was it fear?) boiling out of one of surprise. Bill had never appreciated the world of expressions in between, the way the face oscillated its states as though in dialogue with the mind; eyes and jaw, brow and lips momentarily in opposition, a patchwork of discordant confusion. Eventually this face settled into a consensus of confused terror. Bill felt calm and still yet his clothes and flesh seemed to have a life of their own. He felt as though a summer sun was upon him, warming him to his core. This must be how it felt to conquer; victory was sweet indeed.

Victory would, indeed, be his. This he now knew with certainty. Many thoughts had passed through his mind. Initially he thought he was dying. The enlightened state he felt infused with, a glorious side effect of his spirit taking its leave. Had he been wounded, his life blood ebbing away? Or had his heart given up as his doctor had always warned him it would? No, there was the knife, shining in the moonlight, the white knuckles and fingers of his assailant, tendons straining, blood pumping under the skin. There was no blood on the blade.

The knife began to move in space, cruel, slicing the air, working its way towards Bill's face, reflections of street lights rippling across its surface. For a moment, his own image appeared, strangely blurred, until the blade rotated to reveal the cool moon above. This man had expended love on this malignant shank, had polished it in the darkness to an exquisite shine. He had come out into the cold to steal, to threaten a life and if necessary to kill. His face was changing again, features hardening, tensing, and crystallizing to a hate-filled mask. Eyebrows arched, pushing beads of sweat together. Spittle bubbled round the teeth and dribbled down the chin, droplets slowly spraying into space as he hurled himself forward.

Bill stepped from the path of the ascending blade, his hands folding the wildly swirling expanse of his coat aside like a matador. Even to his own eyes, now so remarkably acute, his movements were a blur. He felt elated, joyful; it had been the performance of a lifetime, every fibre of his being filled with light.

He was out of danger now, his brain confirmed this. Trajectories had been plotted, allowances made for momenta and forces. The roar of his blood subsided and the world returned al tempo. Bill's assailant shot past him into the mouth of the subway, limbs flying into open space. He let out a strange cry, his head twisting up and back as he tried to follow Bill's movements, and then he was gone from sight. Bill heard a strange crunch and a crack, an exhalation of breath and then there was silence. He walked to the top of the stairs. In the darkness below he saw the motionless form of his assailant, limbs comically swastika-splayed, the torso twisted and head snapped back, eyes rolling frantically as if trying to escape their sockets. Bill breathed deeply. Night air flooded in, warm, moist air flooded out; his breath a billowing cloud in the cold, just as it should do, when you are alive.

Perhaps he would catch a cab tonight. The exhilaration

of the preceding moments still coursed through him yet he felt strangely calm. Something remarkable had just happened to him, something unearthly. He would have to think. Had there been something latent within him, something waiting for a trigger such as this: his moment of greatest need? Possibly his gift would only be exposed under conditions of extreme emotional stress. Those born to victimhood would retreat into themselves, frozen in fear, whereas a natural predator, a winner (as he had always found himself to be) could come into their own and discover their reserves of hidden strength. But what of the time dilation he had experienced? Was it possible that it had only been a creation of his mind, a by-product of a brain experiencing impossible demands? Something to do with the drink? As plausible as these thoughts seemed, he still had doubts. He thanked his lucky stars and whoever was looking over him for their protective intervention, mentally drank a toast to the memory of his vanquished assailant (the effects of the alcohol were beginning to return and it seemed somehow appropriate), dismissed any idea of informing the police or an ambulance and for a moment allowed himself to relive the joy of those few split seconds. He remembered the warmth, the remarkable calm, his absolute certainty of his own invulnerability. A cab was approaching, amber light glowing; a tiger's eye in the dark. He would know that feeling again, he told himself. The question was how to control it.

FOURTEEN

'Do you want a cup of tea before you, erm... before...?'
The young policeman looked at his feet. Michael's mother
looked firstly at Suzi then kindly at him.

'No dear, not for the moment. If you would just be so kind
as to show us where to go...'

The mortuary block was quiet, peaceful, and undis-
turbed. A vase of white lilies, almost too perfect, a gentle
reminder of the death all around them. As they closed the
door the world outside became distant. The sounds of passing traffic, the insistent activities of the living, were dead-
ened; the door-seal hermetic against the living. All that
remained was the palpable silence of death.

'If you would follow me...' The policeman led them
through a set of long corridors lined with paintings in
autumn colours. How they contrasted to Michael's works,
winter works, works about space and emptiness and loneliness. It was strange, but somehow Suzi had not seen that
in his work before. She was not a great art lover and when
looking at his work had only the crudest appreciation of it.
It was good, that much she knew, and 'moody', but she had
never really looked beyond that. Now, the contrast of his
work with the bright landscapes adorning the walls could
not be starker. She knew now that he had been trying to
tell her (trying to tell the world) something of his loneliness and disconnectedness. So many deserted estuaries, so
many marshes and fens, never a figure; the viewer was
always on their own. How many times had he thought of
taking his life in those places? Why had he been unable to
share his burden?

The police constable showed them to a waiting room and they were soon joined by an attendant. There were polite introductions, a few carefully practised words. The body was in the room beyond; if they were ready they could pass through and confirm what everyone already knew. They were asked not to touch the body; under the circumstances of the death 'additional' investigations would have to be performed.

Suzi found Margaret's hand and they were ushered through a door into the brightly lit space beyond. Suzi's feet felt heavier and heavier as she approached the steel bed. The air was thick with the smell of disinfectant and artificial scent, somehow viscous and sickly. She paused on the threshold, nauseous, unsteady. Her head began to pound, her temple throbbed, even the subdued, sickly lights hurt her eyes and she thought she might faint. Across the room lay Michael's body. There was no question that it was him; how strange that the mind could store the essence of a person in such a precise way, yet to recall the image of them in their absence could be so difficult. The water had had little effect on him; he had been found soon after death. A dog walker had seen him half submerged and had brought the police to the spot. Suzi did not like to think of those strange hands upon this body. They must have thought his death strange, a bizarre accident, impossible that someone so young, so beautiful should take their own life. Such a man would have loving family, friends, they could not die alone. Each step towards the body, his body, became progressively harder. She wanted to run to him, to throw her arms about his still frame and hug him back to life, but she could not; he had been unable to run to her in life and she was unable to run to him in death. She realised she was crying.

Margaret stepped forward, leaving Suzi a few steps behind. She smiled down at Michael, kissed her fingers and put them to his lips. The moment seemed to last a lifetime. Margaret held out her hand to Suzi and beckoned her to her side. Those last two steps, two small steps, such a short distance was entirely beyond her; and Suzi found she was unable to move. She could not take her eyes from the still body, a body she had known so well. How could he have done this to himself, how could he have left her behind, to carry the burden of life alone? And to leave her with this trauma, something so terrible, she could have survived this time with his help, with his love, but surely not without him. It was a terrible thing to do, malicious, cold, so terribly cold. Her heart was racing now, blood rushing in her ears, her limbs heavy, dragging her down, pulling her to the floor; it was all some terrible dream, a nightmare. In her mind's eye a hand, huge and black, appeared from the ground and grabbed her, crushed her, drew her into the earth. Margaret held out a tiny hand to her, but it was an impossible battle and Suzi felt herself slipping away, drowning in the encroaching darkness. Margaret was distant now, her face obscured by a halo of bright light, her body obscured by nebulous clouds. The clouds boiled together, and Suzi gave herself up to the darkness.

FIFTEEN

Detective Patrick Manee watched the proceedings from the back of the room. It was a habit he had developed: to stand, to observe but not to be observed. As an inspector he had been trained in surveillance techniques, but he had perfected his art in gay bars around the West End. A well chosen spot gave you a distinct advantage; not only could you could pick your quarry, but you could watch the other predators moving in for the kill. The operations room in the department store was remarkably well equipped, so much intrusive security to protect pants and socks, it was frightening. The camera in the underpass had caught nothing but the man's fall as he had come into view, twisting in the air, trying to look back at something (presumably someone). Manee had watched the man fall thirty times, maybe more: the face always obscured by the body, the right hand outstretched, clutching the knife, twisting and falling, falling, hitting the bottom of the stairs and then bouncing to a final stop. He had silently begged the screen for someone to come down the stairs, to check their handiwork, perhaps to pick over the body, but no one else had followed. The murderer had walked away, turned his back. Such a person was cold, calm, dangerous.

The camera had revealed the discovery of the body. Remarkable how three people had ignored it, two giving it a glance, and then leaving the station by the ramp, not wanting to disturb it. One person had stepped over the outstretched limbs. They all must have known the man was dead, even someone with the most rudimentary knowledge of human anatomy would have known that the man wasn't asleep, his head snapped back, the unexpected joints in the arms, the dark pool of blood. Patrick tried not to hate the general public, but it was difficult not to. He would find and question the three, just for the pleasure of giving them a hard time.

This was another lead, a well-placed camera, watching the front of the department store also surveyed the subway at the top left extremity of its view.

The operator, an attractive, dark-haired, well-built lad that had seemed nervous in Patrick's presence (it was probably just the uniform) dutifully wound the tape to the estimated time of death. In fast-forward the usual suspects wobbled across the screen, couples hand-in-hand, the street cleaner with her giant anteater-like vacuum (good, the street had been cleaned just a few minutes before, forensics would be easier), and then, yes, the corpse, the blagger's swagger. How often had it been possible to spot a criminal on the strength of that alone? He appeared for a moment and then ducked down a side passageway, checking the street up and down, exactly the way normal people didn't. Detective Manee asked the lad to rewind the tape a few seconds; they would watch the 'victim' conceal himself and discover how he had met his end together.

It amazed Manee how often criminals overlooked the street surveillance. People rarely looked up in London, and criminals seemed more inclined to keep their eyes down than most. The victim had been a known villain, Manee himself had questioned him a few times, he was habitual, petty, annoyingly predictable, and remarkably persistent, but he wouldn't be robbing on this street again. A few people passed under the camera; a group of three girls, a punk with a Mohican, a young courting couple, had all passed by the hiding place. None had investigated the darkness. None were suitable prey. A large man with a long white overcoat walked purposely into the frame. Det. Manee immediately recognised him as slightly drunk, the single-minded nature of his stride, the slight corrections to his head-long trajectory were clear. The man paused at the top of the stairs, rooted around in his pocket and drew out his mobile phone.

Manley's heart leapt. It was exactly as he had imagined; the narrative from here on so painfully obvious there was almost no need to watch the rest of the tape. The victim broke cover, the knife-blade flashed, his arm encircled the neck of the man in white. Manley's heart was racing. 'Turn round you bastard, come on, let's see your face, come on...' It was as much as he could do not to scream at the screen. For a moment everything went black, a dark grey mass passed in front of their field of view, a blur of movement and then it was gone.

'What the...?'

'It was a pigeon, I think.' The video operator looked back at him. 'See them quite a bit, they nest behind the cameras.' Cute as he was, Det. Manee would have liked to have given him a slap at that moment. On the screen everything had changed, the man in white had stepped to the side and the victim was thrusting the knife towards the gaping maw of the underground. His movements were strange, dream-like; he staggered forward, twisting in space and disappeared headlong into the darkness below. The figure in the long coat glanced down into the pit and then casually walked out of shot.

'Shit! Fuck! I don't believe it!' Det. Manee was livid. His hands slapped against his forehead and he slowly dragged them across his face. 'We got everything except the money shot!' Detective Manee had a very tidy mind. He liked to present his cases cut and dried, no loose ends, and here, in this otherwise perfectly straightforward case, nature had thrown a rat with wings into the mix. Bloody typical.

He shook the disappointment away; there were other cameras, more than a dozen in the street. They would find him, arrest him and place him at the scene. He had been attacked, no doubt, but had he pushed the guy to his death?

'Rewind the tape, and let's see it again, slowly please.' His eyes were on the back of the operator's head (nice crew-cut, black hair); his mind was fogged with irrational pigeon-related hatred. The film rewound, time recoiling, five times the normal rate, and then he saw it, in his peripheral vision: the movement.

'Wo... wo... wo. Wait a minute, play it again, stop it, stop it now!'

The video operator pushed the switches and the film played again. There was a glint of steel, the victim grabbed the man from behind, it looked like words were spoken, probably the usual exchange, there was the flash of grey and then the scene had changed. The victim was moving forward, slowly, slowly.

'The timing is wrong, it doesn't make sense. The tape must have stretched.'

The lad looked at him questioningly. 'I don't see it, what's the problem?'

Manee sat next to the lad, pointing at the screen as they re-ran the tape, a frame at a time. 'Here, look... he is far too fast. From here...' He pointed to the man, knife in his back, facing away from the camera, 'To here...' The grey blur passed; the man had moved two feet to the left, had twisted round and had freed himself from his assailant's grip. There was something else strange: one frame, a single twenty fifth of a second, the view half obscured by the grey blur of the bird.

'And this is too slow. See how he moves? It is subtle, but wrong. I've seen the body, you can see yourself, he chucks himself headlong into the subway, but he is moving too slow... to build up the momentum... can't you see? It's too slow... Now go back a bit.' He grabbed the controls to the lad's dismay, and found the frame he was looking for. 'There... my God...'

In the corner of the frame, partially obscured by the wing-tip of the pigeon, was the face of the man in white; it was caught, for a moment staring in their direction, directly at the camera. The face was surrounded by a swirl of movement, the trajectory of its path through space. The figure had turned and side-stepped, moving like a tango dancer, but had paused mid-turn to look at the camera... no, to look at the startled bird; the movement must have caught his eye.

'There must be something wrong with the camera. It

63

doesn't make sense. No one moves like that. It's all wrong.'
There was silence for a moment; there was something disturbing about the face that stared back at them. Was it the movement? Was it the street illumination? Perhaps, but the face was glowing, smiling, grinning, ecstatic.

'There is nothing wrong with the tape.' The lad's voice betrayed a hint of fear. 'Look, at the time stamp.' He re-ran the frames, one at a time, this time they watched as the tiny numbers clicked over. Hundredths of seconds, dutifully added up; cosmic time was ticking normally.

'I'm afraid I'm going to need that tape.' Det. Manee put his hand on the lad's shoulder. 'Get some experts onto it, might be some explanation we have missed.'

'Yes... of course...' The lad removed the tape and gingerly passed it across. He was visibly shaking. 'Perhaps it is nothing, some sort of artefact.' He felt somehow disconcerted. There was something about that face in the picture, the glory, the pleasure radiating from it, a swirl of movement, inhuman, monstrous. The face of the victim, twisted with confusion. It was vaguely pornographic, the ecstasy, the pain, but a man had died a moment later, his body broken and bleeding. This was a snuff movie and the victim had not stood a chance.

'Are you alright? Would you like to grab a coffee or something?' Det. Manee's face looking down at him was white as a sheet. He had felt it too, something was horribly wrong here.

'Yes, I think I would like a coffee though I might need something stronger.' He smiled weakly. 'But you are on duty.'

The detective smiled back, 'Not for much longer and I know a place we can go.'

SIXTEEN

Agneta Sibilski was a truly remarkable woman. This was the conclusion that Edward had come to after thirty seconds of careful study of her upper thighs.

Not that there was anything wrong with her lower thighs, they were just fine and the transition from thigh to knee to calf was as good as he had seen it. She was also rather good at her job. He described his own day to day working practise, attempting, with significant difficulty, to maintain eye contact. Trying not to mentally undress her (and, as a result, doing exactly that), he intimately outlined his trials and concerns. Agneta seemed to do most of the talking, but after an hour he realised that he was exhausted. He wasn't the fittest man in the building and he guessed that his elevated pulse rate might be putting him under some considerable strain. It was a pressure he was more than happy to bear. Agneta's highly manicured fingers caressed his computer keyboard.

'I'm just going to install a little program for you, Edward. Don't think of it as us spying on you; think of it more as a voyeur. Some people find it enhances their performance'

She said the word 'voyeur' with a rolling French accent, unnecessarily flirtatious Edward noted. The subtle suggestion that she might like things a little kinky sent a thrill through his spine. Edward had never had a kinky girlfriend. Perhaps Christmas and his birthday were coming together this year.

Their interview was completed with a 'lingering?' smile and Edward disappeared to make her a cup of tea. On his return Agneta had moved to the next computer along the row. She thanked him for the tea but quickly returned her attention to her new client, a rather abrasive product developer called Michelle. He tried to keep his eyes off them, not wanting Michelle to despoil the image of Agneta he was propagating in his mind. At one point he heard Michelle giggle (not an everyday occurrence); he hoped Agneta had not used the 'voyeur' thing with her. He was warming to the idea that that had been for him alone. The image of Agneta and Michelle rolling around on a huge white bed flashed into his mind. It was somewhat of a shock to him that it was not such a terrible image and as he sipped his tea he considered dwelling on it. Michelle suddenly let out a raucous laugh and the image evaporated. Edward wasn't one of these men that watched a lot of pornography (he had other types of DIY which kept his hands busy) so he wasn't as knowledgeable about sapphic love as he might have been. He wasn't entirely sure what women did together in such situations; the smuttier possibilities seemed faintly ridiculous to him. He decided to let the image lie.

SEVENTEEN

Mary Weston tried to manoeuvre her chair past the thicket of displays of Valentine's Day cards that cluttered the small newsagent. The wheelchair could rotate on the spot, perform wonderful little climbs up steps and at low speed was remarkably agile, but this year the Valentine's Day grotto was particularly dense and somehow a projection on the chair became entangled with a protruding part of a wire rack. Mary found herself trapped. She tried a few technical turns (nul points for artistic impression she thought), but only succeeded in becoming intimately involved in a stack of 'Love me. I'm your puppy' novelty devils. In trying to extricate herself from this additional problem she put the chair into reverse and sent the stack of greeting cards tumbling to the floor. If things weren't bad enough, several flew open and started chorusing comic promises of eternal love in high pitched voices. Mary was mortified (almost literally) and made a gallant if ineffective attempt to rectify the problem.

'Whoops a daisy!' A cheery shout came from the counter. 'Are you alright love? Let's sort this out.' Now Mary's embarrassment was complete. The owner of the newsagent had always been friendly enough to Mary, though perhaps a little too familiar, but he was invariably rude or dismissive to non-British nationals and Mary suspected he was something of a racist. She had submitted him to her 'economic sanctions' , using the newspaper shop opposite, ironically run by a rather abrasive, though very slowly defrosting, Indian lady, for a full six months, and this was the first time she had lifted those sanctions. There were road works in the street and the whole business was too complicated to even consider navigating.

The shop owner made a sly point of saying how nice it was to see her again, which galvanised her decision to give the road-works a try next time. She bought her normal local paper, a Mail for her husband (he liked to keep up with what the enemy was thinking), a Guardian for herself and a Telegraph for a neighbour. She felt obliged to buy a Valentine's Day card after having written off the owner's display, but she couldn't bring herself to do it. She told herself that it only encouraged the manufacturers and left it at that. She remembered, as she struggled with the heavy shop door, that it was Lilly's birthday in a few days time. She really ought to go back in and buy her a card, in case she didn't get the chance. On reflection, though, it was inevitable that it would prove impossible to find anything that wasn't dripping with bears and hearts, Lilly's birthday coinciding as it did with St. Valentine's. As she placed the papers under the seat of her chair she noticed that both the local rag and the nationals carried the same story. In her experience this was never a good thing. A quick glance revealed that there was a 'gerontophile' stalking the area. A man thought to be in his mid thirties, a man that liked older women. There had been three attacks in as many weeks. He had mainly targeted the very old and infirm. People were being told to be vigilant.

The thought of being ravished in her own bed sent a frisson of excitement down Mary's spine. She would have to read the article more carefully later. Perhaps the man was a bully and a pervert. Yes, it was probably the case otherwise why else be predatory? Surely there were enough elderly women who would not mind the attentions of a very much younger man. After all, what was the Internet for if not for bringing together people of disparate, yet complimentary desires? Maybe the man didn't have a computer. She pondered discussing the matter with Lilly; it might give her a laugh. On reflection she thought better than to worry her.

EIGHTEEN

Suzi slept fitfully. In her dreams she was transformed into an ogre, an enormous monstrous beast that swept all aside around her. Her huge ogre feet crushed a wailing hoard of screaming people, friends from her past, work colleagues, the flotsam of her local circle, family and friends. In her dream she was oblivious to their cries, her head in the clouds, puzzled and disconnected. She saw herself opening and closing giant ogre cupboards with her giant ogre hands, opening and closing, opening and closing. She had no idea what it was she was looking for, but her desperation was growing and her movements became progressively more frenzied. She thought she heard a voice, Michael's voice, tiny, quiet, muffled. Perhaps he was hidden in a cupboard. The doors were slamming now, clapping and slamming impossibly fast. She wanted to scream at herself, she had been here before, why look again and again? She could hear the screams of the people beneath her now, crying and begging. The cupboards slammed shut and she woke with a start.

'Suzi dear, are you alright?' Michael's mother was standing over her, her face full of concern. 'You have been asleep for twelve hours. We had to carry you to a bed here. The staff have been awfully kind. We really couldn't wake you. Here, have a cup of tea.'

Suzi sipped the sweet liquid greedily. The dream was fading now, slipping away as reality slipped in. Had she been responsible for Michael's death? Was there anything she could have done to stop him? It was so hard to hold her love for him, her experience of him, in her mind's eye. He had been gone only a few days and yet he was already fading from her memory, compacting yet diffusing, taking up less space, but tainting everything with his essence. She would never look at a horizon again without thinking of him, never allow another lover to do the little things he had done to her, but at this moment it was difficult to hold his face before her eyes.

'I'm sorry I wasn't always there for Michael, Margaret.' She had to say those words, they did not truly express her thoughts, but they had to be said. She felt a tear rolling over her lips, felt the blood rushing to her cheeks.

'You have nothing to apologise for Suzi dear, I was always there if you had to be away. We cared for him together; he was never alone unless he wanted to be. You have nothing to blame yourself for. He had no right to say the things he said. He was loved by us both.'

So it was true: Margaret had read between the lines too, seen the apportioned blame, and seen how sad he had become in her presence. A strange noise interrupted her thoughts; one of her mobile phones vibrated itself across the bedside table and onto the floor. Margaret retrieved it and passed it gingerly to Suzi. It was a work colleague; her P.A. had regained consciousness.

NINETEEN

Detective Patrick Manee tried to get to sleep. The wind was howling outside the window and he could hear the pain-wracked barks of foxes no doubt digging up his bulbs in his back garden. His head was aching, the same images repeated again and again, the same questions, no answers. The forensic science laboratory were puzzled, too; they had run a series of checks on the tape and found everything to be in order. The time mapped sequences were refractory to their clean-up algorithms and the motion blur caught in the flickering eye of the tape was just that: frozen time, a trapped ballet movement. They had had talks with forensics, the techie boys who dabbled in so many fields. They had done some back-of-the-envelope calculations, speeds, forces. Nothing made sense. Mark Phillippoussis couldn't serve so fast; a humming bird's wing would have been put to shame. Over-weight, middle-aged men did not move like hoverflies round a flower. Physics constrained you. Gravity punished you.

There had to be another explanation. Manee resolved to find the man. He had managed to obtain other images, none perfect but some usable; rewinding the trail of CCTV sightings back through the streets. There weren't so many places to get a late night drink in that part of town. Tomorrow he would ask a few questions, he would follow the chap around for a while. There was no rush. There was no obvious malicious element to the death he had been involved in. He had been attacked hadn't he? It was a mugging, a robbery, he would plead self-defence and the CCTV evidence would only add credence to a claim that he had never touched the man. There might be no case to answer apart from a charge of drunk and disorderly, apart from tardiness in informing the police and a blatant disregard for humanity, having not called an ambulance. He might get a raised disapproving eyebrow from a judge but it wasn't going to send him to jail and it wasn't going to get Manee a promotion. What motivated Manee now was something else; he had to get that smiling face, framed in motion blur, out of his mind. He wanted to be sure the man was human. Something told him deep inside that perhaps he was not.

Manee rolled over, kissed the back of the neck of the lad curled up asleep by his side. Things weren't so bad and he didn't always have a warm body in his bed. He could always save the world tomorrow.

TWENTY

The gym was quiet. Two floors below street level it was only the occasional passing of subway trains that disturbed Miguel's concentration. Even then the approaching hum, the gentle vibration through the floor and the hiss as the train glided away in the tunnels below were all somehow reassuring. Miguel loved this gym. It had changed him from a wiry, shy man who had been in a lot of fights to a muscular shy man who knew a lot about fighting. Perversely he had done far less actual fighting since he had made the conscious decision to make it his career. His peers counted their fights on their bound fingers and toes; Miguel had lost count of his street fights many years ago. It wasn't just the street fights either. There were the fights with his brothers, the fights with his father and, worst of all, the fights with his sisters. That was all in the past. He had another family now. He caught the sight of his glistening physique in the narcissus mirrors. He was looking good, looking sweet, looking dangerous. He liked to do a few sets before the gym opened its doors to the flotsam. This was his spiritual time, his time on the bag, his focus time. He did his yoga (he didn't like everyone to know about that), skipped for a while, the gentle hum of the rope, the tap-tap-tap, tappity-tap, a mantra that soothed his troubled mind and let him concentrate on what was truly important in the here and now, the alignment of bone and tendon, muscle and sinew. It was so difficult to explain to a non-fighter how you could gain unadulterated gratification from hitting another person. Most people never experienced the joy in the moment, when everything was just as it should be, when energy was beaming from your

73

heart, through your shoulders and arms and out through your fists. There was something remarkable about that moment of contact, the intimate exchanges of energy. It wasn't the same hitting a bag. This was the art. This was the soul of fighting. To understand it, you had to do it. Competition provided the motivation that was missing from the normal round of club practise; the change in training tempo. On the streets a fight was motivated by honour and women, drugs and territory. In normal sparring the expression and development of self-confidence and a desire to improve skills provided the usual motivation. In competition you represented your team, your tribe. He wouldn't let them down. He hadn't let them down yet and although it was early days his coach said he could go all the way, he had a natural gift, he was a fighter.

Contentment did not make a good fighter. Poise and skill were also insufficient. You needed a reservoir of anger, preferably mixed with fear, resentment and injustice. Happy people didn't usually make good poets and they didn't usually make good boxers. His gloves thudded into the long suffering leather of the bag, its surface worn smooth by a hundred thousand focused punches and shined by the sweat of a thousand furrowed brows. Today he was sweet, the moves were smooth, and the energy was flowing unimpeded. If he could feel like this on the big nights, every night, he would be unstoppable. It never seemed to work quite like that. The muscles tightened under the gaze of the crowd, and although once you started you were oblivious to their presence, the walk to the ring basted you in their gaze and their fears and anxieties were rubbed into your flesh.

His fists moved faster now as he introduced combinations into the routine. The mind was an obstacle to be distracted from the job in hand. Conscious control was too slow, hesitant and uncommitted. The hands had to do the punching for you, a punch had be unleashed, set free, the instinctive uncoiling scratch of a cat as something runs away, the recoil of a hand from scolding water, reflexes, set pieces, movement unadulterated by the clumsy hand of

74

thought.

Training, of course, was different. To teach your muscles the memory of that perfect punch took time, repetition and strength of mind. To train oneself into the wrong groove would be disastrous. That left you in a hole you had to climb out of, and if it had taken all your strength to climb down into it, you rarely made it out.

Timing was everything. This was the challenge of a real fight, a real fighter. Everyone was different, their quirks, their firing mechanisms. A fraction of a second before a fighter released a punch the thought had to cross his mind. The consciousness refused to release its grip entirely over control of the body and there were diplomatic channels to be passed before the dogs of war were unleashed. A good fighter could conceal this internal dialogue to a degree and read it in the eyes of his opponent. Sometimes it was expressed in a hardening of the lips, sometimes as a narrowing of the eyebrows or a tightening of the jaw. With time and experience sparring with his club mates, Miguel could read them all. This was his forte; this was what made him different from the others. This is why he could be a champ. In competition, without the benefit of previous bouts, things were different, altogether more exciting. The man who learnt to read the signals first, crack the code fastest, would have the element of surprise and the warning radar to anticipate an attack. If the intended punch was expected, the body had time to adapt, and the subtlest adaptation-perhaps a tilt of the head, a slight change in direction, the raising by half an inch of the covering glove, could mean the difference between smelling blood and tasting blood.

Miguel had not had much luck with women. In truth women had not had much luck with him either. They admired the width of his shoulders, the fit of his jeans, the childlike smile, the roughness of his hands and for a week or two that was enough. He never knew quite what to do with them though. They liked him to be rough, but were inconsistent and difficult to predict. Sometimes they wanted him to be forceful, but when he was with them he usu-

75

ally wanted comfort. Sometimes they wanted to mother him, protect him and he liked these times the best, but then they wanted another performance, and that wasn't always so easy. Performance was the right word; in so many ways sex was a performance for Miguel. The re-enactment of pornographic scenes he had watched alone in the dark. Recreations of vignettes he had witnessed: his brothers, his friends, making out on his parent's sofa. It had never seemed real, and when he was alone with a woman it never seemed real then either.

He tried not to think about what had gone wrong, the embarrassments, the spiteful comments but tonight they began to invade his state of bliss. This was his reservoir; this was where his anger lived. His fists were flying now, a tight combination of uppercuts and jabs. Faster and faster, he danced round the bag, ducking imaginary blows, cutting in with a cross, sliding in a sneaky elbow out of the line of sight of an imaginary referee. Combinations, pairs and triples repeated, then morphed into something else; the bag swung, he ducked, moved in, backed off then leapt in with a flurry. Uppercut, jab, jab, cross. He stopped; the room was beginning to spin. He rested his gloved hands on his knees, sucking in breath. No, he shouldn't stop, this was the breaker, this was stamina, this was where losers gave up. He was so warm, so right; he had air in his body all he had to do was use it. Ferociously he tore into the bag again. Emotion was filling him; tears were coming to his eyes, faces, his father, a scorned lover, a priest. He found himself weakening, wanting to stop, to hug the bag for support. His legs could collapse beneath him, any moment, but he released another flurry, uppercut, jab, jab, cross. Then came the omega point, the perfect, clean punch; the white light of orgasm, the flux of energy from stomach and groin, directed by the heart and liver, delivered by the fists. He dwelt in that instant, his mind a point of light in a velvety darkness. He felt the very resistance of the air, thickened and cloying, heating as his fist tore it apart. He saw the contact of glove and bag, the reciprocal deforma-tion, the dust rising from the impact, energy dissipating in concentric ripples; the end of travel of the punch, inch perfect and true, the final destination of a perfect journey.

'Jesus Christ!' The click of the door back onto the latch and the sound of his father's voice-no, no, it was his coach, his coach's voice, for a moment he had been unsure, snapped reality back into the room. His legs gave way beneath him, but he did not fall. The last thing he saw as darkness overwhelmed him, as he collapsed against the stinking leather, was the sight of his own arm, buried to the elbow in the cotton entrails of the bag.

TWENTY-ONE

Agneta Sibilski was a very, very tidy woman. The boyfriends she had let get close enough to see her house often commented that she 'liked her surfaces'. The English boys seemed to enjoy the affirmation of Teutonic clichés. Agneta just liked to have an uncluttered space in which to think. She liked Scandinavian wooden furniture, stainless steel and chrome and technology with lines so slick that the uninitiated would not be able to identify its function. She rather enjoyed having this special knowledge of her personal space. A man let loose in it would not be able to put on a CD or 'make themselves at home', turn on the heating or find the remote control; only she had that power. Sometimes she worried that relinquishing that power would be too much to bear, allowing someone else into that space too disturbing; her house becoming a sleekly designed, gilded cage, condemning her to an eternal existence as its lonely operator. It wasn't that she did not like clutter in other people's lives. The first experience of visiting a man's house, running an eye over the photos, the collected bric-a-brac, the objets trouvés, was always exciting. Here were the clues, the reflections of ego, sometimes laid bare, sometimes subtle. It did sometimes amaze her how some people lived amongst their clutter; chaos invading and smothering, every surface an avalanche of unordered inefficiency. There were times when she had walked into a man's house, well-oiled on white wine spritzers and looking forward to a coffee, a cuddle and a fiddle, when she had seen the pile of boxer shorts in the kitchen and decided there and then that she wouldn't be staying for breakfast. Sometimes, of course, it worked the

78

other way round. Too many surfaces, a few too carefully placed 'art pictures', and it could be a sign that she really had been invited in 'just for a quick coffee'. At the moment that didn't seem too much of a problem. Men and women flocked to her, and she courted their attention easily and confidently. She was too much of an intellectual to allow the vagaries of sexual attraction go to her head and she was aware that such gifts came with responsibilities and associated problems. Men in particular were often sexually predatory. Her looks and sexual allure just gave her advantages in this game. The true skill was in knowing who to beat, when and how. She was yet to find a suitable contender, but she was having a lot of fun looking for one. Of course, the perennial problem was that men in her category, with the same skill set and confidence were not always playing the same game. In this regard she had found the attentions of other women more attractive; with predatory women it was more often the case that you were valued as a quarry, pursued for your qualities. Some men were just interested in adding another pelt to their belt and Agneta did not approve of blood sports.

Agneta placed the cup of steaming cappuccino onto the octagonal glass-topped table, opened up her feline lap-top and began to analyse her assembled data. This job was an exercise in tedium. Kevin was a master of business sleight of hand. She admired his charm, his intellect, but deplored his motives. Once in a while she questioned her decision to stay with the company, but this was just a stepping stone; she would ride Kevin to the bank and then make her own way independently. She might not have been so mercenary had she not recognised the callous nature of his personality and felt no shame in taking as much advantage of her remarkable good fortune as possible. The world was divided into two types of people, predators and prey. Agneta had known from an early age that she was a predator. Being a predator made it easy to identify the traits in others and that was how she had identified Kevin. The truth of this analogy was reinforced with every animal documentary Agneta had ever seen. The buffalo, in their hoards, vast monstrous hulks of sinew and muscle tightly bound in a leather skin were fundamentally prey animals. If a single creature amongst them had the forethought to organise resistance against the packs of lions that circled their territory, picking off their young with cold-eyed precision, they would win a terrible and final victory. A stampede of the animals directed at a pride of lions, all the individuals organised for a moment, focussed on destroying their enemy would crush them into a bloody stain in a moment. A glorious buffalo leader could rid the wide plains of Africa of the larger predators forever. No buffalo would ever have to see their young torn limb from limb again. This never happened. The buffalo accepted their status as prey as the life was crushed from their windpipes. The lions lazed around, aloof and confident in their superior status. It was not fair, it was not logical or reasonable; it was simply the way of things. So it was with small businesses: every single one of them was run by someone who thought of themselves as a predator. Sometimes, of course, this was the case, but more often than not the CEO was in fact a prey animal, alone, separated from the flock. By the time a company like Kevin's was invited to the party, the weaknesses were showing. It was as if the young buffalo was sending an invite to hyenas. A prey animal was always aware of its status as such, they just weren't always as aware of the predators that circled around them. Not one of Agneta's clients had been forced to sign up to their analysis. They walked into the abattoir with their eyes wide open. Often the CEO's own motives for having the work carried out were despicable and underhand, crude cost-cutting initiatives covering management inadequacies. She had seen so many failing businesses making the same errors, the same arrogance, the same 'types' flaying around in the shitty wilderness for someone to blame.

Initially Kevin had made his money simply by operating a genuine service, time and motion analysis, telling the company bosses what any child could have done or telling them what they wanted to hear, whichever was the most profitable path. Often the advice was good; immersed as these people were in a mire of their own creation they were often blind to the simple truths around them. Then of course he had the idea of IIIs. Superficially a means to independently measure the efficiency of any particular employee, it would register every keystroke, identify error correction rates and true typing efficiency, and in combination with other statistics it was genuinely an extremely powerful tool. Of course it could do so much more. On average, the first three hundred keystrokes of any person's day included three passwords. People were remarkably unimaginative when it came to passwords, very rarely having a repertoire of more than half a dozen. Once a week, one in twenty people checked their bank account over the Internet at work, one in twenty-five checked up on an illicit website, one in thirty contacted a mistress, one in fifty attempted some crude form of fraud. Other people's fraud was a particularly rich seam of income.

Initially they had simply taken advantage of the security pennies from heaven, no more sophisticated than a shoulder surfer or a cafe-card duplicator. There was always the potential that they could be caught, however, especially in the banking sector. These crimes left trails and some people were anal enough about their finances to notice. Most extraordinarily rich people had financial affairs so complex that a little parasitism could slide under the radar. Oftentimes, however, the complexity of some people's affairs made the game more trouble than it was worth. This was a decision Agneta felt had been made by the majority of city bankers and analysts. Criminal behaviour was just too much work; there were easier pickings to be made. Blackmail and extortion provided a regular source of income and their targets often worked very hard to make sure that neither the initial crime nor Kevin's secondary, parasitic crime were discovered, effectively doing the hard work for them. It made better business sense to extort the fraudsters than to cherry pick people's bank accounts. There was also some satisfying moral equivalence in the process.

This job was unlikely to be entirely trivial. Agneta had

found Bill difficult to read; his motives for calling their company in were not immediately apparent. He seemed shrewd enough, smart and polite, he and Kevin even had some history together, and that meant that this job would probably have to be a legitimate one, but they did have to have a few legitimate customers. Agneta would have liked to employ a few more staff to run the everyday aspects of the business. They had automated enough of their process- es to bring in some paid help, but it was hard to find can- didates with sufficient talent and spark to do the job with- out them also being too questioning about its intricacies. Kevin was a talented programmer, and the data collection elements of his systems were well hidden to the untrained eye, but anyone who really wanted to know would not have too much difficulty in lifting the lid on their true motives if they had open access to their methods. The more people they employed, the more vulnerable they would become, and besides, it wasn't exactly hard work.

A plan of Bill Morris' office opened up on Agneta's laptop. Names appeared over work stations and data began to upload from the computer's data banks and a stream of micro-drive cards that Agneta inserted into the PC. Agneta performed the task quite automatically. The computer would perform the initial analysis, cross-reference the files and display the data graphically, temperature contours representing hotspots and cold fronts in the office environ- ment; the chilly finger of blame picking out its victims in powder-blue shades. The hard-drive whirred as the com- puter performed its analysis. Who would be the victim today? Agneta suddenly thought of Edward Spinks. She hoped it would not be him. He was harmless, shy, polite, obviously intelligent, but a born prey animal. She had seen the way Bill manipulated him, used the imbalance of power to quietly bully him; the poor man had no idea how he was being used. Agneta's occasional lapses of weakness amused her (which was why she tolerated them). She had watched Edward Spink's eyes moving over her body, seen the dilations of his pupils every time she looked directly at him. There was some part of her that still enjoyed that attention, even from a man like him. The naivety and purity of such behaviour was quaint in Agenta's world, but she wasn't entirely sure if she was motivated by attraction or pity.

The first graph flashed up, a weather map of achievement, parcels of effort flowing around the building as biorhythms and office politics dictated the working vibe. Distant and aloof as Agneta liked to think of herself, she occasionally found delight in watching and interpreting these data. Interesting patterns did sometimes emerge, strange conjunctions of influences warping the normal behaviour patterns. Usually these were dominated by the weather, the season (Christmas being a particularly strong case in point), and oscillations around pay-day and bonus time. Sometimes she knew they had genuinely stumbled on something interesting and useful and sometimes they actually informed the customer. More often such data could be put to better, more profitable effect.

The graphs flashed by, two months of data, the forecast for this weekend will be... sunny... with showery gloom coming in from the east. The patterns that flashed up immediately surprised her; the regularity of the result was something she had never seen before, a nearly perfect mandala, mathematical and incontrovertible, circles within circles targeting a powerful source at its centre. As days flashed past the pattern persisted. The normal dynamics she saw everyday overwhelmed by this other effect. The picture slowly changed, the colours intensifying, disparity polarising. There was a sudden change, a normalising, a swirling of the inks, as though an unseen hand had disturbed the surface of a pool and then it was back, the same as before, if anything more intense; a boiling eye focusing, its gaze increasingly penetrating.

Agneta sipped her coffee; it had become cold. She would make another one. For some reason she felt slightly disorientated. How strange that something which was so every day, so mundane for her could elicit such a feeling. She filled the kettle, her grip unsure. Remarkably, her hands were shaking. She opened the fridge door, its sensuous chrome lines for some reason offering little comfort. Perhaps something was wrong with the program; maybe the algorithm had become corrupted. That had to be the explanation. She would run a few simulations, check some historic data, make a few enquiries. There had to be a rational explanation.

TWENTY-TWO

Bill Morris was definitely not feeling his usual self. He was feeling something altogether better. The past few days had been a whirlwind of self-exploration. He felt like a young man going out on the pull for the very first time, his raw sexuality newly vibrant within him, dangerous and exciting. Whatever it was that was awakening now was not sexual in nature but was made of the same primordial stuff. He felt more alive than he had in years and his senses were heightened and screaming for more.

He sat at the head of his table, his two perfect children busy with their meatballs and pasta, his wife excitedly relating the trials of her day. He had thought of leaving it all behind. His new-found energies did not seem entirely compatible with the safety of a home and hearth. He was becoming a hunter and his blood was now running too rich for the blandness of suburban life. His wife's voice seemed almost distant now, so slow, so very, very slow. His mind was awash with plans and schemes. The business would have to be maintained, of course, he still needed a source of regular funding and security. The external audits would allow him to make a few cost cutting changes, but he would have to make bigger and better changes soon; everything was too bland. He was an entrepreneur, he was their leader; they would follow him or be damned. If he could just pin down the focus of his mind he would know exactly what the new course of the business would be. This was the only downside to his newly acquired powers. His concentration, normally so perfect and focussed, was constantly stirred by the inward pouring of new ideas. He had started keeping a journal to organise his thoughts, but the process of putting pen to paper was too slow, too constraining. He needed a new P.A. Someone to shout at, someone to record this torrent of thoughts and write them up later.

The main course was finished and desert arrived. Bill's wife fell silent, aware that she was not being listened to. Margo Morris observed her husband as he heaped fruit salad into his bowl. Bill had never been an easy man to live with, though it was difficult for Margo to put into words what the basis of that difficulty was. Bill could be kind, thoughtful, entertaining. He was never attentive and that was something that he had passed down to his daughter. Everyone and everything seemed to bore them. Even this assessment was too simple. Their boredom did not express itself as lethargy or disengagement; on the contrary, they were astonishingly busy people, applying themselves to diverse tasks in quick succession, constantly learning, never satisfied. The problem was not inherent within their characters; it seemed to be an inadequacy of the rest of reality to keep up with them. Margo had known for a long time that she was part of this inadequate reality. Bill tolerated her, and she worshipped him at times, hated him at others; the masochistic tendencies she had adopted helped her survive the more difficult moments. It was not that she was a weak woman, nor was she untalented, it was simply that with the arrival of the children, her place in the family dynamic seemed appropriate and comfortable. She was a mother and a house keeper; the order and comfort of their house and the promise inherent in her children (she had been instrumental in their early schooling) was a monument to her strengths. Initially Bill had not been a great father to his son. Margo had realised early on that he had found him dull. As they grew, Jessica had emerged as the apple of her father's eye. Bill never seemed to tire of spending time with her as he had did with her younger brother. Peter was a perfectly happy, well adjusted child, successful at sports, popular and of above average intelligence, but this was not enough for Bill. The same spark was not there; he would never be able to compete with Jessica for his father's affections. This did not worry

Margo unduly; perhaps selfishly she knew that Peter would always be closer to her than Bill, they would become confidants for each other, a family within a family. She would shelter Peter from her husband's dissatisfaction and, when he was older, Peter would champion her if Bill became too oppressive. Such seemed to be the way of things. Margo had read enough Victorian tragedy to know that hers was a common if not unavoidable fate.

She wondered now what was going through Bill's mind. She had thought of leaving him many times and she was aware that he had had similar thoughts; was he thinking along those lines now, planning his escape? He had spent more time away from the family recently, returning home later and later, the smell of smoke and booze lingering on his clothes. It wasn't the fear of losing him that worried her. There had been other women and no doubt there would be again; she understood his need for adulation, she knew she could not fulfil his sexual ambition. If he chose to go she would be more than well catered for, she had not been masochistic in the shared organisation of their financial affairs. To lose him would be a blow, but it was nothing she would not recover from. She worried about the children, changes that might follow their separation. The inevitability of it all filled her with sadness. She shook herself from such maudlin thoughts. So often of late she had found herself tired. Time was passing her by, every day a blur rushing headlong into the next, the tasks of maintaining the home seeming to fill her every waking hour; running behind children and husband was sapping her strength and draining her will.

Surely nothing was inevitable; surely they could hold their marriage together, in spite of the depression that was overcoming her. If things were to fail, it must not be because she had given up; the blame, if blame was to be attributed, would not be hers. Perhaps there was some easy explanation to Bill's new found lease of life. If there was another woman she was certainly making him happy, and perhaps that was the source of her misery. It could be work, some private battle about which she knew nothing.

Years before, she had tried to keep up to date with the politics and intrigue of Bill's work and concerns, but things had become so horribly complex and she had let them slip away. Her own daily routine seemed somewhat empty in contrast to the discussions of money men and contractors, the cycles of hiring and firing and the highs and lows of the business. It was not the complexity of it all that had confounded her, her mind was sharp and she had wanted to know the minutiae of everything. It was simply the pace of it all that had horrified her; it was the main reason she had not returned to work. Modern life was too fast for her and she would sit it out as a devoted wife and a mother.

'How would you kids like to go on holiday with your mother?' Bill's voice shook Margo from her thoughts.

'What about you Daddy? We can't go without you!' Jessica held her father's hand. Peter was beaming. Margo's heart sank. Now it was clear there was some sort of plan afoot, and this was just the start of it. She had allowed him to think alone for too long. She should have made more of an effort to keep up.

'What do you mean Bill?' Her voice quavered. She tried not to show the weakness that had gripped her. 'The children do not break up from school for three weeks, and besides, we've always holidayed as a family.' Bill smiled; it was a warm smile, the sort of smile he had not given her in a long time.

'I know this is out of the blue, but this is a rather special time. I've been making some changes to the business, I might even consider selling up. The thing is I need to work from home for a few weeks and I don't want any distractions, any at all. I know that sounds terrible, but I'm absolutely sure that in a couple of weeks I will have sorted everything out. Money isn't an issue, you can go wherever you like. In fact I've provisionally booked you flights to Las Vegas. You've always said you fancied seeing the Grand Canyon.' Bill was amazed at himself; it had simply come out of the blue. He really did need to be alone. He really did need to find out what was happening to him. He did not know why he had lied; it just seemed the right thing to do. Suddenly the memory of the death of the man in the subway came to him again. He had relived that moment in his mind a thousand times, each time the yearning to repeat the experience was greater. He had even gone so far as to walk past the subway again and again, placing himself in the same position in the strange hope that he might be attacked again, might rouse the same rush. He had no fear of being arrested; after all, what had done? The question that filled his mind now was what should he do? He had tasted the good life, had bitten into its flesh. He was not about to let that slide away.

'Please can we go on holiday, Mum, please?' Peter's face was flush with excitement. 'I've already sat my exams. There is nothing I can't catch up on. It would be wonderful.' Margo didn't know what to do with herself. She recoiled from Bill's penetrating gaze; she could barely tear herself away from his eyes which were burning into her own. She had never seen him so intense. She fled from the table and ran to the back of the house. She needed time to think. She would have to confront him, find out the truth. He would not lie to her face. Perhaps she would take the children; perhaps this would be the start of their separation. She had thought it and now it was happening; had she brought this on herself? Had he read her mind?

She ran into the bathroom and locked the door. She heard her husband's footsteps ascending the stairs; saw his face in her mind's eye, those flashing eyes. She began to feel afraid. The games they had played, the scenes, two consenting adults playing together, now seemed horribly portentous. She needed more time, more time to think, to formulate, to weigh up the options. She had no time. He was behind the door now, she could hear his breathing. She would not let him intimidate her, she would not be afraid.

She took the door off the latch and waited for him to come in.

TWENTY-THREE

Suzi reversed the BMW into a vacant space in the hospital car park, and then realized she could not open the car doors because of the dubious parking of the cars on either side. The BMW wasn't an enormous car, but lately such annoyances were becoming rather too common. She pulled out of the space and found another. The space next to this was half-filled by a Volvo which had parked along the line between two adjacent spaces, giving her a comfortable 'space-and-half'. She threw the car into this gap, glancing back at the embarrassing couple they made. She was still feeling a little bit guilty as she passed the consultants car park next to the wards. Here, rows of Mercedes and Saabs were parked higgledy piggledy as if some toy collector had shaken his display cabinet. A Jaguar XJS had been parked with such exquisite precision that it made four parking spaces unusable. Next time she would park next to the hospital.

It was a bitterly cold evening and she pulled her coat about her shoulders as she followed the signs round the building to the reception. She walked through a few interconnecting corridors completely unchallenged, and eventually found someone to talk to in order to assuage the guilt of walking around unmonitored. The lone night-nurse seemed genuinely pleased to have company. They exchanged a few pleasantries and Suzi was given a long list of directions to get to the right ward. The lifts weren't working at either end of the building, and the remaining operational one only stopped at odd floors, so she would have to walk through the dining hall and take a flight of stairs.

As the nurse's footsteps echoed away, Suzi could almost feel the instructions evaporating from her brain. It didn't matter, she knew the ward number, she was sure she could make her own way there. Hospitals held a special horror for Suzi. The sepulchral corridors, the smell of over-liberally used cleaning products, the white walls and signage, sign posts to disease: this way for breast cancer, this way for rheumatics. Even the children's wards with their brightly coloured toys and hand paintings made her feel ill. Artistic creations born out of the minds of sick children, smiling clown faces watching over the terminally ill. Suzi held her bunch of flowers tightly and marched through another booming corridor whose walls were greasily illuminated by a flickering, fly-blown fluorescent.

She was supposed to be going to cheer up her P.A. She really needed to cheer herself up a bit first. She concentrated on navigation, found the out of order lifts and the stairs behind. There were a lot of stairs to climb. In the stairwell Suzi could hear the crashing of some orderly as they struggled with a trolley. At least she was not entirely alone. The stairs spiralled up and up, floor 7, floor 8, floor 9, the wall decoration changing as she passed through the different disciplines. Gerontology had had a facelift, but genitourinary needed a little bit of affectionate attention.

At last she reached floor 12. She pushed the door and to her dismay found it didn't open. Stepping back she saw a sign. 'Please do not attempt to open this door access to the ward is through floor 12b'. The light in the stairwell flickered ominously. 'For Christ's sake!' She debated going back down, but decided instead to go up, just in case the floor above was the mythic floor 12b. To her delight it was. 12b was some outpost of the hospital; the bare concrete walls hadn't even the superficial smile of emulsion. It was not hospitable, but Suzi felt like Sir Edmund Hilary. If she had had the company of a Sherpa she would have given him a hug. Inevitably Michael's face came to mind and she had to stop for a moment, propped against the dusty concrete, to pull herself together.

The door to floor 12b thankfully opened. The ward was

deserted, everything clean, everything in place. The only signs of life the scuffs on the shiny floor from the door well as life from the floors below had had to scurry through the pristine new space. The room had a skylight; there was carpet in the corridor, paintings on the walls, chairs with soft covers and a shiny new lift (not yet in operation) waiting like a brushed-steel sentinel in the hall. The pastel-blue sign on the door said 'Private outpatients'. Suzi thought 'Telegraph readers' rest room' might have been more appropriate.

She walked back through the looking glass into a sparse stairwell linking 12b with the reality of ward 12. The floor was quiet, but at least there were people about; the beds were populated, though most of their incumbents seemed to be asleep. Around a few beds sat huddles of visitors, though the focus of their attention was often obscured from sight. Suzi found the Night Sister and asked for directions. Her P.A., Miss Julie Wetherall, was in bed 24 at the end of the ward. She was probably sleeping, but it would be alright for Suzi to leave her flowers and sit for a while.

Suzi slowly walked the gauntlet between the rows of beds where Julie lay sleeping. The bed was half obscured by curtains and as she drew them back she was confronted by a battery of monitors and drips. Julie's hair was swept back and electrodes were attached to her forehead and temples. The Night Nurse had informed her that when Julie had woken from her coma she had been lucid but somewhat confused. They were monitoring her brain activity for signs of epilepsy (though she was not to use that word in the girl's presence).

A monitor flashed a set of spiky curves, Julia's life measured in pulses. Dreams registered as sinusoidal waves. Julia's face was calm; she seemed to be sleeping peacefully. Suzi was tempted to leave the flowers and go, standing on the threshold of the bed. She did not want to wake her. There was a big bunch of flowers already there and balloons and a card. She recognised some of the handwriting; the crowd at work had obviously organised a collection.

92

Suzi was slightly relieved. Julia was not the most popular girl at work. She felt an uncomfortable pang of inappropriate envy. She had received no card for her own loss. Perhaps her situation was simply too complicated, too awkward. Hallmark did not make a sorry for the suicide of the love of your life card. She rummaged through her bag, pulled out the vase she had had the forethought to bring and went looking for some water. When she returned to the bedside, her flowers neatly arrayed in water, Julia was stirring. Her lips were opening and closing as if she were speaking in her sleep. One hand, with wires extending from finger tip monitors, lay above the covers and was opening and closing slowly. The monitors were flashing the same patterns, but this time they seemed to be slightly sparser. A flashing heart in the corner of the screen indicated the pulse and was flashing the figure 52. Suzi moved toward the bed to place the flowers on Julie's bedside cabinet, but she stopped short. As she moved closer, the monitor responded with a beep, the oscilloscope lines flickered and the spikes became less frequent. The pulse meter showed 48, 46, 40, 35. Suzi withdrew in confusion and as she did so the monitor responded affirmatively, quickly returning to its previous signals. As Suzi had got closer to the bed she had felt something strange herself, a feeling of lightness and disorientation, disconnectedness, the same feeling she had experienced at Michael's bedside, where he had lain dead in the morgue. She began to feel faint and backed away from the bed. What was happening to her? Was this some kind of panic attack or neurosis? Retreat immediately brought relief. She pulled up a chair and sat for a moment, trying to arrange her thoughts. After a few moments the panic had subsided. There had to be a rational explanation. She was tired, stressed out, in mourning for goodness' sake. She looked through her bag and removed her mobile phones. Yes, that had to be it; the mobiles had interfered with the monitor. All were switched off. It was strange that they should have an effect even though they were off, but then, who knew what 'off' meant these days, nothing electrical ever seemed to allow you to switch it off completely. She threw them onto the bed, for a minute feeling faintly ridiculous that she should have allowed herself to get into such a state over nothing. A nurse eyed her suspiciously from across the room. She must try to remain calm.

Suzi approached the bedside for a second time. She could clearly see Julia's face, peacefully sleeping, but as Suzi approached it was as if a troubled dream started to play over Julia's face: her hands began to clench the pillow, her mouth began to work feverishly, initially as if gasping for air, then forming florid shapes, as if mumbling. With every step the monitors marked Suzi's progress by pulsing progressively slower, the sharp spikes stretching into angular peaks, the periods between them extending almost imperceptibly with every step. The pulse rate monitor flashed, 50, 41, 32, 28. Suzi froze mid-step. It was happening again, fear gripped her and a band of pain seemed to tighten around her head. She slowly recoiled, the curves on the monitor springing back as if some tension were being released from them. The tension in her own head became more bearable, Julia's sleep became calmer. Suzi calmly placed the vase of flowers on a nearby table, arranged as best she could, then, overcome, grabbed her things and ran for the door. The Ward Sister ran behind her for a moment, but she was gone, down flight after flight of stairs, the numbers flying past her as if in a dream, spiralling down. She wanted to run and run into the cold earth and let it swallow her up. This could not be real; it had to be some horrible nightmare. She burst through the entrance doors of the hospital into the cold air, gasping, praying that somehow the chill of reality would wake her from this terrible dream. She sunk to the pavement, tears pooled in her eyes and she started to shake and sob uncontrollably. This couldn't be happening; none of this was real, Michael wasn't dead, she wasn't cursed; she had done nothing to deserve this, nothing...

An elderly couple passed her, unsure of whether to offer sympathies. A young orderly approached. 'Are you alright? Can I get you anything?' He recoiled from her as she spun round to face him. Her face was a mask of terror, her eyes wide and imploring. The air became still, thick and viscous. Through the blurring tears Suzi saw her own hands falling away from her face, the after-images of movement clearly visible. It was happening again. This time she would not leave a trail of victims. She had to get away, to hide. Her hair whipped her neck and throat as she turned to run; the pain was almost unbearable, but the air yielded to her, fizzing and popping as it passed around her body. The orderly slumped to the floor, his legs knocked from under him as if by a wave. He did not feel the transition from standing to falling. His head hit the floor before he had realised that something was wrong. As darkness enfolded him, he had a vision: a woman running, impossibly fast, in the direction of the car park; her body a blur of motion.

TWENTY-FOUR

Detective Patrick Manee woke with a jolt. If he was completely honest with himself he was not really best suited to the type of police work he had become involved in. He really enjoyed his sleep and had the wonderful gift of being able to sleep anywhere and everywhere. No car seat was too uncomfortable, no discreet observation post too cold. Invariably on lookout he would fit himself into a hidden quiet spot, rest his head and then immediately fall asleep. It was for this reason that he always took a keen young officer along with him. This officer was Constable Paul Smith: tall, dark, of Irish extraction, with a good right arm and very, very keen.

It was the good right arm that had woken Manee from sleep and nearly knocked him out of the car into the road. 'Look Sir, he is leaving the house.' Although Manee liked his sleep he had been doubly blessed with the ability to wake up remarkably quickly. 'Come on then, let's go. Don't get too close. Buzz me if you think you have been seen.'

Manee got out of the car, closed the door quietly and followed Bill into the subway. Constable Smith took a deep breath, counted to ten and then followed. This was his first clandestine pursuit and he did not want to muck it up. Being such a large and tall man he had always done rather well in the shouting, running and knocking to the floor stakes. This was altogether different. He had always been rather self conscious and he felt he stood out like beanpole amongst potatoes. Manee had disagreed, said his height was an advantage, people tended only to notice those that looked at them at eye level. Eye contact was everything; if you didn't make eye contact you were as good as invisible.

He had felt reassured by this. Tonight he would try to be as tall as possible. He had found Manee to be very friendly and not too friendly either. They had wound him up a bit at the station; potentially spending the night in an unmarked car with the forces' only openly gay detective did get your legs pulled. Smith felt he was fairly liberal minded, but when people came out they didn't always realise the knock-on effect it could have on their colleagues. Manee was not a very big bloke, but he moved pretty fast, he was getting too far ahead and Smith quickened his pace. The walk from the car to the subway seemed to take a lifetime. As he descended into the station he heard the hum and rumble of an approaching train. He ran down the stairs three at a time; he could hear the doors opening, the sound of people descending onto the platform. A recorded message was giving a list of destinations and changes. He ran down the corridor, police-issue toe-caps ringing out against the tiles. 'Shit, shit, shit!' He skidded round a corner to see the train doors sliding closed, the train gave a jolt and then slid away. 'Shit, shit, shit!' He heard a loud cough and he spun round on his heels. At the platform opposite was another train. Manee stood in the doorway, he gave him a nod. Beeps started to sound and a recorded voice informed the passengers to 'Mind the doors please, mind the closing doors.' Manee held them as they tried to slam shut; Smith dived underneath Manee's arm and, panting, leant against a glass support. 'Thank you!' he gasped.

'You're welcome. That was a close one.' Smith scanned the carriage: their target was not there. He looked questioningly at Manee, who gave a glance over his shoulder. Two carriages down was the white coated Bill Morris, legs astride, rocking with the movement of the train.

Things had come to a bit of a head with Bill Morris. Manee was certain of this. He had kept him under limited observation for the past two months. He was furious with himself for missing Bill's attack on his wife. Unfortunately he had other demands on his time and he was having trouble fiddling his time sheets as it was. On the night Bill had

lain into his wife, Manee had been asleep in the rain outside a coke den. Margo had left a few days later with the
children. They had enough suitcases to be gone for a
month. Margo had hidden her bruising with a scarf, but
whatever he had done, the psychological change was most
dramatic. Margo had changed. Manee had watched her
taking the children to school, watched her leave the house
on her normal round of jobs. The day she had left the
house with the children she was a broken woman. Her
eyes had scanned the road as she had slipped away. She
seemed somehow haunted. She had left the car at
Heathrow, and had not bothered to buy a parking ticket.

They left the train in the West End of London. Smith felt
odd moving through the familiar streets 'in hot pursuit.'
The world looked different when you were on duty. People
became targets, casualties or victims; you were in the
world but not of it, an observer, a voyeur of life. Bill moved
swiftly. For a heavy man he seemed light on his feet; he did
not appear to be running, but Smith found himself having
to scurry to keep up. After three minutes in pursuit he had
lost sight of him. After another minute he had lost sight of
Manee. 'Shit, shit, shit!' He turned a corner and felt a hand
on his shoulder; Manee pulled him back.

'Calm down, there is no hurry. We are unlikely to keep
up with him anyway.' Manee's voice betrayed a hint of
excitement. It was in these moments that Manee understood the thrill of the huntsman; when your quarry was
human you had a truly worthy opponent.

Smith was confused. 'I don't understand? Have you lost
him?' He could not believe that they had let him get away.
A heavy man, big white coat, late forties, surely they could
have kept up.

'You'll understand soon enough.' said Manee. 'I wasn't
sure before, but now I am, I've never seen anything quite
like this. I'm not sure what to make of it. But we don't have
to worry. Not yet.'

'I don't understand. We've lost him. What are we going to
do?' Smith hadn't realised how exhausted he was. His

98

breath was coming in gasps.

'I know where he has gone.' Manee started walking. 'Tonight we are just observers. Do you understand? We need to see how he moves, how he operates. I suspect we won't be able to make an arrest on our own. Tonight I'm gathering information and you are my witness. I want you alert and aware of the target at all times.'

'Yes sir. Of course sir, but what are we going to do now?' Smith wiped the sweat from his brow. He really needed to get back down the gym; rugby on the occasional Saturday he was not working simply didn't seem to be enough anymore.

'I don't know about you, but I'm going for a drink. Come on.'

The club was down a side-street. Not particularly salubrious, some neon, a few chalk boards and a velvet rope with an enormous bouncer. Manee stepped up to the door, and was greeted warmly by the doorman, whose face melted from bulldog aggression to jovial welcome. 'Paddy, who's your friend?' The doorman grabbed Smith's hand and shook it warmly; the two big men weighing each other up as big men are want to do.

'Simon, this is Sergey; lovely bloke, good cook, terrible dancer. Sergey this is my colleague Simon.' Sergey laughed.

'You want to watch him, he could lead you astray!' He laughed a deep rolling belly laugh and slapped Simon on the back with a force that would have knocked a smaller man to the floor.

'You boys get inside, I'd say have a drink on me, but I can't afford to drink here myself and the bastard owner doesn't let the staff drink on the house.' He laughed again. 'See you later, don't start any trouble or I'll have to sort you out!'

They entered the club, coats were checked at the door, security waved them through, and they descended some steep stairs into an underground bar and dance floor. Manee bought a couple of drinks at the bar and scanned the room.

'You come here often then?' Smith took a sip from his whisky and coke and placed the glass down on the bar.

'Not on my salary,' began Manee, 'and it's not really my kind of place.' The music was loud, a DJ was hunched over decks in a corner and a mixed set were moving around lazily on the dance floor. Manee made a mental note of the cocaine dealer in the corner, two female prostitutes at the bar and a nervous lad, who might be new trade, or perhaps an asylum seeker mistaken as trade with an older man in the corner of the bar. Bill Morris was nowhere to be seen.

'We've lost him then.' Smith took another drink. 'I'm afraid I don't dance, so after this I might just go back and write the report.'

'Wait. I'm sure he is here somewhere. He is exploring, you see, pushing his envelope. Perhaps there are private rooms somewhere in the building.' Manee slowly made his way onto the dance floor, stepping into a ring of dancers and finding himself quickly involved in a provocative embrace with a blond young lady who appeared to be having some difficulty focusing on him. He weaved away into the dark recesses of the club and waited.

The very back of the club was hidden behind curtains, and from behind these came the sounds of giggling and a man's laughter. Manee tried to picture the scene: Bill Morris, two, possibly three girls. There was the sound of sniffing and melodramatic sighs. Bill was obviously playing the role of sugar daddy. A brunette appeared from between the drapes, her eyes bright, her face adorned with a broad, beaming smile. She burst through the curtains, poked her head back through the opening and giggled again before staggering round and heading towards the bar brandishing a fifty pound note over her head. Manee's eyes flashed between the young girl and two men at the far end of the bar. They were pale and furtive, with thin moustaches and long leather coats. They were conversing together in whispers, faces almost touching, eyes flicking between the brunette's money and the top of her low-cut blouse. Smith also became inveigled with her as she brushed up against him and started to stroke his nose with the curled-up note. The two men behind shifted their position, sliding back into the shadows. Manee began to worry; he was beginning to understand the play. He did not want Smith to get involved in the cross-fire. A barman came across to the brunette and she threw herself, cleavage forward, against the bar. She appeared to offer Smith a drink, and the barman started lining them up in front of them.

The brunette took three in hand; change was offered and refused. Manee saw the barman drop coins into a jar and slide a note into his waistcoat pocket. The brunette looked back at Smith and indicated he should follow her. Smith smiled somewhat weakly in Manee's general direction, picked up a handful of drinks and followed her swaying form back through the waving bodies. In the middle of the dance floor, drinks spilling to left and right, she stopped to whisper in a girlfriend's ear, and she in turn followed them in tow; her eyes staring fixedly at Smith's firm behind. Smith looked back over his shoulder as he passed through the curtain and then disappeared from sight. The police report began to formulate itself in Manee's tired brain. 'We cunningly infiltrated the accused's circle of friends by feigning interest in proffered drinks, drugs and sexual favours.' It was definitely going to need some work. Instinctively Manee sipped his whisky. He hoped the sight of their quarry would inspire Smith to at least retain some of his mental faculties. The sound of renewed giggling behind the curtain made him begin to wonder if that was likely.

Manee had spent rather more of his life in clubs than he would have cared to admit. The sweaty nights fuelled by the little pills seemed very distant now. He wasn't the boy-man he had been, he could not compete on the open market with the pumped-up pleasure boys that populated much of the gay scene. He preferred to keep his clothes on these days and he was beginning to prefer his men the same way. The straight scene had changed beyond recognition; the truth of this was dancing all around him. If the sixties had reclaimed sexual liberation for the uptight western cultures, the eighties had won us back the freedom to dance. Men and women pranced and preened. The music was now tribal, the beats hypnotic. The volume was increasing incrementally; it was as much as Manee could do to hear himself think. The temptation to just close his eyes and give himself up to the music was acute. The room was warm and the whisky was tranquilizing him on the inside. How many hours had he spent barely awake, sliding between consciousness and sleep in clubs. Where had that time gone? Single tracks of music had seemed to last for hours then, great symphonies of clicks and beeps, the glorious catharsis of repetition. Some things seemed to gain more truth if shouted a hundred times by a thousand voices, a hundred-thousand prayers from smiling boys and girls to the gods who looked after ravers. The faces appeared before Manee's eyes: the open mouths, the wide eyes and their guileless flaccid love. It had all evaporated. The past was a compilation record for the chronically ageing, serving only to remind the complacent present of its naïve lack of sophistication.

The music was struggling to some schizophrenic emotional climax; rapped lyrics tumbled over broken beats, samples pasted clumsily in artless collages of sound. The DJ was looking serious. Someone ought to have told him the avant-garde was a historical movement. Tired limbs were flagging on the dance floor. This was no place for amateurs now; brains addled with cocktails of stimulants and depressants could make little sense of the musical avalanche that was bearing down on them. Another goateed twenty-something took to the decks and mainstream comfort food for the ears was resumed. Manee shook himself awake. This was no good, there were lives at stake. He knew this now. Another young lady slipped behind the curtain, the shady figures at the bar slowly circled the room, moving, pincer fashion, towards the curtained enclosure.

Surely they would not make a move here, inside the venue? Manee had been sure they would wait until the end. Tonight he had just planned to observe, but things were taking another course. The figures circled, slowly, casually, lips pursed, jaws set for violence. It was not looking good. Manee watched their every sleek movement, every look to the left, glance to the right, the signals between them, moving through the crowd like two panthers through long grass. It seemed to take a lifetime for them to reach the curtain. One man passed by so close he could have reached out and touched him. He could smell the man's breath, acrid with cigarettes and garlic, and a pheromone-rich cocktail of toiletries and sweat which trailed behind him.

They paused at the threshold of the curtain, reached into their inside pockets and then stepped into the darkness beyond. The curtains fell closed and all was hidden. How long to wait. It all depended on Smith; perhaps if he was too far gone it might be for the best, they might just ignore him. He tried to imagine the conversation, the practised threats; there would always be threats. Gangsters loved role play, and they all knew their parts. Had five seconds passed or five minutes? The music had faded from his consciousness, reality slid in and out of his perception. He could hear the throb of blood in his ear. It reminded him that he was alive. Then he saw Bill Morris striding through the curtains. He caste them behind him, as a Victorian villain might adjust his cloak. His face was flushed, his hair a dishevelled halo. He seemed triumphant and satiated. Manee could imagine him dabbing blood from his lips with a monogrammed silk handkerchief. He walked forward into the room, gliding between the swaying bodies, the negative effects of his significant bulk negated by the precision with which he chose his path between them. Manee closed in on him, trying to head him off by the corner of the bar, but as he got closer he felt strangely weak. He pushed a drunken reveller aside and tried to focus his gaze on the retreating figure, forcing his legs to obey his will. Running across the dance floor he was no match for Morris who was half way up the stairs before he had even reached the bottom of them.

'William Morris! Stop where you are! This is the police!'

103

Morris span around and glared down at him. His eyes were wide, glittering with internal fire. Manee wondered if it was an effect of the drugs but there was something unnatural there, something feral. The gaze was piercing, pinning him like a bayonet to the stairwell, his heart beating fit to burst. In that moment's eye contact he had felt himself being scanned, committed to memory, studied. The gaze was angry but measured. There was an assured superiority in it; here was a man unafraid, a man with all the time in the world. Bill Morris tore his gaze away and moved away, cat-like, into the assembled crowd, disappearing from sight. Manee shook himself into activity; what was the matter with him? Every movement had been an effort, everything happening too fast for him to focus on. He felt confused and vulnerable, somehow fragile and elderly.

'Sergey!... For Christ's sake stop that man leaving!' His voice didn't sound like his own, it was high pitched and penetrating. He grabbed the stairwell for support.

There was a scream from the top of the stairs followed by another from the back of the club; people started shouting, music stopped and the lights came up. Sixty bleary eyes squinted around, looking for meaning. Manee ran to the top of the stairs, along the corridor past confused onlookers and into the street. Sergey lay on the ground, surrounded by a group of bouncers. Six shaven heads turned towards him, bewilderment written across each face. Someone was calling for an ambulance. Bill Morris was nowhere to be scene. Blood was pooling around Sergey's head, there was blood on the wall behind him. Manee ran to his side and examined the wound; he had been thrown backwards with considerable force. The cut was deep, but his pulse was strong. Manee tore off his shirt, rolled it and told one of the bouncers to hold it as a pressure bandage against the wound. He turned back to the club. Shocked faces loomed up at him, couples hugging close together.

A circle of people had assembled at the back of the dance floor. One of the girls Manee had watched was sitting on the floor, legs pulled into her chest, sobbing. A barman was trying to comfort her. The group was otherwise silent. The curtains were pulled back and as Manee approached a gory tableau was revealed. His thoughts were of Constable Smith. He stepped through the assembled throng. Two bodies lay sprawled, one half over the other. It was the two heavies, their eyes open, their faces twisted in a look of fear and surprise, their necks thrown back, the handle of a knife projecting from each of their throats. The knives had pinned their mouths shut; in one case, the man's tongue was extended through swollen lips, a comic death mask, floating in a frothy sea of blood.

Here also was Constable Smith, spread-eagled on the floor: his chest and groin covered in blood, his trouser flies unbuttoned, his head back, his nose a mess of scarlet. White powder lay in drifting lines on a glass table. Blood spatters had landed upon it, red craters in the snow. A young woman laid beneath him, apparently unconscious, her head on its side, her eyes rolled back into her head. Another woman was draped across his chest. She raised her eyes to Manee imploringly, her face a melted mess of make-up and tears.

'He's dead! He's dead! He tried to stop him and now he's dead!' Manee pulled her aside, and examined his colleague. He was unconscious but alive. A blow to the face had broken his nose, perhaps his jaw, but that was all. Manee felt faint with relief. The preceding few minutes had seemed like a waking dream, now reality was crashing back in. Manee found his radio and tried to request back up, but there was no signal in the basement of the club. He asked for assistance, and together with a barman shifted Smith's dead weight from the woman beneath him. Manee checked her airway, her pulse and her breathing. She would be uncomfortable in the morning, but at that moment was quite incapable of feeling pain.

He rearranged Smith's clothes to make him slightly more presentable and ran back to street-level; what had seemed like an Olympic trial not half an hour ago now barely raised his pulse rate. Sergey had regained consciousness. He was sitting now, holding the scarlet shirt on his head.

'I'm so sorry Paddy, I don't know what happened. The bastard... I've never seen anything so... I don't know.' His voice trailed off. He was confused, shaken. He felt vulnerable. He had not felt vulnerable since the Serbian army had swept though his village in tanks fifteen years before. He had hoped he would never feel such fear again. Manee was quick to reassure him.

'Don't worry mate, there was nothing you could do. I'm sorry I involved you in this.' He guarded his words. There was so much to say, so many questions to ask, so many questions would be asked. He was not sure he had any answers. He heard sirens in the distance; so many of his nights these days ended with the wail of sirens. This would not be the last.

PART TWO
THE GIFTED

ONE

'I'm sorry, I do understand what you are saying Agneta, it's just that it really doesn't seem to make much sense; it's all, all, well, it's...' Edward Spinks was feeling somewhat cornered by Agneta's penetrating glance. She really was a piece of work, and the more cross and concerned she looked the more irresistible he found her. He wanted to pick up her charts, fascinating as they probably were, and throw them out the window. He had imagined gently exposing the milky white flesh of her breasts and ravishing her there and then on the floor of Bill Morris' office. In his mind's eye their thrashings would knock papers and files akimbo, a snowstorm of memos and product designs showering their naked, writhing bodies. They might crawl under Bill's office, roll among the electric cables, become hopelessly entwined in USB bondage and have to be rescued by the humourless I.T. support staff. Edward looked longingly at the coil of printer cable pooled by Agneta's perfectly turned ankle and desperately tried to drag his mind up from the gutter.

'I know... I know it doesn't look real, believe me, I look at hundreds of these a week. I have never seen anything that looks even remotely like this. It isn't normal, it isn't rational.' Agneta was becoming agitated. Edward found that highly erotic. She was possibly even more beautiful when she was agitated.

'Agneta...' He resisted the urge to say darling, but he tried to get his eyes to say the words on his tongue's behalf. 'Agneta... it just cannot be right. What you are suggesting, interesting and potentially as amusing as it is, is quite simply ridiculous and besides...' At this point he coughed melodramatically. 'I come off rather badly in it, don't you think?' He laughed, though there was a hint of nervous self-deprecation in it. 'Especially sitting as I do next to the teacher!'

'No, you are not listening; with you men it is always the same, "me me me me", what does this say about me? Forget about yourself for a minute, can't you? This is important, this is incredible and I am absolutely convinced that it is true. I know it is crazy and bizarre and perhaps I should not have mentioned it to you, perhaps I should've just made something up, fobbed you off with a story you wanted to hear, told you any old lie. But this is true.' Agenta was moving away from being agitated and towards being upset. Edward felt the change in vibe acutely and desperately weighed up the pros and cons of being credulous to her suggestions. On the one hand he might seem somewhat sensitive and concerned; on the other he would appear gullible and naively impressionable. His natural sexual deceitfulness, suggested the latter; his natural intellectual superiority complex balked at the idea. It was an uncomfortable internal struggle. He decided to opt for a third way.

'What does Kevin think of this? Has he ever come across such an... anomaly?' His sexual deceitfulness thanked his intellectual superiority for this artful sidestep.

'He doesn't believe it either. He...' Agneta was choosing her words carefully. In actual fact Kevin had laughed heartily, said 'I've never seen that before!' and asked her if she had gained access codes to the accounts section.

'Look, look...' She withdrew two more printouts which looked rather like the first; the same offices, the same target shapes upon them in various rainbow colours. 'This is the floor below yours, see... the office layout is the same, they are otherwise identical. We got the contact for your marketing department as well... which is why I can show you the data. Can't you see?'

'Well, I can see there is the same pattern, the contour lines are all arranged in circles, all focusing on this office, just with different colours... what is the difference? ...A different scale?'

'No, the scale is the same, the effect is just weaker; different floor, weaker effect. Look...' She pulled out more printouts of the building. 'This is the floor above... and this is the floor above that... The same patterns, the same problem... the effects are just weaker. Weaker as you get further from this office.'

Edward was beginning to feel bewildered. The whole thing had to be some sort of joke, a rouse. This firm was obviously trying to play some sort of trick on the lot of them. It wasn't April the first; surely no one would fall for such a patently obvious play like this. He half expected Agenta to pull a Feng shui frog from her briefcase and tell him that celestial alignments could be achieved by putting the shredder closer to the water cooler. He was beginning to tire of the whole idea. This was either an insult to his intelligence or some kind of test and he was not going to put up with it, even if the bait was as attractive as Agneta.

'Right... so what you are suggesting then, if I don't misunderstand you, is that this room is... exuding... some malevolent force, which is radiating out in all directions, penetrating several floors of the building and preventing anyone within range from reaching their productivity goals. Like sick building syndrome, but concentrated in this single office, a chancre amongst us poor victim staff!' He couldn't contain his mirth. For some reason he was losing the inhibitions that flirtation imposed on him. Who was this woman anyway? Who did she think she was? Who did she think he was? Some oik from sector 27b who fell out of management school last year after daddy bought them a library? It was painful! 'You are seriously suggesting that we are sitting in some Bermuda triangle of an office, some vacuum cleaner to hell focussed on this room, this very chair, where our will to live, our enthusiasm and our perky office productivity disappear into some sort of ambition black hole?' He was warming to his theme now. 'I've worked here eight years and I can tell you that every day I sit at my desk and treat this company with the same disdain that I do every other day. I apply the same half-arsed, barely interested tiny proportion of my mental activity that I feel this company deserves. If you are telling me I should look around for another job where I can feel more fulfilled you are probably right; but if you think you can just get me to go quietly, to resign and bugger off you are quite mistaken. I want a full severance contract and I want to keep my shares!'

Edward Spink's heart was beating like the clappers. Agneta had remained fairly calm throughout. Now she appeared positively crushed. She looked as though she might even cry. Edward had half expected Bill to jump from behind a pot plant and tell him to clear his desk. He had clearly gone too far. Agneta was silent for a moment, breathing deeply, biting her lower lip. Edward began to feel uneasy. He was getting very mixed signals and none of them said 'bed'. After a long pause she started again. She slowly rolled up the plans and withdrew a third set from her briefcase.

'Edward. This is not about you. I'm not trying to get you sacked. I'm not trying to make you resign. This isn't some kind of joke or trick. I've looked at your C.V. if you must know. I thought you might be interested. Your degrees, psychology, sociology, you work here; I genuinely thought you would want to know. I thought you might have an explanation, some insight.' Her voice was calmer now; the kind of 'I'm disappointed in you Edward' voice that his mother had often used when she wanted him to do something for her.

'It's not the room, Mr Spinks. It isn't a sick building. Look...' She unfurled the last set of plans. 'This is what your office looks like on other days.' The concentric rings of colour were morphed into random splodges. The region around his desk was a bright purple, an indication of intense, wilful productivity. He was not sure whether to be happy or concerned. 'This is the office yesterday...' Again a similar pattern, this time the blotches had migrated, the mental weather in the lab was obviously changeable.

'So what's the difference?' Edward tried to regain his composure. 'Why do we work in the office of hell on Monday and a normal office on Tuesday? Is it the air-con, the coffee machine, what?'

Agneta turned to him. Her eyes penetrating into his the

way they had done on the first occasion they had met. Edward began to feel uncomfortable.

'Mr. Spinks. It is your boss. It is Bill Morris. On the days that he is away, your office is like any other office. People have their good days, people have their bad days. If we look over a six month period, we can even work out who the free loaders are.' She was becoming calmer now. She had his interest. He was beginning to see the significance of what she had uncovered.

'On the days when he is here, it is different. I've done the maths. I've plotted the graphs. Your boss does forty percent more work than anyone else in this building Edward, forty percent. And what's more, when he is here, everyone in his vicinity does less, including you.' She was tired, why should she care about this? Kevin was right to have told her to let it lie, some glitch of the program, they would fabricate some data later. Something had stopped her, made her reconsider. Her life had been something of a farce, a series of fraudulent ploys. This was something important, something real; something sinister.

Edward began to feel uneasy. He tried to shrug it off. It had to be a load of old bunk. 'That must just be because we hate having him around.' Bill had been a pretty good boss Edward supposed; but then, who knew? He had not worked for many others; perhaps Bill's particular brand of armchair management psychology was having a negative effect on productivity; the days the boss was in always felt a little different.

Agneta's eyes, glistening with what might have been a choked-back tear, turned to Edward from their full, blue, crystal-clear depths. 'The effects are seen on every floor, Edward, every floor. He is feeding off you Edward, can't you see? He is feeding off you and all your colleagues... He could feed off us all.'

TWO

Suzi slammed the front door behind her, sunk to her knees and sobbed. She did not know how she had managed to drive home from the hospital. The flight from her PA's bedside was a blur. She vaguely remembered seeing a young man, an orderly, vaguely remembered seeing him fall to the ground. She wanted to sob again, but the tears would not come. Who was she crying for: Michael, her P.A., the boy in the car park, herself? What was becoming of her? Suzi had revelled in the distance between herself and others. She was a creature apart, a manipulator, someone perpetually outside the box, observing behaviour, setting up meetings and watching the interactions. Such behaviour was not immoral; surely she was not being punished for using her skills, God-given (if there was such a thing); who could blame her for making use of her natural abilities?

Her mind was racing now, images of her life, flashing before her, each reminding her of her detachment, her distance. She tried to force them away. She could have applied her gifts more thoughtfully, tried to be a force for good, but that never paid the bills. Her family had wanted a successful daughter, drummed into her the importance of dominance and personal strength. They had made her what she was, no saint, a common sinner in the name of Mammon, but no worse than anyone else. Things were different now. These gifts had changed, become more refined, evolved. She had killed Michael without even realising it, of that she was sure. The link was tenuous, thin and fragile, but the condition had been a chronic one. She had wound him in her fragile silk until, too tightly bound, he

113

had suffocated. Now she could not even be in the presence of his body. At the end of the week she would bury him in the cold ground. Should she throw herself in the hole on top of him? Spend eternity wracked in pain, in remorse for the sins she had carelessly and unwittingly committed? The punishment seemed to follow the crime, the two in seamless conjunction. She had nearly killed her P.A. with a single touch and felt like she was dying in the process. Now she and Julia were linked too, the reciprocity of pain a web that tightened as they got closer to one another. As she had fled across the car-park the very air had punished her. She had fought through it as if fighting for breath, fighting the sea. The orderly had been blasted away from her, an innocent bystander, caught in her bow-wave. Her thoughts were frenzied now, bright ripples flashing in the darkness, so many thoughts, so many emotions. She could almost hear the waves in her mind, almost see the coalescing thoughts: bright flashes, broiling, the orb of the sun suddenly appearing in splendour on the horizon. The waves piling one upon the other, the sea becoming choppy, the glorious sun suddenly overcome by scudding clouds. This was the feeling, this was the omega point, this the terrible state of mind which unleashed her new demon. Suzi crawled now, hand over hand, along the pine floorboards of the hall, towards her living room, her personal nest. Each movement was wracked with pain, the air shimmering, humming, squealing its resistance. Suzi wanted to scream, to tear her hair, to put out her eyes. She had to control this thing, or dispel it from her body. She tried to stand but the effort was too much. She pushed the door of the sitting room open; it swung, slowly, slowly. She had roused her elderly cat from slumber. The poor deaf thing stared at her, eyes wide and glowing. It uncoiled and jumped clumsily from the sofa to the floor. Suzi saw every ripple of its of its shimmering fur, the muscles tensing and relaxing beneath the skin, the spring, the recoil, the stare into open space. She watched in fascinated horror the shock and compression of arthritic bones, the ripples of flesh and fur, the light dancing across its back. She saw the flash of pain pass across the animal's face, the shaking of the head, the spittle flying. The animal padded towards her, each paw testing the surface of the floor before weight was applied. She saw the bouncing transfer from one step to another, the coiling and uncoiling of sinews. The cat reached her by the door and rubbed saliva covered teeth along her nose. The full length of its body rubbed against Suzi's face, tip to tail. As it did so the waves subsided in Suzi's mind, the clouds became thinner, the sun appeared and time returned to normal. She pulled the cat into her arms, hugging it tightly, nuzzling into its warm fur. It purred; a deep thrumming purr that Suzi felt through her entire body. It looked into her eyes, its own eyes, green and velvet black, a penetrating, intelligent stare. Suzi could have sworn it was telling her it understood.

THREE

Miguel had hidden himself in the stadium toilets. He loved his adopted family, his coach, the team, the friends, the fans but in the hour before a big fight he needed at least a few moments by himself. Time alone meant finding somewhere to hide, somewhere quiet to assemble his thoughts. For some reason he was very nervous this evening and his bowels seemed to be taking great pleasure in constantly reminding him. He wondered how many boxers had hidden themselves in this same spot over the years. How many great fights had been settled in a fighter's head sitting on this very toilet? The graffiti suggested quite a few.

Tonight was a big, big fight. It was big, not just because of the skill of Miguel's opponent (which was considerable), or the consequences of winning (prize money and a chance to move up the ratings), but also because it was televised. If you looked good on television everything changed. Miguel knew he looked good. If he could box good too...

Miguel gave his bowels one last chance to register their complaints and focused on the job in hand. There were a few things which were sitting heavily on his mind. Only two weeks had passed since he had passed-out in the gym. He had put it down to over-exertion, de-hydration; he had worked himself pretty hard that night. But there was something else as well. He had managed to punch his way through three-layers of cured leather. It wasn't something he had ever seen anyone else do. His glove had been shredded; ribbons of fabric ended up halfway up his arm. He had never seen that before either. There was no getting away from the fact that he had hit the punch of his life. He could feel the heat of it now, feel the connectivity, the joy of it, but he still felt uneasy about it. His fist and arm were a little sore, but he had not broken a bone, had not bruised a knuckle. Was it possible that when you threw the perfect punch you were somehow protected, invulnerable? He had superficially studied some of the far-eastern martial arts. The Tibetan monks, with their incredible demonstrations of physical control and prowess evoked higher powers and spiritual elements. As romantic as these ideas were, Miguel had come from the streets and had always thought these were elaborate circus tricks. In his own chosen art form there were also tricks and feints to learn. Subtle movements were the difference between a bruise below the eye and a few seconds sleep on the canvas. He shook that thought from his head. Tonight he would not be doing any sleeping. Tonight he would make everyone proud. He readied himself for the onslaught of positivism he was going to get from his corner. Everyone would tell him he was going to win. Everyone was behind him. He was a good lad. He would do it for them.

His coach had pulled his fist out of the punch-bag, had carried him to the corner of the room and lain him down on a pile of crash mats. He had fetched him water and bathed his brow (he was burning hot apparently). He had told him not to worry about the punch bag-it was time they got a new one. It was nearly as old and worn-out as the coach was. He had tried to sound reassuring, tried to be a friend. He had played the role well. When Miguel had looked into his eyes, however, he thought he saw a deeper concern; an affectionate concern. Maybe even the concern of a father. There had also been some fear. Fear was something that Miguel could smell. Tonight the only fear he wanted to smell was from his opponent.

FOUR

Bill Morris sat in the shadows under the canal bridge. He thought his heart might burst there and then. Angina had threatened his early demise any number of times and he had wilfully ignored its warnings. In the last few hours he had taken his body to extremes of activity that were beyond human experience and now his heart was complaining. He did not care. He felt he had never lived before this month.

Whatever it was that had awakened in him, he welcomed it now with open arms. It might be the exhilaration of slaughter, the joy of the hunt, the primeval pleasure of extinguishing life that was making him feel so wonderfully satiated or it might be the glorious superiority he was feeling now that made him so complete. It did not matter. It all amounted to the same thing, the same heady pleasure. His blood felt richer now, more vibrant. The swish-swash of his heart was the pulse of a man fully alive, not that of a walking cadaver.

He had fantasised about the previous moments for weeks. The set up, the elements of play were exactly has he had seen them in his mind. The drugs, the women at his feet; the Romans had the right idea. Such idle debauchery was exactly the state an intelligent, powerful man should enjoy. What was the purpose of success if it did not automatically lead to hedonistic excess? It was all right for the moralising clerics to warn against such pleasures, but they found their own ecstasies at the foot of the cross. Each to their own.

All this had charm in itself, the allure of drugs and power, the devotional bright eyes looking up at him as they passed across the surface of the mirror. This was all fine, but it was all an hors-d'oeuvre, preparation for the main course. He knew the drugs would attract the attentions of the drug dealers at the club. He had seen them enough times, young, aggressive, women-hating yobs. He had watched them hunting around the groups of teenagers and business suits; they were creatures of the night and he had become such a thing too. It was only right and proper that he should take his gratification from their pain. He needed a drug and they had provided it. It was the path they had chosen.

He felt the white wave coming toward him as soon as they passed through the curtain, he feared he might even peak too soon; such was the pleasure of anticipation. This edge-play was part of the thrill; he had to know, had to be sure that he still had the power. They slipped into the room, arrogant and confident, as he knew they would. They had shaken their heads in mock disapproval of the scene he had so carefully created. They had started to talk in their faux gangster parlance. He had not listened to the words; they just wanted to go on and on and he could not understand much of what they said anyway. All the time the wave was growing in height and power within him, it was just a question of when and how to let it wash over them. In the end they had made that decision themselves. Next time he would not allow his prey to dictate the time of their demise. But the knives had been exposed, the final insult to reason, animal claws in cold, hard steel. They had wanted to pin him to the wall, put the fear of death in his heart and mind. The thought almost made him laugh. Such audacity, such misplaced confidence in their capacity to intimidate. He had no reason to fear them, he was a successful man, a winner, an intellectual but he had become something else as well. They had not recognised the predator within him. They would not make that mistake again.

The boy had surprised him. He had leapt up between them, trousers round his ankles, face smeared with imprinted lipstick, flecks of white powder dusting his nose. He must have moved like a madman, for to Bill's eyes the motion was almost fast. He drifted up and towards the pair, left arm extended, fist balled ready for impact.

Bill struck him out the way first, carelessly; the crackling air, the coruscating joy of the power unleashed overwhelmed him. It was as much as he could do to control his movements; once liberated there was an inherent momentum that had to be held in check. The boy spun away, blood and spittle Catherine wheeling around his head. Bill then turned his attention to the men before him; he saw the looks of surprise glimmer in their eyes, saw a jaw begin to slacken, a tongue extending. The knives moved towards him in slow unison; they were gifting themselves to him, serving themselves on a platter and offering their own knives for the sacrifice. He found himself unable to resist. He took the knives from their hands, levering them from sweating palms, threw them into the air (why he did this he could not be sure, here just seemed to be some element of theatre that needed to be addressed), caught them as they slowly spun back down and then thrust them to the hilt, up and into their approaching throats. The wave crashed down, the bodies dropped dead-weight to the floor, three simultaneous crashes and reality returned.

The rest of the evening had been something of a blur. He roused himself from his reminiscence. It was cold now and he needed to find somewhere to hide out for the night. He had tickets, an offshore bank account and a fake passport (his connections at the golf club tedious but efficient); but the flight was not for five hours and he felt astonishingly exhausted. He wandered along the tow-path; the moon was high in the sky and everything was bathed in a preternatural light. He looked up at its glowing orb and felt the urge to howl and howl. Laughing to himself, he extracted a cobble from the side of the path, broke a window on a moored narrow-boat, cleared the glass and climbed inside. He found some stowed blankets and hastily assembled a bed. In a moment he was asleep.

FIVE

It had not been easy for Brian Lydon to decide on a career path. He was one of those people who dabbled, for whom life was a succession of exotic fruits to be sampled, ruminated upon and then discarded. He knew that should he have a life expectancy of two hundred years he would have had no difficulty throwing himself whole-heartedly into some subject or other; he could have been a brain surgeon or an art historian, and then trained all over again for the next hundred years.

Unfortunately the four score years that modern medical science promised was not really enough time to do this properly. It was for this reason that he had decided to become an archaeologist. Archaeology was a wonderful subject for someone who dabbled. One morning he might wear a scientist's hat, studying the theories behind geophysics; another day he would be examining pottery styles of the lower Bronze-age. The world was a huge lake of possibilities and he could dip his toe in or go for a swim as he pleased. He had never been particularly practical and if he was honest with himself the field trip open trench, bucket and spade brigade and camping element of the whole procedure filled him with dread. That of itself was a good thing (as he told himself twice a day); he had found the intellectual pastimes interesting without being too taxing. Everyone needed challenges and his were to gain some firsthand experience on how to operate a shovel (not much call for them in the housing estate he had been born on in Highbury), how to cut turf and how to dig a steep-sided hole in the ground without it turning the site into Flanders Fields.

Another thing that he liked about archaeology was the type of people that seemed to get involved in it. For the most part, their common characteristics were an excess of peculiarities. Each of his lecturers had a raft of quirks and personality defects that ran from the comically sublime to the ridiculous. To perform a Christmas revue was almost too easy; the professors seemed to be perpetually parodying themselves throughout the entire year. The students were, for the most part, a fun bunch as well. There were always a few overly keen, humourless, intense ones and a few wasters, but he had always found a group of minds amongst whom he felt comfortable; a few of the girls on the course were even quite fit.

After a few hours digging, falling in holes and accidentally knocking over the trellis table with the camping stove on, he thought he would make himself scarce and help one of the fitter girls with the geophysics. Janet was a punk with a penchant for flint tools. Brian found himself quite excited in her presence and her studious excitement around all things Neolithic gave him a doorway to her affections. Today, though, she was looking for electron magnetic spin anomalies, or some such smorgasbord of scientific terms.

Geophysics itself was a dense mathematical world of modelling and reconstruction. The geophysics tools were the divining rods of the age, X-ray glasses to the buried world. They could detect voids in the soil, water, metals and stone, measure the availability of free water and allow estimates to be made of what constituted the soil beneath their feet. Fortunately you did not have to know how they worked to use them. Janet was quartering a field with a hand-held metering device. Geophys was not her favourite pastime. She could not bear the delay between taking the measurements and getting a result, something that only materialised after an hour and a half with a computer. Janet was not the most patient of people and liked her archaeology immediate, physical and preferably stony. She was waving the device fairly inadequately at the field and was looking into the distance in abject boredom. When she

saw Brian approaching she smiled broadly. 'Ah you dia-
mond! You've come to take over! Thanks!'

Brian smiled back and shaking his head told her that he
had only come to give moral support. This seemed to be a
barely satisfactory reply and they ambled around in
silence for a while. The sun kept disappearing behind
clouds and as it did so the temperature plummeted. The
site was on the top of an exposed grassy knoll and the
wind-chill made them pull their coats tightly around them.
They made small talk and Brian made a few jokes about
their most recent lecturer. He had a bit of a knack for vocal
impressions and their new lecturer in comparative religion
and ethics lent herself to mimicry. Pretty soon he was
walking rather close to Janet, in half an hour they were
talking about her family, in another half hour they were
discussing which pub to go and hide in. Things were going
well. Having nearly finished quartering the field, Brian
ran ahead to fetch his belongings from the rest of the site,
leaving Janet to upload data from the device to a laptop
computer. It was getting dark when he returned and they
wandered slowly into the nearest village. The local pub
was busy but looked warm and inviting and they took
refuge inside, corralling themselves in a quiet corner
between the jukebox and a sleepy Labrador.

After a few beers, a heavy meal and generally putting
the world and their futures to right, Janet took her leave.
They had ended up feeling rather comfortable in each
other's company and such comfort was dangerous. Janet
liked to keep a distance and liked to be seen to play it very
cool. Two other members of their group joined them from
the bar and Janet took the opportunity to make her excuses. She had left a boyfriend at home in Leeds but it was not
a fact that she had publicised whilst at college. The
boyfriend was in a band, had lots of piercings and was the
reason why Janet had adopted her present Mohawk and
boots ensemble. Brian was nice, very nice, far too nice in
fact for anything casual. Casual sex was something Janet
would consider with someone very sexy that she did not
like very much. She had too much respect for Brian to play

that game. Modern morality was a minefield; future students of comparative religion and ethics would have a hell of a job working out what was going on.

Janet artfully avoided Brian's proffered kiss on the cheek, thanked him for a nice evening, refused his offer to walk her home and made her way back to their hostel. A nearly full moon was low in the sky; the wind was now bitterly cold. The moonlight spread shadows of naked trees, withered black hands reaching out across the fields. A dog barked in a farmyard, an owl screeched from the darkness. Janet hurried towards the distant lights of the hostel, glowing orange half a mile up the road. She was warm with drink, but as the lights and music of the pub faded away, she felt the cold air on every exposed extremity, chasing out the warmth, reminding her that it was winter. She glanced at her watch. It was past midnight; she could not believe how the time had flown. In the country it seemed the normal licensing laws did not apply. She cursed herself for letting it get so late. She had to spend half an hour or so looking over the geophys before she went to bed, and bed seemed very appealing now walking in the cold night air. The wind seemed to be getting up; she could feel it now penetrating the very fabric of her clothes. She quickened her pace and hugged the laptop to her chest to block out the worst of it. She was halfway now between the pub and the hostel. There was not a car on the road, nor any sign of life.

As she passed by a high dry-stone wall Janet heard the sound of movement in the darkness. There was a swish and a crunch as dry bracken was crushed under foot; then a deep and rumbling snort. Janet stopped in the road. The wall was quite high, blocking the moonlight, casting the road into a pall of darkness. Janet stood on the threshold of the darkness and peered into its depths. There was silence. She slowly stepped out of the moonlight into the gloom. She was in a dip in the road now, and as she walked down the slope the road became damp and muddy. There was the sound of trickling water, and the lights of the hostel disappeared from view. She heard another swish, a pause, then another crunch. Then silence. She stopped again. In the dip in the road she was protected from the wind. In the still air she thought she could have sworn she heard the sound of breathing. Her eyes slowly adjusted to the darkness; dark figures of battered ferns and ancient hawthorn loomed out at her. A drainage pipe at the bottom of the wall emptied into an overflowing ditch. The water was oily and black in the darkness. Then she heard something rushing towards her, something big, very big. The breathing became louder, short snorts of breath; she heard hooves pounding damp turf. The sounds echoed around between the stone walls; she could not tell where they came from. The thudding became louder, insistent, whatever it was was getting closer and closer, its breathing became an angry snort, bearing down on her, seemingly from all sides. She looked around her. The walls seemed to tower above her, dark against the pale night sky. How high were they on the other side? What if the beast broke through or leapt the wall? She broke into a run, suddenly overcome by her vulnerability. Her legs threatened to buckle; the sweet local beer had made them sluggish and the road was steep and slippery. The hooves pounded the ground louder and louder. In a moment whatever it was would be upon her, she ran in fear for her life; the thudding of the hooves combined with the thudding of her heart. The two became inseparable; she felt the beating of the hooves in the very bones of her body. Her feet splashed through the muddy puddles; water filling socks and shoes. She saw the crawling silhouettes of ancient ivy clinging to stone, caught the wildly rolling eye of a single bright star against the black sky, smelt the musty maul of cold earth and moss. She broke through the shadows at the top of the slope, the moonlight suddenly blinding, the wind newly bitter and chill. She heard almost nothing, the throb of her heart demanding her attention; her other senses working a feverish overtime. For a moment she saw nothing against the glare, but she continued to run; she saw the lights of the hostel, closer now in the distance. She heard the hooves crunch to a stop, and span around to look back the way she had come. She was higher now, and the increased elevation allowed her to see over the wall. In the field stood an enormous bull, glowing white in the moonlight, its huge bulk stretched into an impossibly long black shadow across the field. Its head was held high, its breath forming clouds of steam, which billowed off into the night. Its eyes were pink and wide and glinted with fear and anger. It was awesome and terrifying. It bellowed, a deep and rumbling cry full of frustration.

Janet stood watching the animal for several minutes. For the first time in her life she felt herself a visitor in another creature's realm. The hillside belonged to the bull; she was invading its territory and she was not welcome. The experience was humbling. She left the animal cropping some long grass at the edge of the field and continued up the road towards the lights of the hostel. She ran up the drive, still exhilarated by the chase up the hill, struggled with the key and entered the hostel. As she closed the door behind her she felt an unfamiliar feeling of safety. She was home amongst the comforts of human existence. The moonlight and the stars belonged to the bull.

She climbed the stairs, and made her way through the maze of corridors, strewn with framed maps and empire books, found her room and again experienced the feeling of shutting the world outside. She was in a cocoon within a cocoon. The bull might be standing sentry on the hillside, but this was her secret domain.

She opened her laptop, loaded in the data from the day's geophys and waited for the computer to perform its magic. Any trace of sleep had been dispelled by the rush of adrenalin which was still coursing through her. The algorithm made allowances for latitude, topography and the known properties of the underlying geology that had been established from boreholes and pilot studies of the region. Comparison of these 'crude' data with the precision of her new data set provided evidence of hidden anomalies, caves, and buried objects with densities different to that of the surrounding rock strata. The device was very sensitive, but there were enormous variations imposed by geography and geology itself. Janet had never felt comfortable with the maths of geophysics; there were too many micro-Newtons this and meters per second per second that. She was very thankful for the programs she was provided with that performed these calculations for her. Praise be to the Gods of I.T. As the hard-drive whirred and clicked, she walked to the window, there in the distance was the bull, head up, scanning the road. No doubt he was going to terrorise some other poor, towny visitor. She slumped down onto the bed and looked at the computer screen. The preliminary analysis was usually quite difficult, this was Janet's least favourite task and no doubt her professor would take gleeful pleasure in explaining to her that what she had interpreted as being a putative early Saxon settlement was in fact two Victorian drainage ditches and a buried 1950s tractor attachment. The screen flickered and began to display the day's efforts. The screen was homogeneously green, with an occasional blip of yellow, proof positive that there was nothing of size or interest hidden beneath the damp turf. Half way down the screen yellow blocks became common and then continuous throughout the screen. Such a signal was unusual, fascinating, either something big was buried under the soil or the underlying rock had changed its properties. The screen became a slightly more angry orange as it rastered towards the bottom; then suddenly it was green again and remained so until the end of the run.

Janet spent a half an hour going through the possibilities. It could be some sort of buried wall or footings for a building. If it was, it was enormous; the find of her life, a monastery or a fort. The top of the yellow block was perfectly flat, and she had walked the squares from east to west, so whatever it was perfectly aligned to the cardinal axis. This was a good sign, a very good sign; religious buildings often showed such alignments. She made a note. Whatever it was then stopped abruptly. This run was measuring minuscule changes in local gravity. Iron-rich stone had this effect, as did metals. The local church was of an iron-rich marl; it was a common building stone in the region, just the kind of thing to give this signature. It was looking good; she made another note. The increase in signature might be an external wall, a thickening of foundations or buttresses. Janet was not great on architectural styles, but buttresses sounded good, buttresses could be old. The occasional blips of yellow had to be bits of rubble from the wall, buried in the grass. It all made sense. She decided she had discovered the foundations of a previously unknown ruined Norman chapel of some considerable size. Evidence of Norman activity was relatively rare in this part of the country. It could be something significant. She could become famous. She imagined the Normans, tramping up to a church on the top of the windswept hillside, having to contend with a rag-tag Saxon opposition hiding in their hedgerows and a giant killer werewolf bull which pounced on unsuspecting passers-by in the night. She giggled away to herself, the beer was making her very jolly and tiredness had returned. She saved the data and prepared for bed. It might all be nonsense, but at least she had something to tell the prof.

When Janet woke at seven the next morning, it all made sense. Her head was throbbing and her mouth was dry. She had dreamt of a giant white bull walking alongside her as she quartered the field with a giant swinging pocket watch. How could she have been so stupid? She laughed, rolled over and fell asleep again.

SIX

Mary Weston found herself going home too late once again. She liked to do her rounds, tried to see everyone once a fortnight or so. If she missed a week for one reason or another they tended to panic and worry themselves over her welfare. Mary was not someone who allowed herself to dwell in other people's affairs. She did her bit, and that was all she could do. Worrying never helped anyone, but sometimes the more vulnerable of her friends only had the power left to worry, it seemed to be one of the last things to leave you if you became ill or dependent; yet another bad taste cosmic joke. Her friend Mrs Appleby was a lovely woman, and although she was housebound still managed to keep up with current affairs. Putting the world to rights with Mrs Appleby was always a pleasure, though often it took all afternoon and most of the evening. This evening the on-going conflict in the middle-east and religious lobbying in the Whitehouse had been their subject of debate. It was not a subject Mary knew a great deal about but her friend had managed a diatribe on the subject for the best part of three hours. Escape had been impossible and it had got a bit late. Mary sometimes thought the world would be a better place if people like Mrs Appleby were given the power to make a difference. On second thoughts, some of her opinions were a little right of centre and age had not diminished her. An army of Mrs Applebys would reclaim the streets for middle England, but it would not necessarily be an England that welcomed everyone. Mary forgave a modicum of intolerance amongst her elderly friends. She felt the pace of change acutely herself. It seemed that just as you felt you had mastered the rules of life and had a pretty good idea of how everything important worked, the world decided to change under your feet. Powerless in the face of these changes sometimes resulted in resentment. The powerless young had the same problems. Perhaps some things never changed. Mrs Appleby was a reactionary, but her heart was in the right place most of the time. Mary sometimes put her right on a few points, but she did not like to leave her too excited and overwrought, and sometimes it was better to just listen to the steam escaping.

Mary manoeuvred the wheelchair through the park. This was a short cut that her husband had explicitly forbidden. This rather added to the frisson of whizzing along between the trees in the dark. It really was not so terribly late, but the nights were at their longest and angry rain clouds had been billowing up through the evening which had the effect of advancing nightfall considerably. The wheelchair's hum sounded incredibly loud between the trees. Squirrels and pigeons fled in panic from her approach; she heard the scratching of little claws, the crash as they leapt from branch to branch and the clatter of wings from the tree tops. She felt slightly guilty for disturbing them; they were not to know she came in peace.

The path through the park was illuminated, a misty rain was beginning to fall and the lazy sodium lights picked up the tiny droplets in orange twinkling cones. Mary imagined herself on a dance floor, kicking her heels back under the spotlights, she had never much fancied Frank Sinatra, but he would do at a push. Her husband was not the dancing type, but she was not in much of a position to dance these days either. She was pretty nimble with the wheelchair, but it was not exactly elegant. There had been a time when she was elegant. She and Lilly had strut their stuff on the London scene. The music had been lively then, stuff you could really dance to, music with steps. Mary still listened to music, even the charts. She admired the young women with their energy and confidence, but behind their tarty clothes and provocative gyrations she saw the lecherous hands of sweaty business executives. Such women were no more in charge of their destinies than any other wage slave. Money and fame bought you some pleasures, but artistic control was much harder to come by.

Mary playfully swerved between the pools of orange illumination. She did not think a pirouette was entirely appropriate (she did not want to run the risk of rolling the chair). She would have a go another day, when it was sunny and her husband was around to pick her up should it go awry. She thought of her husband and of her home. She had better get on before the rain really came down. If her husband tried to find her he might not expect her to take the short cut and they could miss each other. He was a sweet man and she hated to worry him. She remembered she had an empty plastic bag under the seat; it would do as a make-shift rain hat if push came to shove. There was a short, unlit section of path ahead. The council had obviously run out of will or money. It corresponded with a particularly dense and dark area of shrubbery and Mary cursed the council for leaving such an open invitation to robbers, muggers and ne'er-do-wells. It was like a red rag to a bull. They might as well put a sign up inviting people to be mugged in the darkness. She would write a letter to her local councillor. He was a nice enough man and she knew his mother quite well.

It was then that Mary realised that she was not alone. The noise of the wheelchair had masked his approach. Perhaps he had been guarding his own steps, sneaking up in the dark. It did not matter, he was there now, just a few paces behind, she was certain. Meeting people in the dark on isolated paths was always a difficult thing, the desire to appear both confident and non-threatening, to be polite and courteous whilst afraid to hear your own voice in the dark. Mary had often thought how difficult it must be for young men just to appear normal to vulnerable people alone in the street. Some people were natural victims. In the next few moments she would establish if she too was a victim. She slowed the wheelchair down to a very slow walking pace. The dark section of the path was only fifty yards ahead. She thought she would make her stand here, in the light, if she could. He slowed his pace in line with hers. She had been right, her radar so acute. How had she sensed him? What clues had told her he was up to no good? There was something about the footfall, something about his approach, directly behind her. Normal people did not do that. Normal people were not predatory to elderly women.

She stopped the chair. He stopped immediately. She could not hear his breathing, but she estimated he was about ten feet away. Her pulse was racing, her mind empty as if listening for inspiration from her heart. Her hands shaking, she slowly turned the wheelchair round on the spot. The wheels turned in opposition, a slow pirouette; she would look her attacker directly in the eye. There he was, perhaps twelve feet away. He wore a baseball cap and hooded jacket, the cowl of the hood pulled forward, his face obscured and in shadow. His hands were in the pockets of his loosely fitting combat trousers. He looked thin and slightly dishevelled. He looked like he needed a good meal. Mary's heart was racing fit to burst. She tried to think; how to act? She did not want to provoke him but she also did not want to appear powerless. She cursed her withered legs and herself for leaving her walking stick propped up against her bedroom door. She tried to speak slowly and clearly, but her voice broke as she tried to form the words.

'What do you want? Why are you following me? I don't have much money, but you can have my purse, here...' She reached down and her fingers found her handbag. They also brushed the metal flask that she always took when she went to visit Lilly. It was hard, it was quite heavy. It might do for a weapon.

'I don't want your money.' It was difficult to say how old he was. His voice was high, slightly nasal, nervous. His hands reached deeper into his combats, his shoulders clenched, pushing the cowl of his hood further forward. Mary realised this was his comfort. He was trying to scare her, but was very nervous himself. Perhaps it was not fear; perhaps it was anticipation. The thought sent a shiver of cold down Mary's spine. She did not know what to say; did not want to play out some clichéd dialogue. She grabbed the controls of the wheelchair and advanced forward, directly towards him.

'I don't care what you want young man.' She stressed the 'young' perhaps she could intimidate him; she hoped it did not arouse him. 'I am going to go home; you are going to get out of my way. My husband knows I am here; he will be looking for me.' Her voice was firmer now. She had to hold it together. She might be no match for this man physically, but mentally she knew she had a chance.

'No he won't.' The voice was flat, matter of factual. 'He won't save you. He isn't here is he? Your lot won't help you this time. You are on your own, like me, on our own, just you and me, together. I'll look after you, don't worry about that.' There was an inflection on the last sentence which was menacing, foreboding. What did it mean? Her mind was racing. She knew his words had betrayed him. This was her way in, her defence, but she was close now, almost on top of him. In a moment she would see his face and fear prevented her formulating a reply. He remained impassive until the very last moment, then he stepped aside as the wheelchair drew level. He ducked behind Mary, out of her line of sight and grabbed her arms from behind. He was wiry, strong; she struggled but was no match for him. He pulled her away from the wheelchair controls. The chair stopped. He held her tightly, his grasp both crushing and intimate. He brought his face next to hers. She still could not see him clearly. Mary felt the soft brushed cotton of his coat against her cheek. His voice was coaxing, seductive in her ear.

'Don't be afraid. No point being afraid. I don't want to hurt you. I want...I want...' His voice cracked, Mary could hear the desperation in his voice, the desire, the need. His hands slid down towards her breasts. She was still pinned against the back of the chair. He turned to face her. 'You don't understand... How could you? You are all in it together. You make me sick. Look at you... gloating in your fucking chair, sitting there, alive and gloating in your fucking chair...' Mary wanted to look into his face, to read his eyes, but she had to twist away. To see his face would be to place her lips in front of his. He pulled her tighter. 'You don't understand what it's like. You've lived your whole life. You don't understand.' His face was so close to hers; she could smell his breath. If she glanced at him she would see his features beneath the shadowed cowl. Perhaps, if he left her alive, she would be able to give the police a description. She had to bring herself to look. It was then that Mary saw the dog-walker entering the park, a man with a Labrador, torch in hand, his light a beacon. Mary tried to scream for help, but only managed a half-muffled cry. The boy's hand was brought over her mouth and nose. Having cried out with such effort, she now needed air. She tried to shake free, but his hand was clamped down too tightly. He tried to pull the wheelchair backwards, along the pathway towards the darkness, but with the electric motor engaged it was heavy and clumsy. He inched backwards but too slowly, the flashlight in the distance flicked towards them but then, to Mary's complete dismay, away again, the man had left the path and was following his dog down the side of the field. The boy's voice was in her ear again.

'You silly cow…What did you do that for eh? Eh? Don't you like me? Don't you? Don't you want a piece of me?' He was agitated, angry now. He pulled Mary back with such force she felt she might break in his hands. Fighting for breath, she knew she might lose consciousness at any moment. Every fibre of her being was crying out for air; she had to breathe, had to breathe now. Time began to slow as the yellow mist of unconsciousness descended. She fought to stay awake, tried not to slip into the dark. At that moment his hand slipped slightly from her mouth. He was adjusting his position to come round to face her. As he did so, Mary bit down with all her might. She tasted blood and felt a bone of a knuckle snap between her teeth. The boy screamed with pain and rage and tried to pull himself away, but Mary remained tightly clamped to his hand crushing it with every ounce of her strength. He screamed and screamed again, then lashed out wildly at her with his free arm. He was off balance and he caught her with the flat of his hand on the jaw. The blow caused her to reel back, releasing his mauled hand from her mouth.

'You bitch! You bitch!' He shouted, clutching his bloodied hand to his chest. 'I'm going to kill you! I'm going...' He lurched forward, but as he did so, Mary brought the vacuum flask up as hard as she could towards his head. Instinctively he blocked it with his damaged hand. There was another crack as a second bone shattered. He squealed in pain and fell to his knees. Mary had swung with such force that she had practically thrown herself out of the wheelchair, it tipped, slowly, painfully slowly and then fell onto its side. Mary's head hit the concrete. The last thing she remembered seeing was a torchlight waving to and fro and the sound of a barking dog.

SEVEN

The music started and Miguel's opponent made his way towards the ring. Carlos Zidanne was the outsider, the visitor; tonight was to be Miguel's night. He had to make it his night. The preceding hour had seemed to last a lifetime. The binding of Miguel's wrists, the prayers, the thumps on the back, eager faces, manly hugs. The introductions, the sponsors, the working-up of the crowd; Miguel would have preferred to have been pulled in off the street and thrown into the ring rather than suffer the drawn out anticipation and psychological torture of the preceding hour. He felt emotionally beaten-up before he had even entered the ring. He watched Carlos bouncing and punching the air, a towel draped over his head, his minders standing behind, dark glasses, huge jaws, sharp suits; it was all for effect. Carlos Zidanne had no need for minders. He was not in that league. In some ways it seemed ridiculous that such a man should need minders anyway; surely a professional boxer could look after himself. Still, it did give the man a certain class. The music played on and on. Carlos was in no hurry to get to ringside, he was going to take his time. The crowd was tepid, polite but restrained. Carlos had a few friends in the audience, but they were not making a lot of noise. The music stopped before he had made it to the ring; he ascended the steps and ducked under the ropes in almost complete silence. Perhaps it was an omen. Miguel's own music blared out, a traditional French folk tune put to an up-tempo hip-hop beat. The audience started singing the words. The crowd roared as the compère shouted out his name. Miguel had a lot of friends and friends of friends in the crowd but still the walk to the ringside was like a walk to the gallows. Most people wanted to see him win tonight, but it was a heavy burden to bear. The crowd jeered and shouted and strange hands slapped him on the back. He kept his head lowered, focussing his thoughts. Twenty paces and he would be in the ring, nineteen, eighteen. He knew he was at the peak of his form, today was his chance to shine, but for a few moments his limbs felt as though they were made of dough. He took a big breath, climbed the steps and entered the brightly lit ring as the music reached its climax. He acknowledged the crowd, tried to smile, tried to avoid looking at Carlos in his corner and shook out his arms. The gloves felt so heavy. He had to snap out of this. He went to his corner; his coach and trainer gave him a few last minute words of advice and encouragement. He soaked up the words, he had to focus, had to pull it all together.

The referee beckoned to him to come to the centre of the ring. Every step was heavy, lumbering; time seemed to be holding its breath. The referee told them to use self-defence at all times, a nice clean bout: the usual spiel. They struck gloves and the two men sized each other up fully for the first time. Miguel tried to look into Carlos' eyes, but he was evasive and did not hold his gaze. Miguel read this as nervousness, weakness he would exploit. Almost immediately his reservoir of strength began to flow into his body. His vision became hooded; he had a prey animal now, a target. He was a predator and his prey was too afraid to look him in the eye. As the bell sounded he was a fighting machine, steady, glistening, focused and ready. He lived for these moments and in this moment he felt more alive than he had ever done before.

EIGHT

'It's you, you daft git. Look!' Janet waved the gravimeter in Brian's direction. The digital counter flickered as it pointed towards him. 'You got some metal in you or something? Hip joint? Plate in your skull?' Brian shook his head.

'No, never even fallen off my bike; nothing like that. There has to be some kind of mistake. I've never heard of anything like that. It's kind of weird. Maybe you've discovered a Brianometer You'll be able to detect me wherever I go. You'll never be able to lose me in crowd!' He grabbed the device and ran it over himself again. Sure enough the signal gently rose and declined. They spent the afternoon running the device over the rest of their friends and colleagues. No one else elicited the same response from it; even their elderly comparative religions professor, who actually did have a titanium hip.

'Could be my animal magnetism.'

'Could be something you are wearing. Get your kit off!' Janet pointed the device at Brian's groin and poked him.

'So I do have animal magnetism!' Brian grabbed the device and ran off to his room to test the theory. He came back with a big smutty smile on his face. 'How much fun was that?!' he giggled. 'No, it is all me and every little bit of me works the animal magic!'

'Maybe you were hit by a meteorite or something and it's embedded in your brain. That could explain it. Maybe you sucked too many pencils as a kid? Have you ever tried leaping over walls in a single bound? You never know, you might be some escapee from some freak scientific experiment. Stranger things have happened.' The two of them

138

decided they needed more test samples. It was a weekend and Janet's geophysics master had pretty much told her she was a waste of space on the course with her plea that her paramagnetic colleague had mucked up her measurements. It was a fine day and Saturday crowds were milling through the streets of the local market town. They mingled amongst the crowds of people in the square, outside the cinema and in each coffee shop, café, tea room and pub they entered for repeated rest-bites. After four hours of discreetly waving their magnetic divining rod around and getting lots of funny looks they had not detected anyone else who gave off a reading. They were about to give up when they stopped by the market square to watch a street performer. He was performing sleight-of-hand tricks with coins, eggs and cards. He had attracted quite a crowd. The device seemed to have a range of around six feet on Brian; on this man its range was more like twelve. The closer they got, the better the signal.

'The force is strong with this one!' said Brian. They watched the street magician for fifteen minutes or so. He wore a black dusty suit, far too small for him, which exposed several inches of dark hairy forearm, a bowler hat and one dirty white glove. His face was clearly made-up, an oily stage-concoction which may have been worn for performance purposes or more frighteningly for cosmetic reasons. The general effect was disturbing. He did not seem to like the attention of the two of them, far less when they pointed the device at him. 'I guess he thinks it's some sort of camera,' said Janet after she received a particularly intense look of disdain. 'People video them and watch the act in slow motion so they can copy their tricks. It's the main reason why this kind of thing has got less exposure on the TV lately.'

The man suddenly interrupted his act and came right over to them.

'Come on you lot! You want to video my act? Come and have a good look then. Don't hide in the crowd.' The two of them tried to plead their innocence but to no avail. He pulled them to the front and started to perform a trick involving royals picked from a large deck of cards. Brian watched his hands intently as he performed the trick to Janet. His movements were careful, deliberate and exaggerated, but there were other movements too, quick, very quick indeed. The magician finished the trick with a flourish. Janet clapped, everyone clapped. The magician then turned his attentions to the one person in the audience who had a pathological fear of being the centre of attention in big crowds. Brian knew his weakness and studiously avoided comedy clubs and cabaret for fear that he should be forced into participation. He felt the eyes of the crowd on him, big round rabbit eyes wide in the headlights. His heart sank. He hoped he would not make a fool of himself. He took a deep breath and decided it would be best just to concentrate on the cards and try not to do anything too clever. He was not a card player and was not entirely sure what the suits were called. He hoped everything would be simple. The cards were shuffled in a blur, shuffled, cut, shuffled, cut, dealt, collected and shuffled again. Brian focused on each movement, the fingers and thumbs moving like a swarm of insects over their shiny surfaces. He saw the play, saw the misdirection but chose not to follow it. The man was fast, very, very fast, but Brian was sure he had seen it, the sleight of hand; the card flicked down and under to his other hand, the tap as it was inserted into the deck, the reshuffle to the top of the pile.

'Where is the lady now then snoopy boy?' The magician passed his hands over the three piles of cards before him. The misdirection had been clear. Brian knew which pile he should point to. But he knew the queen was the third from the top of the pile of remaining cards in the magician's left hand. The question was should he say anything. There was a moment of silence. He looked into the man's eyes, watched his pupils screwing down into tight pinholes. Clowns, magicians, they were all as bad as one another, and he had not asked to be grabbed from the anonymity of the street and ridiculed in front of a crowd of strangers. People shouted out suggestions. Janet squeezed his arm.

He reached out, grabbed the magician's left hand, prized

open the fingers, removed the remaining deck, clumsily counted out the first two cards as he had seen the magician do and turned over the third. To his incredible relief, he was right. The crowd roared their approval. The magician looked daggers at him. The cards were dealt again. The performer was not going to let him get the better of him a second time. He made a show of congratulating the boy; but the steel in his voice was perfectly audible. He would perform a more difficult trick. Brian was on top of things this time. He had seen the misdirection once, the second time was easier. His heart was racing, the light was fading, but he picked it up again; sliding of one card over another, the fake display, very, very fast. This time however there was another level to the trick, the man's hands passed across one another as he swapped and replaced the piles of cards on the table. The movement was so fast, Brian almost missed it, but as the hands passed, the top three cards were moved from the top of the pile in the left hand to the bottom of the pile in the right hand. There was misdirection towards the left hand and the trap was set. The same question was asked. The crowd was silent. To most people's eye the trick was the same. They were not so sure what to expect this time. The tension was palpable. This time Brian wasted no time. He reached out, and withdrew the appropriate card from the bottom of the pack. Quite a considerable crowd had gathered now and they roared their approval. The magician was not best pleased. He thrust his hat into Janet's hands and bid her collect money from the crowd. Guiltily she did so.

There were three more tricks and every time Brian caught the movement. The performer was getting progressively more aggrieved and the last trick was done so nervously and sloppily that Brian was certain anyone in the audience could have picked it out. He decided he had had enough. Who knew what sort of Mafiosi street magicians were connected with? He might sleep sounder in his bed if he got the next one wrong. The question was asked, he saw where the card had gone (in this case behind the man's left ear as he had swept back his hair); but he indicated the misdirected pack. He saw the relief in the man's eyes as he triumphantly exposed Brian's error to the crowd. The hat was passed around again and Brian and Janet made their exit. Unsurprisingly they were not offered any of the pickings as the crowd dispersed.

On the way to the nearest pub they were approached by a smartly dressed man in his fifties.

'I hope you don't mind me asking, but I was watching your performance in the crowd. I was really extremely impressed. Perhaps I should introduce myself. I'm Doctor Martin Gordon. I'm with the university applied statistics department. I'm a bit of a fan of card games. I wondered if you would mind explaining how you did it, you see, I'm writing a book and as you might imagine it is a difficult area to research.' Doctor Gordon was clearly extremely enthusiastic, but Brian wondered how much he knew about street magic.

'I'd happily chat to you, Doctor Gordon, but I'm afraid I don't use any method as such. The tricks the guy did today were all sleight-of-hand, there was no method. I've just got very good eyesight I guess. I'm sure loads of people must have seen what he was doing.' Gordon seemed deflated.

'So you haven't made a study of this? You really do have a remarkable gift. I'm pretty good at watching the hands, but then I've been studying cards for years. I know where to look. I don't want to be a pain, but could I buy you young people a drink? Perhaps I could persuade you to become involved in a little research project I have running at the moment.' They retired to a pub, where they clandestinely turned on the geophys equipment.

'We are performing a little study of our own at the moment Doctor Gordon' Janet pointed the device at him. It gave a subtle, but positive result. 'Ah!... We have another one!' The Doctor was slightly taken aback.

'What are you looking for? And is it life-threatening?' Over a few drinks they explained their results to him. He was enthralled.

'So what is the sensitivity of this thing then? What sort of anomaly is Brian here showing?' Janet had to think for a moment.

'It is measuring electron spin resonance, if that means anything to you, something to do with magnets and microwaves. It can tell you all sorts of things about a person. The street magician gave us a big signal. Brian a moderate one,' (Brian feigned upset at this) 'and you come out a bit less. I don't register at all.' She sipped her third pint. Drinking was becoming bit of a hobby out here in the country but she had developed a taste for the local brew. Doctor Gordon was quite a character and had completely forgotten why it was he had wanted to talk to them in the first place. He invited them over to his offices on the university campus the next day so they could explain their findings to a bio-physicist friend of his. There might be something interesting in it. Who knew, maybe they had stumbled across a new phenomenon? It was the second time that week that Janet had imagined herself becoming incredibly famous; yesterday it was as an archaeologist, today as a biophysicist. Science was obviously not so difficult after all.

NINE

The bell sounded for the first round. It sent a shudder down Miguel's spine. He felt as if very nerve in his body was on high alert. His conscious mind focused on his opponent, what little could be spared reminded him of tactics, last minute advice from his trainer on making him look as inscrutable and threatening as possible.

Carlos bounced and swerved, just out of reach. His beady eyes were now desperately searching Miguel's face for clues as to when and from where punches were to come. Miguel studied his opponent's face in turn. The jaw set firm, the furrowed brow; the man was a study in nervous concentration. He would loosen up that face a little. A jab flashed towards him, it was quick, precise and if he had walked into it, it would have been a nasty one. The cross which followed close behind was half-hearted, a tester; Miguel caught them both on his gloves. He had not expected the uppercut which seamlessly followed. The guy had sent an initial flurry of punches. Such a combination as a first attack was almost unheard of. It was manners to have a few tasters first. The punch landed to Miguel's middle abdomen. He took it well, but it would have been scored by the judges. Bad manners had to be punished and Miguel let go a triple combination of his own. Strangely, he instinctively chose the same combination; fighting fire with fire. With the pique of affronted manners behind them they made an impression. But Carlos' guard was tight, defensive, and slow to open. Miguel's final punch crashed against elbows. He had to withdraw to avoid the next volley of shots. He was half expecting a triple, but the lesson had been learnt, two jabs came in quick succession.

These were distancing punches; Carlos was establishing his reach. It was during these punches that Miguel caught the tick that he was looking for. It was subtle, very subtle and transient, but just before Carlos let off a punch, his eyes, which were otherwise evasive, transiently focused on Miguel's own. He wanted to check if something was coming his way before launching his own attack. To Miguel, who dwelt in such moments the look might as well have been an invitation to a slaughter. The next time he saw it he let out a punishing jab, which caught Carlos completely unprepared. The glove connected nicely, Carlos' head was knocked back, spittle flew and for an instant he lost his footing. He slipped back against the ropes, blood rushing to his face and was propelled forwards against Miguel's chest. Carlos' head went forward and down, and Miguel tried to deliver a downward shot at close quarters but Carlos suddenly brought his head up and back, catching Miguel on the jaw. It was nasty, it was street, it was against the rules and it hurt like hell. Miguel's teeth ground into the gum shield and his own head was thrown back. If he had been moving forward at that moment his jaw would have been broken for sure; as it was he had got away with it, but his head was spinning and he really, really wanted to sit down. The referee threw himself between the two men, sending Miguel to his corner. Miguel obeyed with relief but for a moment his legs nearly let him down. When he eventually reached his corner and sat down it was far more heavily and desperately than he had had to do in a first round before.

Miguel's coach spoke in his ear, advice, reassurance, the usual guff, but he was not listening. His attentions were on the referee's back as he laid the law down to Carlos, and the nodding head of his opponent as he took his dressing down with the wilful disinterest of a naughty boy who knows full well what he has done. The bell sounded. The first round was ended. Miguel's world had stopped spinning but things had changed in his mind. The red mist was descending and when the bell rang for round two he was already on his feet.

They danced around each other for a full thirty seconds. Carlos did not seem to want to stay still for a moment; his nervous energy, aimlessly weaving, was beginning to annoy Miguel. He was no snake to be charmed by such tiresome games. He waited patiently for Carlos to get into a seam, to commence a movement, a repeat, governed by pattern rather than mental agility. This gave him the advantage of knowing where and in which direction his opponent's weight was going. He vectored his punch appropriately; the two masses met smartly. The surprise was that the guard had not come up sooner. The guard was trying to hit his midriff under his jab, and the two punches landed within an instant of each other. Miguel's had the greater force behind it and would have been more readily picked up by the judges, so in spite of a flurry of blows aiming low on his body, he brought in a long and heavy cross. Carlos saw it coming and dug in deeper, ducked under the punch and brought himself in low again to Miguel's body. His head smacked into Miguel's chest as he came up for air and as he rose; an uppercut slipped past his head and onto Miguel's jaw. It landed; it had a lot of weight behind it. Miguel crashed back. As well as the pain was the disbelief that he had allowed himself to be caught twice. He rolled back towards the ropes, trying to maintain his balance, trying to hold it all together. Carlos was unrelenting and tried to follow through his attack with body punches, fast and short. He was wearing Miguel down, tiring him out, he was showing his mettle. Miguel had to think fast. He took punch after punch on his gloves and elbows, trying to gain space, trying to gain a little thinking time. Carlos was focused now, attacking single-mindedly; he had his man on the ropes, he would do as much damage as possible. This round was his. He checked to see if Miguel had pulled it together; did he have space to get a big cross in? As the thought entered his head, Miguel's fists shot between his own. The punch was low on the face, half on the jaw, partly to the throat; it twisted him to the left, away from the judges. They would only see a nicely scoring punch; the slap to the throat on the recoil evaded their gaze. Carlos tried to spin back to face Miguel, but a second punch met him on the way, a long cross from the left hand. It was as much he could do to stand up. The rest of the round was spent in a daze; he held Miguel tightly, sliding in between his arms and hanging on for dear life. He prayed for the bell, but the seconds seemed weighted with chains. The referee tried to part them, like an angry father separating two star-crossed lovers, but he held on for grim life. Miguel lifted up his arms, his face to the judges, to the referee; his torso was slick with sweat, his flesh warm. His strength returning, Miguel allowed Carlos to extricate himself from his grasp. The bell rung and the two men turned away from each other as if their passionate embrace had never been.

Gum shields were spat out, water splashed, ointment rubbed over eyes. Miguel's coach whispered advice, eyes flashing towards Carlos' corner. Miguel heard nothing. They were a team, a family, but he did the fighting, this was his fight and it was he who would win it. He had seen Carlos fighting before on video, he was wiry then, a slimmer man. He had been fast but he had never been against a good opponent. He had never seen him as a street fighter, never noticed that anger, the nasty streak, but it was certainly there. Perhaps he knew Miguel's history; perhaps it had frightened him, made him think that to beat this street urchin he would have to use gutter methods. That was fine. Miguel had lived in both worlds; he understood the street and also knew that his new skills surpassed those he had learnt as a younger man. The fight was won in the mind. The fight was won by the speed of thought.

The bell rung for round three, gum-shields were worked between jaws made tired by the constant scowling. The punches flowed easily from each man. They settled down to a more mature conflict now. Their initial constraining fears evaporated as the desire to win and the beginnings of fatigue took over. Most punches thrown by both men were skilfully avoided, a few were taken on gloves, a few reached their mark. The bell marked the end of the round

147

and both men returned to their seats. There were two more rounds to go. The next round would make the difference. They were probably neck and neck. Miguel was feeling the heat. But the punches were flowing, he had controlled the ring, he felt he was in command now. He was a student of form and he had done his study. There was no telling if Carlos had learnt much from him, but he did not seem to be the empathic type. When the bell went he moved from his corner like an ape. Miguel wondered how he looked himself. Tomorrow he would see himself on the TV; his good sister was recording it, if she could work the video this time. He would make her proud. His coach had said there was no point recording it, it would be over in two rounds; he would wipe the floor with him. His coach was a fine man. He would make him proud too.

Carlos came in immediately, punch after punch. He was trying to take possession, trying to gain control of the centre stage. Miguel was pushed back towards the ropes. He held off the attack easily, slipped in a few body blows himself, twisted away to the right and tried to gain some ground. Carlos was again relentless, firing shot after shot; most were off target, but all had to be fielded. Beneath Carlos' muscular build was the heart of a wiry, skinny man, but this heart seemed to be prepared to fight like a dog. He must be getting tired, but he did not seem to want to let up the pace. Again Miguel lost ground, he touched the ropes, felt the tight chords against his skin. Things were beginning to get serious. Carlos' corner were turning the air blue, screaming their advice. For a second Miguel's mind wandered; they had shouted something obscene, something about his family, his village. He should have kept his eye on the ball. An uppercut caught him hard in the throat. It had slipped through his guard, one punch of so many. The referee turned away to chastise Carlos' corner. He had heard something untoward too and was giving them a piece of his mind. Miguel reeled from the blow to the throat. He could hardly breathe. He pulled back defensively, taking punches to the side of his abdomen. Breathing became painful. With the referee's back turned towards them Carlos brought his head again hard against Miguel's jaw. The pain was intense. Jaw, throat and ribs became one axis of pain. The flurry of blows did not subside. Carlos was going to pummel him into the canvas.

Then Miguel saw the look. The onslaught paused as though the wind had changed direction. Carlos' eyes came up to meet his, a drop of sweat escaped his brow and the chains of time dragged. He was preparing his killing blow, the money shot. But he would be too late. Miguel saw the signal he had been waiting for, the flash of the eyes, the clear commitment. Racked as he was with pain; he knew this was his one chance. He knew where Carlos was going, could visualise the track of his movements; could feel the shift of his mass: the covenant of inertia through space. Miguel released a punch. It came from close to his heart, his hands, tight, defensive against his body. His breath, so hard won, escaped him as if it was his last, rattling through his bronchi, his lungs clinging to wounded ribs. As it exploded from his chest his fist coiled out in sympathy; the breath and movement perfectly coalescing. His fist twisted as it deftly avoided the imperfect defence of Carlos' outstretching arms. His glove grazed both of those of his opponent; plastic against plastic, sliding like hippopotamuses in a pool, sinew and chord, a rush of light from stomach to shoulder, to elbow to fist. The air crackled, shimmered. An image from Miguel's childhood recalled for an instant. His father, disappointed, disappointed again. The blow struck Carlos mid-chest, directly above his heart, but Carlos' body did not move. The foam of the glove compressed, the plastic heated in response, sweat was squeezed between flesh and fist. The sweat mixed with blood and time exploded.

Carlos twisted; spun away as if hit by a car. Both feet lifted from the ground, he rotated in the air, a sycamore elater caught in a draft, then crashed to the ground. The blood, which flew in crimson ribbons, splashed to the canvas around him. There was complete and absolute silence in the room. Miguel heard only the resonant throb of his own beating heart.

The medics rushed the stage; pushing past his now immobile frame. He found himself in his changing room, wrapped in towels, his trainer by his side. He did not know how he had arrived here, could not remember the journey from ringside to bench. His trainer held him tightly, wrapping his arms around him, pulling him close to his chest.

'It's alright, it's alright. Everything is going to be alright.' He said the words again and again. He pushed a tearful face against Miguel's own 'It's going to be alright son.'

Miguel started to sob, but he did not know why.

TEN

The meeting room was oak-panelled and heady with the smell of wax polish and leather. There was the usual ensemble of facial types at the table: the inevitable bald heads and small glasses of the men, tidy hair, plain suits and sensible shoes of the women, but these people did not worry Professor Platt, not unduly anyway. These were people that he could talk to, his kind of people: the old school with years of experience. They had seen it all, put up with every government busybody, watched the fads come and go; they were fundamentally alright. It was the smattering of young people that he had the problem with. They were the new breed of career educationalists. True, they might have been in a school once or twice (hadn't everyone?) but their obsession was not with teaching per se, rather it was ambitious desire to be seen to 'shake down the system' and 'save some tax dollars'. Why such people resorted to Americanisms whenever they wanted to slash your budget and tell you that you were doing your job badly was beyond him. There was definitely a deep-seated insecurity in the country about the supposed greater work ethic of the Americans. Perhaps the Brits just felt guilty for patronizing them for so long.

The suits of the educationalists were just that shade shinier and their ties just that shade more New Labour (regardless of their political affinities). They wanted League Tables; they had delivered League Tables. They decided they did not like League Tables but they wanted Teacher-Focused Development Targets. They had given them Teacher-Focused Development Targets, but when the numbers of new intake teachers crashed into oblivion and the old school started taking early retirement and claiming stress-related mental breakdowns, they had to backtrack and move to Area-Demographic Pupil Development Scores. When this had resulted in swarms of parents upping sticks and moving out of the inner cities, they had to rethink again. They had come up with Individual Student Participation Projection Scores. Professor Platt was fairly certain they were not going to think much of these results either and the consequences of making them available to the unwashed masses was going to introduce a furore beyond anything seen to date. In the corner of the room sat a hack from the newly formed BBC International press associated newspapers. They might be the best of a bad lot, but they could not be trusted not to put some sensationalist spin on the whole thing. What choices did they have in an age of NuMedia? He sighed out loud. It was something he had started doing as a teacher and it was a habit he was trying to break. He should not let them get him down. He knew the desperate need he was feeling to yawn and slump onto the table was his body's avoidance tactic for such meetings. He looked longingly at the dried coffee grounds in the cafetière; a coffee might just sort him out, might just wake him up a bit. There were chocolate biscuits too. He had not wanted to eat before the meeting. In truth he had been too nervous to eat. Most of his public speaking he did in front of a receptive audience of teachers and students. These meetings were different because ultimately the government and associated flunkies always seemed to think that it was his job to get the results they wanted, rather than for him to formulate an honest assessment of the facile tests they themselves had devised.

He also knew instinctively that they were not going to like what he had to say this time. In truth he himself found the whole thing rather concerning, but he had had quite a while to think about the results and very little phased him at his time in life. The assembled crowd would be hearing it for the first time. He looked longingly at the coffee again and caught the eye of a 'not so bad' colleague doing the same. They smiled weakly at each other. No one could have coffee and biscuits until they had been talking ad nauseum for hours and they could not start talking until the minister arrived and the minister was, as ever, running a bit late. There was always some committee meeting of some guild or other that had over-run. Platt wondered what meetings could interest a junior education minister more than the unveiling of the latest educational audit for which said minister was directly responsible. Then he remembered that this minister for education also looked after the performing arts, Cornwall and dentistry or some such ridiculous combination. You could not make it up. Platt looked out of the wonderful lead-light windows of the meeting room across to the London Eye. One well-aimed shoulder-launched missile from the top of the wheel and you could wipe out ninety percent of the highest paid educationalists in the country by firing it into this room. It was a thought he had had before. At the time, taking a class of hand-picked TV perfect five year-olds on the wheel he had been thinking of wiping out the quango set up to establish nurses' wages, but he had been worried that a missile launched from inside the capsule might just whizz round and round and round inside until it exploded. It was likely that the authorities would stop the wheel as well, trapping you. There was also the difficulty of obtaining the weapon, which was probably much harder than the tabloid press seemed to think. He brushed the thoughts away. Who knew what the mind police could pick up these days.

He tried to follow the movement of the wheel. If the minister did not turn up before one full rotation he would be forced to break with tradition and suggest they make a brew. He was not a paid up member of the Socialist Workers Party any more, but he could stand up for his rights for beverage consumption on health and safety grounds. The thought made him smile.

The minister breezed in with the 'sorry I'm late, was caught up in a matter of important state business, you should have started without me' attitude that they always seemed to. Professor Platt had seen them come and go;

political animals were one of the few large carnivores that were not on the endangered list. Other notable exceptions included sharks and crocodiles.

Following the normal round of disinterested introductions, Platt slowly walked to the end of the table, farthest from the minister, where his presentation was set up. They really were not going to like this. He wondered if the minister's proximity to the door would mean he could block it if necessary and thus prevent the hack from getting back to his newspapers.

The concept of Individual Student Participation Projection Scores was not a simple one. Everything about it was designed to obfuscate its purpose in the most abstruse way. It meant nothing, it proved nothing, but it had the wonderful benefit of giving the government the chance to say 'choice' and 'potential' and 'maximize' in the same sentence. Of course, such invasive monitoring of children had only become possible with the massive centralization of education following the restructuring of the whole system on the European model. Centralized data bases could now score every exam mark for every pupil for every subject for every year they were in the system; each and every teacher assessment, each and every essay, module, sports day fixture and pottery class. Calorific values for school meals were monitored and pupil weights, various medical data and behavioural metrics correlated, listed and mined. It was not for the Professor to decide what to do about the data or indeed what any of it meant. To the professor it simply appeared to be fuel for the carousel of blame. It sold newspapers and it sacked teachers but the illiteracy rate seemed to have settled comfortably at the five percent mark and the bureaucrat's inability to understand and interpret rather basic statistical methods seemed to have settled at the ninety-five percent mark. Bad news was looked at blankly, misinterpreted in the most obtuse manner or ignored. Good news, however slight and insignificant, was seized on with the vigour of piranhas on exposed flesh.

He gave his usual preamble, fielded the usual host of

pointless questions from people who should have known better, people who, after all, had been the architects of the whole stupid edifice. He showed them the usual graphs and plots of schools and improvements, of north/south divides, of class sizes, attendances, projected university numbers: both Practical Academic (PAs) and Vocationally-structured Technical Baccalaureates (VsTBs : the practical qualifications always seemed to require longer acronyms). There were few surprises and few things had changed apart from the continued and steady exit of fully qualified teachers from the profession. At last they took a break for refreshments. The professor struggled to get a cup of coffee and a biscuit as he found himself pressed for soundbites by the minister. At one point he was almost tempted to give the man what he wanted, but he resisted. What he had to tell him in a few moments would give him plenty to think about.

ELEVEN

Brian and Janet sat nervously looking at each other in the offices of the biophysics department. Doctor Gordon sat opposite, feet on the table, smiling as his colleagues and friends argued about the implications of Janet's discovery. A brief scan of the members of the faculty had shown a slightly higher incidence of 'positives' than Brian and Janet's scan of the general population. Brian wondered if exposure to high voltages, lasers or magnetic fields had something to do with it. He was tempted to suggest it to the assembled group, but felt too intimidated to speak up. The scientists were working themselves into a frenzy of spin-coupling, magnetic resonance and the heavy metal composition of the human body. Voices were soon raised and shackles rose and egos were bruised. It appeared that the world of biophysics was not only populated by well spoken old-school rocket scientists dressed in tweed. The scientists seemed to enjoy scoring points off each other and almost everything each of them said was contested or refuted by the others. A small, beak-nosed young man with a clichéd explosion of curly black hair seemed most aggrieved. He kept waving the device threateningly at them and mumbling things about the Second Law and Einstein. Brian and Janet were beginning to feel somewhat uncomfortable. They hadn't expected their observations to elicit such aggressive debate; perhaps a slightly patronising discussion and a pat on the back for their enthusiasm, but not this brouhaha. After half an hour, they retrieved their equipment and made their escape. Doctor Gordon walked them to the department exit.

'You know you have really put the wind up these guys. We have no idea what you have discovered, but I can tell you that the research grants are already being written in their heads. These guys are good. They'll have made a big version of your spin resonance devise by the end of the month. I'll make sure you are kept up to date with the progress. I think this is going to be fun! Let me take you both out to dinner in a few weeks time and I'll fill you in on the details.'

They shook hands and walked out into the sunlight. Suddenly it seemed strange to Janet to think that so many millions of people lived their everyday existences without worrying that the behaviour of their constituent atoms was being governed by abstruse mathematical laws. Who knew what would happen if these laws suddenly had a change of plan or decided to take a holiday? Suddenly taking anything for granted seemed rather foolish. The man in the street had no idea what the consequences of general relativity were when applied to the matter in their bones, but some of those people (and Brian felt a perverse pride in this) seemed to be showing unusual subtle gravitational properties and Janet had discovered it. Only time would tell what it all meant. Before Janet knew it they had walked back into the village. Tomorrow they would be sorting through the remains of an Anglo-Saxon latrine. Suddenly science did not seem so terribly exciting after all.

TWELVE

Detective Inspector Manee skidded into the emergency car park at Gatwick airport, crashed through a line of cones and brought the car to a halt by a works entrance at the back of the building. Two security guards gave chase behind him. He shouted back at them explaining who he was; how typical of the police to neglect to tell the airport security what was going on. Manee was light on his feet and quickly lost them as he ran from corridor to corridor. He was heading for the departure lounge; his radio was crackling, the voices of exhausted police could just about be made out over the background din. Bill had attempted to flee the country as Manee had expected. The anti-terrorism squads had sat on the passenger lists for three hours. Now everything was run through Washington there were additional bureaucratic hoops to jump through. By the time he had got the word Bill was scheduled to fly from Gatwick he was already attempting to pass through check-in. When initially confronted he had been calm and collected but once it was clear that security had been summoned he made a run for it. Manee tried to make sense of the crackling radio; they were definitely having a spot of trouble on the floor above. He listened carefully, made a decision and found a service stairwell. This was going to be tricky.

Bill Morris searched the corridor for escape routes. The thrill of pursuit he had come to enjoy was replaced by the fear of being the quarry of another animal. The police were hunting him. They would not understand; how could they? He had killed half a dozen low-lifes, but every low-life had

158

a family and every low-life family seemed to have a lawyer. They would hunt him down and lock him up and not even have the common decency to study him. He knew now that he was very much worth studying. Even following a reasonably comfortable night's sleep, the intense excitement of the preceding day still coursed through his veins. Those moments replayed through his mind again and again, and it was as much as he could do to concentrate on the job in hand. Other thoughts were bursting in on him now. He had killed, he could kill again. He knew he was different of course, a breed apart. The men he had killed were on the very bottom rung of humanity; they did not fully deserve the name. He, on the other hand, was now climbing to new heights. The difference between them was so great they could not be considered to be part of the same species. He had killed, but could it be called murder? Did someone who worked in an abattoir commit murder when they slaughtered a pig? Of course not. The police were gaining; he could hear their shouts and the manic barking of dogs. He had taken a wrong turning. In front of him stretched a long corridor, he was exposed; they might even try to shoot him. He was a big man, not light on his feet and his heart was straining in his chest. He was sweating profusely, and his legs were unsteady beneath him, yet the sounds of the police seemed to recede; the barking of the dogs became faint echoes at the end of a distant tunnel.

In pursuit came four police, two with dogs straining at their leashes. They saw their target at the end of the corridor and sent the animals off ahead. They had been told to capture and contain. Unfortunately that meant they had to carry their guns without the benefit of being able to use them. The bullet proof vests, batons and other assorted equipment were encumbering, but still they were amazed at their target's agility. The dogs ran off at high speed, one following the corridor directly, another leaping onto the travellator, which juddered into motion. The slower dog barked in frustration as it struggled to keep up; their quarry, meanwhile, slipped out of sight. The policemen raced to the end of the corridor to find the dogs leaping and howling at a closed door. These were very bright dogs, but the door catch eluded them. Bill had slipped through to another floor. Gasping for breath the officers threw open the door and the dogs continued their pursuit, their barks echoing up the concrete stairwell.

Bill desperately searched for an exit to the street, but the ground floor was sealed up like a fish tank. Freedom was just beyond the glass but the glass was unbreakable and all the doors were locked. In the distance he could hear the dogs. They were on the stairs now, only a moment behind. He ran from door to door, rattling the levers, his frustrations echoing the jangling of the dog's chains. He dragged a steel ash tray from a corner. It was heavy and mounted on some sort of concrete base. He swung it high and brought it crashing against the nearest window. The window shook and wobbled, but did not break. He tried again and again; his anger building, his mind a maelstrom of fear and anguish. He was feeling weak, his breath now coming in harsh gasps. He heard the clatter of feet on steps; they would be on him within seconds. He pounded the glass with his fists; then continued to run further down the corridor. Then he saw it: a door, slightly ajar. The air around him seemed to be humming as he made his last desperate bid for freedom. His heart pounded, the blood roared, and then he heard another sound, another roaring, from above. A wall of sound flooded the airport, rising to a screaming crescendo, deafening, terrible in its power. It was as if some monstrous creature was descending to devour them. The whole building began to shake; windows and doors oscillated. Bill watched mesmerized as standing vibrations emerged across their mirrored surfaces, expanding and contracting ripples as if a stone had been thrown into a lake. The sound became louder and louder and he suddenly heard it for what it was. A plane was attempting to land on the building. He heard the squeal of engines thrown from reverse and back into full throttle; turbos roared, airbrakes squealed. On board the in-bound

747 pandemonium reigned. Three hundred faces drained of blood as the plane suddenly changed course and soared upwards. Overhead luggage burst open and oxygen-masks deployed. White-knuckled couples found their lover's hands as the pilot and co-pilot wrested the controls from the autopilot. Debris flew around the compartment and two hundred agnostics guiltily prayed to a God they had denied. Seconds behind, a stack of 747s and 737s which followed made similar dramatic course corrections, climbing up and away, pilots suddenly seeing the folly of their descent; the proximity of the planes in front only apparent as they swept out arcs from their common approach vectors. Soon the sky would be full of circling planes, hanging like so many vultures watching the drama playing out below. From the back seats of cars travelling on the M23 children watched the planes coming in to land at Gatwick. Strange how they seemed almost frozen in the air, apparently motionless, then wildly dispersing as if caught in a sudden breeze.

Bill made a dash for the light at the end of the corridor. In this moment he felt more alive than he had ever done in his life. He was acutely aware of everything around him, the air from outside the building blowing in, carrying with it the essences of cut grass and aviation fuel, the sterile chemical vapours exuding from the carpet under his feet, the acrid stench of his own sweat imbued with fear. He heard the shouts of the policemen behind, the barks of the dogs, impossibly dilated into the crunching of boots on fresh snow, could almost feel their eyes upon him. He burst through the door into the light beyond. Impossibly close above him a 747 rose in a wild climb; reflected sunlight from it momentarily blinded him and his hands rose up to his face. The turbulent vortex of air from its wings sent up a sandstorm of dust and debris and it was as much as he could do to remain upright. Through his fingers he saw a parked car not fifty yards from the building. The driver's door and boot were open; a piece of luggage was on the floor by the rear. Bill could not believe his luck. With his last remaining strength he forced his way through the maelstrom to the car, jumped into the driver's seat and to his joy found the keys in the ignition. He tried to fire the engine but there was no response. He turned the key again and again, but to no avail. Suddenly the sanctuary of the car seemed like a prison, the stillness of the air like the cloying stillness of the tomb. His blood ran cold. Frantically he tried again and again to start the engine, perspiration trickled down his shirt sleeves, his feet pumped madly at the pedals to no avail. He heard the door of the airport crash open, saw the police appear in the opening, watched in horror as the dogs bounded across the warm tarmac towards him. He reached across and slammed the door, returning his attentions to starting the car. There had to be some sort of manual override to the starting mechanism. He scrambled around under the seat and steering column. There was nothing. In despair he punched the steering wheel, swearing and cursing. As his eyes rose from over his crossed arms he saw a familiar figure standing at the end of the bonnet. Where had he seen this man before and why was he haunting him now? Detective Inspector Patrick Manee smiled back at him. He pushed a button on his key fob and the central locking of his car whirred and snapped shut.

THIRTEEN

Suzi Rotherman sat alone in the front room of her quiet and seemingly empty home. She was in a black mourning dress. The flowers had been taken to the graveside, the food for Michael's wake was ordered and confirmed. She had organized hundreds of parties, sit down meals, congresses and international conferences in her career. This had been the hardest. Every guest invitation had brought with it a raft of memories; every guest was someone new to be informed of Michael's unexpected death. There were so many questions to field, so many mixed emotions. She had not slept the night before. The ticking of the grandfather clock in the hall, one of Michael's few loved possessions had kept her awake. The deep and echoing machinations of its works gave her no comfort that night. She had wanted to stop it, to hold the pendulum and silence its beating heart. She had been unable to do it. Had she silenced Michael's beating heart in the same way? Instead of covering its mirrored face she had carefully wound the mechanism, placed the key respectfully where Michael always placed it and had sat and listened to it in the darkness.

Margaret had been wonderful, a pillar. She in turn had tried to be supportive of the woman who had stopped her from falling into deep despair, but it was difficult. Suzi felt somehow empty, hollow and she could not see how anyone or anything so desolate could serve any useful purpose. She dwelt now in two disparate words; the surreal present of public mourning and the world of memories. She lived in the shared moments she had spent with Michael, young lovers, the intensity of their lives now thrown into passion-

163

ate clarity by the contrast with her current state. She also reflected upon the recent strange horrors that had pursued her. She thought of the moments in the mortuary, at the hospital and at the moment she had heard of Michael's death. This in particular played again and again in her consciousness. What had happened then, what strange aberration of space or time? She had experienced such time dilations before, of course she had. Under the crushing gaze of English teachers, in her clarinet exam, whilst awaiting the decision on her driving test, waiting for job applications to come back; always anticipation tainted with fear of disappointment or the unknown, the slow rattling of the universe's dice as fate comes down on one side or another. In such moments your future was set, glory or ignominy and you never know which way it was sending you. At these times she had felt almost completely alone, the world contracting and collapsing to a tiny point. It may have been desire to impress her mother, prove herself worthy of love that was so poorly expressed: failure would mean greater isolation, a withdrawal of affection already heavily rationed. She tried to think of less maudlin things. There was something quite different about these recent developments. During these events she felt more part of the world than ever before. The very fabric of reality seemed to drag at her soul. It occurred to her that this implied she was somehow escaping its normal sphere of influence; that she was entering some other realm and space and time were trying to claw her back.

A newspaper crashed through the letterbox and into her thoughts. The terrible weight of Michael's death prevented any meaningful analysis of what was happening to her. Perhaps this was the answer, to ignore it and hope it was only a temporary aberration. She picked up the newspaper, barely scanning the leaders; her mind still undecided as to whether to allow herself this respite of distraction or not. In an hour's time she would be standing at her lover's graveside; should she allow herself to waste valuable grieving time on the headlines? Something caught her eye: a sportsman, a boxer. She never read the sports sections of newspapers unless she was interested in setting up promotional deals for their finance companies. Michael had loudly maintained that it was an opiate of the masses; a thinly veiled scam to divide and conquer; factionalize the proletariat and give them enough distractions so they would never organise for revolution. The strange thing was that this boxer was on the front page. Suzi stared at the photograph in silence. Something reached out to her from the page; the pixellated blur of motion, swirling like a tempest, the face of the victim, head arched back, neck twisted, unnaturally extended as if he were some exotic bird. A moment before death captured for the world to gawp at. The high speed shutter had caught his body, both feet off the floor, the terrible ballet frozen as a force of nature sent him to his death. The contrast between the horrible stillness of the victim and the swirling torrent that was his killer could not have been more acute. Tears fell from her eyes onto the newsprint, spattering words... fatal/blood/widow/400mph/shock.

She looked inside the paper, her hands shaking; here were the faces of the men. Carlos Montoya, smiling, tanned and happy, a holiday shot, now dead. Here also the face of his killer. Miguel stared out of the page towards her, his eyes wide yet unseeing, haunted and hunted. Her tears spattered his face, ran across the image of his cheeks, to the hard line of his mouth. She would have to meet this man. She had to talk to him. They needed each other at this moment. She had to tell him he was not alone. A car crunched up the drive. The hearse had arrived. Miguel would have to wait, today was for Michael.

FOURTEEN

'Poppycock and rot, I tell you! You cannot possibly expect us to believe this... this... outlandish and ridiculous story. Is this some kind of joke, Platt, or have you been got at by some left wing lobby trying to ridicule the government? If you think you can stand there and spout such nonsense, set the gutter press into a feeding frenzy of blame, you are very much mistaken. I'll have your department, your job and your bloody head on a plate before I let this get this out of the room!'

The press representative, who previously had looked like he might make a bolt for the door, stretched his legs and made himself comfortable. Perhaps there was an even better story in the offing. The professor had remained stoic throughout the tirade. He got up slowly, walked to the window, stared up at the London Eye and wished he was on it. He dwelt in that moment as long as he felt was polite and slowly settled his thoughts. He had to try not to lose his temper; it was always this way with the politicos. If you lost your temper you would lose the argument; it was as simple as that. He took a deep breath.

'As hard as it may be for you to understand this turn of events minister; I must regretfully inform you that I have complete confidence in the results of our study. We have carried out the data-collection, mining and analysis entirely objectively, and the nature of the internal controls make it highly unlikely that we have accidentally committed systemic errors. You might not like the consequences of our observations. They may not be in agreement with government projections, desires or expectations, but I can assure you, I can assure everyone in this room, that this unexpected outcome is true. It is outside of our remit to guess at the public outcry this will doubtless cause, or to make suggestions as to what if anything the government should do about this. In the absence of any previous data of this sort we cannot exclude the possibility that this state of affairs has always been like this and the current incumbent government should not be apportioned any blame. Such issues are for the government and advisory bodies such as this one to decide.'

The minister became increasingly agitated throughout this speech. The professor spoke calmly and clearly and this obviously aggrieved him all the more but his final words seemed to pacify him somewhat. If blame was not to be apportioned, this might not be such a terrible result for them. The way things were going, they would not sit as head of the house for the next term of office, or possibly for the one which followed that. This was the kind of thorny problem that would make a diverting poison chalice to pass on to the next education secretary. An image of the shadow minister for education came to his mind. It would be wonderful to knock the smugness off that particular face.

'So, professor.' The minister glanced knowingly at the media representative who brandished a pencil attentively, 'What you are saying is that the current set of statistics, being without a baseline measure, cannot be considered to be the 'fault' of the government. (The inverted commas were clearly audible.) 'In pointer fact, if one looks at the global picture you have presented, we are indeed in line for reaching our ambitious goals for the core subjects'. The professor rolled his eyes. It was futile to rock politicians' boats too vigorously; they invariably then climbed into your own and threatened to drown the both of you.

'Although the current cycle of results are promising and the global picture for education remains consistent with past trends; I believe that this current observation will require careful handling by the government.' Professor Platt hated himself for saying it. Encouraging the present government to resort to spin was inviting the devil to dinner. A hand was raised at the table, attached to the well manicured hand was a smart purple suit and someone who had spent too much time at business school.

'Are you trying to tell us Professor that the government should try to hide the fact that a significant proportion of children in our schools are failing to reach their expected educational goals? Are you trying to suggest that we should condemn these children to a life of under-achievement due to the activities of a minority of, what should I call them; gifted middle-class savants? In this day and age of equal opportunity and common core expectation, I should think we need to root out these individuals and place them in an environment which would be...' She paused.' ...would be more conducive to their personal development.' She seemed satisfied by this. The press-officer raised a hand.

'Could this effect be explained as a direct result of the closure of the grammar schools, professor?' His voice was excited; he was looking for an angle. The professor chose his words carefully, flicked through his presentation and found the relevant slide. He felt tired. These people had no grasp of the beauty of statistics; to them it was just another crow bar with which to attempt to lever in their tired opinions.

'We have no evidence that the minority we have identified in this study are the same subset of pupils that might have previously gone to grammar schools, public schools or indeed any other educational establishment. All we know about them is summarized in these graphs. They appear to be slightly above average intelligence; we are talking around five IQ points. This does not mean they are exceptional, they show a broad distribution. It just appears that the peak of this distribution is slightly higher than other children of the same age.' He paused to let that sink in. He knew it was pointless imagining that it might. Their preconceptions were painfully apparent to him already. 'Let me stress that. They are NOT exceptionally bright. They do however seem to be inherently more successful in a range of the activities that we are measuring. They perform better in exams, in most disciplines and consistently at all ages. This is how the subgroup was initially identified. They are successful without being necessarily bright. The population which performs as well as these children which we have excluded from this population-' (he knew he had lost them at this point, but perhaps the reporter was still on board) '- have significantly higher IQs.'

Another hand slowly went up. It was an old school colleague with whom Platt had dealt in the past. This would tell him if anyone in the room had a hope of understanding the substance of his observation.

'Peter, could you remind us which criteria you used to distinguish these populations again. I know you did explain, but it is a little late and we have heard a lot of statistics. I think some people may have not fully appreciated what you have said.' It was nicely done; the speaker obviously had understood the gravitas of the situation but realised there were many in the room who were not on board. It had been a long meeting, and he was becoming tired of the sound of his own voice.

'Yes, of course. These pupils were isolated because they are all outliers in their classrooms. Their achievements are significantly better than their peers, and not just academically; they are more musical, artistic, they do better at ball games. They appear against the background of their peers like little islands of success.'

'So they are just precocious middle-class kids, dropped into normal schools?' The reporter was banging his own drum again. Professor Platt took another deep breath. He had to try to remain calm.

'No. These pupils come from the same range of socio-demographic backgrounds as their peers. All races are represented in proportions which almost entirely agree with those in the general population. In this respect they appear entirely normal. Their IQs are fairly normal, spatial, mathematical, and that of literary reasoning. The differences we have observed are barely above the statistical noise, the subtle differences in IQ may in fact be a by-product of their positive experiences though school, but this is speculative. The point is they just perform better than their peers with no obvious social or psychological advantages.'

'Could they be different in some way you have missed?' The voice came from another educationalist. 'Could it just be that they are more confident, have more supportive parents, are better-looking or something. Could they be influencing the teachers in some way, cheating or abusing the system?' It was a good question. It was the first thing Platt himself had considered. He answered after a pause.

'This is unlikely, but not impossible. As you all know the exam systems in this country are now centralized and computerized. It is highly unlikely that this many pupils should be able to hack into our databases; though it is possible that an external malicious agent could try to do this. We cannot rule this out. One thing that makes this contention less likely is the fact that much of this data is stored on independent databases and has only been collated by us at the end of the academic year. For the same reason we find it difficult to accept favouritism on behalf of the teachers. Though this is a possibility we cannot rule out, teacher attention and effort is a finite quantity. It could explain some of our results. But there are non-academic differences which need to be explained as well. As for the parents, that is a harder one to analyse as the data is naturally more subjective. The limited metrics we do have pertaining to parental involvement do, however, indicate no significant differences.'

'But why should we care if a few kids do better than everyone else? What does it matter? Just because they aren't brighter or richer than anyone else, why worry? What harm are they doing? Isn't it just nice that the poor old run of the mill pupil should just get lucky by some cosmic good fortune? Doesn't it just bump up the figures? Maybe they just try harder than everyone else. Are we so disabused of the world as a meritocracy that we can't be happy that some kids just manage to get ahead in spite of us?' This was from another educationalist who had appeared to doze off at the point at which Platt had

170

explained this point the first time.

'This is the very essence of the problem.' Platt was ready to sum up. The room was hushed. Perhaps he had got their full attention. 'These children and young people seem to be doing better at the expense of their peers. These people shine because they achieve more than the other children in their classes, but their classes, when compared to other classes in the school or area do worse, measurably, significantly worse.'

'That doesn't make sense. How can you be so sure? Perhaps it is just an unhappy correlation between successful kids and an unsuccessful class.' This was from the old school teacher.

'This is what we ourselves initially concluded. But, as you know we have been collecting and collating these data for three years and it appears that when these...' the Professor paused for thought, 'these "gifted" children move schools or classrooms, they suppress the class into which they enter. They continue to do well, to out-perform peers of their own age across the country, but more importantly they out-perform their local group at its expense. Every class, in every subject these children enter into performs less well than an otherwise identical class of which they are not a member. We have been assessing teacher performance for so long now these anomalies become clear. These gifted children turn a good class into a failing one, a consistently successful teacher into a moderate one, a moderate teacher into a bad one.'

'And you can be sure they don't exert this malevolent effect simply by poor behaviour or class disruption?' The minister was calmer now. He sounded slightly dejected. There were certain truths that even a minister for education could not ignore.

'In terms of social behaviour no obvious correlation has been found. They do appear to be somewhat restless and a proportion show attention deficits, but this may reflect their elevated stature. We plan to study this aspect further.'

Suddenly the minister turned on him. 'How long have

you known about this, without telling us Platt? How long have you bean counters been sitting on this?' There was a sharp intake of breath from the floor, but Professor Peter Platt had been expecting this outburst.

'We have known for some years. We did not inform the minister until we had followed three years of data. We needed to rule out the factors we have just described. We were not certain. We felt we had to get this right. I believe we have.'

The minister was livid. He was tempted to jump the reporter on the way out of the building, kill him and dispose of his body in the liberal club car park. Tomorrow every neurotic middle-class swing voter would want to know if their little Jonny or Nigella had been held back by one of these freakish wunderkinds. They would blame the government and bay for his blood in the streets. He swallowed deeply and wiped the sweat from his brow. One thought which had occurred to him was what would these children be like when they grew up?

'Professor, I'm sorry for losing my temper. You have to appreciate that this is going to be a very difficult matter for the government to handle.'

'I appreciate that Minister; especially so close to the forthcoming elections.' Professor Platt smiled thinly. The minister looked at the floor, out the window, at the press officer, who was holding his pen expectantly. Then back to the Professor.

'What do you propose we do?'

FIFTEEN

Edward Spinks looked across at the man on the other side of his old boss's large pine desk. So Bill had flipped at last, gone mad, threatened his wife and tried to jump on an aeroplane to escape to the Caribbean. It had not surprised him. He had seen almost nothing of Bill Morris for the preceding four or five weeks. It had been a welcome respite from the man's continuous cheeriness and boundless enthusiasm for the mundane and dull. Edward had actually managed to get rather a lot of work done in Bill's absence. It was so typical of the foibles of life that he should at last do some really valuable work at the very moment that the department he worked for was closed because the boss had gone criminally insane. He had fantasised about being made the new CEO himself, to have the chance to wield the power over his miserable colleagues. On reflection, he would be tempted to sack the lot of them and build a new empire in his image. It was a nice thought, but such ideas were nonsense because that was not the way the business world worked. The poor sods that did the work and knew the business would not be involved in sorting out the mess. Their competitors, previously only referred to in whispers, would be approached by the board and no doubt they would be sold to the highest bidder. It was all very sad. The man who sat on his boss's ample leather seat did not look like a member of the board. He was youngish, probably late thirties, early forties, short hair, slightly receding, but spiked up into a youthful style with no attempt to cover the gaps. The face was friendly, the lines around the eyes indicating the man liked to smile, but the brow was creased as well; he was a thinker.

The eyes were bright, blue and penetrating. They had scanned Edward thoroughly as he had entered the room and sat down. The man was measuring him up in some way. It was slightly disconcerting. Perhaps this was to be some sort of interview, or a test, to see if he was CEO material. Edward was beginning to wish he had ironed a shirt when he came in this morning rather than just shaking one vigorously as he pulled it out of the dryer. Well, he might not look like CEO material, but he knew his stuff, had the experience if not the MBA and could sit in the chair opposite in an instant if they needed someone to step in at short notice. Bill Morris might have gone mad, but then anyone who was as patently talented as he was but with so little personal charm was sure to lose his grip on reality in the end. It was just a question of when.

Edward had the talent and he was beginning to think he had the charm as well. At least Agneta Sibilski seemed to think so. Agneta was visiting him rather a lot these days. The thought of her crossed legs in sheer nylons, highly polished shoes poised in front of her shapely calves, made him smile.

'Mr Spinks, thank you for agreeing to speak to me. I imagine you must be wondering what is going on at the moment?' The voice was polite, calm, assured. 'I'm Detective Inspector Patrick Manee of the Metropolitan Police Service. I'm here to perform an investigation on Bill Morris, who I believe is your immediate boss. I wonder if you could tell me what you know of the current situation. At this stage of our enquiries we are interested in any leads that we can get.' Edward felt strangely let down. So this was not to be his big break. If they wanted to find out why Bill had gone wacko, perhaps they should ask his psychotherapist. Such people always had psychotherapists.

'I'm afraid I don't really know anything other than what I have heard on the TV and seen in the newspapers. Bill was quite a private man, a very professional man. I've worked here many years, but I think I've only been to his house once or twice. I really don't know him very well.'

'Perhaps you could tell me what you have heard in the

papers, Mr Spinks. I'm not at liberty to discuss the details of the case, but I would be interested to know what you think has been going on over the last few months.' Edward's interest was piqued; something must be going on. Bill must have had some strange project bubbling away on the side. He was rather cross now that he had not spotted this himself earlier.

'All I have seen in the media suggests that Bill has had some sort of mental breakdown. He appears to have assaulted his wife and then become involved in some sort of fracas at Gatwick. There was a police chase and he was picked up as he tried to escape. Everyone here obviously thought it was rather strange. Bill hasn't exactly been himself for the last month or so, but we haven't seen much of him; we assumed he had just had some sort of mental episode which had been misinterpreted as a terrorist attack: the airport is jumpy at the moment. Bill is a gentle enough man. I wouldn't have thought he was any kind of threat to anyone. I understand he is in police custody. Is he alright?' Manee watched Edward's body language: his fingers constantly drumming the table top, the way he crossed his legs, uncrossed them, then re-crossed them. There was something defensive there; something he was thinking about saying, but was unsure.

'Mr Morris seems quite well. I spoke to him myself briefly yesterday. As you say, he appears to have suffered some kind of mental trauma. Is there any reason why he should have been under particular stress at work at the moment? Do you know how well you company is doing, or how safe Bill may have perceived his job to be?'

'The company is a bit rocky at the moment, but then we are in a poor part of the business cycle. We are in no worse a state than any of our competitors. I'm sure Bill knew this. He was under considerably less stress than many of us. He was after all not at the whim of a time and motion study.' There, he had said it. The words just skipped out; the dreaded time and motion study. He had hoped to avoid the issue; he was not sure what to say if Manee asked anything too specific about this. What would Agneta say?

More importantly what would Agneta do? She had come to him for advice after all. It was his shoulder she had cried on. If anyone had the right to discuss this with an outsider, even the police, it was him. All that had stopped him pursuing this further was his own latent distrust of the whole thing. Agneta was intelligent, ambitious and she did not seem to be a crook. Her boss, however, was another story. Edward had been studying him and there were a few things about Kevin Masters that did not add up. Edward had been hacking into the code of the monitoring program Agneta had installed on his PC. It was definitely more than they had made it out to be. Kevin Masters was snooping on their business. Perhaps he should inform the detective inspector now. He thought about it, but chose not to. What if Agneta was involved? That would throw cold water onto that party. It was not worth the bother. He would wait and see what developed.

'Tell me about the time and motion study.' Manee's eyes did not betray any particular interest. It was as if he was asking about the weather. 'Did Bill instigate this?'

'Bill did instigate it; I'm not sure why. I guess it is just one of those things you do to see if there is any slack in the system, anywhere you might save a bit of money, I guess. Bill was a shrewd guy. I imagine he just thought we could do better.'

'And was he excluded from the study?' Manee's voice was calm, measured, perhaps too disinterested. The images Agneta had shown him came to mind, the hot seat, right in front of him where Bill Morris had apparently managed to do twice as much work as anyone else.

'No, he was not excluded. I guess he was sufficiently confident in his own abilities to think he would come out well in it.'

'And did he? Have you seen the results?' Manee's clear blue eyes focused on Edward. 'Tell me what you know.' Edward stopped to think for a moment. His palms were sweating. There was definitely something going on, something strange. Although he personally had never had cause to distrust the police; he was suspicious of their methods. There was always the danger you could implicate yourself in something, they were always desperate for an angle.

'Look, why do you want to know? These are internal company matters, of no interest to the police, and besides, what sort of inquiry is this? Why would this be relevant? We are a legitimate company going about our normal business. The man wasn't a terrorist, or at least...' His voice trailed off. Perhaps this was it; maybe Bill did have contacts with terrorist groups. Perhaps Manee was of the opinion that the company was just a front for a terrorist organization. They all might be under suspicion.

'Mr Spinks.' Manee stood up behind the desk and slowly walked to the window. 'Mr Spinks, I'm going to tell you something that I don't want repeated outside of this room. You are the most senior employee in this unit. You have had the closest working relationship with Mr Morris. This is a murder investigation. We need to understand the motive. There are...' He paused himself, unsure of how much to say. He had said more than he had intended already. 'There are unresolved issues we need to investigate. I want to examine Mr Morris' behaviour, get an idea of who he spent his time talking to; to try to work out if he had any enemies, that kind of thing. If you have documentary evidence that would allow us to track some of his movements over the last month or so, I would very much like to see it. I need phone records, and access to his computer files and papers.'

It was all a bit much for Edward. Bill Morris, a murderer? It didn't seem possible. Bill was frustrating, bright, annoying, but could he be capable of taking someone else's life? They were unlikely to find anything of interest in Bill's files. In five years of sitting outside the man's door listening to every telephone conversation he had never heard anything that might be of interest to anyone who wasn't involved in advertising.

'Of course you can have access to his files. I'll get his PA to sort out the necessary passwords and find telephone records for you. I don't have the results of the time and

177

motion study, though I have seen the preliminary findings. They are held by the firm we have employed to carry out the study. Agneta Sibilski, the second in command, is coming in this afternoon. I'm sure it can be arranged for you to meet her. I'm not sure what value they will be to you, Detective Inspector.' Again he felt torn between some strange desire to do the right thing by Agneta and the common sense approach of dealing honestly with the police when you yourself have done nothing wrong, the typical groin-brain axis problem that so often faced him.

'Why do you say that? Do you think the data is flawed in some way? Is it not representative?'

'It's difficult to say; the initial conclusions seem rather... How can I put it? Incredible.'

'In what way?' Manee was leaning forward now. He knew there was something Spinks was holding back. Bill Morris was not a normal man. Manee had only been allowed the shortest of interviews before the anti-terrorism unit had pulled rank and whisked him away. Manee was furious. He had made his complaints to the highest authorities and had been told to sit it out, shut up and wait. He would get his chance, but the Americans would have the first shot. During the police chase of Morris through the airport the site's navigation and automatic landing aids had been screwed up for nearly half an hour. There had been a dozen near misses. Thousands of people had been endangered. There could have been carnage in the air and on the ground. The Americans believed the two elements were linked. They were convinced Morris had hidden some electromagnetic device in the airport. They wanted to establish Morris' terrorist potential and needed time to examine links with known terrorist organizations. How much time was the question. People had disappeared into the American system for months or years. Manee had driven straight from the police holding cell to Morris's office. Even if they had stolen his prisoner from him, he could still take advantage of the jump he had already got on them. Bill Morris was no terrorist, Manee was certain of that. The problem was that he was beginning to think he was something altogether more alarming.

Spinks wanted to hold his tongue, tried to keep his thoughts to himself, but he was not naturally deceptive and part of his psyche retained a childhood fear of being exposed as a liar or a fraud. The man sitting opposite obviously had half the picture. Something about his nonchalance, his calm voice but piercing gaze told Spinks that it was not information itself that the man wanted. It was confirmation of what he thought he already knew. He wiped his sweating palms on his trousers, smoothed down the hair on the back of his neck (something which never failed to comfort him when he was under stress), breathed deeply and wrestled with the words he needed to explain his thoughts on Bill Morris.

'Agneta Sibilski has all the details. Her firm have been monitoring us very closely for the last six weeks: work rates, efficiency, typing speeds that kind of thing. The data is supposed to be objective and the data sets are huge. I'm not sure I trust their conclusions; how can you ever be sure there is not some hidden agenda? They seem to imply that Bill Morris is, by a significant margin, the most prolific person in this department.'

'And you think that is strange? He is the boss after all, aren't they supposed to work harder than everyone else? Is he taking the credit for other people's work?'

'The type of data the group collects isn't supposed to be sensitive to that sort of divisive misinterpretation. Bill just appears to get more done in his day than anyone else; he works faster, more efficiently and better.'

'Isn't that just a good thing? Surely there are such exceptional people. Isn't it possible that the man is just incredibly good at his job?' Manee's eyes were twinkling; this was the crux of the matter. Bill Morris was exceptional, but was he abnormally so.

'That is not a problem in itself. There is something else, some strange effect. I know this is going to seem crazy, I'm not sure I believe or understand it myself, but when Bill is here he seems to suppress the efficiency of everyone else around him. The closer you are to him, the stronger the effect.' Spink's voice trailed off. Saying it out loud made it seem so patently foolish. It had to be some elaborate joke.

'And you sit just outside the door. So you must be affected more than anyone else.' Manee said it so calmly, so matter-of-factly. There was no hint of sarcasm or mockery in his voice. Spinks was taken aback.

'Well, yes, that's right. The company's models seem to show that when Bill is here, in this office, my own productivity crashes.'

'And when he is not here?'

'It increases to levels at least as high as everyone else. Everyone's productivity increases, especially those sitting in his vicinity. It has to be nonsense.' The more he said the more foolish and uncomfortable he felt. But Manee remained impassive. 'It really isn't for me to say. I'm one of the subjects of the test; I'm not responsible for it.'

'Well, it seems from Bills notes that you are somehow responsible for it. He asked you to supervise the work didn't he?'

'He did.' Edward thought back those few weeks. So much had changed since then. It was a time before Agneta, before that red dress.

'And you seem to know a lot about the preliminary results.'

'Agneta has been keeping me up to date.' He could not hide the slight frisson of pleasure that thought gave him. Manee changed tack.

'Have you noticed the effect Bill has on you? Do you feel somehow different when he is around?'

Edward reflected in this. It was something that had gone through his mind many times of late. In the darkness of the night he had chased the thoughts away with images of Agneta, but the memories persisted. Where had that time gone? Where had it leached to, slipped and slid from his reality. Years he had given to this firm, but so much of that time had sublimed. The more he thought about it, the more he could almost feel the ache of it, the wasted past crying for him, but he had let it slip away.

'I don't know. I sit here, I do my work, I drink a cup of

coffee, I wander around the building to clear my head. I don't notice any difference. There is always a sense of childish relief when the boss is away. We might leave work a little early, take an extra half an hour for lunch, chat about the weather a little more. That is what seems so strange. You could ask anyone here the same question and they would all say they did less work when he was away. Agneta says such management effects are common. In good companies, bosses often improve work rate, presumably by energizing people to get on with things. In poorly-managed firms the opposite can be true.'

'So you are not surprised then; maybe your firm is of the second type?'

'No, I don't think so. And you see, it isn't just our department. The effect radiates out, to other departments, to other floors; people who don't even know who Bill Morris is. There is something weird about him, if all this is to be believed. He seems to have some malevolent effect on us. It all seems just too implausible. Do you think we are being deceived?'

'No, Mr Spinks, I don't think that at all. I'm just not sure what the alternative options are.'

SIXTEEN

The headlines were a mixed bag of sensationalist humbug and confused intellectual outrage. 'Freaks crush spirit of our kids' roared one tabloid. 'Bright lights put other kids in the shade' declared another. 'Examination disparity accentuated by mixed ability classes' opined the worthier broad sheets. The Minister for Education slammed the papers down one at a time in front of Professor Platt.

'Look at what you have done! For Christ's sake. This is going to cause a war. Have you ever stood in front a room full of angry parents who think your policy is going to fuck up their kids' education? Have you? These people will want blood, they'll want my head on a pole. Christ. Christ. Christ!'

The Professor nodded gravely. 'Yes, I suspect they will. Unfair really as it's hardly your fault. But then it can hardly be considered to be our fault either. We collected the data; you put the policies in place. You chose to monitor every cough and sniffle of every child in the country; we just collated the maths. I'm sorry Minister, but the cat is out of the bag.' He scanned the papers. 'I would suggest your best bet is to obfuscate the issue, accentuate the positive and try to hide the problem in the statistical noise. I agree it is a difficult one. Try and hide it under the carpet and you might get dragged over the coals; try to address the problem and the left wing will crucify you. I have to admit that I'm very glad I haven't got your job minister.'

'You are enjoying this, aren't you Platt. It's all a big intellectual joke to you isn't it? You might well be laughing on the other side of your face if we look into this and find you have fucked up. If there is any shit that will stick to you,

182

believe me I'll make it stick.'

'There is no point getting worked up about this, minister. You aren't going to pacify the electorate by beating up your civil servants. You should have learnt that by now. I think what is more interesting is why this happens. Don't you think it is an interesting phenomenon? Don't you wonder why it is happening?'

'I couldn't give a rat's arse as to why it is happening, Platt. I just want to know what to do about it without losing my job and bringing down the government with me.'

'I'm sure it won't come to that. I'm sure, given a bit more time and resources; we can sort out what is going on here. Personally I'm fascinated by this result. It goes against accepted psychological doctrine. I think there might be something profound here. Something, well, frankly rather concerning. If this has been going on throughout history, it might have implications for the whole of society.'

The minister pushed his face up close to the professor. 'If this is some crude ploy to pull in more funding for your intellectual mind games, I'll personally see to it that you are destroyed. Believe me. You've got a month. I'll try to stamp out the media fire storm. If I go down in flames, I'll make sure you burn too. Come up with answers. Something that puts the government in a good light or there will be trouble. Read the papers, Professor, read the bloody papers.'

With that the minister left the room, slamming the door behind him.

SEVENTEEN

Lilly Anterton lay in the darkness. Tonight the dark seemed more penetrating and threatening than usual because Lilly felt more helpless and alone than usual. Her helplessness was not drawn from self-pity, it came as a result of news she had received from her least favourite nurse at the home. Why did such news always have to come from her? It was almost as if the nurses had sat around distributing the day's news and the miserable, humourless nurse had cherry-picked the most sour or bitter fruits for herself. Mary had sent a message explaining that she would not be able to visit for a few weeks. Lilly was not to worry, but she was somewhat poorly and couldn't make the journey in the wheelchair. Lilly knew her friend well enough to know that this was a nonchalant, kindly covering letter. Something was wrong, Mary was sick and Lilly felt sick with worry in return. She had tried to call the house, half a box of Cadbury's had secured the use of a mobile phone, but no-one answered. Lucy had left a message on an answer machine, tried to sound cheery, trying not to allow any inflexion of desperation to colour her words. Lilly hated telephones, especially talking to answer machines. She had left her up-beat message, her voice nearly cracking, her heart pounding. Knowing her friend could be laying somewhere, sick or dying. These could be the last words they shared and their distance had infused the words with insincerity. Lucy listened to the sound of the clock and for a moment allowed herself a few maudlin thoughts on the frailty of human existence. The clock measuring out life, threatening to slow as it had done before. Lilly had sat in the darkness before and tried to influence its horrible monotony, but since the first time she had been unsuccessful. There was always the initial sense of success, the first few agonising ticks and tocks as the rhythm imprinted on the mind, but after the initial insecurity it always seemed to settle. Tonight it was metering the beating of her heart.

Lilly woke with a start. She had drifted off to sleep; images of dancing and a swirling of long gowns slowly faded as the dream floated away. Of late she had tried to hold these dear memories, to prevent the morning from stealing them from her, but cold reality slid in. She felt unusually alert. Her body, weak as it was, was tense. It was still dark, very dark, so why had she woken? She felt a draft of cold air on her face, heard the sounds of occasional traffic outside, too loud. Her brain tried to make sense of the level of the noise. Surely this was wrong. She was momentarily confused. The home was normally sealed tight like a Tupperware sandwich box. It saved money on the heating and thus was an immutable law. The window was ajar. A hand, a black silhouette against the slightly paler darkness outside, pushed the window closed. There was someone in the room.

For a healthy, young person, fear has the effect of overwhelming the body with signals, paralysing the limbs with a torrent of demands, solidifying the blood with a cocktail of endorphins; the conflict between fight and flight holds the heart in a crushing embrace. For Lilly, trapped in an unresponsive body with barely the strength to lift her arms, fear merely served to shake the cage in which her spirit lay. Now her mind was crashing itself against her prison, a canary in a jar, frantically fluttering.

The silent figure before her was hooded, in dark, loose-fitting clothing. White lines ran along the edges of his jacket and trousers, the feeble light from the window illuminating this outline, giving him a preternatural glow. A hood covered his face. The whites of his eyes peered out from the darkness.

In the midst of the turmoil of anxieties and thoughts which convulsed in her mind, Lilly saw an image, an

185

engraving in a book: a terrified Ebeneezer Scrooge, sheets pulled up to his chin, the cowled ghost of Christmas-yet-to-come, a boney finger extended, ghastly, towards the future. But Lilly had had no warning of this apparition and had not the strength to sit up in bed or pull the covers to her chest. The silence was terrifying. The figure just stared, drinking up her image in the darkness, still, yet charged with menace, poised between the state of withdrawing and the state of advancing. She wanted to speak, to try to reason with the thing before her, but she knew her body would not obey her. She knew also that there was no discussion to be had with this particular spirit.

'Don't be afraid.' His voice was low, reverential, as one might speak in a church. 'Don't want to hurt you. I never want to hurt anyone.' He began to move forward, slowly. His hands touched the bed, the springs responded to his weight, deforming, compressing; measuring his approach with nearly inaudible screams. He crawled slowly towards her, straddling her form, pulling the covers tight, mummifying her legs and lower body in a cocoon of polyester. As he moved up the bed, his face entered deeper shadow. Lilly was not now confronted by his eyes, which had glowed in the sodium illumination from the street, but by impenetrable night behind the hood. She felt the man's warm breath on her face, heard his breathing. This creature was of flesh and blood. He had not come to collect her soul or show her the error of ways. He was a man like any other, and Lilly understood men. She knew what it was he had come for. She opened her mouth to speak, but he leapt towards her and placed something over her mouth. She tried to turn away, tried not to breath, but she was too weak to resist. The solvent vapours stung her eyes and throat.

'Don't struggle, don't struggle. The other one struggled. Mary hurt me. I had to hurt her back. I don't want to hurt you though, I want to be your friend.' She tried to break free. His head lay upon her chest; his hot breath almost came in sobs. The rolled up rag now muffled any cry. Lilly felt consciousness slipping away. It was then that she heard the ticking of the clock. The sound so familiar, she

186

had heard it a million times before. But this was different because it was slow. Time was holding its breath as she tried to hold her own, clinging to the moment as she was clinging to life. For a second she had thought of giving up, breathing out her life into the cotton over her mouth. What was left to live for trapped between these four oppressive walls? But now she was infused with new strength. This man had attacked Mary, had tried to kill her friend. This realization set off an explosion of fury within her. She slowly, painfully, placed her hands on the man's face, and the back of his head, folding the hood down so it smothered him, an echo of her own desperate state. In her youth she could have wrung his neck like a turkey. She had been shown how and more than once behind enemy lines she had nearly had cause to do it. But those days were long gone and she was so terribly weak and at this moment the air itself seemed thick and viscous. Her skin crawled with invisible turbulence; the air fizzed around her hands. She was losing consciousness and the blackness of the room roared towards her. She pushed with every last ragged fragment of her strength, felt her old bones complaining, chalky pain on chalky pain. The clock ticked but no answering tock came. Blue fire seemed to play around her hands. There was no struggle, no resistance; the world was momentarily perfectly peaceful. Then, as darkness passed across Lilly's mind, time reasserted itself, but the second was marked not only by the clock but also by an explosive retort, the sound echoing and reverberating in the confines of the room. The skull between her hands cracked and splintered into a million tiny shards.

ONE

Professor Sutcliffe was fifty-eight, more than moderately successful and obsessed with gadgets. As a professor of physics he had his fair share of boy's toys to play with at work, but in all honesty, in spite of the two million pounds' worth of supercooled, glistening, chrome-plated futurism which was in the basement of his laboratory, he had most of his best ideas in the bath. He was in the bath now. Sometimes his bathing took several hours and his wife would call up the stairs in a concerned manner, always fearing he had fallen asleep and drowned among the flotsam and jetsam of his ideas. There was something annoying about this because once a really good idea had been interrupted, even by a well meaning wife, it was always fogged or castrated. The beauty of original thought was that it oozed out of a very shy part of the brain; any loud noise and it would scurry away into the darkness. It was also nice to know that his lovely wife cared enough about him to leave her gardening or her astrophysics long enough to check that he was still alive. Professor Sutcliffe's children indulged his passion for gadgets with great enthusiasm. The professor's bath was surrounded by a battalion of sophisticated, battery-powered children's toys in various bright colours. The professor could amuse himself with a small radio controlled submarine though the bath provided limited space (especially with him in it) and there was always a minor risk of getting something caught in the little propeller. The professor was getting quite good at fine manoeuvres and had some control on the rather fiddly business of controlled dives and surfacing, but he had definitely decided that he would get the technicians at work to replace the periscope mechanism (which was only amusing for the first hour or so) for a potentially infinitely more satisfying spring loaded weaponry system. With such modifications he could have a very good go at attacking the yellow submersible Thunderbird 4 craft which he had previously delivered from his favourite toy, the sleekly retro-modèrne Thunderbird 2. His wife called up from below.

'Do you want a cup of tea, dear?' He thought about it for a second. Should he interrupt the current state of war in the bath for a cuppa? He decided it wouldn't hurt and recalled some of the craft to base to make room for his floating radio-controlled coffee mug and biscuit holder. He fancied that such a device was originally designed for the super-rich so that their staff could send over gin and tonics and petit fours when they were lounging around in their swimming pools in the Algarve. He found it was more than adequate for motoring round a cup of instant coffee and two Hobnobs.

It was at that moment that he had a realisation. He had naturally been amazed and bemused by George Spink's demonstration with the ground penetrating atomic resonance probe. It had caused quite a controversy and it did not look like it was going to go away, but it suddenly occurred to him that he had the perfect system in which to examine the effect. Fred Sutcliffe was about to extricate himself from the bath in a classic Eureka moment, when the door opened and his wife appeared carrying coffee and Jammy Dodgers. The world would have to wait a few minutes more. There were some things more important than nuclear physics.

TWO

'I am sorry, Miss Rothermann, but you must understand Miguel is in the middle of... how do you say... a media feeding?... and I don't want him disturbed. He is my responsibility now, and I do not want him upset by anyone else. He is having too many problems right now.'

Suzi persisted with her broken French. She could hear the note of anguish in her own voice, she hoped Miguel's coach would hear this too. It had been a series of snap decisions. To go immediately to France, to the city where Miguel trained, to ask the local people where she might find the small boxing club that had created this phenomenon, to bribe the caretaker to give her the coach's private number. She had to do this. She had to speak to the man. She knew this now more than ever. As she had driven through the quiet streets of the outlying villages, she had seen something in the eyes of the local people. When she had asked for directions that look had intensified. Some refused to talk to her, but others were only too happy. They did not seem to care who she was or why she had come to their little corner of France, but they also seemed to feel no loyalty to their most famous sporting son. Several had spat on the ground when she had stopped to talk to them. She was not sure if this was custom or disdain.

'Monsieur Gavroche, please, you must not misunderstand me. I am not from the media, I want to help Miguel. I think I know what happened to him. I need to see him. I might be able to help him.'

'How can you help him, Miss Rothermann? Can you bring that poor boy to life? Can you put his heart back in his chest? I don't think so Miss Rothermann, I really don't think you can do that.' He was going to hang up; Suzi could hear it in his voice. He was going to finish the conversation there and then. There was only one thing left to try. How much did this man know his charge? How closely had he watched him?

'Monsieur Gavroche, Miguel is not like normal people. He is... he is different.' She did not know how to phrase the spiralling emotions which threatened to steal her voice. She scrambled around the wreckage of her French vocabulary picking words from the debris. 'Miguel is different, he sees things differently. Time is different for him. I understand now, I know.'

The line went quiet, for a moment she thought the man had hung up, but she could hear laboured breathing at the other end.

'How could you know, Miss Rothermann? How? You do not know my Miguel. You have not watched him change from a boy to a man as I have. You know nothing apart from what you have seen in the papers.'

'No Monsieur, you are wrong. I know Miguel, I know what he is going through, I understand, because, because... ' Her voice cracked. She could hardly bring herself to form the words, her arms started to tremble involuntarily. She thought she might faint. Images of Michael's funeral passed through her mind, the accusatory glances from the splinters of his friends, the constancy of Margaret.

'How can you know, Miss Rothermann?' The man's voice was quiet now, calm. 'How can you know?'

'Because, because, I am the same, Monsieur Gavroche. Miguel and I are the same.' There, she had said it. Though she did not know exactly what it was she had implied. She was the same as what? In what way were they the same? She was a successful businesswoman and entrepreneur, he a successful boxer from the streets of southern France who had just made himself infamous by slaughtering an opponent on live television. Yet they were the same where it mattered. She had known it as soon as she had seen the photograph. The realisation was painful, but there was no point in running from it. Perhaps they could help one another; perhaps together they could understand what it was that had happened to them.

There was a pause, more breathing, a sigh.

'Okay Miss Rothermann. You can see Miguel. But if you upset my boy, you will have to deal with me. He is like a son to me. You understand? Like a son. Come to my sister's house number 245 Rue de la Seine. At eight o'clock this evening. Miguel will see you then.' The phone went dead.

Suzi leant back into the phone box. She had come this far. She would see it through.

THREE

The crowd outside the small inner-city school was ugly. As soon as the minister's Daimler turned off the main street and was visible to the crowd they let out a roar of angry disapproval. They had placards; placards were bad. The minister took small comfort in the fact that they did not appear to have an effigy of him. The crowd was composed predominately of women, many with young children holding their hands or clinging to their legs. They were being harangued by a semi-circle of teachers who had formed a cordon on the front gates. There was a smattering of police in attendance and they formed a thin blue line between the two parties. As the Daimler came to a halt the crowd moved away from the school gates and began to redistribute itself, amoeba-like, around it. It was soon engulfed by angry middle-aged, middle-class faces. Placards threatened to make a mess of the paintwork; lenses appeared in the crowd as journalists and a camera crew jostled to the front.

'For fuck's sake! I knew this kind of shit would happen; fucking unbelievable, thoughtless irresponsible bastards. I'll find out who did this and smash them to pulp.' He spoke under his breath; only the driver heard the outburst.

As he stepped from the car his face automatically adopted the calm, half-smiling, firm-set mask he had practised for such occasions. He hoped to God there would not be too many more of them. His thoughts flashed to the Prime Minister's office. The smarmy bastard had brushed off the warnings. 'Your job is to protect the policy, John. Protect the policy: that, John, is your job.' It was rare to see the PM out and about in the thick of things these days. He

195

sent his minions and minions were fundamentally expendable.

'Ladies and Gentlemen, please, if you will just let me get through to the school.' He wanted to shout 'Get your filthy hands off the bloody ministerial car, you hysterical nonentities', but that probably would not go down well. He scanned the crowd for the most prestigious microphone and gravitated towards it, ignoring the independent companies and newspapers. He grabbed the arm of the anchorwoman who brandished her microphone as if she were warding off a vampire with a cross. It was not anyone he recognised. Christ, they hadn't even sent out a half-decent interviewer. He cursed their house a second time. Being interviewed by a nobody never looked good. Nobodies were ravenously hungry for a story, always wanting to prove something, these days invariably rude and often pig ignorant. They could sometimes be intellectually crushed. He dragged her through the police cordon; the bobbies smirked as he asked them to part the ways. He hated happy policemen. If he ever got that particular office they would smirk on the other side of their redundancy papers. Their hilarity related to his much publicised appearance in the press following his alleged assault on a local bobby in a public convenience. John Saviour-Smith was moderately happily married with two moderately pleasant children. The recently passed changes in 'Defence of Entrapment' meant that it was easier to get mud to stick than ever before. The 'Good Citizen's Charter' with its associated raft of 'Inclusive and Exclusive Behaviours' had placed a sword of Damacles over everyone's head. The only question was when or if they chose to cut the wire suspending it. He had stepped out of line on a few policy issues (most notably the Good Citizen's Charter itself), and the sword had fallen. There was no proof of wrong doing, the policeman had been sloppy over collecting data and over enthusiastic when pushing for a conviction. The case had been overturned on appeal. Fortunately his children had been too young to suffer the ignominy of the whole thing. His wife had ridden the storm; she knew enough about the game he was in. He was a very minor player then, he thought his career was at an end, but it never worked like that. The powers that be had demonstrated their reach. A few ministers stood by him to ensure there was no confusion as to whom he owed his salvation. The problems were cabbies and policemen. They seemed to have longer memories than most. He had not been able to use a black cab for five years.

The anchorwoman was now talking to camera, introducing the piece. The crowd jeered appropriately; placards and children were hastily brought to the front of the assembled group.

'With me today is the Minister for Education and Child Potential, the Right Honourable John Saviour-Smith. Mr Smith, do you concede that the events unfolding around us today come as a direct result of the government's overzealous collection of psychometric and biometric data?'

His lawyer's mind awarded her points for the use of long words, obviously the broadcast was going out to an ABC audience, but he subtracted a hundred points for contracting his name. He was suddenly annoyed that he had not taken the time to note her name. It always looked good on screen if you used their name and he might have been able to score a few points by a reciprocal over-familiarity. This appealed to his natural childishness, but in some ways it was good that he had not had the chance. Sometimes his childishness got the better of him. He had to concentrate on the job in hand.

'No, it is quite clear to me and I'm sure to any sensible, reasonable member of the general public' (he had almost said proletariat, he really should spend less time down the club), 'that this unfortunate incident has arisen due to the pernicious and wilful misrepresentation of data by the media.' There was an angry ripple of discontent from the crowd. On the way to the school he had toyed with the possibility of winning the crowd over, but his disdain for them was such that he could not lower himself to that. If he could not browbeat a crowd of hysterical, unreasonable Islingtonites he really did not deserve his job. The anchorwoman withdrew the microphone before he could elaborate.

'Minster, are you suggesting that the concerns of families that their children's schooling could be adversely affected by the presence of gifted children are unfounded? The published data does appear to be quite clear on this.'

'If one looks at the larger picture of education in this country, one can see that the government's targets, on areas such as literacy, numeracy- as my parents would have said, the three R's- are being brought in line with the other member states of Euro...' The crowd roared in disapproval.

'But minister, these families are concerned with this particular issue. If I can just bring in a concerned mother...' An angry, anxious woman with a clinging child was brought into shot. 'Mrs Wilson, you are Gareth's mother, perhaps you could explain to our viewers and to the minister your concerns.' Mrs Wilson's eyes glanced nervously round the circle of faces and at the cameras; the child clung tighter to his mother's leg. She turned towards Saviour-Smith.

'My Gareth has always been at the top of his class. His writing has always been good, he writes very good stories.' Gareth's face disappeared into the folds of his mother's coat. 'His teachers have always said he was a very bright boy. His scores have always been excellent; but since Mitchel came to the school...' The anchorwoman broke in at this point.

'Mitchel; having been identified as having rather exceptional scores?'

'Yes, since... that boy... came, Graham's scores have deteriorated by nine percent. This boy is holding my Graham back. In this day and age that can make a difference. I'm not happy with it, and I'm not going to put up with it.' Her voice had been progressively rising in pitch, she began to shout. 'I'm not going to put up with it. Either my son goes, or he goes!' The crowd took up the cry. 'He goes or we go! He goes or we go!'

'Minister, what do you have to say about that? Surely it

is your responsibility to address the concerns of worried parents?' The microphone was thrust back in his face.

'I think the natural jealousy of one set of parents when they find there are other, more successful pupils in the school is both understandable and sad...' The crowd began booing loudly. Things were not going well. 'In every class-room there will be dynamics between pupils and teachers. Very bright or successful children will affect these dynamics. It has always been like this. We lived with this before...' He was drowned out by the noise of the crowd. 'We have lived with this before, it is nothing new, and we will continue to provide the best possible educational environment for all children in our care.'

The crowd were looking nasty. The problem, as was always the case, was not the collection of data; there was nothing wrong with that at all. The problems had only arisen due to the release of that data to the unwashed masses that had neither the inclination nor the mathematical knowledge to understand them properly. The screaming left's demand that the data be made public had eventually triumphed and this mess was the inevitable result of that. The strange effect of these occasional weird children on others was something that the government was investigating with some vigour. Initial discussions with educationalists from Europe and America indicated that the UK was not alone. The effects were subtle but consistent. The problem was that in the absence of historical data there was no way of telling if this was a new or fundamental phenomenon. The minister himself had not really liked to think about the consequences of the data should they be found to be correct. In his arrogance he rather suspected that if such people did exist then, presumably, he would be one of their number. He was a golden child, an achiever; his meteoric climb through local government and Westminster had marked him out as such. Did it really matter if the proles were disadvantaged any more than they were by the vagaries of being born into a particular social demographic or genetic pool? The same successful minority would still enslave them as they always had. The barriers to self improvement were as economic as they always had been. Economic envy was still the fundamental drive of growth. The middle-class at the school gate were already winners in the big race. They should thank their lucky stars and shut up about this minor, if surprising, setback.

'Are you suggesting minister that there is nothing that can be done? Surely if such children can be identified in a class, they can be moved away to other classes or another school?'

'The core of our educational policy is equality for all. Mixed ability schools are a central part of this culture of fairness. In the past the intellectual elite have been creamed off the top of our schools. We feel this is inappropriate in a fair and just educat... ' The crowd suddenly let out a roar and started to run up the road. The anchorwoman signalled to the camera crew to follow and set off in the direction of the noise. The minister found himself abandoned.

The crowd rounded on the back of the school where a small cordon of teachers and police were surrounding a small and scared little boy and his father. A police car slowly edged towards them but its progress was hindered by the assembled mob. They were chanting and shouting, placards were being shaken, the little boy was crying. The anchorwoman tried to get past the cordon but was repulsed by the police. The car edged closer, its siren was turned on, unbelievably loud and penetrating at such close quarters. The crowd was momentarily subdued. People were shoved aside as the boy was guided towards the car, but just as he ducked down to climb onto the back seat a projectile hurtled from behind the crowd and struck him on the side of the head. It was a glass-bottle. The boy screamed, his father pushed him headlong into the car and threw himself on top of him to shield him from further attacks. Another bottle struck the car and shattered into a shower of twinkling shards. The police cordon closed, batons were drawn and the car began to reverse out of the school gates. Some people stood stunned, their hands limp by their sides, but others attempted to batter the car with their placards; their faces twisted into angry masks.

John Saviour-Smith slowly walked back to his car. His head was spinning, he felt sick and confused. What had just happened? The image of the boy's face, the look of disbelief and fear was imprinted on his mind. He thought of his own children. It was not so difficult to superimpose their little faces on the face of nine-year-old Mitchel. He slumped into the back seat of the Daimler, slamming the door and sat momentarily unsure what to do, his head in his hands. Through his closed eyes he saw the flashes of cameras. There was a tap-tap-tap at the window. He knew the anchorwoman was trying to get her thirty seconds of his misery. Without looking up he told the driver to drive on. 'Let's get out of here; I can't bear to be with these people.' The driver looked back towards him.

'But Sir, don't you think you ought to give the press a comment on...'

'Just drive the fucking car!" He slapped his hands against the security panel and the car gently rolled slowly forward. The crowd was flowing around the car and police and camera crew were flocculating into little groups. Flashes illuminated the interior of the car; there was repeated tapping at the window. Saviour-Smith turned his face away. He needed to extricate himself from this depressing cloud of mob anxiety. There was nothing to be afraid of in the little boy's face, only confusion and fear itself.

He needed to think, to clear his head. He would visit the child in hospital. He would take his camera calls on his own terms. The little boy needed some protection; he would phone the local chief of police. He would speak to the home secretary. Yes, this clever little boy would need protection. The question this posed was how many others would there be and could they protect them all?

FOUR

Suzi paid the taxi driver, tipping him heavily. She needed every little bit of good karma she could attract today. It was dark and raining heavily and the streets which in earlier sunshine had appeared to be ageing gracefully, characterful and attractive, seemed Amityville-depressing in the miserable downpour. She ran from the car to the imposing steps of number 245. The curtains were drawn, but a lamp had been placed in the window. The curtains shivered as someone observed the taxi pull away. The cold night air and anticipation made Suzi pull her coat tighter around her shoulders. She looked around for a bell. The door was large and covered in elaborate door furniture. She reached for a large brass art nouveau door-knocker, but the door opened before she could place her fingers on it. She was greeted by Monsieur Henri Gavroche. She had seen his face many times in the papers in England and France, his brow furrowed with concern and misery or twisted into an angry mask as he spurred his charges into greater effort. The face before her was neither of these caricatures. He was around fifty, with an expressive face, kindly; his muscular build softened by a loosely fitting shirt. He held out his hand and guided Suzi out of the rain.

'Come in my dear. You have braved a horrible night. I did not know you would come. I must apologise for my... intensity... on the telephone this afternoon. I had to be sure. Miguel is a good boy and the press have been very, very cruel. You must understand that.'

Suzi was wrong-footed by this sudden change in Monsieur Gavroche. The feelings that tormented her were intense, but private; how could this man have any idea of what was going on in her mind? How could he be so assured of her integrity when she was not sure of anything herself? She was shown into the dining room. The lighting was subdued, the furniture antique, encrusted with Ormolu excrescences, the walls adorned with romantic scenes in elaborate picture frames. Suzi was introduced to a well-dressed lady. Monsieur Gavroche's sister smiled and in perfect English invited Suzi into the drawing room.

'Miguel is quite distraught, Ms Rothermann, I'm sure you can understand that. Please don't tire him out. I'm very glad you have come to see him. I'll make some tea, or would you perhaps prefer coffee?'

Suzi thanked Madame Gavroche and upon entering the drawing room, came face to face with Miguel. His eyes, so dark brown they appeared almost black, were red ringed. His face, handsome and rugged, was flushed with tears. He sniffed loudly, ran his fists down the front of his legs as if to wipe away tears from them and shook Suzi's hand. His grip was very strong, almost vice-like. He sniffed again and relaxed somewhat as if remembering where he was. His English was broken and hesitant and after their initial eye contact he seemed shy, averting his gaze. Suzi did not know what to say. She sat herself in a chair next to him, feeling suddenly awkward. She had needed to see this man so badly, needed to establish a link with him, but had stumbled selfishly into his grief and despair. Again, she thought of Michael. Was being here in some way connected with his death? Was she trying to make amends for it? The tea arrived and Mme Gavroche and her brother left the two of them in peace, sitting in silence, each studying the designs on their cups and saucers. It was Suzi who spoke first. Her French was hesitant and she felt more nervous than she had done in years, tongue tied and unsure, like a girl on a first date. Miguel was powerfully attractive to her; his physical masculinity rippled beneath the cotton of his clothes, his unbearable sadness, his acute vulnerability, made her want to pull him into her arms. She thought of Michael. How could such sentiments be coming into her mind with Michael newly gone? It was obscene. She drove the thought away, but was aware there was something other than sexual magnetism that was drawing her to him, something subtle and perhaps even more powerful. She had felt tiny elements of this before, in glances across smoky bars and crowded tube trains, in hotel corridors, on quiet beaches. She had put these things down to chemistry, something animal, something base. But in this man, sitting this close, and in her current state of mind she was prepared to think it was something else. She had come here to find a difference, some element that set them apart. In the muted sadness of the sitting room her senses were alive now, frantically searching for what this might be. The thing she had identified in the photograph, the phenomenon she had discovered in herself; these flashes were just fragments of a greater power. It was becoming clear to her that she had identified this in others, at a distance, and perhaps they had seen it in her too, but only now was she certain it was something that could be named. She was desperate for a vocabulary to describe it.

'Miguel. I know you will find this strange, what I have to say to you, but I think we share a...' She paused, searching for the right word in English or French, but there seemed to be no suitable word, the consequences being such a curse on both of their lives. 'I think we share... a gift.' Miguel turned away.

'I have no gift! I killed a man last week with a single punch. Six hundred kilometres an hour they said. Six hundred kilometres an hour! It is impossible! No man can punch that fast, no man has ever punched that fast. They say I am possessed by a demon!' He beat his hands on his face, and rocked forward, sobbing uncontrollably. Suzi reached round him and placed her arm over his broad shoulders. He began rocking back and forth, child-like in his despair.

'Miguel, it is not your fault. You are not to blame. We are not to blame.'

He turned to face her. 'What do you mean we? What have you done? What can compare with my crime?' His eyes

204

were huge, almost pleading.

'I nearly killed a woman.' She said the words slowly, the realisation of what she was saying slowly blossoming as the words rose to the forefront of her mind. She had made these connections in waking dreams, and the dreams came to her now; parts of the puzzle, melting into place. 'I nearly killed a woman just by touching her.'

'Nearly? Nearly? What is nearly? I did not nearly kill a man. I killed him. The blood, oh the blood; there was so much blood.' He began to shake again.

'I nearly killed a woman, and I killed my boyfriend. I killed him slowly and I did not even know I had done it.' She said the words, and knew them to be true, but she did not know at that instant the underlying meaning of them. The thoughts slowly gelled, morphing from one to another as new truths emerged from the confusion. Had she killed Michael? It seemed impossible, but it had to be true. She had drawn the life from him slowly, in the smallest drops, but she had weakened him irrevocably. She had used the same powers with which she had stuck down her P.A., frozen in a space and time, hit with an irresistible bolt that nearly sent her to her death. Her life borrowed, stolen so that she, Suzi, could live, live in that moment, live to observe, to dwell in the cracks between the seconds. Suddenly realisation came to her, so simple, so keen-edged; she felt faint as its consequences rift her thoughts in two. The revelation made her heart race wildly. She found herself reaching for Miguel's arm for support, and through the fabric of his shirt felt the pounding of his blood in time to her own. 'Miguel, our gift is time. We don't see time like other people. We don't use time like other people. We are different. We take time, steal it, and use it for ourselves.' It was so clear to her now. She had absorbed Michael, slowly, little by little, drop by drop and she had not realised it. He must have been aware of this, whether consciously or otherwise. His need for solitude, his discontentment and fear of dying unfulfilled, his acute awareness of his mortality all pointed to this. Had Michael been afraid of her? She did not know and now she would never know. She held Miguel's huge hand in hers. He looked into her eyes.

'Miss Rothermann. I don't want this gift any more. I am frightened of myself. I fight. It is what I do, but how can I fight now? My trainer, he is like a father to me, but I know he is frightened too. This thing, I can't control it. I do not have the power.'

Remarkably, at this moment Suzi felt closer to Miguel than she had done to any man. She had spoken the words, and he had accepted them, completely and unquestionably, as a truth he only had the power to express with his hands. She felt acutely aware of his misery and despair; connected to him through hand and mind. She wanted to hold him and wash away his fears with the wave of affection that was welling up in her. He gripped her hand tightly, put his head on her chest and began to sob. She held his head in her arms and drew him to her, resisting each shudder of his body, running her fingers through his curly black hair.

'Don't be afraid, Miguel. We have no reason to be afraid. We will learn how to control our gift, I know it. There must be others like us, fearful like us. I am sure we are not alone.'

FIVE

Professor Fred Sutcliffe practically galloped up the stairs into the surveillance headquarters at MI7. The British branch of the new Aligned-Nations Anti-Terrorist Observation Laboratories (ANATOL) shared office space with MI7 to maintain lip service to the Americans, but operationally they maintained a gloss of incompetence that kept the Americans at a comfortable distance. Professor Sutcliffe felt a twinge of guilt every time he visited ANATOL. They were among a number of targets of left-wing criticism dubbed the 'British Big Brothers' and were accused of intrusive state monitoring. Although this was probably true, Fred, like so many of his contemporaries, assuaged his own left-wing guilt by telling himself that it was better for people like him to involve themselves in this inevitable monitoring than to hand the baton on to less scrupulous individuals from the right. It irked him that it had been thought necessary to coin them the British Big Brothers: Big Brother being, after all, the creation of a British mind. We were the originals, if not the best. The other annoying thing about his situation was that he rather enjoyed the work and it was wonderful to actually see the efforts of your theorising placed in the public arena and used for practical, if unpopular, purposes. He would still have difficulty explaining his involvement with ANATOL and MI7 should it become widely known in student circles. It was for this reason he always turned into the department at the last possible moment and ran up the stairs without looking back.

The security guards were polite as ever, performing the normal retinal and hand scans and asking the same pointless yet carefully constructed questions which were guaranteed to annoy even the most calm and comfortable visitor. Fred was never a calm and comfortable person except when he was in his bath, and today he was particularly on edge because he had the rare and wonderful opportunity to test a scientific hunch and get an almost immediate and potentially satisfying response. Once through security he found a friendly face in I.T. gave them his clearance and began to trawl through the data bases. In an instant he was accessing the national files of personal achievement and development that had been assembled by his friend and ex-colleague Professor Platt. Such information was usually available to everyone, but with the recent scaremongering in the newspapers the database had developed 'technical difficulties'. Fortunately these difficulties did not extend to government agents but the data had to be accessed through rather restricted portals. The professor quickly assembled macros to sort and sift the enormous resource. He then accessed his personal files and those associated with a project he had been working on in secret with ANATOL. The idea was simple. They used high resolution ESR-electron spin resonance to scan passengers as they passed through customs. All matter had a signal under atomic spin resonance and different materials had unique and characteristic spectra. The average human body, composed as it was of a multitude of different elements, produced a complex spectrum, but it was possible to distinguish this with modern computer algorithms: from clothing, metals, ceramics and large quantities of relatively pure compounds. This included knives, guns and plastic explosives and the sensitivity and power of the technique to identify things missed by conventional scans had made Professor Sutcliffe very popular with the anti-terrorist police across the globe. To date many thousands of gates had been installed in numerous countries. They had proved useful for identifying drug runners and antique smugglers as well as the original targets and Sutcliffe had walked through one himself to enter the MI7 building. Now he was accessing these files, looking for a new signature, something like those he had seen with the geophys equipment. Tiny peaks in the spectra; anomalies that may have flagged a problem but proved groundless at the time. In three years of operation they had hindered two point six million people in their daily movements from country to country. Sutcliffe told himself that at least this was in the public good. Of these two point six million people, one point nine million had been subsequently cleared by conventional magnetic techniques; belts, buckles, toe caps and piercings. Four thousand six hundred and twenty individuals had been found to be carrying illegal substances, most of which were wrapped drugs they had swallowed and were smuggling internally. A tiny minority were carrying guns. For this the professor felt a twinge of pride. The needs of the many outweigh the needs of the few, or at least the minor inconveniences of the many... A thousand minor inconveniences prevented the occasional tragedy. With no way of measuring suffering, there was no way of telling if this was a fair exchange. This still left a group which were largely unaccounted for. Approximately seven hundred thousand people whose atomic spin profiles caused a blip in his device. He set the computer the task of downloading and establishing the mean of all these spectra that were still in data storage and comparing it to seven hundred thousand spectra drawn at random from the population. It was an onerous task but it gave the Professor time to have a cup of tea. As he pushed the 'return' key, Fred Sutcliffe thanked the silicon Gods which allowed such mind-bending processing to occur.

In the tearoom of MI7 Fred bumped into Professor John Platt.

'Fred, I hadn't expected to see you here.'

'Likewise, I didn't think they liked people taking a cut from both ministries.' He had not wanted to sound so sarcastic, but his own dismay at being caught in the lion's den had made him defensive.

'There is a certain "function creep" possibility that MI7 want to discuss on the child profiling. I'm here to persuade them that it is a bad idea.'

209

'I see, and I suppose you are looking for another job after the hot water with the education minister.'

'The minister creates his own problems. I just take the measurements; he does the fitting.'

'He'll fit you up good and proper if you aren't careful, John. I've seen it before. The so-called caring ministries are the worst.'

'Which is why you are with MI7.'

'ANATOL actually, just a bit of pin money to keep the lab open. What clearance do you have here?' He was quite surprised to find that his friend had a higher clearance than his own. 'In that case, after another tea I'll show you what I've been up to. It's funny bumping into you; I was planning to access your data set. Now you are here, I'm sure you'll make a better job of it.'

'I've got a meeting with the Ministry of Love at seven, but I'm free before then.'

'Asylum and Repatriation as well? You really do get around.'

'I only come here for the chocolate biscuits; in Asylum and Repatriation it's digestives if you are lucky.' The two friends made their way to the I.T. suite. On the way, Fred continued to ask about developments in what had become called the 'gifted child problem'. The media had gone on a multi-layered feeding frenzy both whipping up hysteria and then covering the unpleasant consequences in gory and uncomfortable detail. Several tearful children had already been withdrawn from inner-city schools. Tight-lipped mothers sheltered their charges from angry crowds in Greenwich, Sutton and Potters Bar. The data analysis required to identify the 'gifted' minority was quite complex and beyond the scope of most people, but one paper help-fully published the names of the three hundred children in the country who had shown the most potent effect on their co-eds. The government was looking into charging this newspaper with acts leading to incitement to violence, but no action had been taken to date. Without an accompany-ing list of addresses any child with a name matching any of those on the list was immediately threatened. The ready availability of the data was also an invitation to any vested interest to draw their own conclusions from it. Everyone had an opinion, and anyone with a computer could back their claims with an impressive list of statistics drawn from the data. When the data were withdrawn from circulation such individuals simply made up their own results. The unions were talking about closing schools across the London boroughs for fear that the teaching staff would come under attack from frenzied parents. Information from moderately reputable sources had suggested that teachers as well as pupils in classes with 'gifted' children suffered the same oppressive forces. The unions were concerned about this as well. A ballot was to be called.

By the time the two men got to the work station Professor Sutcliffe's calculations were complete. 'Here we go. I'm looking for an anomaly in the NRI spectrum. We picked it up using Geophys equipment. I wanted to see if the same thing had been measured by the security arches.' He ran his fingers over the complex patterns of peaks and troughs on the screen. 'Look there! Compare the data from the false positives with the background. It's subtle, but can you see a difference?'

John Platt stared at the screen over the top of his glasses. 'Hmm, there are a few differences, but are they significant? How many people have you had a chance to zap?'

'Seven hundred thousand. I think you'll agree that is a hefty number.'

'Lord above, and we wonder why the students are up in arms. What you get away with in the interests of national security.'

The dig was ignored by Sutcliffe who was tapping furiously at the keyboard. 'I'm subtracting the background from the anomalies. There!' A graph appeared with three clear peaks rising from a becalmed sea. Sutcliffe withdrew a piece of paper from an inside pocket.

'And now, Professor Platt, if you would be so kind as to read the three numbers on this piece of paper.' Grumbling, Platt unfolded the paper and holding the paper at arm's

211

length read out three four digit numbers. 'And if you would now be so kind as to read off the peaks on this graph.'

'Well I'll be... they are the same. But what does it mean?'

'I don't know, yet... that is the point. That's what I need you for. I want to run the names through your database and tell me if there is anything odd about them.'

'Like what?'

'Anything at all. Disease outlook, genetics... anything.'

'To what ends? I don't see the point. We have enough of this do it yourself statistics from the mindless punters out there.' He waved his hands expansively. 'Do you want to give them something else to worry about? What exactly have you measured anyway?'

'It's their ESR spectrum: electron spin resonance. It's like NMR only more sensitive. We've got so much computer power now you'd be amazed what we can dredge up. Interpretation isn't trivial though; the spectra are sensitive to a whole raft of issues, small scale things like local nuclear interactions, the variations in abundance of atomic isotopes, but also to macroscopic things like the hydration state of the individual. It all operates on so many different scales. The remarkable thing we have here is a group of individuals who have a blip, a signature, something different from everyone else and unique to them. Your data might not be able to tell us what is different about these people, but it might give us a few clues. What do you think?'

Platt was quiet for a few moments. 'It could be interesting. Might be a cancer marker, Alzheimer's marker, could be anything. It's a shot in the dark, but why not.'

'Marvellous. How long do you think it will take?'

'Now I have my database almost to myself, not as long as you may think. I'll run some initial analyses and get back to you in a few days.' The two men shook hands and parted company. Fred Sutcliffe was beaming. Seven hundred thousand people, uniquely labelled, moving through life like everyone else, not knowing of each others' existence, yet all somehow linked in the vibrations of their atoms: a lost tribe of Israel? Werewolves? Perhaps they were vampires- no, that could not be true as most flights occurred during the day. In a few days he might get a clue. He could not wait for Professor Platt's phone call.

On returning to his office he phoned Doctor Gordon from the statistics department. He was bound by the Official Secrets Act not to divulge his work in connection with ANATOL, but he had to tell him that he had a made a minor breakthrough. If anything interesting panned out, he would invite them all over for a sherry, including the students who had discovered the effect. It was the least he could do. He had barely put the phone down when it rang back. It was John Platt. He was very excited. He would not say what he had discovered. Fred was to meet him first thing the next morning at the MI7 building. The phone went dead. The anticipation was almost unbearable; he would not sleep tonight. As he sat on the bus on the way home he looked around him at the motley collection of passengers. He wondered if any of them carried his anomaly. Perhaps he himself carried it; he had not thought to check if his own name was on the list. This sudden realisation made him feel momentarily uncomfortable. Perhaps he should find out first if he was included before John told him his news. If it was good, he would hate to be disappointed if he did not carry the marker. Similarly, if it was a bad thing, a prescient of morbidity or mortality for example, maybe he would not want to find his name on the list. Then of course there was the question of his family, his wife, and his children. Would he want them to be on the list? These were difficult questions. He needed to sit in the bath to think about it.

SIX

Suzi lay in the flat ivory glow from linen-covered windows. The house around her creaked and groaned in dark ecstasies as the warm sun dried its sodden timbers. The night before now seemed dream-like and surreal. She had comforted Miguel until the early hours. They had taken tea together and then something stronger and in the glow of Dutch courage they had felt closer and calmer. Miguel had asked her to stay. There was something he wanted to show her, but she would need all her strength. It would have to wait until morning. When Madame Gavroche left the room to make up their spare bedroom he had taken her hands again in his and looking deep into her eyes had thanked her for finding him and for saving him from his isolation. He had kissed her gently on both cheeks then and retired to bed. He had not slept for three days but now he felt that perhaps he could. There was a tap on the door and Madame Gavroche entered bearing a tray with the day's paper, coffee, orange juice and steaming croissants. Miguel was still sleeping and she thought it better not to disturb him. She was so grateful for the help that Suzi had given him. She kissed Suzi again and left the room, clearly emotional. Suzi lay back on the scented pillow for a moment; the lavender barely masked the musky sweetness of Miguel which lingered on her. It was strange how another person's scent could persist so long and after such transient contact. She was hungry and read the headlines as she ate. With her imperfect French it was difficult to work out exactly what had happened during the preceding day but it appeared that a child had been crushed in a fracas outside a country school. A mother, trying to protect her own child from the mob, had reversed her car at speed through school gates, inadvertently running him over. There were related stories throughout the paper. The French ministry for education had decreed that the parents of all children identified as 'gifted' should contact their local authorities. Special schools were to be set up to accommodate them; they needed to be protected from society and there was a call for society to be protected from them.

Suzi pitied the poor children. They had done nothing wrong; they could not help what they were. They were not so different from her at that age. She had always shone at school, achieved in spite of or perhaps because of the less than perfect classes she had found herself in. She was good at games, the hockey, the basketball; she had captained both teams. What was wrong with that?

The penny dropped into place. How had she been so blind, so self-obsessed to have not made the connection? For a moment she could not think, could hardly breathe. The ramifications were enormous, terrifying. These kids were just like her. They were her kind and they were being placed in ghettos. She felt furious and afraid and then sick. But then she thought of the mothers of the other children, of Michael's mother, of Carlos, his blood splashing the front row of the boxing crowd. What was to be done with them? She let the paper slip to the floor and pulled the covers tightly about her. The light became dim at the window as a cloud passed across the sun. Suddenly the room had become colder. Suddenly the whole world had become colder.

SEVEN

Gavin Breedon woke from an erotic dream as the tube train squealed as it passed over a particularly sinusoidal part of the Central line. He squinted at the station name as it passed outside the window and swore. He still had another eight stations to go. He was not happy and when he was not happy someone usually had to pay. It had not been a good day. He had pissed off the foreman by arriving late on site and he had got ticked off again for not wearing the appropriate safety gear. How he hated them, with their soft, work-shy hands, their clean white hard-hats and their clip-boards. He had bitten his lip this time. In the past he had been a wild one, he had even done a little time. These days he kept a tighter rein on his temper. The shrink was dosing him up and the red fog now came upon him far less frequently. He found the drink helped as well. He would be a bit agitated for a while, but if he could quietly drink through that, he would become docile again, sleepy. He sometimes drank at work to get a head-start. It made the whole day that little bit more bearable. Gavin did not have a lot of friends. He rarely stayed in a job long enough to get a drinking circle together and when he took an angry turn he often frightened them away. There were a few guys he called mates, but sometimes he wondered why they hung around with him. Such evenings were rarely just going out for a drink and a laugh. There was always someone they wanted to give a good kicking to, someone they wanted to put the frighteners on. He had had a few drinks tonight and there was a bottle waiting at home to finish the job off. He was feeling fairly calm, but he had eight stations to go and the bottle seemed a long,

216

long way away. He had been laid off much of the last month and work was becoming scarce. There were a lot of eastern Europeans in the job market now. He hated them even more than the Asians. They knew each other, they spoke each other's strange languages and they seemed to know how to do everything. The sparkies could plumb, the chippies knew bricking. There was not much left for the likes of him to do. The carriage was nearly empty; only two other passengers remained. One was an Asian city girl, a fair bit of thigh in tight nylons, sharp suit, totally engrossed in some book or other. He felt like spitting. Opposite him was a youngish lad in tight jeans and bomber jacket. The boy's eyes glanced over the top of his newspaper at him and then went back to carefully study-ing the editorial. Gavin rolled his fists into two tight balls. The guy had held his gaze; he was sure of it. It was not for long, just too long. Perhaps the guy was queer. These days it was hard to tell, but Gavin did not think so. Gavin was no pretty boy. Labouring had made him strong, but drink-ing had made him heavy. He had had attention from a gay bloke years before. A gym partner he had met off a site, an enormously big, hairy bloke. Gavin had felt small fry next to him and could barely lift the weights the guy used for warming up. He had told Gavin he needed to bulk up and had shamed him into partnering him at the local club. They had taken a lot of pills, even injected some steroids, and he had found himself bulking nicely. The mood swings were exacerbated but he was part-timing as a doorman and found the edge helpful. It was three months before the guy made a move on him. That was what had shocked him most, that the guy had waited so long, building up the friendship. A little too much body contact here, a little too long in the shower there. The guy was even married. How was he to know? Then the guy had just come out and said it. He had not known what to do with himself. Looking back he regretting never hitting the guy, never venting his anger there and then. The shock had just been so great he had become muddled, confused. He had just dried himself off, pulled on his clothes and had walked out of the gym without saying a word. When he got home he had sat in the bath for an hour, punching the wall. He never saw the guy again. He had never spoken to anyone about the incident; even thinking about it now made him anxious.

The guy opposite had looked at him again. He was sure of it now. He was reading a broadsheet rag stretched out on his knees like some architect with his plans. Gavin reserved a special kind of hatred for architects. He watched the lad now, he could not be more than twenty-two, reading the Guardian like some shell of superiority; stuck up little prig. What was wrong with reading a man's paper, a tabloid paper, like everybody else? Who did this guy think he was? What was wrong with a bit of tit and arse? Was he different or somehow special? Perhaps he was gay. Then he remembered something he had seen in the papers and it all made sense. The lad had to be one of these weird kids with their psychic powers. That was why he could read the broadsheets; that explained why he was looking across the carriage. With no one else to feed on his was the only available brain. He did not know what to do; he felt confused, frightened. This kid could just suck out his mind and he would never know. He felt his palms and back sweating, his legs started to shake as they had done in the bath on that terrible day. And it was true he was feeling a bit odd. It could have been the drink, but he was feeling fucked-up, more gone than usual. The lad must be sucking his brains out. He could almost see the red mist descending. There was a foggy sticky substance to his thought processes as if he had some horrible head-cold. Something was trying to contain his rage, block the air which was feeding the fire. It could be the tablets but it could also be the mind of this lad. He tried to breathe calmly, deep breaths to still himself, but the air in the carriage was thick with choking filth. He had never realised before this minute, but now he could taste it, taste the black filth and the grime permeating the very air. The train shuddered into the next station and the Asian girl clicked and clacked onto the platform. The lad looked up from his paper and suddenly realised he should have gotten off. He grabbed his bag and made a run for the door but was too late and they closed in his face. He laughed in Gavin's direction and slumped back into his chair. The train gave a disparaging shrug, whined and headed into the next tunnel.

The boy had actually laughed in his face. Gavin got up, jaw set firm and went over to him. The tainted air around him fizzed with his rage. The boy looked around him and up at the lumbering figure coming at him. He saw the blur of muscles moving under grimey overalls, felt a shockwave of warm air hit him as the figure leapt, supernaturally fast. In a moment Gavin's hands were locked around the boy's throat. He tried to protest. 'What the fu...,' but was silenced in an instant. His thin bony hands clawed at Gavin's massive wrists. Legs kicked out under a flurry of newsprint but after a few seconds were stilled. As Gavin squeezed the life out of the boy the train slowed and then stopped in a tunnel. The lights flickered off and on, fluorescent flashes in the boy's wide, staring eyes. Gavin heard a crack and a gurgling hiss and he knew instinctively that the boy was dead. He let go his grip, concentrating hard to peel his fingers away from the boy's throat as if they belonged to someone else's hands. The boy slumped to the side, mouth lolling open. Gavin returned to his seat. The train started again with a jolt and trundled into the next station where it terminated. The doors slid aside and Gavin walked off without looking back.

EIGHT

Patrick Manee had been very busy. Busy like he had never been in his life before. He never really imagined himself in the style of the television detectives, though he had a soft-spot for Columbo and anything by Agatha Christie, but there were times when clichés were simply concentrations of reality. In the past week he had been thoroughly dressed down by his boss in the manner of every TV detective's boss. They never appreciated the significance of the poor detective's remarkable yet circumstantial evidence; they wanted something that would stand up in court. There was also always pressure from some unseen yet vaguely suggested third party that was brought to bear on the investigation. 'You have got into things you couldn't possibly understand Maguire/Japp/McFee... You should let it lie; it's out of our hands now...' In this case he knew who the faceless ones were: The American or should he say 'Coalition of Aligned-Nation's' Anti-Terrorism Agency. They had flambéed his Bill Morris investigation and his superiors were still smoking from the heat. Thankfully he had had a chance to interview Agneta Sibilski and her strange boss Kevin Masters. Agneta had essentially backed-up Edward Spink's story about Morris but was obviously nervous about his snooping into their business interests. He had watched her legs crossing and uncrossing. Beautiful women often had trouble with him, relatively insensitive as he was to their advances. Most simply gave up after the initial assault, but Agneta had more resilience than most and had turned the heat up to full. He could not blame her for trying. She was a very smart woman and he had found her fascinating. Once they had started to talk openly about Bill Morris she had been extremely forthcoming. There was passion there, intellectual concern and like him she had made the connection. The news was full of 'gifted' children but few people had seemed to accept the fact that gifted children might grow up to become gifted adults. It was clear to Manee that Bill was one of these creatures and he had seen with his own eyes the consequences of that gift in an adult. They had not spoken directly about it, but he knew she knew. Like him, she was wrestling with the consequences of this strange phenomenon and wondering who to tell.

Kevin Masters was another story altogether. He appeared to be intelligent and his answers indicated a remarkable precision and attention to detail. This clear personality trait was, however, being obfuscated by a feigned disinterest. It was as if Kevin Masters was too important or too busy to concern himself with Manee's line of questioning. To the untrained eye it would have been interpreted as traditional arrogance, but Manee knew better. People like Kevin Masters were interested in everything, if only because any line of discussion could lead to business opportunities. Kevin Masters was also, at heart, a sales person, someone specialising in the projection of positive, warm attitudes. It was a hard habit to break and feigned disinterest was a role that he obviously found uncomfortable. Manee could tell immediately that he was a crook, he could spot that a mile away, but he was not really interested in the man's motives or petty criminality, it was what the man was or was becoming that interested him more. He wondered if they had ever run their profiling on their own company. He had seen the flash of light in Bill Morris's eyes and there had been a similar one in those of Kevin Masters. He had watched his slightly feline movements as he moved around his office, noted a subtle measured accuracy in his vocabulary and grammar. There was definitely something there, something different.

He showed the pair to the front door of the building, carefully watching their body language. There were definite sparks between the two, a veneer of professional confidence, disconnected superiority, feigned bonhomie, but beneath the surface It was obvious to Manee that Agneta was slightly afraid of her boss. She felt trapped by him and it was clear he enjoyed this power. As they left the lobby Kevin rushed forward into the traffic to hail a cab, angrily chastising the first car that refused to stop at the busy junction. When he had secured a ride, he looked back at Agneta and gestured for her to join him.

Manee arrested Agneta's departure with a light touch to her arm. She swung back to look at him, momentarily caught between the twin demands of good manners and her gesticulating boss. In that second he saw a flash of vulnerability, a fault in the smooth veneer. 'You would think he was a man in a hurry, a man without time on his hands.'

'No, no, he is a busy, busy man.' She looked slightly confused.

'That's not what I mean't.'

'No, no... I really must be going.' She politely drew away and ran towards the car, not looking back and keeping her head down as they pulled away.

Manee left work early that evening, moving through the expressionless mass of commuters rather than slinking home with the nightcrawlers and jettisoned pub-goers as was his usual fate. London was awash with fallout from the initial discovery of the gifted children. The response had been vulgar, violent and vindictive. There had been numerous attacks on the gifted and their families after they had been identified in the press. A family of four Romanians had been bludgeoned to death in Norfolk when their eight-year old had come first in class in the end of term exams. When the police arrived at the scene, alerted by neighbours who had heard screaming, the perpetrators were still there, washing their hands in the sink. Two fathers of other children at a neighbouring school had coldly and calmly taken baseball bats to their neighbour's house. It appeared they showed no remorse, no guilt for what they had done. They had murdered for the good of their children, and the other children in the school. Neither had any obvious connection to any violent group; none had any previous convictions.

Manee was worried, very worried. History provided examples of ferocious societal brutality based on the flimsiest of differences. It had always seemed to him that the more similar the two groups, the greater the shared culture and experience, the nearer the neighbours, the hotter the fire when it started to burn. What would be the response of the current society when it realised there was a fifth column in its midst? He just prayed to God that no government developed the means to identify these people in his lifetime.

When he returned home he found a Dear John letter on his kitchen table. His most recent love-interest had left him. The letter was kind, but was similar to several he had had before. He scanned it for the phrases 'nice guy' and 'never see you' and 'need to find myself'. They were all present and correct. He glanced at the clock on the sideboard. It was six-thirty. The irony that he should have picked up such a note on the one day he actually returned home at a sensible time almost made him smile though his heart was sinking. Who was he working for? When was he going to sort his own life out? His official work-load was crippling enough; his other investigations were leading him to who knew where. He was sure to get no thanks for his work. He could easily spend the next few years protecting the gifted children. So far the consequences of this did not look good, besides; he suspected that the gifted, ultimately, and if cornered, could probably look after themselves.

NINE

Monsieur Gavroche walked Suzi through his winter garden. The sun was bright and after the night's rain everything seemed gloriously renewed. Dogwoods and spindle berries created a startling backdrop to the exploded flowers of Hamamelis. An enormous contorted hazel dominated a bed of narcissus spears just breaking the soil, its Art Nouveaux agonies glittering with dew. A stand of Ghostgum trees stood sentry in one corner of the grounds, their silky white boughs scantily draped in twinkling silver and green-grey vestements.

They returned to the warmth of the house for coffee and were greeted by a smiling and vibrant Miguel. He was a different man from the one she had held the previous night. He seemed twice as broad, twice as tall and his black hair was combed back in glistening curls. They spent a pleasant few hours and after a light lunch Miguel asked her if she would be prepared to join him for a walk. The sun was hidden behind a bank of cloud and the air had become chill, but there was a sparkle in Miguel's eyes which could not be resisted, and wrapping herself against the cold Suzi followed him through the town and among footpaths between fields of sprouting winter-wheat.

'I want you to see something, I want your opinion.' His hand found hers, almost childlike, pulling her closer. She did not resist. 'You may be the only one to understand.'

Suzi was not afraid in his company. She felt only his warmth and his need. The winding path eventually brought them to a large cluster of old farm buildings and an enclosure. From within, Suzi could hear the stamping and snorting of cattle; the air was thick with the smell of them and of silage and straw. A large grey building formed part of the complex and outside it was a large refrigerated lorry.

'This is the abattoir.' Miguel's voice was low. 'I used to stop here when I was training during in the winter, to stretch my legs and catch my breath. I was watching the animals and I saw something. I would like you to watch with me.' Suzi was taken aback by his request. But one look at Miguel's face assured her that she had to comply. They walked beneath vaulted corrugated iron roofs echoing to the lowing of the cattle and the shouts of farm hands. They came to a fence and Miguel held her back.

'We do not need to see any more than this. I have seen more, but not today.' He pointed towards the containment pens. The cattle were large, almost completely black except where they were spattered with the muck and filth of the yard. They had been focused together by the alignment of fences, funnelled into a narrow passageway. Forty or fifty animals in disordered array were crushed together, flank against flank, nose to tail, steaming and stamping in the cold. A boy with a stick lazily whacked them as they reached the front of the queue so that they marched into the shed head-first.

'Now watch.' Miguel's voice was little more than a whisper. Suzi looked at him and for a moment saw him as a little boy, face pressed against a butcher's window in fear and amazement. Suzi was no tree-hugging vegetarian. In her line of work only the prey animals ate lettuce, the models, the actors and the creative advertising gurus. All the important people, the financiers, the bankers and the lawyers were organ-eating carnivores. It was an unspoken rule. Suzi liked her game well-hung, her steaks blue and her paté fois gras. She did not have a delicate constitution and was prepared to watch the slaughter, if that was what Miguel wanted but she could not for the life of her see why. For a horrible moment, she wondered about his motive. Could it be that he found this death somehow arousing? She tried to put the thought from her head. Instead she watched the line of animals stamping and complaining, slowly making their way towards the shed, a captive bolt, death and the meat wagon. The air was cold and Suzi was becoming uncomfortable, but still they watched in silence. She felt Miguel's hand in her own. A cow was taken from the front of the line and walked into the shed. Another stepped forward to take its place; patient, mechanical, logical death. There was a pause and then Miguel squeezed her hands. She looked on his face and there was a tear in the corner of his eyes. What had he seen? What was the problem? She looked back at the herd, their breath billowing, eyes bulging, bodies writhing one against the other, jostling each other in the turbulent eye of the storm of their bodies. Occasionally one would rise up out of the herd into a clumsy mounting position, caught in the mêlée like a tree sucked into a whirlpool. She tried to concentrate on the swirling mass of beef, tried to look beyond the immediately apparent, tried to see with Miguel's eyes. She watched the glistening sweat on the animal's bodies, the steam from their breath appearing then whirling and disappearing, the rolling of their eyes. She observed the rhythm of their circling, learnt the timbre of their calling, watched their tongues, lolling, jaws chewing the cud, muscles contracting and relaxing in endless cycles and then she saw it. The time-dilation twisted the focus gently; a distortion of lenses, oil on the water. It was like a gun-shot caught in every eye, a momentary holding of breath, a flinch that ran through the herd and rippled back and across them. It was caught in the blinking of an eye, the sway of a head, a tightening of jaws and then it was gone. The revelation hit Suzi like a wave almost as if the emotion had transmitted itself across the distance between them and struck her, in spite of being tucked up in Miguel's arms behind the fence. The herd continued its tormented procession; another rotation of flesh, another roll of the dice. Then it happened again: the shock, electric, passed through the herd and across to them. In that split second each animal responded; another wild stare, a lamenting cry, a stamping of hooves.

'What is it Miguel? Please don't tell me it is the gun, they cannot tell, they cannot understand, surely not?'

'I call it their 'premonition,' Miguel said wiping away another tear. 'I do not know if they hear the bolt-gun, or hear the death of the animal. Perhaps they sense it in some other way. But, yes, it coincides with the shot. Once you have seen it once, you will always see it. It makes you wonder how men have never seen it before.' His voice was sad and calm, but he held her hand firmly. 'I knew you would see. Now I can be sure.' They walked back in silence. The sun was now low in the sky. In the distance they heard the lowing of the cattle, diminishing, diminishing, into silence.

TEN

'I'm so sorry; the lady on the door didn't tell me you already had company.' Detective Inspector Manee tentatively opened the door and came face to face with Lilly Anterton and Mary Weston. 'I don't think she liked me very much, or at least she didn't seem very happy to see me.'

'Please come in, detective,' Lilly's voice was surprisingly strong and clear for someone who, by all accounts, had been through some appallingly traumatic experiences in the last few days. 'I'm afraid she doesn't like anyone. I'm just happy that I don't have to get past her. Or at least, the next time I do, I'll be in a box and won't have to look at her sour face!' Lilly motioned to him to sit on the bed. 'I'm sorry there isn't more room. Detective Manee isn't it? This is my best friend Mary Weston. Anything you may want to say to me you can say in front of her. She has my complete confidence.'

Manee shook both ladies' hands, placed a bunch of lillies he had brought with him on the bedside table and made himself comfortable on the end of the bed.

'Please feel free to tell me to leave if you feel in any way uncomfortable talking about what happened, Ms Anterton. I imagine your experience must have been quite shocking, in spite of your... ', he coughed, 'career history.'

'I can see you have done your homework, inspector. That was all a long time ago and now alas I can't remember very much about it, which is probably for the better.'

'You apparently remembered something of your... training a few nights ago. Ms Anterton.' He suddenly remembered. 'And yes, Mrs Weston, if I'm not mistaken, you gave this character something to think about as well.'

Mary looked down at her hands. 'Well, we do what we can. I'll just put these lovely flowers in water.' She operated the chair round the room, retrieved a vase from the sink and filled it with water. On closer inspection Manee could see the marks and cuts on Mary's face which she had cleverly disguised with make-up.

'I read your statement to the police, Mary. You were extraordinarily brave. This man was dangerous. He left a trail of distraught victims.' He turned again to Lilly. 'I know it is easy to say for someone who has no experience of such things, but you should feel no guilt for dispatching him Ms Anterton. You did the world a service.'

'Please call me Lilly, Inspector. I'm afraid I can only feel remorse because, you see, if I hadn't been so frail I might have been able to restrain him, to call for help, to contain the situation. As it was, I was just trying to protect myself. I did not mean to kill him; I'll tell that to a judge if I have to. Mind you, they'll have to find a Divan chair to take me to the courtroom.'

'Please call me Patrick, Lilly. I don't think that will be necessary. But please, if you don't mind, can you tell me more? Can you tell me how it was that you found the incredible strength to do what you did?' As he said these words, he was mindful of the police reports. They had moved Lilly to another room; it had proven to be impossible to remove the traces of gore from the walls without completely redecorating. 'You seem remarkably calm. I'm not sure I could have dealt with the experience as well as you have. You really are a remarkable lady.'

'Patrick, flattery will get you everywhere.' Lilly laughed. 'But in all seriousness, it is only because I have such a wonderful friend in Mary that I have managed. As I say. I cannot feel any compassion or involvement in what happened that night. I was then, as I am now, as weak as a kitten. I am not a religious woman, Patrick, but if I was, I might have thought that someone was looking after me.' Her eyes flicked to the clock on the wall. 'I guess it just wasn't my time to go.'

Manee followed her gaze. He was silent for a moment, inwardly contemplating. When he spoke, it was quietly and without guile. 'I know this may seem strange Lilly, but there is something I want to ask you, something which I have been investigating. It is difficult to explain, but perhaps you can help me. Have you ever experienced periods of... how can I put it?... time dilation? Moments when the world seems to change tempo, go slow when you yourself are dancing at a different speed.' He was not sure where this insight had come from. It just seemed so right, so perfectly fitting that Lilly too should be one of the 'gifted'. Lilly herself was silent for a while, studying the clock, tentatively taking herself back to those strange moments when she had momentarily slipped sideways from reality.

'Patrick, I don't know if you have ever been bedridden for a period. I hope you never have and I pray you never will be. But I can tell you that being trapped in a sick body, on your back for twenty-four hours a day, is a terrible, terrible thing. If I had known this would be my fate, I'm not sure I would have chosen to live for so long. But we are not always party to such decisions are we? The will to live, to persist, in hope for something better is not something you can placate. The only sacrifice it will accept is your own and in that there can be surprisingly little choice. I live for my friends and for my memories, what is left of them. Sometimes, sometimes in the dark, sometimes in moments when you are at your most quiet, time has less meaning. Life flashes by when you are young, detective, but for me, there are times when a day has seemed to drag to a week, an hour to a lifetime. It is a dreadful irony of life, Patrick, that those of us with most time on our hands often have the least ability to spend it productively. You realise then that your youth was so precious you should have spent it more wisely. How I would have loved to gallop to my grave.'

There was a crashing from outside the door. Tea was approaching loudly and with a fanfare of plasticised crockery.

'Here,' Mary Weston reached down into her wheelchair and withdrew a flask and three cups. If we are quick we might not have to suffer the stewed tea.' She passed a bottle over to Manee. 'You might want to hide that from the nurse, I'm sure she wouldn't approve.' Manee glanced at the label. It was single malt; taken aback he sequestered it in a spare blanket.

The tea-lady was new, evidently on some sort of work experience and smiled sweetly when she saw they were happily picnicking without her help. She supplemented their high tea with chocolate biscuits before smiling again and making her way.

'Let's have a quick shot. We won't tell anyone if you are on duty, Patrick. I'm sure it will be interesting; Mary's husband has excellent taste.' Lilly slowly, painfully retrieved three shot glasses from a bedside cabinet. It was as much as she could do and she fell back spent against the pillow. Strange to think this woman had crushed a man's head between her delicate china hands.

'Lilly, I was thinking perhaps of something more dramatic, more extreme. I was thinking in particular of the night you were attacked. Did anything strange happen to you?' He thought he saw a flash in her eyes then. It was the same light he had seen with Bill Morris and Kevin Masters. She did not have to say any more than that, given her training; she would never make such a mistake. It meant that she would tell him everything. After a few sips of whisky she was ready to continue.

'That evening was very strange, Patrick. I was frightened. I don't mind admitting it. Fear affects how you perceive time. Fight or flight I guess. I know you have read the report. He tried using chloroform on me; that affects your mind as well. I was losing consciousness, I cannot be sure; I don't really know what happened.' Her voice trailed off.

Mary held her hand. 'Perhaps you should tell him dear. He knows already, and what harm can it do?'

ELEVEN

Professor Fred Sutcliffe entered the back office of ANATOL's operation centre in MI7 expecting to have a quiet meeting with his old friend and colleague John Platt. He had an eventful trip in on the bus, giving a young man who had been busy scratching some meaningless hieroglyphics into the windows a piece of his mind. The lad had not taken the professor's artistic criticism well and had referred to him as a 'muppet', but the window remained relatively un-spoiled and so the professor felt he had at least won the war if not the argument. When he eventually burst through the doors, somewhat late, he was taken aback to find the room full to bursting. Every seat was filled and numerous suits were stood leaning against the wall. At the front of the room, at the end of the long meeting table facing them was the only vacant chair. Slightly horrified, Fred realised it was for him.

John Platt got up to meet him in the doorway. 'Fred, I'm sorry to thrust this on you like this, but a few things have come up and a few other things have rather been taken out of my hands. The powers that be wanted to meet you face to face and I was not in a position to refuse them.'

'You might have given me a bit of warning.' Fred hissed back. 'I haven't prepared anything, I don't even know what this is about.'

'You soon will Fred. But don't worry; I think you'll find this interesting.' He stepped to the front of the table and introduced Fred to a rather sweaty, suavely-dressed man who Fred immediately recognised as a member of the cabinet. 'Fred, I'm sure you recognise John Saviour-Smith, former Minister for Education, recently moved to Asylum and Repatriation.' The minister shook Fred's hand gingerly. He looked older and more tired than when he appeared on the television. Fred wondered if he wore make-up on TV. It was possible they always did. 'Pleased to meet you.' He had never thought much of Saviour-Smith when he was at the education ministry; he did not have much time for politicians of any variety and was quite outspoken on the subject. He had not expected to be thrust in front of one today. John Platt took the centre stage and the room settled down. Fred poured himself a black coffee, took a biscuit and tried to fortify himself for whatever was to come.

'Thank you everyone for coming. I know this must have come as something of a surprise to some of you and I realise it was at short notice, but some information has come to my notice and others, which I believe may have some considerable bearing on your research. As I'm sure many of you know I have been involved in the government's Child Profiling and Prophylactic Anti-Terrorism Unit'. He glanced at Fred, who was already looking at him with a puzzled expression. 'We have identified over the last three years a subset of children who apparently have some unusual gifts. They are high achievers at school, often succeeding beyond the expectations of their IQs or demographic backgrounds, yet they seem to do this at the expense of their co-educationalists. As you all know, this has lead to a social backlash, which I believe we are only seeing the beginnings of. We have been formulating various plans to contain this problem and protecting those so-called 'gifted' children that might be affected. I would like at this point to introduce you to Professor Fred Sutcliffe, who is an old friend of mine form many years back. Fred is an expert on nuclear and electron magnetic resonance. He is a lecturer at the University of Staffordshire and has been availing his services to ANATOL where he has contributed significantly to the development of high definition ESR gateways, which have allowed us to unobtrusively examine travellers who cross international borders with a

233

degree of precision and differentiation which was previously impossible.' There was a smattering of vocal appreciation around the room. For a moment Fred wondered if he was in line for some sort of lifetime achievement award. His technology had indeed done a great deal of good, but somehow award ceremonies did not seem to be appropriate behaviour for a department of intellectual spooks.

'Recently Fred has identified an aberrant ESR signal associated with a subset of passengers who have been subject to monitoring through airports across the country. I have some information for Fred at this point and I'm afraid, ladies and gentlemen, that this information is classified to Secrecy code 3 level, so some of you will have some form filing to do, but Fred's ESR machines have been installed in numerous other sites that he was not aware of and in total we have now isolated one point eight million people globally with this unique signature. I think I'm right in saying-' at this point he looked in Fred's direction. For his part, Fred was rather annoyed that he had not been informed of the proliferation of his device into new applications, but he kept quiet. '-that the underlying cause of this unique signal may be difficult, if not impossible, to ascertain, and I'm sure you will have many questions to ask him in this regard. Over the last eighteen hours I have been comparing Fred's data set with our own and we have come to some very interesting conclusions.' He paused at this point for dramatic effect. The room was entirely silent. 'Of the one point eight million people that carry this anomaly, two hundred and fifty-five thousand are children which fall into our child profiling population or similar study group set up by others across the European Federation.' He paused again. The room was silent, eyes bright with anticipation, but Fred had already made the connection and his mind was whirling. 'Of these children, some ninety-five percent fall into the category we have described as 'gifted'. This means, in short, that we now have a means by which we can identify gifted individuals in our population.'

After a hushed moment, the assembled crowd broke into

whispered conversations. A hand shot up from the back of the room. 'Professor Platt. You told us that only a proportion of these individuals fall into your study group. Does this imply that the others represent false positives?'

'Thank you for that question as it brings me on to my next point. Only a proportion of the total individuals identified as having this anomaly fall into my study group or those of the Europeans. That leaves a large number of children from regions outside the European Federation for whom we do not have educational or demographic data, but if we assume that the incidence of gifted children in these populations is comparable to that in Europe, this would account for a further five hundred thousand individuals worldwide. As for the remainder... nearly one million people. These are all adults. Although our adult data set is much more limited for these people, some interesting correlations have already been identified. Firstly...' The noise level in the room had slowly increased and Platt raised his voice correspondingly. 'Firstly, these individuals tend to fall into the higher socio-demographic groups. That is to say, compared to the control group, they tend to be more successful financially.' He had to raise his voice again. 'Secondly, of their numbers, a higher proportion are successful sportsmen, linguists and scientists, a higher proportion are divorced and a much higher proportion have been implicated in criminal activity and violent crime than the rest of the population. In short, ladies and gentlemen, I believe we have identified the adult population of 'gifted' individuals.' The room was buzzing now. Questions were shouted from the floor. Professor Platt remained calm. 'There will be plenty of time for questions and discussions later. I'm sure you will have many for myself and for Fred, but there is more. There are numerous high-profile individuals and indeed a few low-profile, high-status individuals that will be familiar to many of you in this room who also appear on these lists. Some of these are known terrorists, some are religious leaders, some are military leaders others are heads of state. There are a few names that are even in this room among us.' At this the room became almost silent. Currently this list has been classified as security level 7 and as such I am afraid it is currently unavailable to you.' There was a chorus of dismayed cries. 'At this stage I would like to propose a twenty minute recess to give you time to digest this information. Hopefully Professor Sutcliffe and myself will be able to take questions from you after that period.'

Fred Sutcliffe nodded slowly but, for the life of him, could think of nothing to say.

TWELVE

Suzi waited in line at the airport. Her mind was fogged and fractured by emotion but she tried to resist the constant impulse to cry when confronted by the slightest inconvenience. She was sufficiently self-aware to realise that her particular torment was a result of conflicting emotions. She had lost her boyfriend, had discovered she had strange, unholy powers, had found the same powers echoed in the traumatised shell of another and now found herself falling in love with him. Her thoughts seemed structureless, atomised and dispersed. In time she knew they would settle, but at the present they were only dunes and quicksand. It would be only too easy to allow herself to be sucked in.

The queue stopped again and Suzi resisted the desire to unleash her fragile temper for the thirtieth time that day. Her passage through French customs had been delayed by a succession of sullen immigration officials who had taken her aside and asked her long lists of intensely dull questions. The metal detector had bleeped in spite of her experienced approach to it. She had packed her shoes with the high steel heels in her luggage, a plain leather belt substituted for the chain-links she normally wore with this skirt. Her jewellery was minimal and had never tripped the machine before. She considered herself seasoned and experienced, someone who moved through the bureaucracies of international travel with the skill of James Bond, secretly dangerous but flying under the radar. That she should suddenly be singled out from the flowing crowd and questioned about her links with international extremists was almost too much to bear in her present state of heightened anxiety. They had eyed her strangely and with a curious lack of professional conviction that had disturbed her. Although she had been very careful to keep her temper, she had feigned enough professional displeasure to make them realise she was not happy about this personal intrusion. When pressed as to why she had been detained, they had been evasive and dismissive, muttering non-committal things about global security. She had missed her flight and only a carefully controlled outburst had secured her an upgrade on the next flight. Naturally her luggage had been misplaced but she always travelled light. She had hoped that this would be the end of her trauma, but on landing she had been singled-out again and found herself plucked from the stream of anonymous humanity and thrown into another holding net. She had flown into Heathrow and the crowd in which she found herself was an eclectic mix of international travellers. Fur coats, leather jackets and expensive sunglasses abounded. All nations seemed to be represented and the common humanity of man was expressed on the drained, passively angry faces that slumped over their luggage trolleys. There was a unique form of misery reserved for those inconvenienced by irresistible state bureaucracy. As the minutes dragged and stretched, and the luggage shuffled forward, painful inch by painful inch, she found herself sustained by thoughts of Miguel. The last few weeks had passed in a soft-tinted happiness that made every act seem like some treasured memory. They had not allowed themselves to fall into each other's beds, but they had fallen into each other's arms. She had allowed herself to find comfort for her recent loss in that powerful embrace, but had resisted yielding further. Miguel seemed to understand, but the magnetism between them was powerful and it had not been an easy detente.

She eventually found herself at the front of the queue. A highly preened woman with pencilled-on eyebrows asked her to come in and sit down. Once again Suzi was asked a seemingly endless succession of inane questions. Had she heard of this terrorist organisation or that religious leader? Suzi prided herself on her knowledge of current affairs; in her job it had paid to be up to date with world machinations. Her clients could pass from wealth and fame to political despond by the fall of an obscure despot or the redistribution of oil-rights. She had learnt from her experience in France that it was better to deny all knowledge of global affairs. An answer in the affirmative, when questioned about the former Saudi Royal family, had lead to a French eye-brow so severely arched that she had thought the man might rupture something. Suzi was fearful that a similar response from his English counterpart might result in some catastrophic make-up crisis. Before the interview was concluded Suzi had tried to establish why she had been interrogated. Had her name been included in some list of undesirables? Was some member of a fundamentalist sect masquerading as her whilst plotting to blow-up Liberties? If this was to be the future of air travel she would have to move permanently to France to be with Miguel. What reason did she have to stay in England? Her job? Her house?

As she burst through the doors in arrivals she was struck by how self-absorbed she had allowed herself to become. Alone and asleep against a pillar was Michael's mother. She must have waited for her for three hours.

THIRTEEN

So it was true. It was amazing and remarkable but when Lilly had spoken to him, her damp, clear-blue eyes shining with intensity and passion, Patrick Manee had found himself believing every word she said. Lilly, like Bill Morris, had a special gift. Somehow, under certain conditions, she could manipulate time. Her desire to stretch subjective time leaked out and the world bent to her will. Her apparently superhuman strength must have come as a consequence of this temporal distortion. As Manee had gently squeezed the parchment skin of Lilly's skeletal hand, he realised that he was in contact with one of the most powerful beings that had ever lived. It was a terrifying thought that someone, even someone as sweet and kind as Lilly appeared to be, should wield such power. He had asked her what she proposed to do with her gift, now that she had discovered it. She had told him that such skills were of no use to someone in her position, but as she had said the words her eyes flashed with an inner light that sent a frisson of fear through Manee's spine. They had spoken for an hour and Lilly was becoming tired; thanking her, he accompanied Mary back to her home. They spoke candidly about her attacker and of Lilly. There would be further investigations; such things were unavoidable. Lilly had told the authorities everything she could with the exception of her knowledge of her gift. Manee imagined the forensic nightmare and the raised voices that would accompany them back in the office. He admitted to Mary that he was not directly involved in the case. He had read the reports and put two and two together, wanting to see

240

Lilly for himself to try to link her case with others he was investigating. It was possible that Lilly was not the only one with these powers. He felt unprofessional for sharing such information, but the candour with which the women had shared their thoughts deserved some reciprocity. He had kept some facts of the case to himself. There was no doubt that their attacker was damaged goods, an unstable and dangerous individual; but it appeared he had had a twisted logic in his unprovoked attacks. Both his younger brother and his mother had died in a road accident. In an instant his life had been destroyed and his future rewritten. The hit-and-run driver had been in her seventies. She was on her way to an exercise class, was running late, and had hit the mother and child on a zebra crossing as she had been raising a number on her mobile. She did not realise her mistake until the police knocked on her front door. She had the wrong pair of glasses on in the car and had neither noticed the young family or the double flash of the speed camera as it recorded the accident in all its grainy horror. It was a truth that might come out in the press; but Manee did not want to be the one to tell Lilly and Mary. For such blameless victims of crime, the personal tragedies which often explained the twisted logic of the criminal, like tree roots steeped in poisonous ground, only served to choke their recovery.

He assured Mary that if there was anything he could do for either of them they were only to ask. As they neared Mary's home, he saw her husband nervously peering out of the kitchen window. He waved to him reassuringly, and made to leave. Before he could, Mary stopped him and turned the chair in the street to face him.

'Good luck with your investigations, Detective. Lilly has entrusted you with her burden, she trusts you, as do I and you must do with that what you will, but be careful.' She looked around her and her voice trailed to a whisper. 'Lilly is a remarkable woman, Patrick, but I am sure she cannot be the only one with this ability. Let us just hope that the others have half the control she has. Think of what could happen if they do not. What would that sort of power do to a disturbed mind or a vengeful one? It could destroy you, Patrick. Power like that could destroy us all and we would have to be very, very careful not to make them angry.' She smiled and turned away. 'Patrick, please keep us informed.'

As Mary whirred away into the house, he contemplated her words. Something had changed the balance of Bill Morris's mind. The gift had twisted him, made a good man bad. Was there some inherent difference between the two, or were the different outcomes just some reflection of the spectrum of human behaviour? He would keep an eye on Lilly. Perhaps the gift had only just begun to work in her; perhaps even she would succumb to its negative influence. Time would tell.

FOURTEEN

'It's got out of hand. I don't want to be party to this. I don't understand where the government wants to go with it. I'm getting nervous of their motives. My security clearance has been withdrawn for data management and I can smell the American influence over the handling of it.' Professor Fred Sutcliffe folded his arms defensively, unfolded them, took a swig of tea, crossed and uncrossed his legs, picked up a document and then threw it back onto the table. He got up and walked to the window. The sun was setting behind a bank of purple cloud; a line of pearlescent silver topped them with regal glory. 'I'll tell you something, John; this has always been my greatest fear, ever since I was a student. I've always been aware of the danger of getting mixed up in some dastardly governmental plot or other. Inadvertently giving the bastards some secret weapon, some insight into the human condition, a knowledge of our secret workings that would let them get inside our heads that little bit more than we want them to.'

'And do you think that is what you've done?' Professor John Platt sat opposite, leaning back in an expansive leather chair, the very model of a university don. 'We are all pawns in this game, Fred. Don't cut yourself up about it. You know how it is. You apply for funding for your pet project and it gets knocked back, again and again. Then in desperation you apply for something else, something maybe a bit more mainstream, a bit more 'target orientated', and suddenly you are on the gravy train. We are all in the same boat. They give us big shoves here and there, and gentle pushes one way or the other. There is no conspiracy

243

though. You have to believe that. It is the greater consciousness, the shared goals of humanity that direct us. The Greek Gods do not sit on high. We are the collective committee. Peer pressure, peer review, peerages, egotistical massages and displacement activities for old men. You are not a victim of the system, Fred. We are all in it together.'

'That might be the mantra you tell yourself as you are sweating through the long nights, John, but it just doesn't cut it for me. I came to you with an idea, a thought. It was pure, unadulterated and untainted by politics and you took it out of the bounds of our friendship and waved it at the lions. You should have consulted me, should have given me a chance to think about the consequences. Perhaps we could have foreseen all this. You have connections in the right places. You know how these people think. You should have known.'

'You flatter me. No one knows the mind of the politicos and no intelligent person can predict the response of a government to a crisis. They don't think like rational people en masse. Put one in a room on his own; he'll be fine; two, with a lectern, and you have entertainment; but put a few behind closed doors and there is no telling what the outcome will be. And besides, there may well be things that you and I aren't party to. There are a lot of clever people in this building and there are people on your list that have been the subject of intense study for years if not decades. You've thrown them a bone; you can't expect them not to go into some sort of feeding frenzy. It's what they do.'

'That is my point! You knew this would happen. You could have prevented it. Could have given us some time to look a bit deeper, think a bit harder.'

'To what ends? Would you ring round all the gifted? Tell them all to move to Greenland and out of Euro-American jurisdiction? There are nearly a million of them Fred. They are embedded in our society. They are our families. They can't be separated out, sifted, wheat from chaff. You and I don't have the power or the influence to make any sort of difference. Do you think we could have discussed the issues with the home office over beer and sandwiches? Excuse me minister, but one in a thousand of your population has some strange effect over the rest of us, screwing with our minds and exhibiting weird paramagnetic properties when energised with powerful magnetic fields, but don't worry about it and don't do anything too radical. I don't think they would have listened, I don't think we could have made much of a difference. Do you?'

'No, but we have made them naked, John; we did not have to do that. We've blown their cover and they can no longer co-exist quietly. We have no idea how long they have been among us. They may have always been here.' Fred Sutcliffe held his head in his hands. He sighed deeply, the breath taking with it the guilt driven anger that was welling up in him. 'Think of the Cultural Revolution. Think of Rwanda. We have seen it before. These things can happen again. People need the flimsiest of reasons to turn on their neighbours, John. You know that. Do you not think that running through every family, every business and every government office or public sector organisation there isn't enough pent-up jealousy and spite to set them against each other?'

'We don't know that will happen. The gifted look the same as us. Hell, for all we know we could be gifted ourselves. There is no cultural or religious distinction, no tribal or physiognomic differential. How will people know? On what grounds will they differentiate?'

'We have handed them the tool, John. No, YOU have handed them the tool. The government is frightened. Every department is on the defensive; every MP's back is against the wall. The general public want to know and they want to be protected. Either the incumbent powers will give them what they want or the people will vote for someone who will. It is the way of things. I think you have unleashed a...'

Their discussion was interrupted by a knock at the door; a colleague known to the pair entered. 'You boys should put on the TV. The Minister for Internal Affairs is on the box. He is giving some sort of address. The department

245

advised him only last night, but you know how it is with these people; they always go off on a tangent and they so rarely seem to get the point. I thought you might want to see what sort of an arse he makes of things.' He opened an oak panel on a wall exposing a flat screen. At the push of a button on a remote control the screen slowly positioned itself so that it was visible to all in the room. The Internal Minister appeared, seated behind an imposing oak table not unlike the one they themselves were leaning against. Shots of the minister were cut with video footage of violent crowds and close-ups of women's faces snarling into camera. The minister's voice was calm, soothing and edged with carefully trained sincerity.

'Following the identification of a remarkably gifted group of children within our school system, the country has seen a period of unrest and confusion. A vocal, confused minority have disrupted schools and colleges, and have made impossible the day-to-day business of educating and caring for our children. This mindless vandalism of our schools is based on the misconception that these children exert some bizarre negative influence on other children in their classes. This in turn has come about due to a wilful misrepresentation of recently acquired statistics by the unprincipled right wing press. In spite of repeated clarifications from this department and others, public confidence has been difficult to re-establish. As a result the government feels it must take unprecedented steps to protect this minority of talented individuals and to re-establish the rule of law in our schools. Tomorrow morning the Prime Minister will make a statement outlining our plans to remove all gifted children from mainstream education. The Prime Minister's announcement will be given simultaneously with similar announcements from the American President, the president of the European Union and the Prime Minister of the Allied Eastern States. I am afraid I cannot elaborate at this time.'

The screen flicked off and slowly retracted into the dark panelling. For a moment there was stunned silence.

Professor Fred Sutcliffe sunk into his chair. 'It's begun.'

FIFTEEN

The face that sat opposite Patrick Manee was barely recognisable. The call had come in the middle of the night. He had just dropped off into a pleasant dream after many hours of fretful wakefulness; trying to get inside the mind of the gifted, to try to understand how their gift might distort them. Any impurities in the metal of their personalities would be sure to cause them to twist in such heat. Now the man himself was sitting opposite. Two day's stubble criminalised his jaw; sunken eyes, all spark gone, implied something had left the sullen shell. The Americans had at last relented. They had nothing on Bill Morris to warrant keeping him secured under their new anti-terrorist legislation. It was not that they needed anything in particular- the law of connectivity meant that everyone was directly related to a terrorist or knew a terrorist through a chain of no more than six people- but the prisons were getting full and the backlog was a national embarrassment. The British Police had a murder case to present and the foibles, vagaries and impossible slowness of the British legal system meant that he would be locked up at British taxpayer's expense until such a time as new information became available. The prisoner exchange had gone ahead at midnight; one set of Rock-plastic manacles in the faux-antique American style had been replaced by a genuinely elderly stainless steel British pair. An orange jumpsuit had been replaced by a grey T-shirt and jeans. The prisoner had not tried to escape. The drug regimen had maintained him 'healthy' and 'compliant'. Everything had passed off as expected. Manee was disappointed, bitterly disappointed. Initially he had been overjoyed that he had the opportunity to question his prisoner face-to-face; for a while he thought the man would disappear into the American penal fog which had enveloped one in twenty of their population and a tenth of their immigrants. It appeared, however, that although Bill had come through the fog, some of it remained with him, inside him, inside his mind.

'Bill, I know you can hear me. I realise you have had a very difficult time. I know you must blame me for that, but if it had not been me, it would have been someone else. You could not have gone on the way you were, you needed help.' The face that looked back at him was expressionless, resigned, sullen. 'I can't imagine what the last month has been like for you, Bill. The Americans mistook you for a terrorist. We know you aren't. You are in safe hands now. We can help you.'

Bill tried to bring his eyes into focus on the man sitting before him. The face stirred a memory, but memories and dreams had become one and the same, and there was no point worrying about dreams as they were not real. Reality had indeed taken on some new forms of late. Bill was aware that he had been drugged. He had heard the questions they had asked of him and heard himself babbling in response. They had not been happy. They had done something to him that made him wince and cry. He had not cried in years. The tears had flowed from him in a manner he had not thought possible. He had cried like a child and had not the slightest inhibition in doing so. The pain was transient and tolerable, but it had induced fear. Surely there was no limit to what they could do to him, no torture too fiendish; in the absence of compassion there could be only dissection, scrutiny and death. It was in these moments and the long periods of sensory deprivation that he had turned within himself. He had looked for a quiet place, a refuge from the discomfort and the grinding trauma of the psychological games they had played. In time he had found that place, the gap between thoughts, the drawing-in of breath before a barked command, the moment when a hand was placed on his shoulder to guide him, blindfolded through a door. He had lived in these moments for what had felt like an eternity. The turning of a key in a lock was not the end of freedom. It was a study in friction, of mechanics, of motion; a chorus of low frequencies humming and oscillating, weeping and moaning. He must have slept a great deal and it was almost entirely when unconscious that time had seemed to return to normal. In sleep people moved at a pace he could understand. In sleep there were things he could recognise; only when he was awake was the world hopelessly abstract.

At one point they had not drugged him. They had found his behaviour too refractory and puzzling. They thought they might have damaged him. As the narcotic warmth left him numb in its wake he had retreated further from the inquisition. The noises and crashes of reality were no less inharmonious when heard clearly. There was also something else he had discovered as he made this inner journey. He had learnt how to tap the reservoir of pleasure activated by his gift, the thrill that had driven him those mad few weeks. Initially the experience had been like a mainline injection, blinding, all encompassing, driving his conscious mind before it. Now he had learnt to control that release, maintain the high by restricting the outpouring, saturating his mind whilst rationing the pill. The time dilations he had experienced were restricted to his subjective mind, with the internal floodgates closed to a trickle; he could slow internal time as he wished but he had not noticed any effect on his surroundings. In moments of lucidity he had damned his gift. In a prison cell the last thing one might desire would be to extend the experience of suffering. This would have been true for a man who existed fully in that world; but Bill Morris did not. His dreamscape and pleasure-fuelled fantasies did not revolve around his tawdry present. Reality was becoming a blank canvas on which to paint them.

The face of Detective Inspector Manee congealed into concrete reality. He knew this man and some part of his mind was reminding him that he hated him. With every passing moment the drugs were wearing thinner and the stale air in his lungs was reminding him that he was a prisoner. He allowed himself to settle back into his old skin, to focus on his breathing, to feel the old pains. Yes, he knew this man. For a few moments he wondered what he was doing, his face distorting and changing, sounds, vaguely familiar, somehow provided the rhythm for their dance. He found himself fascinated by the opening and closing mouth, the tensions in the jaw, the wrinkling around the eyes. Slowly meaning attached itself to the motions. The man was speaking. He was speaking to him.

Bill wanted to tell the man to stop, to wait, but the voice in his head could not remember at that juncture how to make itself heard by others. It raged like a bull tormented, but then became still as a new sound crashed into his ears; the sound of his own screaming.

'I'm sorry.' Bill was calmer now. 'I have had a difficult time. I am not sure I am entirely sane.' Manee sat back on his chair, nursing a cup of black coffee, his eyes focused on Bill's face, catching his every movement. He had seen this man move like a cheetah through a crowded room. Now he looked as if he needed help to stand.

'Please, take your time. Start where you like, tell me what you can. I know this must be very difficult for you.'

Bill looked at Manee in a way he had never looked at anyone or anything before. There was a time; was it six months ago? Was it a year? He could not be sure, but he would not have looked twice at this man. Now he was studying him with the eye of a student, the eye of a scientist, a behaviourist. Manee was a good man. He really did want to know what had happened. He really did want to help. The signs and symbols were there to be read if only you could be bothered to allow yourself to read them. He watched Manee turning the coffee-cup between his fingers saw the unease, the excitement in the flickering movements.

'I'm not like other men.' It seemed a good place to start. It was the fundamental truth that had imprinted itself on

250

his mind in those first heady days. 'I see things that other people don't see. I see birds flying, really flying and air, I see the sparks in air.' How to describe them; the shimmering blue and purple distortions of light when his powers were manifest? He was no poet; he did not have words for mirages such as these. 'I only killed because I could. The first time was an accident. I didn't even touch him, you see, I was just afraid; but it was so incredible to feel like that, to feel alive like that. I just had to do it again. I had to see if I could, you see, it was just so, so wonderful.' For a moment his eyes glazed over and Manee thought he had lost him.

'Have you always had the skill, to... do the things you do?' Manee could not help himself. He looked at his partial reflection in the reinforced glass suddenly angry with himself for being so reckless. The guard standing behind him in the doorway was picking his nose, thinking himself unobserved.

'No, I don't think so. It is so difficult to say.' Bill was with him again, sentience reasserting itself behind his eyes. 'You can live forever trapped in a moment, or your life can pass before your eyes. People say that all the time, don't they? Maybe we all have the power, I don't know. It's just, when I'm excited,' -his eyes were flashing now- 'very excited, I can control it, you see, control the flow just for a moment. But in here,' -he tapped his skull- 'I can control it all the time.' Manee felt sweat on his palms, felt his coffee going cold in his hands, saw the pleasure radiate across Morris's face.

'How does it feel when you are manipulating time Bill? When you are watching us from the outside?' He could hear the nervousness in his own voice, felt the trembling of his heart. Was this natural excitement or was Bill manipulating him now from across the table, through the glass?

A smile slowly spread from Morris's mouth to his eyes; he slowly leant towards the glass. Manee heard the guard suddenly tensing at his post.

'Wonderful, Detective. It feels wonderful.'

251

SIXTEEN

'I don't understand it and I don't want to go!' Brian Lydon threw an officious looking envelope onto the table, picked it up again, re-read the contents, then screwed it up and threw it into the fireplace. 'It doesn't make sense. This isn't China. They can't do this to me. I'm happy where I am and I haven't had any trouble. I haven't hurt anyone. No one has said anything; I had no idea myself. You don't think I'm odd, do you?'

Juliet sat opposite, the light from the fire momentarily bathing her face in a warm glow as the envelope caught light. 'Of course not... well, maybe I thought you were a bit odd, but in a good way. You've always been a bit too bright for your own good, a bit too spoddy, but you are basically okay.' Brian looked away into the flames. There was a hollow gnawing in his stomach. He hated to admit it to himself but he had grown very fond of Juliet. Sufficiently fond that she had had to tell him she had a boy waiting for her at home. She had then proceeded to give him chapter and verse about the boy, whilst all the time intimating that he wasn't really everything she wanted, but she was rather confused as to what she really wanted. It had not made him feel much better. Now some computer in a dark airless government office had spewed out a list with his name on it. He was officially 'gifted' and that meant he had to leave his studies within the next week and head to another university site in North Wales. It was for his own protection. His studies would not suffer and every provision would be made for him. College fees would be waived for the duration and accommodation would be provided. Brian had seen the Prime Minister's statement the week before and the sinking feeling had begun to take hold of him then. He had giggled at some of the more fantastic articles in the papers and on the Internet about the 'gifted' and like everyone else had laughed with the satirical comedians who had lampooned the hysteria and the government's response to it. He had not thought it applied to him. He had never demonstrated any overt powers, though like every child of his generation he had attempted to fire spider webs from his wrists as a child. He had always quietly assumed that his superpowers would come to him on his twenty-first birthday. Bruce Wayne would call him up and tell him he was his lost son, spawn of a night of passion with one of the lesser-known Marvel heroines. Now it appeared there really was something odd about him. He had read that people with this so-called gift had a nasty effect on those around them, but could see no obvious change in his friends and colleagues. The fire burnt itself out; the embers glowed and disintegrated. Perhaps the fire that burnt twice as bright would burn itself out twice as fast. Maybe he was gifted, but only mildly so. Most likely there was just another Brian Lydon in the system with a wonderful house a wonderful sexy girlfriend and a wonderful job with a whole bunch of miserable ape-like friends and there had been some sort of computer mix up.

'What are you gonna do?' Juliet had quietly crept up behind him and placed her arm over his shoulder.

'I don't know. I could just make a run for it I suppose, but it's getting harder to hide out. You need I.D. to buy milk these days and I'm not sure where I'd go.' Juliet was silent for a minute, gently massaging the nape of his neck whilst staring at the glowing coals.

'You could go and stay with my dad, my real dad. My mum doesn't know I know where he is, but I go and see him every now and again. He lives in Llangollen, near where they wanted to send you. It might be a good place to hide out. You'll be able to follow what goes on there, but from this side of the wire. It's the last place they'd think of looking for you. Right on the doorstep.'

'But, I don't know, what would I do for money? I'm loaned up to the eyeballs as it is, my folks will go spare.' Juliet was quiet for a moment as if having some internal discussion as to what to tell him.

'Don't worry. My dad is a bit of a colourful character. That's why my mum left him. He has done a bit of time and knows a bit about faking IDs; he'll look after you. I'll phone him now; he can scan your face from the phone. He'll have a card and a name for you by the end of tomorrow. He is very good. He hasn't been caught a second time.' She slipped her hand into his. 'It'll be all right. I'm sure this will just blow over. People are crazy but they forget things quickly. Something else will come along, a war or an election or a new girl-band and they will forget all about it.' She kissed him on the cheek and withdrew an ID card from her wallet. 'See this? This is my other ID; on it I'm Miss Juliet Arkwright, twenty-five, able to buy hard drugs over the counter and single. Perhaps it is time I got married.' She looked at the card. 'How do you fancy being Mr. Arkwright?'

SEVENTEEN

The rain spattered the apple-blossom and caused the glossy leaves of bamboo and Cordyline to shimmer and tremble. The borders were full of bright tulips and wall-flowers and tight bundles of leaves thrust promise from warmed earth. Normally such a sight in the garden would have filled Diane Spinks with joy, but today she could take no pleasure from the scene. Diane was a single mother with an only child and today the authorities had taken her son away from her and sent him to a remote part of north Wales. She had tried to convince herself that it was for the best. God knows the last few weeks had been a terrible trial. Her son Daniel had been bullied mercilessly at school having been identified as gifted. Initially Diane had react-ed by telling him to stand up for himself, thump anyone who was threatening him and she would back him up with the teachers if there was a problem. Bringing up a child without a father can lead to difficult judgement calls and she felt that that would be the advice a father would have given. Diane's husband had not stayed around long enough for her to have a particularly informed idea of what his advice might be, so she second-guessed the thoughts of an idealised man that she hoped, perhaps, one day would come into her life. There had been fights and a bloody nose and angry letters from frightened teachers, but Diane was never afraid of such small-time authority and had put them in their place. They had a responsibili-ty to protect her son and if they reneged on that responsi-bility, he had to look after himself. Failing that she would come up to school herself and teach the monsters a lesson and woe-betide any bully's mother that got in her way. The teachers had muttered about the difficulties of intervention and their own powerlessness, but Diane had told them in no uncertain terms that such issues were not her concern. The safety of her son, who had done nothing to deserve such unwanted attentions, overruled everything else. The weasel woman of a schools complaints officer had nearly sent her into an apoplexy of anger when she had asked to speak to Daniel's father. It was with the greatest difficulty that she had explained that that was not currently possible without also telling the woman where to put the telephone. Her brother Edward was not much use as a surrogate father, though he did try. Edward was a sweet man, but his poor luck with women and his unfulfilled work ambitions did not make him the best role model for his nephew. Edward was sufficiently deconstructed to talk openly about his continual disappointments and frustrations. Diane did not much care for filling Daniel's mind with angst before the boy had had a chance to acquire his own. Daniel was bright, pleasant and sensitive and she was not sure how he would deal with being thrown into a strange environment away from home. She had tried not to be over-protective of her charge, but she had not let him stray far. Now he was being deported over the border. The headmistress had phoned whilst the letter was still lying on the table, moist with her tears. The government-backed security firm had arrived in a van to take him to the coach station; it had been the kind of van they used to transport high security bank-robbers and paedophiles. The government spoke of sensitivity and concern, but their private finance cost-cutting now clothed every walk of public service with the dehumanised, grey disinterest of the lowest bidder. The driver had a list of names and addresses; he had thrown Daniel's rucksack and suitcase into the back of the van as if he'd just collected a delivery of tinned-peaches. She had seen one last glimpse of Daniel's white, frightened face as the driver had slammed the doors. The windows were darkened, sparing her the additional horror of watching him wave goodbye. That was an hour ago and now her heart felt like stone.

The back door opened and a voice called up the hall. It was Edward. She tore herself away from the window and met him in the kitchen. Emotions welled and she flung her arms around him and sobbed. 'They have taken Danny away.'

The tears helped and over a cup of sweet tea and a double brandy she recounted the series of events to him. He listened attentively, trying to hide his growing dread. The government had acted swiftly, in the first week following the Prime Minister's televised speech they had 'taken fifty thousand children into safety.' Although some had gone voluntarily; there had been scenes of anguish on the television as parents packed their children off. Reports of widespread public disobedience had not appeared and it was this absence that worried Edward. When the media colluded with the state the sky could get very dark indeed. There had been continued persecution of gifted children across the country and there were a number of wild reports of gifted children lashing out in self-defence. In Daventry a fifteen-year old girl, hounded into a corner of a classroom by jeering classmates, had hurled a boy through a plate-glass window. Eyewitness reports had described how she had shoved him away from her. They all confirmed hearing the sound of his ribcage cracking before he had flown through the air. They were confused as to what had happened next. Somehow the girl had escaped from the scene. In another school, a boy had taken refuge in a cupboard. When the crowd of children had eventually torn the door off to get to him he had lashed out at them. Police had questioned him but he was at a loss to explain how eight girls and a boy had come to be knocked unconscious. Five were still recovering in hospital, the doctors seemingly unable to establish the cause of their condition.

'When can we go and see him?' Edward slowly paced the room, desperately trying to organise his thoughts. Perhaps they could liberate Daniel from the place. There was no telling what foolishness the government could embark upon under these circumstances. Edward Spinks had always prided himself on his knowledge of history and his-

257

tory provided endless examples of situations when the general public had failed to read the writing on the political wall. He had always promised himself that he would never let that happen to him. He would buy his tickets and get on the first boat out of there. Something else was also troubling him. Edward's intellect was of the kind that quietly pondered problems in almost total secrecy from his fore-brain. The times were countless when he had woken from comfortable sleep with the answer to some problem or concern fully composed in his mind. On other occasions he found himself blessed with both the question and the answer, delivered, as it were, from thin air. In some cases even the inspiration for such puzzles eluded him, but he had learnt to accept such gifts gladly. On the way to Diane's house another such revelation had come to him; a sudden blinding realisation that now seemed so patently true and right that it shocked him to think he had not made the connection sooner.

'They say there will be an initial period of two weeks during which they'll do some tests on him and give him a chance to settle in. After that, they say we can visit, but the rules are complicated; they cover three pages.' She started to sob. 'I haven't been able to read through them properly.' She pushed a damp sheaf of paper towards him and he began to flick through. It was pretty much as he had feared. Security would be fairly tight; they did not want too many angry parents in one place at the same time. It would be policed by a specially-appointed branch of the National Security Corps; a police-based squad who would be armed in case of 'terrorist threats.' Both parents and children would be monitored before and after any exchange for psychological or physical changes. The government wanted to assess the effect the children had on their families at close quarters. Enclosed was a list of psychometric tests which the parents were asked to complete. He scanned the questions. Things were beginning to come together.

Bill Morris was gifted. This was the revelation that had come to him driving round the London orbital. Agneta had been right to be afraid of the oppressive shroud he imposed around himself. She had recoiled from it instinctively and he had not fully understood the significance of her reaction. He had been too selfish, too involved in his own intellectual affairs and the distracting yearnings of his own arousal in her presence, to give sufficient thought to her concerns. The papers, of course, had been full of speculation about the gifted children, their subtle subversion of their environments, but as time had worn on he had begun to grow tired of the speculation. There had been some misunderstandings and the government had dragged out a host of scientists to bore the public into dull acquiescence. The Prime Minister's speech had shaken him from this lethargy and now his own nephew was being sent away. There were so many questions in his mind at this stage. He knew so little about what Bill Morris had become, and if the truth be said, he had not really cared. It was strange how someone once so important to your daily happiness or general malaise should so quickly seem irrelevant to you. The coverage in the papers had been slight; Bill had been branded as a terrorist but at this time terrorism-fatigue had swept through the media. Terrorism was now so rife throughout the Western world that it barely counted as news. There were only so many distraught bereaved and burnt-out wreckages the public could tolerate and profiles of strangely-haunted-looking suspected terrorists did not warrant many column inches. Edward knew what he had to do. He held his sister's hand.

'Don't worry Di, I've got a few ideas. I have a few connections; I might be able to pull a few strings. I'm sure Daniel will be alright. He is a bright boy, a strong lad and he'll know to keep quiet and keep his head down until we can get him out. Don't worry about the forms, just ignore it all. If the authorities want something from you they'll have to work to get it; but it's probably best for Daniel at this stage if we keep a low profile. Better to go over the heads of the people at the camp rather than dealing with them head on. Local government employees don't have any authority anyway. Be strong. I won't be long.' He kissed his sister on her forehead. She smiled weakly at him through her tears as he waved goodbye. Once in his car, he turned on the video phone. Searching through his wallet he found, with relief, the numbers of Agneta Sibilski and Patrick Manee. Three minds were better than one and something had to be done.

PART FOUR

THE HUNTED

ONE

Daniel Spinks surveyed the long line of children who formed the rag-tag queue in front of him. Instinctively he looked for a friendly or familiar face. There was no-one there he recognised, but it was strange how many echoes there were of people he had known in his short life, facial elements seemed to have been copied and pasted into slightly different frames and several times he was almost convinced there was someone amongst them he knew. Every face featured tell-tale signs of fear. Some of the children's eyes were red with tears; others were glassy, impassive to the environment around them. Daniel was fifteen and as he surveyed the line he realised he was one of the oldest there; the youngest was probably ten. For the first time in his life he realised that he was just a statistic on someone's form: a gifted ten-to-fifteen year old, his name purely a device to identify him; no emotional elements being associated with it. The thought choked him for a moment, but he managed to subdue the welling fear. Getting upset was not going to help his predicament and he was the oldest one here after all. He had to set an example and be brave.

The reception area was a beautiful old private school, built of pale stones in shades of orange and pink. The collegiate atmosphere, the quiet quadrant surrounded by such pleasant buildings calmed him somewhat and he tried to think of the whole experience as some kind of adventure. He had not spent much time away from home and he had travelled very little, his Mum having to work all the time to keep them. The journey from home to the first pick-up site had nearly scared him out of his wits, sitting in the dim police van, swaying from side to side; unable to see where they were going. The sounds of traffic perilously close, the driver's angry swearing and general resistance to questions shouted to him. Although the journey seemed to last a lifetime, they could not have gone far because Daniel recognised the motorway service area where he was transferred to a small bus. This driver was more forthcoming and friendly but was unable to answer many of Daniel's questions. The other passengers were all children of between nine and twelve. There had been little conversation, save an hour or so when he had found himself having to comfort a nine-year-old boy called Stephen who had suddenly gripped his hand in fear as their bus had been passed by a large lorry. The boy was a very nervous traveller and they had had to stop several times on the side of the road whilst he retched into the roadside beds of spring bulbs. They had passed through some beautiful countryside: rolling fields and farms, which had excited some of the children who had apparently never seen such wonders. As the day wore on though, the countryside had bubbled up somewhat into more dramatic hills and the children had become subdued and intimidated. The road began to climb and swerve and Stephen's eyes became wide with fear. He held Daniel's hand tighter than ever before eventually falling asleep against his arm.

The bus climbed a great purple arc of road, the ground sweeping away to a river and nestling villages. The sun burst through ominous cloud and illuminated the tops in a warm, golden light. Daniel pressed his face to the window and looked horrified at the precipitous drop below. The engine struggled in low gear and they slowly reached the summit, closely followed by a line of frustrated motorcyclists.

They had passed through a number of small villages with progressively stranger-sounding names. Daniel recognised them as Welsh and had practised rolling his Ls and guessing the vowels. He tried to glean vocabulary from the Welsh road signs in case he had to try to communicate with the locals in their own tongue. He was somewhat surprised they had not had to pass through any kind of border controls or customs. They had approached the town from the east (he had tried to navigate as best he could in case the opportunity arose to escape). It was partially-encircled with a double barbed-wire-topped fence, which was still in the process of being erected as they came through the security check-point. Outside the gates a large crowd was assembled, carrying placards and chanting. They were kept back from the road by a line of police in riot-gear. Daniel saw the black barrels of foam guns and entanglement snare RPGs, but the crowd was too far away for him to read the placards. A refrain of their chant came across on the wind; it was strangely harmonious. He had seen a short media clip about the resistance of the locals to the acquisition of their town by the police. The TV had mentioned several hundred, but there seemed to be at least a thousand people gathered. Some people had been allowed to stay in their homes to provide services to the police. He had heard heated debates and some talk about striking and scabs (words he did not understand).The guard was polite and smiled at the children as they passed through the gate. Daniel did not smile back, but took the opportunity to see that the guard was armed and carried a baton, radio equipment, binoculars and handcuffs. He wondered if they had night-sight capabilities. They were waved through the barricade and the van slowly climbed up through the quiet streets towards a reception centre.

The sun was now low in the sky and the air was cooler. The dramatic ruins of the castle on the top of the hill cast a jagged shadow over the town. For a moment Daniel imagined himself high up on the battlements, firing burning arrows down on the heads of a besieging army of the National Security Corps. They would not take him alive. Shortly after they had arrived Daniel had been separated from Stephen as the two boys fell into different age-groups. He told the younger boy not to worry, to be brave. They would meet up later. Not knowing if it was true, he had the distinct impression he had conspired with the enemy, something that made him feel queasy inside. The queue shuffled forward and he found himself at the front desk.

The suited official at the desk was friendly and polite and told him not to worry. He would be safe here and looked after and hopefully he would be able to go home to his family as soon as things got back to normal. The man told him he was lucky, he had been assigned a nice room in the old school, right at the top, closest to God. He would have to share with a couple of other lads, who would arrive in a few days, but it should be fun. Daniel asked him if he could explore the town and go and look at the castle. The man had answered that he was free to go anywhere he liked within the boundary of the fence. He was not a prisoner; the fence was purely there to keep the weirdos out. All the children coming to the 'camp' were gifted, he was sure Daniel would make some interesting friends. He could explore the castle any time he liked. You could walk the remaining walls of the old town and somewhere, though the man was coy about exactly where, you could get down into the old dungeons of the mediaeval city. There was a lot to explore; he would have a great time. He had to answer a whole raft of questions and was then given a set of keys, directions, a mobile phone and a map. If he had any problems he was to call a particular number on the mobile phone. He could use it to call his family at any time. He was told that the surrounding hills interfered with normal mobile phones and Daniel had been unable to fix on any local signal with his own phone, in spite of repeated attempts on various networks. He was not convinced by this at all and wondered how they had blocked the signal. He was sure he had seen them do something similar on the TV.

He thanked the man, his hard-wired politeness overcoming his anxiety with this disturbing authority, and slowly walked towards his assigned block. The heat of the day still radiated off the stone but the air was now distinctly cold. Perhaps when the moment came and his troops of archer-children were ranged across the battlements he would not have everyone killed. He would spare the clerk on the desk and perhaps the bus driver; but the van driver would have to go.

TWO

Patrick Manee stared at the letter in front of him. He turned the radio down and instinctively pulled on some clothes. Some letters were best read dressed. He was being reassigned. He dreaded the word. Reassignment for him was synonymous with waste and frustration. He was to be frustrated and his previous efforts wasted. He could not believe it. The letter was of the half personal-half computer generated variety that he had come to expect. The technology had been cultivated in the advertising business but had spread into so many other walks of life. The junctions between the human and the digital now smoothed by such sophisticated algorithms that only rare and peculiarly personal foibles often betrayed the human hand. He read between the computer generated lines.

'Dear Paddy
...blah blah... Following the not entirely unsuccessful completion of your current mission and the intransigence of your friend and ours (ref. 0089-787849-8989)
I am afraid it has been... blah blah... reassignment... blah blah...

What followed was an almost entirely computer-generated description of his re-deployment to Denbigh in North Wales. He was to act as part of a coordinating team of the 'Gifted-child Secure Zone' as they now described it, policing the internal affairs of the community. In particular he was to head-off potential child abuse within the compound but he was also assigned to look for signs of organised escape plans, interpreting tapped communications from within the compound as an early-warning for the half-dozen security firms and the National Defense Corps who provided the bulk of the site's security.

Manee was angry, very angry. He was angry that his boss should resort to a semi-automated letter to tell him his life was going to totally screwed-up for the foreseeable future, he was angry that the man had called him Paddy (which he only did to be provocative) and he was most angry that his job should have come to this: gathering tittle-tattle for mercenaries and keeping children under house arrest. This was after all, what it was all about. He had been watching developments in Denbigh with a growing malaise. It would never work, the public would never allow it, it was too difficult to police, and who would police the police? The echoing warnings from internment camps of the past were surely too loud even today. Even with the best of intentions the parallels were too stark. Now it appeared this poisoned chalice was to be passed to him. It was a nightmare. He was not even qualified to perform the task. What did he know of policing regular children? It was hard enough chasing after the hordes of wild-things that were terrorising the inner cities, but these were juvenile delinquents and they knew the game better than the police did. They played the system, baited the police, committed their petty crime and acted out their little power fantasies whilst the left-wing bleated and wrung its hands and the right wing turned away behind their iron barricades. The police and the thugs had a 'special relationship' like cowboys and Indians shooting at each other from behind rocks. There was almost legitimacy in the whole process, as tedious and mind-numbing as it often seemed.

Regular children were different; they still had a residual respect for the police and as such had to be treated with proverbial kid gloves. It was not that Manee did not like children. He was very fond of his nephews and nieces; but you could always give them back at the end of the day. The street kids were only his responsibility for as long as it took to get them to their parents, a police cell or a social worker. There was also the more pressing question as to

267

what on Earth the government was up to. How long did they think they could protect the children from the masses and who were they protecting from whom? Links had begun to form in Manee's mind between the gifted children and his recent investigation. He tried to put the idea out of his mind. It was too fanciful, too outlandish. His thoughts were interrupted by the bleating of his phone. The rude disturbance left him feeling suddenly cold. It was Edward Spinks. It took him a few moments to place the name, the metal in the voice initially incongruous with the self-assured yet evasive man he had met in Bill Morris' office. He wanted to arrange a meeting with Manee, to speak off the record about the gifted children and Bill Morris. The juxtaposition of the two delivered with a voice that was shot through with tension and fear felt like a blade drawn along Manee's spine. He was to come alone, but Spinks would arrange for Agneta Sibilski to join them to bring corroborating evidence for his conjecture. They arranged to meet by the Embankment at 8:00. As he put down the phone he felt his heart racing. So, Edward Spinks was thinking along the same lines as him, but what did he have in mind? The image of Bill Morris's milky blue eyes burning into his suddenly appeared before him. He felt the man's penetrating gaze, felt its almost physical pressure. What was a man like that capable of? And what of the children; thousands of lost souls, their fragile minds separated from their families, exposed perhaps for the first time to each other's gifts? Perhaps this was not such a disastrous posting after all. He would be in the thick of things; in a rare position to actually make a difference. He really wasn't sure if he was ready for it. Manee re-read the letter and poured himself a double whisky. He placed the glass to his lips, inhaled the first breath of peat and smoke but was rudely interrupted again by the phone. He slammed the glass down and accepted the call. 'Yes? What is it?'

He slowly replaced the telephone on the receiver and picked up his glass. He took a deep draught from it, his hand trembling. Bill Morris had escaped.

THREE

'What do you mean you don't know how long ago he escaped? What sort of idiot are you? Didn't they teach you to tell the time in your idiot school of higher idiot education? How difficult is it to stand still for a few hours and watch a man in a cage? Is it asking too much? Did I ask you to perform strange alchemical calculations to solve the deep mysteries of human thought? No! I asked you to stand still, eyes forward and watch a man in a cage sitting still looking back. I wouldn't have thought such a thing was beyond the capabilities of someone even as dumb as you.'

'Excuse me sir, there is a Detective Manee to see you.' The messenger ducked back behind the door like a frightened rabbit before the Head of Security could answer.

'I'll deal with you later, and if this Detective Manee gives me a hard time over the fact that you have allowed his prisoner to slip out of the building under your very nose then I will use your scalp as a floor cloth. Do you understand me?'

'I doubt that will be necessary, Mr Hargreaves; I'm afraid the prisoner's escape was probably inevitable.'

Patrick Manee strode purposefully into the room followed by the sheepish messenger. 'I'm sorry sir he just pushed past me.' Hargreaves gave the man a stare that would have melted an Amsterdam bollard.

'As you can see, I was just trying to establish the sequence of unfortunate events that lead to Bill Morris's escape. We have a large force of our own, plus the local bill in pursuit with dogs. He can't have got far.'

'Thank you for your co-operation, Mr Hargreaves. I

would like to have a brief interview with everyone who was around the prisoner at the time of the escape. I'm sure it won't take long and of course I would like to see all video footage of the moments prior to, and during, his escape.' Hargreaves seemed taken aback. He was not used to people making direct demands of him; even the pen-pushing pencil-necks who were his bosses never asked him for anything directly.

'Well, I'm sorry, Detective, but my men are out looking for the escapee. I'm not prepared to pull them back and I'm afraid there is little point looking at the tapes.' His voice trailed off.

'Why?' Manee's voice was calm, collected.

'Because...' The man was clearly having difficulty forming the words. 'There seems to have been some problem with our security cameras during this period.' The poor man looked as if he might choke on his own tongue.

'I'll be the judge of that, Mr Hargreaves.' Manee walked up to the man so that he was only six inches from his face. 'And as for the security who are running around the fields like so many kids on half-term.' His voice was loaded with menace. He could see Hargreaves could smell the whiskey on his breath. The man seemed slightly horrified. 'I delivered a perfectly good prisoner to the British and American combined forces six months ago and your people have just given me a piece of paper telling me you have lost him in the woods. Now I am going to have to go and capture him for a second time and you and your men can go into a quiet room and lick each other's wounds. I just asked you to do a little bit of baby-sitting, and you couldn't be trusted with the job. I suggest you get out of my face before I begin to tell you how angry I am. I'll use your office for the interviews, I'll start with this man and I want an orderly line of everyone my prisoner walked past before he decided to have a jolly in the Surrey countryside.'

He turned to the guard who was staring into the half-distance as if his very life depended on it. 'Lead the way.' He turned back to Hargreaves. 'Milk and two sugars please and not out of a machine. Thank you.'

The guard gave a fearful look at his superior, flinched from the look he received in return and led Manee down the corridor to a large, tidy side office. Once inside Manee closed the door and asked the guard to sit down. When he spoke it was kindly and politely. There was no trace of the steel that had been there a few moments before. He took a notebook from his case and a pencil.

'Before you start I want you to know that I don't blame you for what happened.' The guard's body seemed to stiffen as he said the words, his eyes came up to meet Manee's. 'I want you to tell me everything you remember from the moments prior to Morris' escape; leave no detail out. I want you to tell me what he was doing, what he said and, most importantly, what you felt.'

FOUR

Bill Morris slumped backwards against a tree. His breath was coming in strained gasps and his heart seemed to be about to slip through the bones of his ribcage and spew itself at his feet. He was sliding between his internal utopia and reality between breaths. By losing himself in the white fog of his internal ecstasies the acute physical pain became a distant irrelevance. His conscious mind still strove to stay in command of his actions, but now he relied upon it as an old but distant friend: familiar and trustworthy, but most definitely 'other'. The white heat of pleasure was his new calling; perfect and sublime, sensuous and sexual; turning every frantic, giddy step into a rhapsody. He was not sure how long he had been running, but his clothes were drenched in sweat and covered in the bodily fluids of countless unsuspecting plants and insects. He had watched the duty guard carefully, dwelt in the man's very essence, knowing his movements and his foibles with a depth and insight that the man himself would never have understood. He knew how he moved, how he paused between pulling the door to and inserting the key, between checking the shackles and turning towards the door, before picking his nose and examination of the objet trouvé and, most importantly, between looking, seeing and understanding. These moments could be extended, could be teased and stretched into a window of opportunity, a window a prisoner could slip through. Getting past the man and onto the other side of the perspex wall, trapping him inside, had been child's play, but he had had to exact another cost from his captor. The guard had been pleasant enough, professional enough, distant enough. He had shown no malice or attempted to take any advantage of him or his predicament or indeed to take any sadistic pleasure form Bill's vulnerability, which had made extracting the man's time more difficult and distasteful.

Bill had felt himself flushed with the man's time, could almost feel it humming within him. It was not as if the man missed it, sitting as he did, for hour upon hour outside Bill's perspex cell, wandering up and down the corridor, reading the same pointless article in the paper again and again, scanning the same pointillist nudes, creamy plastic breasts described by ten thousand smeared-ink dots. Such behaviour was not living, was not life. He had initially absorbed a few seconds, then a few minutes. He had assumed that the man would feel pain and fear in proportion to the pleasure and joy that had been transfused into him, but this did not appear to be the case. A few times, when Bill had drawn more heavily from him, taking as much as he felt he could bear without slipping into some sort of ecstatic trance, he had seen the man swoon slightly, but that was all. It had become clear to Bill that his powers were all borrowed from those around him; he was malignant, pernicious, a parasite on unknowing victims, but he himself had been blameless in the beginning. His skills were in his essential nature. He had used them like a baby uses its voice, with only the rawest emotions, plaintively and crudely. Now he had developed a little control he could charge his powers, store them and channel them. It was a start. At the final moments the guard had looked at him, wide-eyed, almost pleading through the plastic. He read the anxiety on the face, dwelt in its confused emotions whilst drawing the required time from him. The voyeuristic pleasure this had given him was almost divine. When he allowed himself to pull deeper on the vein; the air had crackled blue and green. His eyes had rolled back into his head. Pleasure stacked against pleasure, the outside world folding in on itself, manifold and tortuous. Then he had started to run. He had turned to look back at the guard, one hand slowly reaching down towards his gunholster another reaching up to his brow, his face distorting and twisting as the blue fire played across it. Timing was everything, knowledge was power and Bill Morris had a surplus of both. He had heard the bolts withdrawn from the automatic barrier, the whirr of their stepper-motors, the whine of their hydraulics: that was when he had made his move. A rare conjunction of the arrival of a new prisoner with a meal-time; for a few moments everyone with a key to every door between his cell and freedom would be perfectly positioned. He had been in luck: the first door in the corridor was open, two guards and prisoner were passing through them. He ran between them, drawing off time as he went, vibrations of air tinged with blue flickered between them. For them the moment must have been but an instant; they could recall little, perhaps a blur of movement, but it was so, so transient. Another corridor, another door to unlock, to push a man through, to lock behind. They had performed the action a thousand times, why dwell in one such meaningless repetition of so many. For Bill, however, sliding between the figures and the door-well each second was drawn into minutes; he heard the rumbling of their clothes, the groaning of hinges, the chiming of keys. The second door was closed but the guard on the far side was still engaged in operating the lock. Bill moved towards him, keeping out of his line of sight; he would be a peripheral shadow, a trick of the light. The key was turning in the lock, slow, so slow. The mechanism crashed and collapsed, girders grinding into place. Bill grabbed the man's forearm through the bars and reversed its motion. The air flashed, the lock mechanism squealed, bones splintered and tendons shattered.

Bill pushed the door gate open and slipped through the gap. The man's head was turning, an expression between astonishment and pain formulated itself on his previously non-committal features.

The remaining gates were gloriously easy. Manned posts, armed guards, chatting, laughing or staring into space: he ran past them all, carefully keeping out of their direct lines of sight. He drew time from them as he slipped by, a little from each; they would lose track of a thought, the flow of a conversation, fail to hear a few words or suddenly wonder why they were doing what they were doing at that moment. They would be distracted by the cries in the corridor beyond. Alarm bells would be rung, lockdowns activated. By this time Bill Morris was out of the main gate and half-way across the yard. This was his most dangerous stretch. A wide and clear expanse of concrete, he could be seen by anyone and everyone, but he was lucky. A police van was leaving the site at that very moment. He ran to it, opened the side door and slipped inside. To his ears the rolling mechanism of the door sounded like a great ship coming into harbour, great hollow metallic booming, tortured bearings, screaming hinges. He drew time from the policemen sitting up front; he was in and hidden, crouched behind their chairs in a moment that they would never recall. For them time collapsed; one minute they were strapping themselves into their seats, then a blur, then they were off and down the road. Perhaps in a dream they would see the figure approaching, eyes staring, blue light playing over his body. They would see him grab the handle to the police van door, concentrate and with all his strength draw it back far enough to slip inside. All this might be remembered by their subconscious mind, but only if they awoke in the night in a cold sweat would they ever recall it happening.

The van had stopped at the gates, pleasantries were exchanged and they were soon driving towards freedom. At a turn in the road the wind carried the sound of a siren but the men's chatter and laughter drowned out its sad refrain. After ten minutes they stopped to refuel. Bill had slipped from the van and into the Surrey countryside, closing the van door behind him.

Now he was a wanted man, a fugitive from justice. He had no money, no ID and his photograph would be dispatched to every pattern matching surveillance camera in the country. It did not matter. He stood looking at his dishevelled frame. He had lost weight in prison; he was not sure how much he had eaten, having spent much of his time in trance-like inactivity. He would have to find shelter, clothing and supplies. He would hide low for a few days whilst the initial flurry of searches blew themselves out. Whilst his image was fresh in the mind of every policeman in the country he was extremely vulnerable; he might even appear on the news. In a few days things would settle down and he would be able to move more freely.

The warm sun illuminated a glade of cow-parsley and late blue-bells. A white and orange butterfly floated between the confetti umbels. Liberty was sweet. At the top of hill, rising out of a glade of exotic trees, was a roof-top. The house was secluded. It would be perfect. He could feel a hunger gnawing at his insides, but he did not know whether it was motivated by the need to feed or his newfound addiction.

FIVE

Patrick Manee emerged from the airless underground into the crisp evening of the Embankment. People drifted away from him towards the glittering lights of the West End. Not for him tonight such careless pursuits. He slowly walked towards the river. The languid blackness of the tide on the turn hid fast-moving undercurrents; a drowning man had perhaps ten minutes in its inky clutches. The lights of the far bank and the illuminated façades of the buildings were almost perfectly reflected; warm lights dispelling the cold from London's dark and stinking heart. The cobweb of Hungerford Bridge marched towards him. Delicate fibres sticking the banks of the river together, ready to draw the wound closed and forever heal the city. Manee gazed into the melancholy waters below. It had been a terribly trying day. He had gained little insight from his interviews in the prison. The emptiness he felt reflected the white emptiness of the cell. Had he allowed himself to seriously entertain the ideas he had been formulating about Bill Morris he could have foreseen his escape. Somehow there had been some barrier, a denial of the evidence that had prevented him talking openly to the authorities. It begged the question who to tell. Society was not composed of a hierarchy of the learned and wise. Bureaucracy seemed a woeful substitute for the Wisdom of Solomon's court; but who was in a position to measure reality against mythology? The guards all had the same story. They had been vaguely aware of Bill's movements, of seeing a form approach them, his prison garb so familiar to them, moving in and out of their peripheral vision; but they were all confused as to the exact course of events. The only man Manee had been unable to question was a guard whose arm had been broken. Surgeons were apparently going to have to work through the night to stabilise the splinters of bone and reconnect severed nerves. The radiographer had said that the wound looked like it had been sustained in a car-crash.

For Manee this element of the escape fascinated him. At certain times Bill seemed imbued with super-human strength. The same had been true of Lilly. Police records had given numerous examples of such feats. People had lifted cars off trapped children in accidents, alcoholics and drug abusers had overcome innumerable police in moments of frenzy, but well documented events were rare. One report, from a coroner in France had described the accidental death of a boxer, killed by an apparently super-human punch in a competition. The whole thing had been televised. Manee decided to pursue this link at a later date. In the here and now he had other things to worry about.

'Detective Inspector, I'm sorry to keep you waiting.' Edward Spinks must have approached from the underground. Manee had been so absorbed by the gentle ebb and flow of the water and his own thoughts he had not seen him approach. He glanced at his watch. Eight fifteen, where had the time gone? He inwardly chastised himself for poor observation.

'I have only been here a moment myself.' He looked around. 'Was Ms Sibilski unable to join us?'

'I have arranged to meet her on one of the restaurant boats on the water; it is a little colder than I had anticipated, but I thought out in the open we could talk more freely. There is one a little further upstream. The food is actually quite bearable. Have you eaten?' Manee was taken aback for a moment. On reflection he had not eaten since the night before.

'No, come to think of it, I haven't. Lead the way. I'd be intrigued to hear what conclusions you two have come to.'

After a short walk, they came to a large vessel moored at

one end of a long system of connected jetties. On board, wrapped up in a long wool coat, was Agneta Sibilski. She was alone on deck, in the prow of the vessel, in one of three metal chairs arranged around a circular table bearing bread, olives, bottles of red and white wine and assorted glasses. She rose from her seat as they approached.

'Mr. Manee, thank you for joining us. Edward seems to have an eye for the melodramatic. But when the wind dies down it is almost romantic.' She held out her hand. 'I hope you don't mind me starting without you.' They took their seats.

The bread was still warm and the wine was infused with spice. The water lapped gently at the sides of the boat and Manee allowed himself for the first time that day to relax a little into his chair.

It was Edward Spinks who began. 'Detective Inspector...' Manee interjected.

'Please, call me Patrick. As soon as I start drinking I'm off duty.'

Edward began again. 'Patrick. The authorities have taken my nephew into care in the last few days. The government is setting up a camp for gifted children, and my nephew is one of these. He has never exhibited any remarkable talents; as far as we were aware, he is a perfectly well-adjusted, happy, normal child.'

For a moment Manee began to worry that he had been brought here on a false pretext; but how could they know of his new posting? He was not yet in a position to help this boy or interject on his behalf anyway. Spinks continued. 'No one seems to have a proper explanation for why the government has taken these children away. They tell us it is to protect them, but this can't be the whole story. The children could be protected by their families, at home. We believe that the government is worried about their potential, what they might become. Nobody in the press seems to be asking about gifted adults.' Agneta Sibilski took up their argument. In the subdued electric light on board ship, her silky voice seemed all the more exotic and alluring.

'We believe that Bill Morris is one such gifted adult. We

have come to the conclusion that he has the ability in some subtle way to locally control subjective time.' The vowels rolled off her tongue, their warmth and that of the wine were a heady mix.

Manee leaned towards her. His eyes looked deep into hers. 'Go on...'

'Such a man is dangerous, powerful. By distorting our view of reality and stealing our time he makes us vulnerable. Time is always an advantage in argument, in combat. We think the government knows this and is afraid of the children. Perhaps they want to use them, to control them, to harness their power in some way.'

A waiter politely interrupted them. They ordered and when he had left them in peace, Spinks continued.

'We want to know what happened to Bill Morris. If we are right, this could be the future of my nephew, Daniel and goodness knows how many others who are at risk of turning into him, becoming some kind of beast.'

Manee looked at the two of them over his wine glass. 'That isn't everything, is it? You have already told me you know nothing of Bill Morris. How can you be afraid of something you know nothing about?

He saw Edward and Agneta exchange conspiratorial glances. It was Agneta who spoke first. 'If we share what we know with you, you must promise us you will share with us in return.' Manee nodded slowly.

'I will tell you everything I can, though you must realise I am bound by certain regulations.'

This seemed to satisfy them and Agneta continued. 'We believe Bill Morris is not the only adult with these powers. My colleague and boss, Kevin Masters, is another such creature. After you interviewed us both following Bill Morris' disappearance I decided to analyse our own company. It was something Kevin had expressly forbidden but he was clearly going off the rails and something you said to me that day made me go the extra mile. I have studied our business in the same manner as I have studied so many others and the parallels are clear. Kevin is a ruthless man, Patrick; a man that lives outside the law, he has amassed a great deal of money through dubious practise and for my part I have indirectly assisted him.'

'Is this some sort of confession, Ms Sibilski? You must realise that I am first and foremost a policeman.'

'What I have to say transcends such trivialities.' Agneta's face remained calm. 'Kevin has been acting strangely for the last few months. He has had no interest in the business. He has neglected things. A few days ago he came to the office. He was dishevelled; he had lost weight. He was distant, confused. I thought he was drunk or drugged, but when I went near him, he changed. He bore down on me, close, as if trying to kiss me. I was going to fight him off, but I became weak, tired. I don't remember what happened next but perhaps I passed out. When I awoke he was gone. I was alone on the floor of the office. I did not appear to have been molested but I was bruised and confused. Perhaps I had fallen, dead-weight, from my chair, I don't know. I was so shaken I called Edward.' Instinctively she reached across the table and touched his hand. 'We went to Kevin's house that night together. I wanted to confront him, to demand an explanation. We found his door open, no lights on inside. Somewhere in the house we could hear a radio, but it was de-tuned, just hissing static. Kevin was there. He was catatonic, staring forward, in some kind of ecstatic state. Across his lap was draped a woman. Her eyes were open, but she seemed unable to see. We thought perhaps she was dead, but her breathing, though shallow, was steady. When we touched her she was cold like a corpse. We tried to rouse Kevin but he was insensitive to everything we tried. We carried the woman to our car, covered her in blankets and tried to revive her. She started to shake uncontrollably, presumably in some kind of shock.'

'And Kevin, Did you go back to see what happened to him?'

'Yes, we went back to the house. By the time we arrived the house was empty. His car was gone.

'This is all very interesting, Ms Sibilski, but how can you be sure they were not just under the influence of some kind of drug? Any number of things could have had a similar effect. I'm sure the hospital will tell you the same.' Manee motioned then to silence as food arrived in a fleet of steaming dishes.

'At first the hospital treated us casually. They thought the same as you, but this was three days ago and they have been in contact with us several times since then. The woman has not recovered properly; they think she may be in some kind of coma-like state. They say it is something they have seen only once before. A young girl, transported down to them from another hospital in north Wales where they had run out of beds. The girl had been attacked by a gifted child. It took her three weeks to wake up. She remembers almost nothing of the whole period. It prompted the hospital to look for similar cases. They have found two dozen. There is more.'

Edward Spinks placed his cutlery down carefully on his plate. 'Yes, I went to see Bill Morris's wife, Margo. I'd met her once or twice before; nice woman, successful in her own right. She had left with the family to the States, but she came back last week. She phoned Bill's office and ended up speaking to me. She seemed distraught, a mess. I offered to meet her, to offer some help. She wouldn't let me come to her house and instead insisted we meet in a park.' His eyes were flashing now. His hands moved excitedly, animated. 'She told me Bill had attacked her several times. She doesn't remember the details, she can't put into words what happened, but she was so frightened that she ran away.' Manee recalled Morris's face against the perspex and shuddered. There was something in those eyes that was fearful.

'Whilst she was in the States she had another shock. She caught her own daughter one night in a hotel room attacking her son. She described seeing the girl standing over the boy in the same way Bill had stood her. He was sleeping or unconscious, and the girl was in some kind of ecstatic trance. She said the sight had nearly driven her from her wits but somehow she had found the strength to get across the room and break the connection between them.'

'Could it not be that the daughter was merely copying something she had seen her father do? Some sort of game? Children are natural mimics.' Manee said this but he knew the answer already. Bill Morris's daughter had to be another gifted child. Perhaps the condition could be inherited. The image of this child absorbing her brother's precious life filled him with horror but he had to be sure they believed what they were saying.

'No, No...' Spinks was even more animated. 'She described how the air between then and around her daughter had become dense, she described it as 'sticky' when she tried to pull her daughter away from her brother, but as soon as they had made contact she felt herself becoming overcome in the same manner as when her husband had attacked her. She broke free and pulled her son away by his ankles.'

'And what happened to the children?'

'The daughter wouldn't speak of what happened. She was in some kind of daze for several hours, but when she regained full consciousness she was tearful and reticent. The boy woke up and seemed to be completely unharmed. It was the next day that Bill's wife decided to return to England.'

'And where are they now?' Manee spoke through a mouthful of spaghetti and meatballs. 'I would like to interview them, especially the girl.' Agneta broke in.

'When they arrived at Heathrow the three of them were taken aside by the airport staff and interviewed for an hour. They told Margo that her daughter was at risk in the country, though they refused to elaborate as to exactly what the threats were. Margo asked to return to America but they refused, stating something to do with national security. They took her daughter into care. You can imagine there was a terrible scene.

'We believe she has been taken to North Wales with the other gifted children. Margo has been told very little. She refused to go back to their old family home; currently she is living with me.'

'And you have been told nothing about the girl?'

283

'The authorities are being evasive; they tell us she is well and being looked after and will be in touch soon, but you can imagine what this is doing to Margo.' For all Manee's hunger the food before him was beginning to lose its flavour. He had to think, to arrange his thoughts. How had the authorities been able to pick up the girl at the airport? What were the government's ultimate plans for the children? Did they perhaps know more than he had credited them with? He pushed his plate away.

'Edward, Agneta, you have been very helpful. I want to help you and I think I can. If you will excuse me I will make some phone calls. I'll try to find out where the child is and then I would like to speak to Margo Morris. Edward, are you in contact with your nephew?' Edward nodded in the affirmative. 'Say nothing to him of this. All lines into the compound in Wales are tapped. As soon as I know more I will call you.' He placed some money on the table. 'And thank you for dinner. I will be in touch soon.'

Agneta rose to follow him, but Edward held her back.

'Give him time. We don't know if we can trust him. Perhaps he doesn't believe us. Perhaps he knows a lot more than he is letting on.'

As Patrick Manee walked back up the jetty his mind was in disarray. The sooner he was in Wales, the sooner he would understand the children. He needed to get access to someone higher up the food chain. First Bill Morris and then Kevin Masters had turned bad. It was not a lone occurrence. How many more of them were there? As he walked up the dark streets he could not help looking left and right into the darker alleyways. Tonight the streets of London were teeming with hundreds of thousands of people with time on their hands. Unbeknown to them there were at least two hunters out there who would be more than happy to relieve them of that luxury.

SIX

'Tell me about him, love; I know you want to, but you are too shy.' Margaret Darmer placed a toasted sandwich on the table in front of Suzi.

'Tell you about who? Margaret, really there is nothing to tell you.' Suzi looked away from her former fiancée's mother and concentrated on the steaming bacon and egg sandwich in front of her. 'This is lovely, thank you. It's just what I needed.'

'Come on now. You can't hide it from me. I'm old enough to be your mother, you know. You are a beautiful woman and beautiful women do not walk around France for long without attracting attention.' For Suzi, Michael's death now seemed a lifetime ago, so much had happened since she had lost her poor dear man. She had taken him for granted much of the time, but she had loved him. If only she had known the effect she was having on him, she could have sent him away; he might have been saved. But now he was gone and his mother was sitting in her house, making her egg and bacon sandwiches and asking after her new love interest. It was so very wrong.

'You know Michael would not have wanted you to be alone Suzi. You are a good woman, a strong and kind woman. You will make someone very happy some day. My Michael was happy. He just did not always know it.'

Suzi looked across at the kind woman sitting in front of her. They were seeing a great deal of each other lately; they were comfort for each other and had taken solace in each other's arms numerous times over the past month. In such moments memories of Michael had flooded back to her, making him briefly real again. There had been times immediately following his death that she had been almost unable to see his face in her mind's eye. Thankfully that time had passed. Margaret was the concrete manifestation of Michael in her life. His memory of late had however to share space with that of Miguel. Suzi was desperate to tell Margaret of Miguel, to keep him secret seemed a cruel disloyalty; but it was too soon, feelings were too raw and in spite of her deeper understanding of her own special relationship with time; convention and propriety still instructed her feelings of guilt.

Miguel had shown her sides to the gift that she had only been dimly aware of. In moments alone, her cat snuggled into the crook of her arm, she had practised controlling it. The throb of the central heating, with practise, could be separated into the individual heart-beats of the water pump; the whine of a distant police siren slowed to a comforting lullaby. In these times her own mind had remained free to think at its normal rate; she could make a night last for a week or hold the moment before the dawn in a glorious, patient limbo. There was a downside to this practise. She had always found the experience emotionally and physically painful and although her control over the process was become more refined, the pain was unrelenting. Miguel had never described any feelings of pain associated with his gift. For him it came in the guise of a peaceful, restful equilibrium, a sanctuary from the anger and misery that had tainted his youth and, in his lowest hours, pierced his present.

Suzi was not naturally a cold, logical thinker. She had tried to apply logic to Michael's suicide in the fuller knowledge of her gift and had come to the conclusion that her own success and skills had been, at least in part, to his expense. She had unwittingly parasitized him for twelve years. On hearing of his death she had unwittingly drawn from her PA. This much was clear. The poor girl had now made a full recovery, but had chosen to find employment elsewhere.

It was during one of the gift-extended dawns that Suzi realised that what was true of Michael and Julie was also true of Michael's mother and this realisation filled her with cold horror. Margaret was a font of kindness, a dear, sweet woman for whom personal sacrifice was a commonplace event. Recently Margaret had seemed slightly wan and tired, but Suzi had attributed this to their recent loss. The possibility that she herself might be contributing to Margaret's condition filled her with a sudden and violent self-loathing. At first she had avoided Margaret, making excuses until she could put into words the tangled mess of thoughts that were keeping her awake at night. When it became impossible to hide away any longer she only allowed herself to come into contact with Margaret when she was acutely aware of own thoughts. It was during such soul-searching that she had felt herself reaching out to Margaret. The desire to feed, albeit at a low level, seemed immediate and automatic and once the process had begun she felt the gentle chronic pain that came with it. She realised she had always lived with that familiar pain. She had stepped into it every day with Michael in the same way as she might step into a favourite pair of shoes. The dull ache could not be denied, but it could be controlled. When it has initially fired within her, the horror had made her physically sick. But amidst the confused emotions was the control she needed, control she had harnessed in those lonely hours. The ache could be disciplined.

'If you can't tell me about your new man now, dear, I'll be patient. But you know where I am if you need me.' Once again Margaret had been a rock.

'I don't think I have emotions spare for someone in my life at the moment.'

'I know dear. You need a little time to become content with yourself. I feel rather the same at the minute.' There was something in Margaret's voice that made Suzi look at her more closely.

'Hang on you... all this talk about me is just an overture, isn't it? Have you got something to tell me?' Margaret blushed immediately and leant across to grab an escaped piece of bacon.

'Well, that would be telling, wouldn't it? And as you are

so secretive, I'm not sure I want to tell you. Besides, it's probably nothing, just the fantasies of a woman who has missed the bus!'

'Come on, you can't wheedle out of it that easily! Tell me who the lucky man is. You dark horse! Is he a dark horse?' The two of them rolled up into laughter. It took Margaret a while before she could speak again.

'I don't know, it all seems so silly really. I mean, here I am, nearly fifty-five and this very smartly-dressed man bumps into me in the supermarket, discusses the price of coffee with me and then asks me on a date.'

'My God, how crafty you are! And when is this date?'

'Crafty? What rubbish. He was ever so sweet, well-spoken and terribly young. He can barely be forty-five, far too young for me, obviously. I can't imagine what he could see in someone like me, but there is no accounting for taste!'

'And...'

'Well we had a date, actually, last Friday, just a little drink, down by the river. The old Anchor. We had a nice evening, very relaxed; I don't know where the time went. It got to eleven and I asked him to take me home. He seemed very gallant. I asked him if he wanted to try some of that coffee we had been talking about and he refused, on the condition that he would see me again soon.'

'And does this toy boy have a name?' Suzi was smiling broadly now. Margaret's eyes were more alive than she had seen them in ages.

'Yes, his name is Kevin, Kevin Masters.'

SEVEN

The Anglo-American Ambassador for Security Co-operation leant back on his chair and put his feet on the table.

'Containment, George, containment: one word, very simple and straightforward. Re-read the legislation, which, I might add, your own interior minister was complicit, nay, indispensable in drafting. Containment is part of the package and that is the line we have been following up to now and will continue to follow until such a time as it becomes indefensible.'

The British Minister for internal affairs looked at the man's patent-leather soles resting on his two-hundred year old table and sighed heavily.

'You know as well as I do that it is not as simple as that. You can't classify these children as terrorist threats. They aren't, for Christ's sake! They have no connection with terrorism, they aren't colluding with terrorists and they don't belong to any identifiable racial or religious group. The people of this country will not buy it. Europe will not buy it. There will be riots; we have already seen some. It won't work in the states and it won't work here.'

The General pushed himself further back in his chair. 'This is the problem with you, George. It has been the problem of Western Europe for a very long time and it really sticks in my throat that you still haven't got it.'

George Norton-Smith looked at him blankly. 'I know what you are referring to and I'd rather you didn't talk about it here. There is no telling who might be listening in this building. In Europe every wall has ears. You should know that by now. Most of those ears have been put there by your lot.'

'Who cares? This is your problem, you don't seem to realise that it isn't just a few fruit-loops at the top of the pile who think along these lines. It is the entire establishment. Economics, power and control: nothing else matters. Money buys you the economic position, economic positions give you power, power generates fear and this gives you control. In the west we use this mantra all the time, but every now and again we can short circuit the process. Fear leads people to hand over power. They are totally predictable. In the gifted children we have a wonderful opportunity and you are wasting it in Europe with your pathetic mincing and prevaricating. You put the gifted into care for their safety. Foolish, ridiculous, totally wrong! We will put them into care because they are dangerous. Don't you read the papers? Don't you have secret intelligence in this country? Some of these kids screw with your mind. They need to be locked up. They are a threat to society.'

'I've heard all this before. But it doesn't cut any ice here. You can't put fifty thousand kids into custody like that, it's madness. It'll cripple the country and God knows how many you will have in the States once you have completed your study; a quarter of a million, half a million, who knows?'

The General got up and paced the room. 'Therein lies your inherent stupidity, George. Totally fucking stupid, so literal, so little imagination. We have absolutely no intention of making some stupid bloody by-the-book study of every scraggy kid in the states and then locking the whole lot of them up. What good is that for Pete's sake? Where is the economics of that? Where is the power? No, it'd be a disaster. No, it's much simpler than that. We'll put a few thousand gifted into care: mainly Blatino kids, mainly poor kids. Then we'll put a few high profile kids in there with them: a few sons of heads of industry, a few pop stars' kids; it will put the fear of God into the whole rat's nest. That's what makes it worthwhile, there is your power. Any number of sons of senators will be gifted. There must be hundreds of Blue-chip gifted kids. Don't you understand? It's leverage George, unbelievable, incredible leverage. We out your child, we get to keep it. You pull the party line, everyone is happy, no-one need know.'

'You are mad. You can't possibly mean what you are saying! The American people will never fall for that. You won't turn a whole population against the best in their society. It is ridiculous, impossible.'

'We have done it before, Minister, and we'll do it again. Remember The Crucible and McCarthyism? The poor multitude doesn't clamour for economic equality; they only want equality of misery for the upper echelons of society. They might scream whilst you take their child away. But they will scream a bloody sight louder if you don't take a senator's child away for the same crime. Don't you see? The gifted are godless. They are an abomination and they are a threat to the very fabric of our society. Given half a chance they will murder us in our beds. They are the antithesis of fair play, of decency and everything that is good about my country. That is the story we are going to tell the press, that is the story my boss the President is going to tell the American people and that is the story I suggest you tell the British people.'

'You are totally mad. I am certain the Prime Minister will have something to say about this. It is unspeakable.'

'You are a funny man George. I know your politics; I've been studying you for a while. This mock shock horror is so much smoke. You should blow it up your own ass, not mine. And as for your boss; I think you'll find he is in remarkable agreement with my boss. It's just a good job there are a few people in this world with some political balls. Think about it George. If you don't there will be any number of your scurrying friends who will.'

EIGHT

Brian slung his rucksack high on his back. He had maps, a compass, pencil, note book, binoculars and a digital camera with mirror lens and three-times tele-converter, a torch with spare batteries, fake ID, food and a flask. He was wearing several layers and carried waterproofs just in case he had a long spell up on the hill. He cycled from Llangollen to Ruthin avoiding the high passes and then cut across country. The day was fresh and beautiful; visibility would be good. The country roads were busier than usual; the misplaced residents of Denbigh had holed up in the houses of neighbours and family in the surrounding district. Many were driving to the barricades to shout obscenities at the police. He had thought of riding with the crowd, but had not wanted to make himself known to the police. The fields were green and fresh with recent rain and the paths were muddy but passable. He carried his bike over a few stiles and low dry stone walls covered in white-flowered blackthorn, checked his map and left his bike tied up against a tree. There were sheep in some fields but otherwise there was not a soul around. After another two miles skirting mainly empty fields he came to the disused quarry which was his target. He slipped beneath the barbed wire and past the pre-requisite 'Keep out' and 'Danger' signs, through swathes of bluebells and the last few wood anemones. Their heady scent was almost intoxicating in the still air between the beech and birch trees. He approached the far side of the copse and slipped down steep banks of spoil from the quarry. He had to be careful not to burst through the wood into the space beyond. The woodland stopped abruptly at the man-made precipice that was the quarry edge. Through the last remaining trees he found the rudimentary seat he had made on his previous visit. He made himself comfortable, pulled out his binoculars and scanned the scene.

Through the swaying branches of scantily-leaved trees he had a fairly good view of the approach road to the town, the main barricade and the maze of streets that filled the extended apron of what had been the mediaeval city. On the top of the hill the crenulations of the thirteenth-century castle wall were illuminated in a crisp spring light; the remains of the great portico with its multiple layers, now toothless with neither portcullis nor gate, still grinned down over the town. The castle walls were echoed by the remains of old town walls, winding along a broken contour. To one side the strangely sad aqueduct-like arches and lone tower of the unfinished church of St David, unpopular protestant erection of Robert Dudley, The Church of St. Marcellas, the Eglwys Wen and St. Mary's. The grand design was knitted together with rows of neat houses of various periods, arranged in swirls from the main street. The whole was nestled in the Clywd valley; the Clywd Range stood as a backdrop of green and purple sentinels guarding the town from the infinite distance of the horizon. It was a beautiful spot, but Brian knew he had to look beneath the idyllic veneer. He watched the movements of children and policemen, moving in loose groups around the town streets. In the middle distance was a school recreation ground and a large number of young children were noisily playing games and chasing each other and various balls and frisbees around the field. There were a few adults among them, wandering slowly between them, seemingly friendly but rather bored. Around the High Street sat gangs of slightly older youths, some smoking, others laughing and pushing each other around. Another group of children were flying kites from the lawns outside the castle; brightly coloured deltas in reds and purples dived and soared. The scene was generally one of lazy tranquillity. The peace and quiet was however marred by the shouting and chanting that came from the main gate.

The crowd was tightly corralled together; their bristling placards like porcupine quills. A bus approached the gate from the south and the volume of the crowd rose several notches. This was the third occasion Brian had spent his vigil in the quarry. He had mixed feelings about the camp; part of him was horrified that such a group should be effectively under house arrest, having done nothing untoward, part of him longed to be with them, his special status recognised amongst them. There was some strange attraction that tugged his heart strings as he sat in the half-light of the beech-wood. These were his people, distinct and apart, though he guessed his own gifts must be weak compared to some of the more outrageous things he had heard on the news. There was something else there too, drawing him in, a need, an emptiness, some great unseen attractor. He shook off the idea. Tonight he could walk back through the quarry and return to freedom. These children were prisoners. Through the binoculars he could see that the assembled crowd carried placards with mixed messages. Some demanding access to their property, others access to their children. Brian had watched small groups of parents walking through the barricades under armed guard. The families all walked the same way, like mourners at a funeral. They met their children in a red and ochre building in the shadow of the castle. To Brian it looked like a public school or finishing college. After an hour or two they would be paraded out again, mothers constantly looking over their shoulders as if trying to catch a last glimpse.

It was wrong, very wrong, but the question remained: what could he do about it? Brian scanned the view again. Perhaps if he could capture some misdemeanour, some brutality, he might be able show it to the press. He searched through his bag for his camera, placing flask and sandwiches amongst the leaf litter.

'You have come well prepared.'

The voice nearly made him jump out of his skin. He turned on his seat and came face to face with a man in his early thirties. The shock of this unexpected intrusion caused him to lean back sharply, his makeshift seat collapsed and he fell backwards towards the edge of the precipice. He was about to call out when strong hands fell upon him, grabbing him and dragging him back into the cover of the leaves.

'Watch it young man! It's a long way down if you go that way.' Brian shrugged free of the man's grip and defensively grabbed his belongings to his chest.

'I wasn't doing anything, just walking through the woods, wondered what was going on.'

'That's okay; you don't have to explain anything to me.' The voice was calm, disinterested. 'I noticed you up here a few days ago. I just wondered what you were doing. Are you some kind of investigative journalist?'

The reference to him as a professional pricked Brian's ego. 'No, actually I'm training to be an archaeologist. I was studying this old quarry. It's very interesting from an archaeological point of view.' The man nodded in agreement.

'Yes, I'm sure you are right. The town is also very interesting from that point of view as well. Have you noticed anything that interests you... in the town?'

Brian's insides felt like snakes in a barrel. He glanced back towards the castle, trying to avoid eye contact. 'Yes, well, very interesting ruins, 12th century I would guess, built to subdue the Welsh, by the English. I'd like to get up there to have a closer look, but the town is all sealed up.'

'Yes, like a siege really. Would you like to have a closer look? I can get you in and out. I have some authority there.' Brian looked at him sideways.

'You some sort of security then, for the compound?'

'Yes, in a way I am. Though I guess the authorities are more worried about people getting out rather than stopping people like yourself getting in.'

'I'm fine; I'd rather not go in there to be honest.'

'Are you nervous? What do you think is going on in there?' Brian swallowed hard. Who was this guy and why wasn't he just arresting him.

'Look, if you are going to arrest me just do it will you. Otherwise I'm off home. I haven't done anything wrong, I haven't taken any pictures. If you don't mind I'd just like to go.' The man smiled.

'Brian, you are free to go whenever you like. I took the liberty of looking you up. You'd be amazed at the face recognition facilities the police have these days. You are on our records as someone who should be in the complex. I can let you in now if you want. But something tells me you'd rather I didn't. I think you are right to be nervous. If I were you and I was as resourceful as you obviously are, I think I would have done the same. I think you are staking us out; keeping an eye on us. I think that's the best thing you could possibly be doing. I have no intention of interfering with that. Just try to be a bit more discreet.' Brian was shocked.

'Who are you and why are you saying this?'

'My name is Detective Inspector Patrick Manee. I'm here as part of the police presence. I'm studying the place myself, but from the inside. I have as many misgivings about this as you do, but my name is not on their list.' He smiled reassuringly. 'Your secret is safe with me.'

'Like Schindler?' He did not know what had inspired him to say it, but it seemed somehow appropriate. Brian looked at the man sitting on the tree stump before him, piercing eyes, an honest smile. Manee was silent for a moment. 'Lets hope it doesn't come to that, shall we?' He handed Brian a card with a number on it. You can call me here, but don't say anything incriminating over the phone. Just say hi and I'll give you instructions if the coast is clear. You might be useful to me, being on the outside of the security cordon. I might need to get messages out.' Brian was taken aback; this was not what he was expecting at all.

'I'm not sure I want to be some police patsy on the outside, but if I notice anything I'm worried about I might give you a ring.'

'That's just fine. I wouldn't expect you to say anything different. Here, take these. You might find them useful.' He handed Brian a pair of slim binoculars. 'I think you'll find these are a bit better than what you've been using. They're anti-glare as well, so they won't be able to see you from the town.' Brian gingerly took them; they were superb.

'Are you sure?' His instinctive, reflexive manners annoyed him, he suddenly felt like a child again.

'Yes, I might need to get them off you when the police want them back. But I can always say I dropped them down the ravine. I'm supposed to be checking out the new intake, sixteen to eighteen year olds. The age range is creeping up.'

'What would they do if they wanted to imprison adults? Do you think that is going to happen?' Manee ran his hands over his stubble.

'I don't know. It would be difficult. It all depends on numbers. The prisons are full to bursting already; I can't see them attempting it. It also begs the question of whether or not they could contain them. Don't you agree?'

'What do you mean? Do you think there is any truth in these stories about the gifted? I can't say I've noticed that I've got any special talents.'

'Maybe you just don't know how to use them yet.' Manee smiled wryly. 'To be honest I'm not sure what to believe. From what I've seen it might not be a good idea to develop your skills. There seem to be side effects, problems. If I were you, I'd keep my head down and not try too hard. Right, I'm off. Keep your eyes open and if you see anything untoward, you know where I am.' He turned and began to walk back down towards the village.

'Thanks!' Brian called after the disappearing figure. Things could most definitely have gone a lot worse.

'No problem, take care, good luck!'

In a few minutes the wood was silent. Brian scanned the streets of Denbigh with his new binoculars. Up on the hill a policeman was arguing with a small group of kids. He now had a job to do. Was this guy genuine? Or was he playing him for a fool? It was a difficult one. He un-wrapped his sandwiches and took a mouthful of coffee. There was a frantic crash and the sound of claws on wood as a pair of squirrels chased each other around a tree. The human world might be going to pot but nature carried on regardless. He rebuilt his makeshift seat and prepared for a long afternoon of observation.

NINE

Suzi looked at her watch for the hundredth time that evening. The airport was quiet now, and the vast space just served to make her loneliness more complete. They had decided that Miguel should fly into a small airport thereby avoiding the circus of security checks that awaited passengers at any of the central hubs, but that had been a mistake. Now it appeared that the peripheral airports went through the same pointless procedures but with a fraction of the staff and resources. The thought of her poor, gentle man, struggling with his less than perfect English to answer such facile questions filled Suzi with rage. They had chosen to stay apart until the coroner's report on Carlos's death was complete. They were worried that borders might suddenly close down in the present climate of fear that was sweeping across Europe. The papers were full of terrorism and stories about the gifted and in some less salubrious journals the two had begun to merge together. It was now clear to Suzi that the government had established new ways of identifying the gifted. Her own powers were becoming somewhat more attuned and sitting for the last four hours perched on a ridiculously uncomfortable plastic chair she had been identifying them herself as they came through customs. Whatever the government was using was obviously very accurate, because the initial flood of jetsam never included a gifted individual. Only an hour or two later would they pass through, eyes down, fatigue written on their brows. It was difficult for her to explain how she knew who they were. There was something about the way they carried themselves, the way their eyes scanned you, dwelling, just a little too long.

There was also some strange attraction there, familiarity, recognition and comfort.

Miguel was the last to appear. She imagined him, polite as ever, motioning the pretty girls and the elderly to go ahead of him in the queue, standing aside for the bossy business people. When their eyes met it was as if chains had snapped around her heart. Her eyes filled with tears and she hugged him to her with every ounce of her strength. They stayed like that, locked together for the longest time.

TEN

Daniel sat in the sunshine on the grass banks of the slope under Denbigh Castle. It was another beautiful bright spring day and the town, full of children and youngsters, was like some sort of holiday resort. Things had turned out surprisingly well. His room-mates, James and Michael, were around his age, quite well-to-do and both had been sent away to public school. They had helped him to settle in; knowing the ropes of living away from home, they were well prepared and had brought lots of things to while away the time. They also understood his homesickness. Lessons had begun but the children were at such mixed levels and abilities that it had soon become apparent that grouping them in terms of age was pointless. The school chose to open its doors to everyone and the children went into whichever lessons took their fancy. That was not to say they were free to do whatever they liked. They were constantly monitored and their progress and understanding checked and assessed by a small army of researchers. It was clear that they were in some sort of grand experiment. Daniel had been giving some considerable thought to this. He was aware that the gifted children were believed to parasitize their peers in some way, though he had never noticed this ability in himself. He had wondered for a while if they had made a mistake. Perhaps he was there as some kind of 'negative control' or maybe he was the token normal boy on which all the others would feed. If that was the case then he had not noticed it and everyone seemed very nice. Problems with the staff, however, had emerged. He'd noticed issues developing after a week or two. Initially they had been friendly and helpful, alert and involved, asking their seemingly innocuous questions as if they really cared. This had slowly changed. Many of the staff had become short-tempered and abrasive, impatient and temperamental. James and Michael had said they were probably feeling the effects of homesickness themselves, they had seen it in the masters at their old schools. They had, after all, been separated from their friends and families too and after the first few weeks the novelty of being in a new place wore off. This had satisfied Daniel for a few weeks, but it soon became apparent that many of the staff were mentally deteriorating whilst their charges seemed to be thriving. Daniel himself felt remarkably well; when he phoned home he almost felt embarrassed, hearing his poor mother trying to be brave whilst he was enjoying the time with his new friends in this big medieval playground. He was woken from his thoughts by the sounds of a crowd shouting. There was the constant noise from the gate and sometimes, when the wind gusted in a certain direction it would seem much closer, but this was different. It was definitely coming from nearby. He heard another roar, children's voices, laughing. He jumped to his feet; all around him people started running down the hill. Something was happening and he did not want to miss it. He took a shortcut down some an alleyway and across several gardens, jumping fences and skirting along walls. It was part of a complex web of escape routes he had been considering if he ever wanted to make a run for it, and this seemed to be a perfect opportunity to try that section out. As it was, he had no intention of leaving in a hurry, but he had always prided himself on his preparedness. This rat run eventually circled back onto the main street and it was here that the disturbance was centred. He burst through a hedge into the garden of the Hope and Anchor pub, ran up the old delivery alleyway and found himself in a crowd of teenagers who were jostling and baiting a strange, dishevelled figure. At first Daniel did not recognise him; his clothes were in disarray, his eyes wild and pleading. He was bleeding where he had fallen and vomit and beer soaked his shirt. He wheeled around at the assembled crowd.

'You did this to me... Look at me you bastards... Look what you've done!' He pointed madly in all directions, lost his footing, slipped and fell again.

It was the old man who had initially welcomed Daniel to the town. He watched him, sliding around on the floor, in horrified amazement, frozen to the spot with fear.

There was a squeal of wheels, a clattering of boots and the sound of sirens as a police van pulled into the main street and half dozen police jumped out in riot gear. They fanned out across the square, insectoid and intimidating, their shields and batons clattering, their faces hidden behind tinted visors, respirators covering their mouths. The crowd withdrew from the unfortunate man and he was quickly lifted up and placed into the back of the van. Daniel had seen the same police at the barricade but he had not imagined they would be policing inside the perimeter. An eerie silence fell over the assembled crowd. The police returned to their vehicles and, lights flashing, sped away. Two familiar faces appeared out of the crowd. James and Michael, their faces flushed, picking their way between the bigger boys amongst whom Daniel had found himself caught.

'We hadn't expected you to be hanging out with this lot.' Michael whispered through gritted teeth. 'That was horrible, baiting the poor old boy.'

'I wasn't with these guys; I've only just got here.' Daniel took them aside. 'I didn't really see what happened. What did they do to him?'

'Well, nothing really, you know, just the usual. He'd been drinking very heavily, all morning. I guess they just pushed him over the line.'

'What do you mean, just the usual?' Daniel looked between their two faces. 'What is the usual? Why do that?' He could feel his face reddening; he had to try to calm down. He didn't want to cry in front of the boys.

'Some of us can... control the gift, a bit better than others.' James placed an arm round Daniel's shoulders. 'I've been talking to lots of people; it seems with practise we can all do it. I'm pretty rubbish, but some of the older boys can focus quite well.'

'But what does it do?' Daniel was beginning to worry now, all around him were older children and young adults; frightening enough at the best of times, but some of these really did have strange powers.

'It's all about time. You know that. We borrow a little here, a little there, just a little, you understand, and no one notices. But if lots of people focus on one person, that's different. It messes you up.'

'But why did they pick on him? He is such a nice guy.'

'Some people are very sensitive; they almost bring it on themselves. You'll notice this yourself soon enough. Don't worry, I'm sure they'll sort him out, get him away from this place and he'll be fine.' Daniel fell silent for a moment, he was thinking through different possibilities.

'This is bad, very bad, don't you see?' He looked them straight in the eye. 'This will get out, soon everyone will know. People will panic; there'll be more attacks, everyone will hate you, will hate the gifted, they'll want to wipe you out.'

'Hang on, hang on.' James's face was close to his. 'Not so much of the you, you, you. You are one of us as well; you might not know it yet, you might not realise, but we know.' He looked at Michael, who was nodding sagely. 'Soon you'll be able to tell too. If they come for us, they'll come for you too. We are all in this together.'

All in this together. The phrase hung in the air between them. This was the question; what exactly were they involved in?

ELEVEN

When Bill Morris first entered the grounds of the house in the Surrey hills he knew he was not alone. He could not hear anyone moving within, and there was no car on the long gravel drive, but occupied houses always 'breathed' in a way that empty ones did not. He did wonder about leaving the property for another one; things might be so much easier if he could find some city banker's weekend retreat rather than have to take over one with a sitting tenant. Still, he was tired and very hungry and a house with people in it would be more likely to be stocked with supplies. Even in his confused state he knew he should lie low for a while. The perimeter was defended by a high wall topped with broken bottles, the front a mediaeval assortment of railings and spikes. He opened the gate and walked through. As he crossed the long drive he sank into a dilation trance, dwelling in every footfall, gently adjusting each pebble as his feet made contact with them before applying his weight. If it had not been for the joy that accompanied the release of the gift, the journey would have felt interminable and the exposure, terrifying. Had anyone been watching from the house they would have seen a heavy man in a grey T-shirt and jeans run cat-like and silently across to the side of the house. The likelihood of anyone actually staring out of the window at that point in time was small and he glanced in through the dining room windows as he passed. There was no one. He crept to the rear of the house, keeping himself pressed against the pebble-dash. He glanced into the kitchen windows; again nobody to be seen.

He gently tried the back door, and to his great satisfaction found it open. A twist of the wrist and he was inside. He closed his eyes and breathed slowly. In a few moments he would have food, real drink, maybe a bath and a shave and then a sleep. First he had to sort out whoever else was in the building.

In the large front bedroom, sprawled on the bed, lay the lady of the house. Jill Heurvey had somehow managed to close the curtains and build a nest of cotton sheets about her body. She lay in a half conscious, torpid state. She had felt the migraine come on the moment her ex-husband drove away with the children. It was not so much seeing them go that upset her; she and her husband had split amicably enough, they had been almost callously grown up about it, she still liked him and he deserved to spend time with the kids and heaven knew how hard she found it to look after them. They tired her out. In many ways she blamed them for the breakdown of the marriage. Motherhood had turned her into an obsessive harpy. She knew that and who wanted to be married to a harpy? It was not the stress of seeing her husband happy after her own less than successful attempts to find his replacement. He had slipped off with another woman as soon as the papers came through. She had got the house and the four-by-four and the kids, but had not found a novel comfort zone to slide into. In fact she quite liked to see him. He was always friendly enough and they usually had quite a laugh. The problem had been the glare off the car's rear window as it drove down the street. It had only flashed for a few seconds, but like a fool she had not been able to draw herself away. She knew herself so well, knew the triggers, but maybe in a pique of martyrdom she had let it happen. The sun flashed in the rear window, and then the lights and pain flashed in her head. As her eyes had 'gone' she had crawled upstairs and lain in the darkened room, hoping to salvage herself from it, but to no avail.

Her head was pounding, thumping with every surge of her pulse. To place her head on a pillow unleashed a cacophony of pain. Instead she bundled the sheets into loose folds and nestled into their warmth. A moment ago she thought she heard the back door. It was only for an instant, but then there had been silence. She thought that her ex had perhaps returned to the house for something or other; there was always something the children had forgotten, something they needed beyond all human understanding more than anything else in the world. She did not want her ex to see her like this. It would only evoke pity and stroking of the hair. If anyone touched her hair for the next three hours or so she would scream. But then she had not heard the car. No, it couldn't have been the back door.

Jill awoke to find her arms and legs tied together with the very sheets she had been laying amongst. Her mouth was full of something large and spongy and as soon as consciousness returned fully her body convulsed into retching to get rid of it. As her legs wrestled with her bonds, her mind wrestled with the concept of how she had come to be there. It soon became apparent that her mouth was both gagged and taped. Her migraine was much less intense and the lighting in the room somewhat faded implying several hours had passed since she had lost consciousness. She struggled against her bonds again, screaming her frustration and anger into the wadding in her mouth. She stopped; listening. Whoever had done this to her could still be in the house. The thought nearly made her gag. She lay, stock-still, angry that her own heartbeat now seemed so loud that it could cover all other sounds from below. Then she heard it. The sounds of a body of flesh moving in the bath, the squeak of skin and the reflux of water.

Bill Morris felt more human than he had done in many months. The necessity of slipping back into corporeal concerns and making good his escape had saved him from himself. It would have been all too easy to slide into madness during his time in prison. The memory of those halcyon days, his mind immersed in light and sound flooded back, but he shook it away. He had more pressing needs. He stepped out of the water and began to dry himself off.

It was wonderful to use a well-laundered towel and for a moment he almost slipped into a trance as he concentrated on its softness, feeling the caress of each individual fibre on his naked white flesh, ten thousand little lovers, twenty thousand gentle hands. He was startled from his thoughts by the sound of a car on the drive. He had not heard the gate open, but now he heard the crunch of wheels. He almost allowed the old habits of his body to overcome his newly found control. His instinct was to flee or hide. His heart-rate leapt; what should he do? Where could he hide? What would they think? These foolish notions did not persist and the steely coldness that had dominated his thought processes in prison reasserted itself. He had all the time in the world. He was the hunter, the night creature. His had the power. He would fear no man. He pulled on his trousers; some habits died slowly, ran down the stairs and peeked through the closed blinds. A large four-by-four was parked in the driveway. A man, presumably the husband, was still in the driving seat; two little girls had disembarked and were running towards the house, the youngest with a big bunch of coloured balloons which streaked along behind her.

Something strange tugged at Bill's heart as he saw her. There was some sort of physical recoil, revulsion. He shook the thought away. She was nothing but a child. He ran to the back door and double-locked it. Throwing bolts across at the top and bottom. He ran to the front door and did the same. Perhaps they could be discouraged, perhaps they would just leave. He had made a cursory survey of the house and he had seen the signs of the divorce: the slightly odd arrangement of photographs, the father placed to the back of the shelf, prominent photos of the girls with their mother, alone. It all added up. The family pictures echoed any number he had had taken of his own family. The images had stung him. His own wife had never visited him in prison. He had not seen his children since the day they had left for America. The image of his daughter came back to him now, so clever, so smart, his own little girl. Where was she now?

He hid himself out of view and listened to the giggling of the girls as they ran up to the side of the house. They crashed into the back door, expecting it to yield and then made a chorus of complaint when it did not. Hands went to foreheads and they peered into the dark. They lifted the letterbox and shouted up to their mother. From upstairs came the sound of muffled cries. It was unlikely that they could be heard outside. A car door slammed, central locking clicked and whirred and beeping alarms announced that that little bit of middle England was secure. Bill could hear the crunching of gravel underfoot. He followed the sounds as they circled the house and the man came into view. He was averagely built, quite muscular in the chest and arms (mirror muscles from being newly single) and was showing a little grey around the temples. He banged on the door.

'Bee! What's going on? Come on, open the door, we need cake!' The girls started laughing and shouting for cake. He banged again and found his keys, operated the lock and gave the door a push. The bolts resisted. He tried again. He peered into the darkness of the house.

'Your Mum must be in the bath. Come on, let's go in the front door. There was a crunch of feet, the sound of struggling and moaning upstairs. Bill slinked through the house and listened. Keys jangled, the bolts held.

'I for...' There was the sound of a man's head thumping against the door. The girls began to giggle again.

'I tell you what; you run round to the secret door. Go and scare your mother in the bath and then let me in. Off you go.' Suddenly Bill's mind was thrown into turmoil. There was another door. Little footsteps scampered away. They were racing, running in different directions round the house. It had to be diametrically opposite.

Bill ran helter-skelter through the hall and into the kitchen; there was no door. There was no other way into the building. Then he heard a crash and more giggling and the thunder of little feet on wooden stairs. A cupboard door under the stairs opened and a little girl's head began to emerge. Bill threw himself against the wall. He had not been seen, but now they were in the house. He could over-come them all, there was no question of that, but it made everything so complicated. They were little girls, damn it, he did not want to hurt anyone; he just wanted a bit of home comfort. He thought of running out through the front door; but there was a woman tied-up upstairs and he did not want the police on his tail again so quickly. He would be hunted from their door step. He had to work fast. Fortunately this was something he could do well. Little feet thundered up the stairs and doors banged in the bath-room and then the bedroom. By the time Bill had reached the top of the stairs they had found their mother. There was a gasp as the two children stopped on the threshold, momentarily frightened by such an unfamiliar scene. He ran behind them and pushed them headlong into the room. They let out a piercing scream and tumbled to the floor. As he slammed the door closed he thought he saw the elder girl spin back to look at him. Her angry piercing eyes drilling into his own. He grabbed a chair and thrust it under the door handle and then began to run downstairs. The girl's scream had set their father running and there was much crashing and banging as he fought his way through some unseen obstacles in the passage behind the stairs. Bill looked about him for a blunt weapon, found a glass ashtray and waited behind the door. The cupboard burst open and the man emerged through the small open-ing, falling to his knees. As he struggled to get up, Bill struck him with the ashtray; he had not meant to use excessive force, but somehow he had been unable to help himself. The man's head shot back and to the side and he slumped, immobile, to the floor.

Bill felt the rush of the gift subsiding. It had risen up in him without being summoned. He felt the pleasure of its gentle caress, its vapours soothing his racing mind. He recovered his breath. The exertions of the previous day had taken more out of him than he had realised. He looked down at the body slumped before him. Was the man dead? Should he check? Did it really matter? He looked at the body with complete detachment. No, it did not matter; this man was one of many. There would be many more. He heard the creak of a window from upstairs. They were trying to escape. Heart racing, he ran back upstairs, two at a time, knocked the chair aside and entered the room. His eyes immediately fell upon the elder of the two daughters, those eyes, blue and piercing. The girl's mother was leaning out of the window, still half draped with knotted sheets, half in, half out. The little girl was nowhere to be seen. Bill's mind re-created a picture of the front of the house, there was a porch above the front door; the little girl must be on the top of that. He ran across the room, the air flickering blue and white sparks and grabbed the woman from behind. Her scream hit his ears as a drawn out wail; he heard every nuance of fear, grief and hate. Its emotive power almost prevented him from his task, but he dragged her back, her arms still reaching out towards the window.

He was not a particularly powerful man, but his advantages were manifold. As the air sparked, he danced around her, cotton sheets billowed; her hands flew out but never found a target, her hair whipped in circles about her face, a face twisted in fury, confusion and fright. To Bill it seemed as if she moved through water, a delicate ballet. He did not give himself entirely to the gift as that would be too dangerous, he had to stay in control, and when his hands fell upon her it was not with the fearful freezing power of one who controls time, but rather the soft and gentle touch of one who can dwell in a caress. She struck out again, an explosive punch towards him, fists and spittle flying. He ducked the blow and allowed her momentum to project her into his arms; she spun on her heels and slowly, slowly, fell.

As he sunk to catch her, he felt something strange at his forehead: at first a pressure, then a sharp pain, cutting deeper and deeper. He reeled away, involuntarily letting out a scream; his hands reaching up to his face. With time dilating and expanded, he felt every nuance of his misery, the scrape of metal on bone, the tearing of individual fibres of muscle, flesh parting, nerves screaming.

He turned to look into the face of his adversary. It was the girl. Both her hands were wrapped around the end of a metal comb; she had driven the handle into his forehead with all the strength she could muster. He moved to brush her aside, allowing the gift to flood his veins, but she was too quick. Her wide eyes seemed to become even wider, and she slipped under his flying arm. Her blue eyes flashed and the air about her sparked in the same pale hue. She glanced back at him and then made a dash for the door. His initial imperceptions rapidly clearing, Bill Morris now understood what his instincts had been trying to tell him: she was a creature, just like him. He could barely contain his excitement. He dragged himself up from his kneeling position, pulled the metal comb from his flesh, squealing as the pain intensified again. He was trapped under the weight of the little girl's mother, and as he tried to pull himself free, he found her hands on his arms, her nails, biting into his flesh. She reached towards his eyes but he batted her hands aside, kicking and twisting to be free. She was a dead weight and it took all of the remaining energy he had just to wrestle himself free. Even as he staggered away, he found her hands on his legs. He kicked her away; she moaned and fell silent. He heard another piercing scream; the little girl had found her father. Bill hurtled through the bedroom door and practically threw himself down the stairs. His heart was screaming at him, his chest tight, but he had to stop her. The little girl heard him crashing down the stairs, knocking pictures from walls, stumbling and sliding. She glanced at the back door, but there was no way she could reach the high bolt. She kissed her father, and dived through the opening behind him.

Bill saw two legs, bathed in shimmering light, disappear into the cupboard. His chest was on fire now. He gasped for breath, each harder won than that which preceded it. He thought for a minute he would follow her, but the gap was small. He grabbed the still figure of her father and tried to drag him free of the doorway, but his strength was failing him. He roared in anger and turned his attention to the backdoor. Immersing himself totally in the fire of the gift he launched himself at it. Space shimmered; the world around him became a blue and white blur. His shoulders struck the resisting timber, flesh on wood, bones slid between muscles, organs compressed and rebounded, ligaments became wire-taut. The fibres of wood in the door bent and bowed, molecular bonds, their scintillant vibrations stilled in the distortion of space-time became momentarily fragile. The door exploded outwards, glass and timber splinters hurtled through space, a violent cloud with Bill Morris in its epicentre. He crashed headlong into the side of the parked four-by-four, his flying body buckling side and door panels, the impact sending his limbs slapping against its toughened glass, a road accident recoiling in surreal reverse.

As the dust and glass settled around him, he thought he heard the sound of children screaming. He tried to pull himself to his feet but had no strength; somewhere in his body something was very wrong. His legs collapsed and slid from under him. Through the haze of dust he saw two little girls, hand in hand, running away. He felt the blood-clot slide into place, felt the change in blood pressure, the muscular spasms, and the hand of death closing around his heart. His heart beat for the last time and the gift held him in that moment, the evening sun on his face, the tinkling of glass, frozen, a bird in flight, morphing, slowly twisting into darkness, a distant light and then he was gone.

Five hours later Patrick Manee's phone began to ring.

TWELVE

In a small corner office in the astrophysics department of a small English University a small group of post-doctoral students and their supervisor were huddled around a collection of monitors showing an ever-lengthening list of eight-digit numbers.

'What do you think? Is it too early to tell? Has anyone got the ability to do the projection in their head? Sandra, you are good at this kind of thing. What do you reckon?' Sandra looked across at her over-excited supervisor with mild amusement. They had been awaiting this data for six months and now he could not even wait the two days it would take to input it into a computer simulation and give them an easily interpretable model. The data was coming from X-ray measurements from a region of space they had suspected of showing profound gravitational lensing. If this could be verified then it would provide evidence for Einstein's General Theory of Relativity. The delicate and rather beautiful cluster of oval galaxies seemed as good a place as any to look for such effects. The early pictures from Hubble had already tantalised them. In this study they hoped to attach some numbers to the phenomenon.

'I'm not sure. It's tricky; you know how complex the sky is in that region. You get a pretty complicated picture.'

'Oh go on, tell me so I can go to bed happy tonight!' The irascible doctor would not take no for an answer. 'Your best guess, looking around the bigger galaxies; have you noticed any shifts?'

'Well, as I say, it's tricky, and to be honest I'm a bit worried about the feed.' She looked sidelong at her boss, who was looking even more agitated now than usual.

'What do you mean? Doesn't it make sense? In what way, luminance, colour?' Everyone in the little room was looking at her now. Sandra had been biting her tongue for the last half an hour, but the pattern had been clear from the initial low resolution scan. Filling in the numbers was only confirmation of what she had already convinced herself. She walked over to the magnificent Hubble picture of their favourite corner of the universe and ran her hands over its surface.

'This region here may well be showing gravitational lensing but something else has distorted the region.'

'What? Come on, I've got a conference to talk at in three days and I want to tell them good news!' The Doctor was almost beside himself; the slightly embarrassing tic, which all his students had had to learn to deal with, was beginning to make an appearance at the corner of his eyes.

'There seems to be a significant region of red-shifting, over here...' She swept her arm across a region of space which included several bright galaxies...and another region which is blue-shifting here...' she indicated another region of space. 'which, I suppose, would imply that this region of space was travelling towards us at this moment in cosmological history, whilst in this region it was travelling away from us.' She paused, slightly embarrassed by having to state that which would have been perfectly obvious to all around her had they her very high spatial IQ and the ability to visualise the numerical data as well as she could.

'No, no, that can't be right.' The doctor was looking even more excited. 'That would imply some sort of localised collapse or a massive gravitational wave; we can't have been that lucky, surely?'

Another student spoke up. 'Perhaps space isn't spherical there? Perhaps there is a ripple?'

The doctor's mobile phone suddenly broke the silence. Fingers shaking, he wrestled with the controls. 'Yes, what is it?... oh, Michael, it's you... oh... yes... I see. Well, that's exactly what we were thinking.' There were a few moments of silence whilst he listened to the murmur with growing excitement. 'Yes Michael... this is wonderful, I'll be in touch tomorrow, when the full data set is in. Yes, wonderful, I'll speak to you then.'

He closed the phone. 'That was Michael Valence in Honolulu. They have confirmed your observation Sandra, and apparently something similar was observed last week by the Richmond Hill Battery. Ladies and gentlemen, it looks like we no longer live in a spherical universe. Go to your beds tonight and try not to let the horrendous mathematical consequences of that get into your nightmares!'

THIRTEEN

Margaret looked at herself in the full-length mirror and smiled at her reflection. She would never be twenty again; hell, she'd never be forty again, but the happy woman looking back at her did not seem to mind. Tonight she was on a date. She did a turn. The dress was long, elegant, refined and bright, bright red. Tonight red was the right colour. It showed off the richness of her skin and spoke of luxury.

Kevin Masters was not the kind of man Margaret would necessarily have seen herself with. He was suave and ruggedly handsome with a penchant for suits which Margaret would have thought might have better suited a younger man. Kevin was quite young, of course, but, to Margaret's mind, people reached a comfortable plateau and tended to stay at that level until they regressed to childish playfulness as they entered their dotage. The question was when to slide into such misbehaviour. Margaret felt she was ready to make that move, perhaps starting tonight. She sat herself back at her dressing table not peering too close into the glass; these days she had learnt not to. The general effect was marvellous; the details did not bear too much close scrutiny.

She glanced up at the clock; seven thirty, he would not be late. He was that kind of man, of that she was certain. A meal somewhere nice, and then a swanky dance-bar was all he had told her. It sounded perfect.

The front doorbell rang. Margaret pulled her shawl about her shoulders. Tonight she could not wear a coat; a few glasses of wine would have to warm her up. She opened the door to a smiling Kevin. His hair was slicked back to reveal a broad and slightly greasy forehead. His

316

eyes were dark-ringed and he looked unbelievably tired. There was something not quite right about him: an underlying stress, a tension. Margaret wondered if he was perhaps extremely nervous. They had met on only two previous occasions and in neither case had she noticed even the slightest hint of self-doubt in the man. He oozed confidence. Tonight, however, his eyes were missing a certain shine; he had dressed quickly, his shirt and suit; immaculately tailored, but neglected.

'You look wonderful.' Kevin looked Margaret over slowly, breathing her in. It was a remarkably sensual look, one that she found arousing, but somehow intimidating. 'I have a car waiting across the street to take us to the restaurant. I hope you'll like it. I've wanted to go there for a while but I've not had suitably beautiful company to join me.'

He spoke slowly; the words were well practised. He was obviously comfortable in this line of flattery. From the first moment she had met him, Margaret had been aware of this element to his character and it was not something she found attractive. For some reason, at this particular moment, the words rang particularly hollow. His heart was not in it. That was the bottom line. Perhaps he was having second thoughts; perhaps he was just ill.

'That's very kind of you Kevin. But, if you don't mind me saying so, you don't look quite yourself. Send the car away, if you like. We don't have to go anywhere if you don't want to.' She looked past him into the street. She saw a line of cars, but none seemed occupied. 'I think the car must have already gone dear. I can't see your driver.'

Kevin looked back up the street. 'Oh yes. He must have gone.' His voice was somehow distant; he seemed unfocused, disinterested. Something was definitely very wrong.

'Kevin, let's do this another day; shall we?' Margaret's heart was sinking, but she had the wherewithal to hold her emotions in check. 'You look like you need a lie down, dear.' All of a sudden she was not sure she wanted this man in her house. 'Go home tonight, dear, and have an early night. Call me in the morning.' How could she send him away without being rude? He did not appear to be drunk; at least she could not smell booze on him. Perhaps it was drugs. These sharp dressers often took drugs, didn't they? She did not want a druggie in her house, especially these days when she knew nothing of the modern drugs. It was all so confusing. There would be other men, other times, men who did not stare at her in quite such a strange way.

She was not sure how long she had been standing at the door, but she suddenly realised she was cold. Kevin had not moved; he just stood there, watching her, on the threshold of her hall. She had to make a decision. She made it. As she began to close the door Kevin's hand shot forward and held it firm.

'You are a remarkable woman Margaret. Do you know that?' Now she knew something was definitely very wrong. His voice was strangely slurred, the syllables sliming together like snails in a box.

Across the road in a grey Ford sat Agneta Sibilski and Edward Spinks. Manee had given them strict instructions: they were to follow at a distance; they must not put themselves at risk. If they suspected anything was amiss they were to call him, or in a more pressing emergency his colleague, a man who had had some appropriate experience already. If that failed, they should call the regular police. They should tell them they had seen an armed man; they should specifically mention a gun. Such elaborations would ensure they got the attention they needed. Manee had given them elementary instruction on clandestine surveillance. As he peered over the top of a flamboyantly spread roadmap, Edward Spinks felt his heart beating in his chest. This was the most exciting thing he had done in a while. A stakeout, who would have thought?

'Who is the woman, do you think? They seem to know each other. She is dressed up. I guess she thought she was going out this evening. Shit!'

'What is it? What's going on?' Agneta reached out and

pushed the paper aside.

'He's gone in. I hardly saw him move; he's inside and the door is closed.'

'Do we call Manee?'

'No time, get the crowbars; we are going in.'

Kevin had crossed the threshold in a single step. He closed the door behind him and slid the bolts in a single movement. As they snapped closed it was as if two shots had rung out. Margaret backed away, turned and ran towards the kitchen; this was her space, her domain. She knew where the knives were kept, knew the layout. Armed she had a chance. The back door was locked, and Kevin stood between her and the only other exit from the house. She would have to fight her way through him to get out. So be it. She had seen the flash in his eyes in that split moment and it was this that had sent her running for her life. That strange animal stare was not human, was it blood lust? His eyes had rolled back, sexual, wanton and perverse. It was as if he were tasting her. Her fancy shoes nearly caused her to stumble as she skirted the kitchen table but she held her balance and victoriously drew a cleaver from the block. To Kevin Masters the 'zing' of the knife against the steel reverberated in a glorious symphony of harmonics. The blade hummed and vibrated in Margaret's iron grip. Monotonic decays of sine-waves, rolling and boiling to silence. He had no need to rush.

'Margaret, please, don't fear me.' He stopped on the threshold of the room. Margaret stood before him, knife raised, eyes glaring with a fearsome intensity. He felt her passion washing over him; drank it in and gently allowed his gift to connect with her.

'Don't be afraid. This is so right. Can't you see?' He found it difficult to control the timbre of his voice, the syllables impossibly drawn out; they slipped into nonsensical gurgles. 'You and I are perfect for each other. You are a well, Margaret, a font of life. You always have been and you always will be. You were put on this Earth to give yourself to the rest of us. You are a gift.'

Margaret glared across the expanse of the breakfast table; just four feet of pine between her and a madman. The knife felt good in her hands. She could dismember a knuckle of lamb in a few choice cuts. Surely it would not be so different to mete out the same blows on a homicidal maniac.

'I was put on this Earth for something else. I am a predator, a carnivore, and I was put here to feed on people like you.' He was silent for a moment, pensive. Margaret did not allow her eyes to leave him for a moment. 'It's strange really, I've always been like this I suppose, but I never really realised my potential, or the strength of my calling. I have always taken advantage of the weak and the foolish, but now I can do it directly. We are all parasites on something. We use and abuse our animals, our land, our workers and our friends. You are different, Margaret. You are like some lamb that longs for the slaughter. You give of yourself, you give and give and all around you take from you; a little here, a little there. You should thank me. I plan to take everything you have and unlike the rest of them, I won't waste your time. I will absorb your time, charge myself and evolve to a higher state. Your life will become pure bliss. You always think of others, Margaret, you want to give pleasure, comfort. Through me you can give the most sublime pleasure. Please, come here, let's do this together. You cannot possibly hide from me; you are like lead, heavy, slow and malleable. I am quicksilver. Don't you want to be part of that?' He edged towards her, moving round the table; he was lithe, quick and his eyes fixed her with a steely glare. Margaret kept him at a distance, moving round the table, one hand holding the knife, the other holding the pine table top, partly to feel its comforting edge and partly for support. He had said she was as lead and at this moment her every movement seemed to confirm this.

Suddenly he was upon her. Time contracted in upon itself, her limbs suddenly too heavy, held taut by some invisible pressure. He had disarmed her in an instant; the blade had trembled in her hands, but she had not seen him move. He placed it onto the table and encircled her in his grip. His face was close, his breath acrid and warm. He held her tightly, intimately. She tried to struggle, but somehow she knew it was useless. You could not fight the sea. She would drown in this man's arms as her own son had drowned in the arms of the river Thames. The thought of Michael brought Suzi to her mind. Her dear Suzi, where was she now? And what would she think? She felt a terrible chill running through her body. She turned her head away from the monster. He would not see the fear in her eyes. She would not give him that pleasure.

There was a crash at the front door, the muffled thud of human flesh against the timber; then the sound of wood tearing, glass breaking. For Kevin the squeal of tortured wood reverberated into his reverie. He heard the glass shatter and splinter, traced the lightning scars of its disintegration. Like an icebreaker crashing through an Arctic sea, they rifted the perfect blinding purity of his dreamlike state. In fury he pushed Margaret's limp body away from him and turned towards the intrusion. Dreamlike, he saw two figures enter his field of view; they advanced so slowly, their movements hideously laboured, the fear and anticipation apparent in every lumbering step. They twisted to look at him, eyes wide, and mouths stupidly agape. He wanted to run, to slip unseen between the two drones, but he was engorged with time. He had drained Margaret quickly, though incompletely, and the pleasure of it and the dilation he was experiencing were affecting the balance of his mind. He could attack the two of them, of that he had no doubt, but as he turned to move his legs refused to respond, his own body not yet equilibrated with the burst of time he had absorbed. He stumbled and slipped and grabbed the table for support as Margaret's body slowly hit the flag-tiled floor.

The two figures were approaching; he knew one of them, of that he was sure, a woman, familiar, attractive, but what did it matter? There was no past, no history only an ever-lasting present, an exquisite moment that persisted and persisted.

Agneta brought the crowbar down towards Kevin's head in a mighty arc; his eyes were glazed, he looked right through her, his body shaking and twisted. She struck at him with every ounce of her strength. The sight of this poor woman cast aside like some used carton filled her with a sudden loathing and hatred. She had heard Kevin speak of a society of victims, dolts exposing their throats to those with genuine business acumen. To her shame she had laughed with him then. She was not laughing now.

Kevin saw the crowbar descending; saw the hate in those eyes. He knew them now; he had gazed into their icy blue-depths before, looking for recognition, looking for a spark of love. This he had never seen, only a cool distance. He brought his hand up to defend himself and from some-where in his being he felt the gift defend itself too. For a moment the air crackled with blue light. The crowbar slowed and stopped. The release of this energy sobered him like a cold bath. He threw himself to the floor, scram-bled under the table and bolted for the door. He saw the figure of a man he did not recognise turn towards him, but he was past him and into the hall in a split second. He careered from wall to wall, throwing his momentum from one side to another, barely able to control his flight.

Five minutes later he was standing in a shop doorway nearly two miles away. His mind was torn between misery and elation. He had chosen in that instant to run, but he was not entirely sure what he was running from. He could have killed them all in an instant, of that there was no question, but how many would he have to kill and how many did he want to kill? Where would it end? He slumped into the doorway, his reflection gaunt and sickly. What was he becoming?

FOURTEEN

There was something about Dvorjak that constantly amazed Daniel. Every piece seemed unique, crafted from air, not grounded in the classical clichés of so many other composers. Daniel had no remarkable musical talent; what he had was the result of hard work and practise, and music lessons had been sporadic and far between. His life at Denbigh had been quite stressful and strange; the separation from home, the immersion with the gifted, the newness of everything mixed in with the normal traumas of adolescence amounted to a heady cocktail. He had found some respite and sanctuary in music and for the first time in his life he had found himself surrounded by a legion of talented youngsters, fine instruments and numerous teachers for many of whom the gifted school at Denbigh had seemed a delightful change from their conventional daily grind.

He was sitting at a particularly fine grand piano in an oak-panelled room in the old school's music room. His music teacher over the last few months had been a very kindly old man, patient, artistic and thoughtful; he had helped Daniel lose a few bad habits he had developed over years of learning alone and had introduced him to some composers who had stretched his technique to the limit. It was remarkable how a few well chosen bars could trip him up time and time again. 'When you can play that without falling on your face, you will be ready to enter discussions with Rachmaninov, but not before! Liszt could play this at five, Rachmaninov could play this and transpose it at four. You have ten years on these children... how easy should it be for you?' As he eventually taught his fingers to obey, he was introduced to new musical wonders. Passages which he had stumbled through, he now skipped through; for the first time in his life he was listening to some of the sounds that came out of the piano rather than just wrestling with his own insecurity. He was also getting over the musical vertigo and the converse fear of depth that the extremes of the instrument tended to give him. He had been forced to play familiar pieces in odd registers, send his hands on adventures into unknown territories and hours had been spent transposing melodies to stratospheric heights to familiarise himself with the precarious notation. His advancement had been quick and his teacher had not been slow with praise. Today the man had been detained by illness and Daniel sat and practised with some trepidation whilst he awaited the arrival of a stand-in teacher. He hoped his old teacher had not succumbed to the pressures of the gifted. Many familiar faces had disappeared from among the staff and those that disappeared seldom returned. He closed the Dvorjak, the notes still ringing in his ears, and began to run through sets of scales and arpeggios, something he never usually bothered with, preferring instead to loosen up with Clementi or a familiar piece of Mozart. Today, however, he felt obliged to perform this chore. It might look better when the teacher arrived to see him involved in some studious task.

The door opened and Daniel was confronted with a rather humourless, pointed face framed in swept-back black hair.

'Daniel Spinks? I am Doctor Vickers; I'll be directing your studies for a few weeks. Mister Hardy tells me you have not deigned to take your grades, but your ability places you somewhere around grades six or seven. Is this correct?' The man's voice was surprisingly high-pitched and nasal. His hooked nose and long fingers made him look somewhat vulture-like. As he approached Daniel from behind the bleached bones of the open grand-piano the image was greatly enhanced. 'I'd rather you did not play with the lid up like this.' The Doctor worked the catches and gently lowered the lid, apparently diverting his eyes from the piano's entrails. 'It gets dust in the mechanism and I want to have my piano back in one piece for the school when this ridiculous experiment is finished.'

'Did you work here before, Doctor Vickers, at the girl's college?' The Doctor gave him a slightly venomous glance.

'Yes, I was the senior music master here before we were invaded by this rabble. Everything was peaceful and organised here until we were overrun by the police, the army and this menagerie of so-called gifted. Well, I'm afraid it is for me to be the judge of just how gifted you are. Let's see, B harmonic minor scale please, ascending and descending, legato, four octaves.' Daniel took a deep breath and ran through his scales as directed. Doctor Vintner picked him up on every error of fingering and style, his hawk-like eyes scanning Daniel's fingers like a falcon looking for voles in long grass.

Eventually the ordeal by scales and arpeggios was completed. 'What has Mister Hardy got you learning at the moment?' For 'Mister Hardy', Daniel assumed he meant George, the kindly man who Daniel was fast canonising in his mind. He would have to visit him, if they let him out of the compound; anything to hasten his recovery so he did not have to deal too long with the carnivorous Doctor Vickers. Daniel pulled out a Mozart sonata; it was a piece he knew well, he did not want to show himself up. He ran through the piece carefully and precisely; strangely, today his fingers were behaving themselves. Returning to this piece after a month of technical practise demonstrated the significant improvements he had made. When he finished the final bars he was rather pleased with himself.

'Adequate I suppose, but your phrasing needs some work and you need to count your trills more carefully, it's not a licence for laziness. Please go back to the beginning and we'll dissect it as we go.' Daniel's heart sank. This was going to be a long hour.

After Mozart had been fully deconstructed and criticism levelled at every bar, it was the turn of Liszt's 'Consolation number 3'. The gentle rippling arpeggios, gently coaxed into uncertain emotional waves as Daniel explored his own insecurity and concerns through its subtle variations.

'No, no, no. I don't know if Mister Hardy has discussed tempo with you, but there are limits to what is acceptable interpretation and what is simply laziness. Lento placido, cantando, not 'self-indulgent', you do understand the difference I hope.'

Daniel bit his lip. This was the reason he had avoided music lessons at his previous school, the hairy-faced and humourless Mrs Trevithik had sucked the life and pleasure out of everything he had ever attempted to play in her presence. She was like a spider, drawing out the light and goodness and leaving only a dry musical husk. Daniel's youth, respect for his elders and the insecurity that followed from that meant that such experiences were always one-sided frustrating affairs where he would have to passively accept criticism whilst secretly knowing it to be unjustified.

'Play it again, and try a little attention to timing. From the top, one-and two-and three-and four and one...' Doctor Vickers drew a baton from his coat pocket and beat time on the casing of his precious piano. Daniel played the first ten bars with as much sarcastic and robotic precision as he could muster, the abrasive clacking of the baton jostling the tune along as if it were a captured prisoner of war. 'Yes, that's it, much better. Improvisation has its place, but not in Liszt.'

Daniel tried to maintain this militaristic precision for a few bars more, but the music was too beautiful; he allowed his mind to wander between the notes, listening to the suspended emotion between them, the anticipation of gentle emotive evolution. He played a few staccato bars clipping the notes and extending the vitrified silences to breaking point. As he entered the emotive climax, he was oblivious to the man standing behind him, baton limp, face twisted in confusion. He danced his way through the development, dolcissimo, and swept towards the gentle finale, cadenza, smorzando, his heart dancing and his mind with his mother and friends. Time held its breath as he tripped down the last few intervals, perdendosi, to a final peaceful resolution. His mind was momentarily blank; strange how the music had carried him, just for those few moments. He felt tired and light-headed, satiated but drained. He opened his eyes to see Doctor Vickers leaving the room.

'If you will not take instruction seriously then I will not waste my time with you!' He opened the door, glanced back into the room, his eyes full of anger and fear, and then was gone. Daniel shrugged and opened the music to Beethoven's Moonlight sonata. He ignored the first movement; Liszt had satisfied that particular urge. Today he would master the second movement.

As Doctor Vickers passed under the music room window he heard the rippling scales of the sonata. Impossibly fast, the notes scrambled and buffeted one another, ascending in cruel spikes before coruscating down in syncopated avalanches. He had never heard anything like it. He drew a deep breath, feeling dizzy and disorientated. He had studied piano for thirty years, performed and taught for twenty five. What he had just witnessed and the profound effect it had seemed to have on his psyche was like nothing he had experienced before. He turned his back on the college. These children were not natural, not normal. George Hardy was right, the children's gifts were becoming more pronounced. He would make his report to the committee as soon as possible and get away from these freaks as soon as he could.

FIFTEEN

'I don't really know how to thank you. I can't tell you how important Margaret is to me.' Suzi hugged Agneta to her and the two women held each other for a long time. Miguel and Edward looked on, slightly uncomfortable, not really knowing what to say to one another. Suzi walked back to Margaret's bedside. She was sleeping peacefully, sedated following her ordeal. In spite of the fact that she looked comfortable, the sight of her still sent a shiver down Suzi's spine. She sensed the temporal weakness of her friend and mentor. A monster had attacked her, drained her, of this she was sure, a vile creature with a dark gift that she also shared. Her own exquisite sensitivity to the change in Margaret's strength disturbed her. Her unspoken fears that she had somehow drawn upon Margaret's inherent generosity, tapping her selfless temporal vein, came back to her now. Weakened as she was, Suzi was aware of Margaret's waning appeal to her; it was crude, purely animalistic and subtle, but none the more disturbing for all that. When she found herself this close to her sleeping friend, she felt a slight revulsion; it was similar to the feelings that had overcome her when she had tried to visit her personal assistant in hospital. Her very presence might be dangerous to her friend. She turned away, frightened of undoing any good that rest and time might be putting right. What was it that separated Miguel and her from the monster that had attacked Margaret? Was there any difference?

'Tell me more about this man; what do you think he wanted from Margaret? I never met him.' They turned from the bedside, and walked out into the hospital

328

grounds. The day was warm and the flowerbeds were full of fragrant peonies.

'Kevin Masters. I used to work for him. He always was a slightly strange man, very highly driven, successful and interesting. He had a criminal mind, always looking for ways to make easy money. I have to admit some involvement in that myself.' She looked at Edward who was now in deep conversation with Miguel some distance behind. She wandered what he would think of her if he really knew what she was like. She also began to worry why she cared. She shook the latter thought away. 'He started behaving strangely about six months ago; I didn't see him for weeks at a time. I assumed he had some business interests that he didn't want me involved in. Then Edward got in touch with me, and introduced me to Chief Inspector Manee. Manee was worried about Edward's old boss Brian. Manee had arrested him at Heathrow airport in some kind of anti-terrorist raid. He seemed to suspect that Kevin was somehow involved and could be dangerous. We followed him and found he had attacked a woman; he had left her in a state similar to your friend.'

'And this Manee character; he just left you to your own devises to follow this lead yourself? Why didn't you leave this to the police?'

'Well, there is something else, something bizarre. Both Brian and Kevin seem to have a strange ability, they... I don't know how to put it; they don't appear to be entirely normal. I think both ourselves and Manee thought the police wouldn't fully understand. He did give us back-up, though, colleagues on the inside who we could contact in the event of an emergency. Obviously the police are involved now; it's unavoidable. We gave descriptions and statements. I'm sure it won't be long before Kevin is arrested.'

Suzi was quiet for a moment. What should she say to this woman, how much should she share? Reading between the lines it was clear that she had firsthand knowledge and experience of the gifted. Should she say that both she and Miguel were made of the same material? No, it would be foolish. She would be handed to the police. She needed to speak to this Chief Inspector, to find out what he knew.

'Where is this Patrick Manee now? I'd like to hear what he has to say; I want to know what we are dealing with.'

'He is in North Wales, in Denbigh, protecting the gifted children I guess. I'm in regular contact with him; I'm sure he would be happy to talk to you.' It was all beginning to make sense to Suzi. This man understood the connection between the gifted children and the attacks. There were others like her in the world, who knew how many? Some of them were going off the tracks and Chief Inspector Manee was hunting them, either directly or through his minions.

Edward could not stop himself swelling with pride as he regaled Miguel with the details of his experiences the previous evening. His daily grind of product and promotional development left little room for derring-do. The prolonged stake-out, breaking into the house and his subsequent, if belated, chase out into the night was the most exciting thing to happen to him in years. The fact that it was Agneta who lead the attack in the more pressing moments did not dull his enthusiasm. Agneta had warrior written all over her. He was more than happy to hold her coat in the tighter moments. Miguel listened to the details of the attack with mounting fear. He saw his own powers twisted in the actions of this madman, and dwelt in the miserable recognition that in spite of his own moral complexion, application of his own gift had resulted in the death of a young man, albeit an accidental death.

He had looked down on Margaret's vulnerable, immobile body in the hospital bed and anger had welled up within him, but guiltily he had had to pull his eyes away. Instinctively he was aware that should he chose to he could draw strength from her as easily as her attacker had done. The thought repulsed him and terrified him. Edward's description of Kevin Master's escape, distorted through his naturally excited exaggeration and the contraction of subjective time that had accompanied it, enhanced its supernatural properties. Miguel feared this man more for what he represented than as a creature of itself, but as Edward described Kevin's cat-like movements, his impossible turn of speed and his apparent demonstration of momentarily and locally freezing time, a shiver ran down his spine. What was this man capable of? And did normal men have the power to stop him? Perhaps more importantly he wondered if he himself had the power. Over the course of their time together Suzi had explained her desperate desire to find him, to learn from him and if possible to establish that she was not alone in the world. Now he felt a similar feeling welling within him. He needed to find this Kevin Masters, confront him, try to establish what humanity remained within. Perhaps, by finding and punishing this man, he could atone for his own sins.

Suzi had become Miguel's rock, and he hers. Retiring together to a café was like returning to port; once together, they were home. They held hands over milky teas and discussed the details of what they had learnt. Suzi and Edward could be useful allies, but they needed to see the lie of the land. There were worrying developments concerning the gifted children, leaks of various sources suggested problems within the compounds and clashes between parents and security firms. The government was under pressure from all sides; political pacts that had maintained a precarious balance of power were slipping apart. Across Europe international borders dissolved during the expansion of Europe, were becoming re-established, the political temperature was increasing everywhere. The western world was on high alert and the police appeared to be everywhere and with increasing powers. There were worrying stories of large numbers of people being taken in to custody; there was talk of an outbreak of an aggressive virus, spreading across Europe, enforced blood tests, quarantine and unexplained disappearances. Suzi and Miguel spoke in whispers. As they looked out of the window of the café, the world of humanity outside seemed an ugly one. They were different from nearly everyone else and others like them were running amok. Should the world turn against them, where would they hide? And where should their allegiances lie? If the gifted children represented their kind, their future, then they needed to get to Denbigh. They would contact Patrick Manee and test the water. Every gifted person had been part of a community, a family; surely the whole population could not turn against them. Walking through the underground, however, on a wet weekday evening, examining the empty faces of the sleepwalking commuters, almost any horror seemed possible.

SIXTEEN

In a dark and listless region of space, in the shadow of larger cometary debris, a diffuse cloud of interstellar dust particles silently drifted. Sol, our own sun, was but a bright star in their heavens, and the particles barely felt its gravitational enticement. The solar wind was equally enfeebled and they had moved little in many hundreds of millions of years. Suddenly they found themselves caught in a swirling vortex of forces. A buffeting wind that pulled them a million miles in an instant, then flung them away again. The ferocious forces obliterated many of their number and their demise was marked by a sudden release of short wavelength radiation. Had any of the particles had any kind of self-awareness, they might have caught in the tormented maelstrom the weakest echo of light and sound, an image of bright sunlight from a much closer sun, of pale warm stone and perhaps the sound of birdsong or gunfire. In a moment they were still again, the wave passed on and they were left to gently diffuse in their quiet corner of the universe. There was no intelligence amongst their number to ponder the wonders of what had just occurred. They continued their journey in silence, the universe around them radiating their billions of tiny deaths into the darkness.

SEVENTEEN

'You have got to be kidding, George, this is political suicide. We'll be torn apart by the opposition from both sides
and the bloody liberals, who are wavering already, will
jump ship in an instant.' The Prime Minister stood aghast
in front of his Minister for Internal Affairs. George Norton-
Smith had shown signs of progressive insanity. The dark
circles around his sunken eyes; the sallow complexion and
hollow cheeks spoke of many sleepless nights. 'You are my
friend and colleague George, I'm beginning to worry about
you, you don't look well. Has someone been putting pressure on you? I know you take the brunt of much of the
American interference with policy, but you know I'll support you. We're in the middle of a bloody mess, there is no
denying it, but we have the support of the party and in
spite of everything there has been no descent into civil war
which, to be honest, was what we all secretly feared. We
can ride things out; surely we don't have to resort to this?
It is unspeakable.'

George Norton-Smith looked at his friend and boss
through tired eyes. It was true the Americans had been
putting a great deal of pressure on him, but ultimately it
was his own conscience that was causing him the greatest
discomfort. In Italy the general rounding up of gifted children had lead to widespread anger and civil disobedience;
hundreds had died in spite of the improvements in non-
lethal crowd control. Most of the injured had been tram-
pled underfoot when corralled demonstrations had turned
ugly. A similar pattern had emerged in some former soviet
states, factions blaming the abduction of their children on
some perceived western plot. At the time these knee-jerk

responses had been unfounded, but as time wore on they were becoming all too appropriate. There were appalling suggestions on the table and according to various sources time was running out.

'Anthony, I've known you for more years than I care to think about and what I am saying to you I am saying with the heaviest of hearts.' He spoke slowly and carefully, like a teacher explaining something to a slow but favoured child. 'You haven't seen what these people can do, you haven't seen the victims.'

'But the connections are not there. We don't know that these individuals and the gifted children are part of the same spectrum, do we? We don't have any conclusive proof.'

'That is where you are wrong, Anthony.' Norton-Smith withdrew a ring-bound file from his briefcase. 'I received this only this morning. It's a joint report from ANATOL and the FBI. There is now no question that they are one and the same. The Americans are far more advanced in this regard than we are. They are already bugging the homes of all the gifted. They have had to take on thousands more operatives. They are infiltrating them at every level. I am getting alarming reports from them and these are being confirmed by ANATOL.'

The Prime Minister stared at the document with mounting horror. So it was true; the gifted children grew into gifted adults and there were hundreds of thousands of them. He had seen reports from many departments and they all said the same thing. A group of individuals were emerging: monsters in human form. They were hunting amongst the general population, selecting victims apparently without motive or reason and the victims were left dazed, confused, many close to death, overcome by a weakness that neither they nor the medical profession could understand. There had been a dozen fatalities in Britain alone and similar reports from France. The French foreign minister had confided in him that they were considering going public with what little information they had to prepare the ground for the bigger and more terrible course of

335

action that might be necessary in the future. The philosophical French would be a test case but it could not be contained. The European wide 'pandemic' of East Indian influenza had also been a French ruse. The government had spread a story that the influenza was a particularly nasty avian variety, often fatal and requiring urgent prophylactic treatment. Anyone with as much as a sniff should present themselves for a blood test; the biohazard control teams, now spread liberally through all major cities and towns would then identify the gifted from the records provided for them by ANATOL. Some were quarantined; those that would not be missed found themselves in much deeper water. The more salubrious gifted were tagged with surveillance devices; some disguised as paramedical equipment, others microinjected directly under the skin or into personal belongings. The universal distribution of passive radio-frequency tagging and the core government involvement in its deployment and maintenance meant such surveillance was now a trivial process. This was not necessary for a significant proportion of the gifted as many of them were already under close surveillance. Their powers had often brought them success, and this in itself was sufficient reason to attract government monitoring in the modern world. Many of the gifted had also been attracted to crime, and these individuals represented a further subgroup for whom surveillance was already in place. Artificial intelligences were already identifying unusual patterns of behaviour in these groups. The God of metrics was not omniscient, but his all-seeing eye was gaining in power.

'What do you propose we do?' The Prime Minister sank back into a chair. The true weight of the decisions he would be forced to make in the next few weeks would define his political legacy. It was unlikely that history would look back on him favourably.

Norton-Smith sat down beside him. He opened another file and began to sift through it feverishly. The Prime Minister reached across, took the bundle from his hands and in one sweeping motion threw it through the open window of the office. 'For fuck's sake, no more fucking papers! Just tell me what the bloody Americans and the French want us to do. I know more about this than you probably realise. We need a solution and we have to act soon. Just tell me what the fuck they want us to do.'

George Norton-Smith watched the pile of top secret documents fluttering from view. Perhaps the PM was right, what good did all the paperwork do? In the end what did time and motion achieve? It did not make the decisions any easier and, in the final reckoning, didn't every oppressive regimen attempt to destroy the paper-trail of its misdemeanours? This was, after all, what they had become. It was a slow and steady transformation but every capitalist liberal-democratic government was thinking along the same lines.

'We can't live with them, Anthony. It is as simple as that. They are a destabilising influence, useful of themselves, but damaging to others. They are superior to us, there is no question of that, and that makes them dangerous, extremely dangerous.'

'But Denbigh? The study centres? Have they given us nothing to work with? Do we know they can't be controlled or cajoled?'

'Believe me, we have been trying, and the Americans have been characteristically rigorous in examining all options. The gifted are not different from us in many ways. They are susceptible to everything we are susceptible to, to disease, to drugs. They have tried different types of radiation, magnetic pulses, infra-sound, you name it. The gifted respond much like we do. But it is in time they excel. They control it, manipulate it and some of them, when they reach maturity, seem to get off on this, become uncontrollable, sliding into other mental states. The Americans see them as a threat to their national security and their economy. They have modelled the gifted's impact and they have concluded, without putting too fine a word on it, it is them or us.'

'That is madness. You can't just exterminate point one percent of the human population. There'll be civil war.'

'The American's say it can be done. They have devised a strategy.'

'And how do they plan to dispatch these people?' The PM's mind was racing; for a moment he thought he might be sick.

'In the compounds they would use gas; it's cheap and these days very quick. But they have other weapons. They suspect the best solution would be one of a number of viral agents they have developed. The current health scare smoke screen had always been put in place for this purpose; you must have realised that, Prime Minister, surely. We have put a story about that the gifted are particularly susceptible to this avian influenza; we slowly work through the gifted population and knock them off, one at a time if we have to. The children we can deal with in a few quick strikes, after the event. The weapons people are really very, very good. The bugs and chemicals are so well-tuned, no-one would suspect anything, possibly for years, possibly never; a worldwide pandemic, to which the gifted have no resistance. It's terrible, horrific, but there really is no choice. You will see that in time Anthony. It is inevitable.'

'Get out of my office! Just take your shit out of my face. Do you hear me?' The Prime minister suddenly lunged at his friend. He grabbed him by the lapels and dragged him, protesting to the door.' As he threw the man into the corridor, he heard a last strangled cry. 'Think on it Anthony. Just think on it. If you haven't got the stomach for it the cabinet will find someone who has!'

This could not be happening. There could be no 'final solution'; it was an abomination. He tried to phone home; he needed to ask after his fostered niece, she was in Denbigh. His wife had been hysterical at the time she had been taken away from her sister, but he had had to be cold, distant and strong. It was only going to be for a few weeks, only for a few tests; there was nothing to worry about. The children would be better cared for than they ever had been in their lives. Besides, the government had to be seen to be fully committed, both publically and privately to their policy course. Now he knew his folly. He tried to push the buttons but he could barely see the numbers for the tears that streamed across his face. He gave up in disgust and sank to the floor, sobbing. Let the hidden cameras watch him now, let them record his discomfort, let the future see the horror of this moment.

EIGHTEEN

Manee scanned the distant line of the quarry, pink and gold in the evening sun, the trees faded to greys, like some romantic Victorian fantasy. Without his binoculars it was difficult to make out anything amongst their charcoal depths. Then he saw the flash of a torch, a single glare in the gloom. He set off in its direction.

The evening was warm and pleasant, the streets quite busy with the gifted children and their remaining teachers. Things had slowly deteriorated in the camp over the preceding few weeks as the side-effects of the children had become progressively more intense and debilitating for the non-gifted. Depression and mental collapse seemed to come swiftly to some, slower to others. Manee had watched, fascinated, as first one, then another, of the less popular masters in the school had succumbed. Some had escaped before things had progressed too far; one had left in a body bag. The pattern of 'attacks' implied some focus on behalf of the gifted, but their abilities were broad and varied. A focused tantrum from a particularly powerful eight year old girl had lead to one PE master impaling himself on railings. Apparently the girl had some serious connections in government and she was removed from the compound forthwith. In other cases the effects appeared to be slower and more gentle; an almost perceptible hum from the gifted that radiated from them, a hum he now felt was powered by his non-gifted colleagues. Many of the staff had left of their own volition, others were given extended periods of rest and recuperation away from the site. This had not helped everyone. Depression was rife and counselling of limited value. It appeared that for the non-gifted, local temporal distortion was poorly tolerated by many. He had found himself only mildly affected. His normally introverted demeanour and his morose dissatisfaction with his currently vacuous love-life was piqued more than usual; being trapped as he was, in this goldfish-bowl did not help. He spent as much time as he could off the base, travelling to a range at which he felt he might escape their reach. He had been trained to make himself invisible and this, he concluded, had been his greatest strength. The gifted did not notice him; he moved between them like a ghost, watching but only rarely interacting. He had become acutely aware of the passage of time. The days had begun to tumble together and this of itself was like some element to a nightmare. The lost time showed on his tired, unshaved face when it stared back at him from the glass. The lost time reminded him of his loneliness in the unfurnished room he had to call home. He could see how simply one could be pushed over the edge. He had made contact with Daniel Spinks at the behest of the boy's uncle. He had proven to be a very likeable and talented boy. He was acting as Manee's eyes and ears in the dorms. If plots were afoot he would know better than any crude surveillance would allow. Young children seemed remarkably adept at avoiding surveillance and the gifted were not normal children.

He walked across the school playing fields and began to climb the bank opposite. He had no fear of being observed. It was one of his many jobs to occasionally check the perimeter. There were fewer of his police colleagues on site now, and the command structure had thinned dramatically at the top of the tree in the last few days. The management were leaving the ship to the rats. He was experienced enough to know this was a dangerous development, but suspected that it was the insidious effects of the gifted that had sent the high-brass fleeing. From an open window in the school he heard a lyrical refrain; Lorentzen's 'Hunting Concerto', dark and mysterious. His foray into the woods must have been observed by young Daniel. He smiled as he entered the sanctuary of the woodland glade.

In a moment the drifting sounds of the piano were muffled by the enveloping peace of the leafy glade.

Brian was sitting cross-legged up a tree. He was wearing camouflage fatigues and various bits of assorted herbage were stuck to his body.

'It's good to see the home guard still on the job!' Manee said, suddenly stopping and looking up to Brian's hiding place.

'What? I hope you aren't being funny; I've been here for six hours.'

'I'm sorry, no offence meant. I hope your efforts have not been wasted. I appreciate what you are doing, I really do. You said you might have some news for me.' Manee drew several chocolate bars from his deep pockets and threw one up to him.

'I've been watching them setting up some sort of post on the far hills. They have listening equipment and what looks like radar. A few days ago I was nearly caught on my way up here. There is a whole bunch of military hardware building up in the next valley. It's hidden under tarps. Some of it has been stored in a cow-shed in Ruhin.'

'Have you any idea what any of this might be?' Manee was worried; his superiors hadn't mentioned anything about this. The government-run projects were bad enough, too many suits and accountants, but the military per se had kept a fairly low-key involvement in Denbigh to date. If the army were coming in then that meant the police would presumably be pulled out. The two made uncomfortable bedfellows.

'No idea... lots of it was in boxes. There was nothing recognisable as a weapon, just Jeeps and trailers and stuff.'

'Have you any idea how many men?'

'No, I only saw a dozen; four up at the listening post, four came up through here on some kind of recce, I think they were looking for a platform to get a good view of the town.'

'And they didn't see you?'

'No, I just climbed round the tree as they went past. They were busy being stupid, and mainly talking about

342

girls and beer. I don't think they expected anyone to be up here.'

'Thank you. You've done very well. This changes every-thing.' Manee looked out towards the quiet town. What were they thinking of doing here? What was the plan? It did not bode well. 'It's probably best if you get yourself away from this place, as soon as possible.'

'You can't be serious?' Brian slid down the tree and dropped to the floor. 'Not now, when it's all going off?'

'I'm deadly serious. We've got no idea what they plan for us here. Things could get very dangerous very quickly. I don't want you caught in the crossfire. And besides, you've been lucky once; next time you'll be arrested and before you know it you'll be in the compound. You should make good your escape as quickly as you can.' He tried to keep his voice steady, not to betray the mounting dread that was overtaking him. Why hadn't he been told about the army? Perhaps they never had any intention of telling him. Over the last few weeks numerous members of the families of the gifted had replaced the Denbighites and the police in support staff roles. He himself had been involved in their security assessments. Family members seemed to be prepared to accept the potential hazards the gifted en masse afforded, but not even they were entirely immune. If the government was planning some sort of drastic action, putting the families of the gifted in the blast zone might be a way of containing some of the backlash.

'There is something else.' Brian began to remove the herbage from his clothes. 'When I was a student, my girl-friend Juliet and I noticed a strange effect that I had on a geophysics device.' The word 'girlfriend' seemed reason-able, though he was not sure what Juliet would say to it. 'It measures electron spin resonance...' He eyed Manee for any sign of comprehension; Manee nodded that he should continue. 'Kind of flukily we got talking to this guy Doctor Gordon who got very excited about what we'd found; he took our ideas to a bunch of Professors at the University to see what they made of it. Well, we didn't hear much about it until the other day. Juliet got called up by Gordon who had promised to keep us up to date on any developments that came out of our discovery. We met up with him a few nights ago, down in a pub in Sheffield. After a few drinks he got quite upset and told us pretty much that our ideas had been taken out of his hands and taken up by the Ministry of Defence or something.'

'Why was he upset, do you think?'

'Mainly because we weren't going to get any recognition for it, I think; he kept going on and on about papers he was going to write. It was all a bit embarrassing. Anyway, he said a biophysicist had linked the ESR signal to the gifted and the gifted could be detected now, when they walked though those detector things at airports. It meant the government knew how many there were and everything. There would be lists of the gifted, children and any adults who had travelled by air in the last year or so. Juliet reckoned it could have been how they found me, though it could have been my SATS or something. You have to go through a bloody metal detector to go on a coach now. I had to thumb a lift up from Sheffield, because I would have been traced on the way back.'

'Do you have enough money? Are you going to be alright for the next few weeks?' Manee looked at him anxiously. 'I've got no idea how much longer I'm going to be here; in fact, the more I think about it, I imagine they'll want to get rid of us as soon as possible. They won't want their preparations being exposed to the rest of the world.'

Brian looked out over the quiet town. From their distant viewpoint no individual voice could be heard, but the streets were busy with children and the green of Castle mount was covered with them, lying on their backs, looking up at the colouring clouds.

'Have I ever told you that they know I'm here?' Brian looked up now at Manee. 'I've noticed it more and more recently. I can feel them too. It's like a gentle tug; it feels so natural. Several times I've just wanted to walk down the hill and climb over the barrier.' Manee was taken aback.

'You all communicate?'

'No, not exactly; it's more instinctive, cruder than that. I guess the gift isn't very strong with me, I've never really noticed it to be honest, but when I'm close to them all, up here, I can just feel them. It's like they want me to join them. I think they are getting stronger every day.'

'I don't think you should join them, Brian. I think you are better off where you are.'

'You think they are going to kill us all, don't you Patrick? They are going to kill us all, because they don't know if they'll be able to control us.'

'I... don't know, Brian, I really don't know... It seems impossible that they should try something so barbaric. We should be fostering the gifted, helping you to assimilate; you might be the next stage of our evolution, who knows? Maybe you will end up replacing us. It's possible. Maybe that is what world governments would be afraid of.'

'But wouldn't you do away with us all, if you are honest? You've been living with them; you must know what they can do, what we can do. My gift is weak, but I can still see what they have done to you; I can feel the difference in you, Patrick. You couldn't put up with that forever. In six months you'll be dead, even if you carry on the way you are going now, taking time away. If I go, you have to promise me that you'll go too.'

Manee looked away from Brian's searching eyes. 'I'm not sure I can make that promise. I have responsibilities here. I have responsibilities to the children here.'

'Do you think it will make any difference in the end? If this is what they really want to do? If they want us dead, they'll hunt us down in every town and village, they'll come with the detectors we've given them. If anyone is to blame it is me.' He bowed his head and wiped a snotty tear from his face. 'It's the only reason I haven't gone to join them.'

'You can't mean that; you can't blame yourself for what's happened. It was an accident, from what you've told me, a fluke. You didn't sell them out. You've been watching over them; you've been their guardian and you still are.' Brian's tears had turned to sobs and, though he tried to disguise them, he began to shake uncontrollably. Manee wanted to place an arm over his shoulders, but felt unable to.

'We can't see into the future Brian, we really don't know what is to come. There is one thing, however, that I do know. The gifted are remarkable and their powers pretty much untested. I dread to think what could happen if the army attempted to attack this place by force, and it wouldn't be just the gifted they would have to fight either. You are not alone in this. There are lots of people out there worrying about their children, their families and their friends. We won't forsake you. If we go down, we go down together.'

Manee did not allow himself to dwell on the horror of what he was saying. He had phone calls to make, people to warn, children to rescue. No, surely not, this was unthinkable. He needed more information. As he walked back to the town through the fading light, however, he felt as if the sun was going down on all of them for the last time.

PART FIVE

THE END OF ALL THINGS

ONE

'There is a road block. What do you think we should do?' Miguel looked out the sun-roof of the MG and scanned the road ahead.

'Turn round, there has to be another way. There is one of those magnetic gate things set up; I can see it on the side of the road. Manee was right to warn us, they want us all dead.' The desperation and misery in his voice was hardened with an edge Suzi had not heard before. It was a voice tempered with anxiety camouflaged as anger, the type of voice he might have used to his colleagues before a big fight, the kind of voice you might use in the trenches. There were no atheists in the trenches. She had read the phrase a few days before, but now they were all in the trenches she really had no idea what to believe in. News from the US came thick and fast. There had been a terrible fire in a gifted enclosure in one of the southern states. Initially it had been called a tragedy, a terrible accident brought about by poor building practices employed by immigrant labour who had built the camp. Later it had been blamed on a rogue Christian fundamentalist terrorist group, who called themselves 'God in our Image'. The GIOI had been festering in an Illinois backwater. The sect leader had denied the allegation but had apparently committed suicide a few days later. A note found beneath his swinging, lifeless body asked forgiveness for his sins. Miguel said it bore all the marks of a CIA job. The number of dead in the fire was yet to be established. The horror had occurred at night: a gas explosion. The fireball had been visible from space. This had been the first of a series of attacks by the GIOI sect. The current wave of road-

348

blocks and cordons was supposedly to prevent further attacks.

Suzi swung the MG back down the opposite carriageway. She hoped the manoeuvre would not be noticed by the policoid uniforms on the roadway. 'Policoid' was a phrase that had grown out of a rising wave of liberal disgust at global developments in security; the army were too busy protecting the oil reserves to perform any home-guard function, and the police were for the most part either chasing the manic gifted or engaged in sorting out cases of identity theft. Now home security was almost entirely in the realm of the private 'policeoid' firms. The wannabe soldiers and failed policemen of the world had at last found their spiritual home. What they lacked in experience and power they made up with intransigence and inflexibility. Suzi had had to restrain Miguel on several occasions. His powerful build, swarthy complexion and physical presence was a red rag to this herd of testosterone-fuelled bulls. His rich southern French accent made baiting him entirely irresistible.

'If it comes to it we'll just have to hire cars on the other side of the cordon and cross the checkpoints on foot'. Trains and coaches were off limits now. You had to walk through a scanner just to buy a ticket. In policoid England even breaks in your paper chain could lead to suspicion. Failure to renew an insurance policy almost guaranteed a knock on the door from some burly youth in a nylon-serge uniform.

They drove through rambling countryside, through little villages and border farms. Their intention was to reach Denbigh by the following day, but now they would have to find a Bed and Breakfast, somewhere in the country that still accepted cash. The government's tax breaks for cash-free transactions had made real money a rarity. Bills could also be traced in an instant, but bills needed to be scanned and people that still insisted on handling the antiquated things were not always the most keen to advertise that fact.

The Bed and Breakfast was upstairs over a pub. The

glass-eyed fox's head mounted over the fireplace, the faded, mis-matched chintz and the total absence of rustic charm immediately identified it as the genuine article. The landlady, a big-armed woman who filled the cut of her dress like toothpaste in a tube, eyed them with barely disguised suspicion. A child in a baby bouncer, with swollen puppy-fat arms, screamed for attention in the mix and match stick-furnished hall. Suzi did the talking as they stepped over discarded toys: breakfast at nine would be fine, no, neither of them had funny dietary requirements, no, they didn't mind dogs and no, they probably would not be wanting dinner this evening, they appreciated the kitchen would be quiet, what with the difficulty with travelling at the moment and no, Miguel was not a traveller, he was just French.

The room was small, the angles of roof and floor both disconcerting and structurally remarkable. The bed must have had springs at some point in its history, but was now more an artist's impression of a bed; a montage installation of wire, dumped timber and fluff. They sunk into it and into each other, rolling together exactly as the previous thousand couples had done so on the bed before them. Gravity and the metallic memory of tired wires held them close and slowly, gently, they yielded to its coaxing and the desire that had been simmering between them throughout the day. The raw sexuality of Miguel had inhibited Suzi from the beginning of their relationship. His need, so childlike yet wrapped in his powerful frame, seemed to cry out to her. She wanted to release this child, hold him to her heart and tell him everything would all be okay. The need had asked her to wrestle with the muscular frame before her, fight it and slay it, but there was a voice in her too, who wanted the masculine frame to wrestle her to submission. The conflict had made their sex disjointed, passion and fear exerting themselves in violent waves. They had also sensed something else, hiding in the space between them: an invisible phantasm, sexual but tainted, an intimate voyeur excited and jealous in vindictive turns. In this moment the creature made itself known to Suzi, a thought caught in between the angles of their bodies, the angles of the bed and the folded up room. They held each other tight, hands exploring, hardness on soft, softness on hard.

'We are the same: two positive forces, two norths together. We glide over each other, we never really touch. You have felt it, haven't you?' Suzi spoke slowly, breathing in Miguel's musk; studying the coiled black nest of hair on his navel, soft on hard. 'I want to use it, the gift, I know you do too. But together we can't, one of us must yield, one of us must take the chance.' Miguel held her tighter to him, kissed her neck, her throat, her breasts. The man asked her to yield, but the boy spoke to her through his eyes. She kissed him on the lips and gently whispered. 'Tonight you will give yourself to me. Tomorrow, I will be yours.' His body shuddered and his eyes became damp. The boy reached out to her and she felt the gift reach from her. It was soft; like the merest touch of fingertips at first; mirroring her own gentle caress, tracing the lines of muscles, rolling off sparks from shoulder to curving biceps, from the curve of his long fingers to her own fondant whiteness. Miguel felt himself lifted, his body, taut and vibrating, but light as a feather, caught in a maelstrom, rising then falling as if he had been dealt an unimaginable blow. There was no pain, just unbearable lightness. He braced himself for the impact but it did not come. His mind experienced incredible forces, but his body was warm. Suzi morphed into a vision of succulent motion, a thousand fluttering butterflies, a thousand silk caresses. Her every move so gentle, but their combined effect as irresistible as an avalanche. He was buffeted, and carried, helpless in a cloud of pleasure. Bewildered as he was, his arousal almost came a surprise. It was like nothing he had experienced before, the yearning did not build in intensity, but appeared fully formed crashing into his brain like the sun bursting from behind a cloud. He found he could reach out and pull Suzi towards him, her quicksilver body shimmering beneath his arms. In sexual union they were as if fused, a continuum, the ancient four-armed god, rolling in on itself, engorged on its own atavistic pleasure. Sweat suddenly erupted from their bodies, a twinkling in blue spectra; he found himself sinking, falling though waves of light. The world exploded in a glorious explosion of unbearable joy and he found himself crying out. Then everything became dark.

TWO

A lone long-distance lorry driver lay on the roof of his cab on a dark stretch of desert highway. He had had to pull over; the flicker of the road markings, the rolling of the cab, the gentle rocking of the Country and Western radio station were conspiring to send him to sleep. As he lay draped over his cab, he thought of his wife and his little girl, only twelve, but already so bright. She had been taken to the Santa-Fé Institute when the troubles had started. They had said she was special in some way, gifted if you like. He had visited her in the institute, overawed by the equipment, the professors, the maths. His little girl had smiled and shown him fantastic games and puzzles he could not have begun to understand himself. She had explained things patiently, encouraging him when he got something right. Somewhere in his heart he felt every man would eventually be overtaken by the progress of his children. In your dotage you ultimately threw yourself on their mercy, such was man's lot in life. He had been superseded at thirty four. Somehow it did not seem entirely fair. On her last visit they had driven into the desert on a night like this. She had wanted to show him something, but they needed darkness and a clear sky. She had asked him to turn off the cab headlights and had held his hand whilst she pointed out the constellations and the planets. He searched the sky now, trying to remember some of what she had told him, but the world was constantly turning, and things didn't look quite the same. He found the river of the Milky Way as his eyes became accustomed to the darkness. It had reminded him of the path of a fish he had seen from his father's boat when night fishing in the bay.

As it glided along it had elicited a sparkling trail of luminance in the water. He wondered at the magnificence of a
fish that could leave such a trail in the sky.

He found a bright light that he thought he recognised,
yellow-orange and low in the sky. His daughter had pointed this out as Jupiter, the biggest of the solar system's
planets, too small to be a sun, unimaginably more vast
than the Earth. Her eyes had lit up when she had told him
of the storms that raged across it: tornadoes that lasted
eighty years. At first he had not believed her, it all seemed
too remarkable, but in the middle of the night on a lonely
road not so different to this, he had got into conversation
on the CB with another driver who had an almost disturbing knowledge of the night sky. How they had got to talk
of it, he could not remember, but the trucker had confirmed everything. He had found strange comfort listening
to this voice, miles away up the road, telling him that his
daughter was so bright and so right. Telling him that she
and Jupiter and the whole world was real; because sometimes, on the open road at night in the dark, it felt as if you
could be alone in the universe. To think of space all
around, was terrifying, it was a cold, black blanket populated by monsters.

The insignificance of man in this picture had never
depressed him. He had been brought up in the Methodist
way and he was happy to leave the maintenance of the
clockwork universe to God. The CB man had tried to tell
him that the universe was not as cut and dried as the popular scientists would have you believe. He had spoken in a
sing-song way about Anthropic Principles and paradoxes
and used German words which could have meant anything. He had listened to the CB man as the road hummed
beneath the tires and he had not really understood anything save that the man's soft voice seemed to be telling
him that many futures were possible and man's place in
the present was a wonderful happy coincidence. He looked
at Jupiter and thought of his daughter. Perhaps the CB
man would be on again this evening; he had some questions he wanted to ask.

At that split second in time on a world populated by nearly eight billion people, only three hundred were looking directly in the direction of Jupiter and of those only forty five had an unhindered view. Of those few, only twenty-one knew what they were looking at and none had a telescope powerful enough to resolve any but the largest cyclonic systems. If they had, they would have seen two deep-red storms, each as large as the Earth, coalescing into a single, swirling, bloody eye. They would have then been amazed to see them just as quickly twist apart, resolving back to their former states, recoiling as if their merger had caused them sudden and unexpected pain. An observer would have seen a ripple pass across the face of Jupiter momentarily disturbing the balletic flow of clouds, then just as quickly leave. Jove continued to dance and no one saw him stumble.

THREE

Manee looked at the orders on the scrap of paper in front of him. All non-essential personnel to leave the enclosure by the end of the week. His job was considered non-essential; knowing what he did, he should have been overjoyed.

He threw himself onto his single bed and stared at the cobwebs decorating the corner of the room. He was suddenly and acutely aware that the following few days would come to define him for the rest of his life. He had experienced many moments of fear and trepidation in his career. The police were exposed every day to the raw meat of society, the guts and gore of its underbelly, things which somehow seemed as if they should be kept hidden from the light of day. He had lived through times when he knew his aspirations were at stake, when he had to show he could deal with the fear and the gore. This current situation was not about his aspirations, it was not about his future. It would colour his future and his past and quite likely would lead to his imprisonment or death. It was about everyone. How far would the government go? This was the question, how terrified were they of the gifted? The magnitude of this fear would determine their course of action and ultimately his fate. It seemed outlandish that the government could consider eradicating the gifted; such a crime against their own citizens would lead to civil war. The attacks by GIOI could be a cover for their activities, but this thought itself seemed ridiculous, unbelievable, the fantasy of a conspiracy theorist gone mad. Western governments did not exterminate swaths of their own population at a whim, did they? Though history was not his strong point, the answer kept coming back: yes. If the GIOI were a cover for the military, they had to be exposed. Only then could he be sure that his perceived threat was real. Extraordinary claims required extraordinary evidence. There had to be other things he could do, contingencies in case his worse fears should be realised before he had chance to obtain the proof he needed to expose them. His mind was working overtime. Schindler had put the Jews to work, he had used the system, worked it from inside. He understood it. That had to be the answer. In one place the children were vulnerable; they had to be disseminated, dispersed, ideally amongst their families, but any redistribution would be better than none. A health scare? The Asian flu? If an outbreak of that was suspected, could he get children distributed to hospitals for check ups? Manee had made friends with a few of the medical staff, one doctor in fact had taken quite a shine to him. Perhaps he could bring them onboard, explain the situation. There was a danger that he could start a wild rumour. If word got out to the authorities, the army might move immediately. The consequences of his blowing the whistle would inevitably be his arrest, and who knew how many spies there were inside the enclosure. He himself was effectively working undercover.

Then an idea came to him, fully formed in his mind and perfect. He would use the threat of an attack by GIOI themselves to evacuate the centre. In the ensuing panic he might be able to get some of the children away. He would need a fleet of buses. It would not be easy. The idea reformatted itself. He would warn the newspapers that there was the imminent threat of an attack on the centre, and then stage a small explosion. If the information was released to the press, the parents would arrive and demand the release of their children. The parents would supply the vehicles. If the government wanted to stop them they would have to do so very publicly and in full view of the nation's press. Yes, the media seemed to be the answer. He would blow up a building and blow up the secrecy surrounding the camp. He had enough experience that the causing of an explosion would not be difficult, but there were protocols to be followed. An anonymous warning to the papers would not ring any alarms unless accompanied by a code sign, the key to validate the warning.

The realisation dawned that he had not been informed of any such key. It was normal police practice for the commanding officer to receive the code in case the terrorists should give warning of an attack. With the slimming down of the force he was now the most senior regular uniform on site. He should have been given the codes. Every terrorist used police codes, it gave them kudos; even the crummy anti-vivisectionists with their wire-cutters and their car-bombs gave cryptic warnings accompanied by a code-word. Without a police code you were a nobody, an also ran, not considered important enough to constitute a real threat. According to the press and the limited briefings he had had on the GIOI, the government were in dialogue with them, but there had been no mention of codes. It was an astonishing procedural error that pointed to one thing. Why would the GIOI need a code to verify a warning if the government itself was the GIOI? It would hardly need to warn itself.

There was a loud knock at the door. It was the Camp Governor, a Mr Langerton, a rather nervous, chinless man whose eyes seemed constantly to be looking for an escape from the room. He introduced Manee to two men in matching black suits. 'Detective Inspector Manee, I would like to introduce you to Ser... I mean... Mr. Howard and Mr Wolfowicz. They have been assigned here to facilitate the transfer of the camp from our hands to those of our replacements.' Manee looked the men up and down. It was clear that their beautifully tailored civilian suits, whilst fitting their ample frames perfectly, were somewhat uncomfortable for them. 'I would appreciate it if you would bring them up to speed on any procedural elements they may need help with.'

Manee tried to read the governor's eyes, but they were busy exploring the window catches and the fire-escapes.

'And who exactly are we handing over to Mr Langerton?' For a moment the Governor's eyes flicked in Manee's direction, and Manee thought he caught the subtlest flicker of embarrassed displeasure.

'That is not for the likes of us to worry about, Detective Inspector. We are all servants, are we not, of His Majesty's Government.' He turned on his heels and Howard and Wolfowicz slunk away.

Langerton looked back over his shoulder as if making a final inspection of his escape route. 'I trust you will give your full co-operation to these two gentlemen, Detective Inspector. A lot depends on a this transfer going smoothly. You wouldn't want to find yourself stuck here in a week's time after everyone else has gone. Our baby-sitting job here is over. There are other things to be done.'

As Manee closed the door, he cursed himself for rousing the Governor's umbrage. He should have played it cooler. If he was to discover anything about their plans he would have to do it stealthily. He collapsed onto the bed, but was immediately disturbed by his mobile. It was Suzi Rothermann.

'Detective Manee? This is Suzi and Miguel. We did not want to impose on you or concern you, but we have driven up to North Wales. We are staying in a village about twenty miles south of Denbigh. Agneta Sibilski and Edward Spinks lead us to believe you were going to try to help the gifted children...' The line became silent for a moment. Manee realised his heart was racing. He needed more time, he was not ready for this. 'As you are aware, Edward's nephew is among the gifted in Denbigh. We want to help him; we'd like to help you.'

'I'll meet you in the Bull Inn on the outskirts of Ruhin at 8:00pm.' He turned the phone off. The message could have been intercepted, but they had said little that would immediately arouse suspicion. He needed time (or was it space?) to think. There was precious little of either. He did not know if Suzi or Miguel would be of any practical assistance to him. But in the preceding moments before their phone-call he had felt more alone than he had ever done in his life. Maybe, just maybe, he had not been lying when he had reassured Brian on the quarry hill. Perhaps the gifted did have allies after all.

359

FOUR

The transition to a wretched life on the streets had been seamless for Kevin Masters. His mind was addled, of that he was acutely aware, but it didn't seem to matter. Self-worth now had a whole new world of meaning. His previous vanities, his clothes, his nice car, his education and his merciless parasitism on those less well educated now seemed pitiful travesties in a meaningless froth of existence. He knew now that he was something altogether different and separate and this new-found perspective elevated him over trivial human concerns. His silver suit, which at one point had delighted him, was rank with the accumulated grime of several weeks. The world was basically filthy and true immersion in it left you sodden and stinking. His ability to roam, detached and distracted, filthy and fetid amongst the rest of society amazed him. He had railed at people in the street, screamed into their faces, to tell them who and what he was. They had walked away without looking back. Stiff little arses, eyes front, knuckled white hands caressing valuables. He had shouted like a madman at their retreating forms. 'I don't want to rob you; I want to eat you!' But they had not looked back.

Now he found himself in a piss-soaked alley, sitting under a painted sign.

'Please spare some change, this man is shy.' Amongst the winos he was invisible. No one looked for filth; everyone glanced at you, but not a single person saw you. Occasionally he caught his reflection in a shop window, but he tried not to look. He knew he was becoming confused as to who or what he was. That ragged face was barely recognisable to him. He did not want to be that man, he was not even sure he had pity for him. The winos were easy prey. They were a mixed bunch and he had been surprised to discover the wealth of their pedigree. He was not the only former company director checking the pizza boxes in the dustbins for crusts. One of the regulars outside the all-night Lebanese restaurant still had a seat on several boards. There were druggies too, of course, but they were rarely of any interest. The world could be divided into sources and sinks and the young druggies were sinks. Time ran into them and through them. In their presence he felt the pull of their desire. They were like him, feeding on those around them, sapping the thoughtful and the selfless; gaping bird-mouths, yellow-lipped and insatiable. He hated them. He had been there himself, seeking in the chemical haze to dull the yearning pain. His new life had opened his eyes to this. He now cast scornful looks on those shooting up around him. He despised them with the particular passion of one who could truly despise their own past life. It was a particularly clear and pure scorn, the distillate of wasted time.

On one occasion he had actually met a creature like himself. He could have so easily missed the signs and signals, the man had been little more than a shell of a living thing, a skin inflated with acrid smoke and emphysemic inhalations. So weak was the man's grasp on the mortal coil that his gift had appeared to shimmer, but the signs had been there. Their eyes had met for the briefest of moments, a gaze like a flicked cigarette from under a shuffling duffle coat. Their mutual recognition had caused them to freeze, gazes locked together in feral measure, all movement in space frozen in their joint displeasure. Kevin saw the skin around the man's mouth wrinkle into the beginnings of a sneer, but he was weak and the hoods of the eyes descended and he withdrew. His immediate and intense recoil from the creature shocked and appalled him; here after all was one of his own kind. The sight of another creature, so desperate and weakened, had filled him with horror, but some long forgotten memory of territorial behaviour told him that was how it should be. As he sat in the shadows, slipping down the cider and slowly absorbing the elemental time of the down-and-outs, he felt strangely satisfied. He had managed to evade the authorities so far and in spite of having been reduced to feeding off the weak, his gift was growing in strength and complexity. Like Bill Morris before him, he had begun to understand its benefits and subtleties and as the light faded and the shadows stretched he ignored the cold by sliding past the cider-haze and slipping into the glorious warmth that timelessness provided.

He was woken by a sharp knock to the back of his head and his disorientation was further compounded as lights flashed into his eyes. He recoiled from a boot that crashed into his stomach and instinctively curled into a ball as a flurry of punches rained down upon him. He was drowsy with booze, physically weak from lack of food and the greater part of his conscious mind was floating in a warm place between the ticks of the clock, but anger began to dispel the mists and the gentle heat began to pulse in brighter hues. As the boot came in for another blow, he allowed his gift to fly from him; the tungsten light was dismissed in a flash of blue. He slid from under their slow ballet, and found his feet, pain hit him in slow waves, pulsed and sickening, but without its raw sting it could be ignored. He rose to his feet, delighting in the pleasing wave of crackling light that played over his ragged frame. The outward discharges were accompanied by an ecstatic internal flame that rose in response to the gift as it fed from the hapless policemen that now faced him. Unable to bring his eyes into focus, Kevin was unable to strike out with any precision, but he had enough control of his powers to know that accuracy was unnecessary. As he unleashed the gift again he found himself staggering backwards into the darkness, the exploding envelope of time hitting him like a wave. Time dilated and curled around him and he danced before it like a conductor before the shock wave of an orchestral hit. The two policemen could not enjoy the spectacle. His catlike escape may have registered on their retinae; neurons may have fired in response to the preternatural light that glowed from him, but time for them suddenly span away impossibly fast. Their minds were caught in its sweep and sentience was wiped from the surface of their brains. Their lives could not pass before their eyes before the veil dropped, there was insufficient time for such brain chemistry to act. Electrons hung in quantum stillness, vibrations held their breaths and the playful knot of space-time that was their conciousness became suddenly brittle. As the universe collapsed in on them, it splintered and exploded. The most meaningful alignment of energy in the universe dissipated into incoherent heat.

To say that their bodies were lifeless when they hit the floor would have been untrue. Every cell of every organ at that brief moment was as alive as it had ever been. The spark of life that each cell contained, the product of thermodynamic engines making order from chaos, continued unabated; cells respired but the bodies did not breath. The brain too was not stilled, activity would have been detected by ECG or NMR, but the mind was gone; all that remained were flares and waves, ripples on a lake, decaying patterns, remarkable and beautiful, but not alive.

Kevin was no longer aware of the bodies slumped on the ground. He staggered away, only dimly aware of why he had to leave. The white light was in control now, glorious and warm; it saturated his senses and all other cares fled before it. He had tried in the past to climb out of the glorious light, to dwell on the threshold of the door of perception that opened in such moments. Time dilation allowed him to experience everything with a clarity that was itself sublime. Unfortunately the glory that accompanied it this time, drug-like in its purity, was too powerful a draw. He allowed exquisite reality to slip away and fell into the arms of hebetudinous joy.

FIVE

It did not make any sense. Brahma Sikurda stood in the middle of his greenhouses and shook his head. No terrible damage was done as such, they would just have to go off in the trucks tomorrow rather than today. Initially he had got angry with his subordinates; perhaps someone had left a door open, or forgotten to turn on a heater, but that really didn't make sense. It had been a wonderful warm and humid night and the rose buds, which were showing the first blood of promise, should have burst to reveal their spiralling hearts. He had been growing roses for fifteen years and the one thing that had dominated his thoughts over this time was the timing of flowering. Timing was everything, it was the difference between making a single delivery or setting up a contract, it was the difference between success and failure of a small, independent company. Nature had been tamed in this greenhouse. Nature was predictable- in colour, in size, in length of stem and density of thorn, in blush and stamen, in burnish of leaf and most importantly in compactness of blossom. There were the occasional sports and mutations, of course. A lonely white, single rose amongst a greenhouse of crowded purple extravagances. They were weeded out and destroyed. This was different. Fourteen thousand roses in a giant swathe in a greenhouse the size of ten tennis courts and half the population in the greenhouse next door, had decided they would hide their beauty for another day. Today should have been the day. It really did not make sense. There had been a lot of flapping of hands and shouting, but it simply could not be explained rationally. A rose does not begin to open and then suddenly change its mind and coyly decide to hide its beauty away again. There would be some difficult phone-calls to make. He picked one of the tight-lipped blossoms. He studied it, as if hoping it could tell him something, but it had nothing to say.

SIX

The Bull Inn in was a modern symphony of stripped-pine, chatty chalk boards and assorted 'rustic' objects. Mining paraphernalia was mixed with obscure farming and cockling equipment; modern public house interior design did not concern itself with the aesthetics of utility. The pub had just opened after the refurbishment and the handful of locals who had supported the former business were not yet sufficiently desperate to return, so it was not difficult for Manee to find a quiet corner. With a Victorian sickle and a grubbing-eye mattock hanging precariously from the ceiling above them, Suzi and Miguel introduced themselves to Manee.

'It can't have been easy for you to get across the border.' Manee passed frothing pints around the table. 'Security is pretty tight now. There is practically martial law throughout the country. It is amazing how far the government has been able to go without declaring a state of emergency. It makes you wonder how far they could go.'

Suzi and Miguel eyed Manee suspiciously. This man was speaking exactly as they might have allowed themselves to hope for. But they were not convinced they could trust him.

'This is our worry, Patrick. We have become concerned for the children; there have been too many accidents and concerted attacks by the GIOI; we are suspicious that the government is not doing everything that it could do to protect them.' Suzi resisted the urge to look over her shoulder but she lowered her voice nonetheless. 'We feel that the government is complicit in the attacks on the children. It makes sense: the gifted are a dangerous liability that I'm sure they would love to wash their hands of.'

366

'And how much do you know about the gifted?' Manee watched their eyes. He had been burned by the gifted before, and the intensity of Bill's gaze was clear in his mind's eye. As Suzi's eye's flicked around the room and came to rest on him he knew he was right. He felt the weakest echo of that which he had felt with Bill. Something within him recoiled from her gaze. Could it be that he could detect them now just by being exposed to them? It seemed incredible.

Suzi was about to speak, but he could see the internal conflict written across her face. He saved her the trouble. 'Suzi, I know you are one of the gifted, why else would you be here now.' Miguel slid back in his seat and, as their eyes met, Manee felt the gentle probing of Miguel's mind too. 'You have nothing to fear from me. I have no desire to hand you over to any authorities, I'm not even sure the powers-that-be are interested in adults yet, though it is only a matter of time, I guess.' The way he had said it, so matter-of-factly, there seemed little point in denying it.

'I'm not sure that question is relevant, Patrick. I can assure you our motives for helping the children have not come as a result of fears for our own safety. If the police want to attack the gifted they will have to come in force.' Her mind flew to the image of her love in the paper, the blur of speed, power unleashed between the blinking of the camera eye. 'The gifted adults can look after themselves, if it should come to that. It is the children we have to worry about now. You have been working with them, Patrick. You have seen them, you must know what they are capable of. You must also have some kind of idea about what the authorities plan to do.'

Manee shook his head. 'I will be relieved of duty very soon. And yes, I have have seen the gifted in action on several occasions, and I do fear for their safety. I agreed to see you today because I want to help, whilst I still have the opportunity to do so. The regular police are soon to be replaced with another policoid group. I have only met a few of them, but everything about them screams of the army, or a paramilitary organisation. They are sponsored by the government, of that there can be no doubt, but they could be from any number of organisations and at the moment I have no idea what they plan to do in Denbigh.'

'How much time do you think we have?' Manee's mind flashed back to his conversation with the camp Governor, 'You don't want to be here in a week's time.' It had been a blatant warning. 'We have a week. If you want to help we must move quickly, perhaps tonight. There is much we have to do.' Every cell of Suzi's brian was aching with the desire to trust this man. She so wanted to trust him, it was almost unbearable, but it was not just herself she had to think of.

At that moment Miguel pushed his beer aside and leaned towards Manee. He glanced over his shoulder at Suzi. 'We can trust this man.' He spoke with complete authority and coming from the lips of the man she was growing to love, the words rang true.

'But how can you be sure?' Suzi reached for his hand and gently squeezed it.

'Manee is one of us, can't you tell?'

Manee stared back at them in stunned amazement. He felt his world falling away from him, it could not be true, could it? He had seen Bill Morris escaping through the crowds and had watched in stunned amazement, he had seen the sullen looks of the gifted teenagers, seen the mental anguish they had unleashed on those that crossed their paths. He had felt the power of the gifted mind and he watched Bill Morris' catlike movements time and time again in slow motion. If he was honest with himself he had wanted to taste that power. He wanted to know how it must feel to be able to defy nature itself. He had wondered what it would be like to be feared. Now this Frenchman with flashing eyes was telling me he was one of their number. It was too much to believe.

'We can trust him, because he must help us. We are of the same kind. Ultimately society will turn against us and he will be thrown amongst us. He must join us now or suffer with us later.' Miguel spoke with such quiet authority.

There was an uneasy silence around the table.

'Can I get anyone another drink?' The pleasantly smiling barmaid woke Manee from the turmoil of his thoughts.

'What, sorry, another drink, yes... yes, please.' The barmaid waited patiently. 'What would you like Sir?'

'What...? Oh, anything, anything at all. I'll have a whisky, make it a double, make it a good one.' He downed the remaining dregs of his glass and looked around the table. What would you like? I think I need one more and then we should get busy. We have much to do.'

Over the course of the next hour he outlined his plans. They listened carefully, interjecting where necessary. They had skills he should know about, they could help him more than he could imagine. Miguel assured him that in spite of being unaware of his own potential, it was just a question of time before the powers that the gift implied would reveal themselves. When he said goodnight to them, his mind was ringing with a song from his youth. It was The Smiths or Morrissey, he could not be sure: 'When your gift unfurls, when your talent becomes apparent, I will roar from the stalls, I will gurgle from the circle. The saints smile shyly down on you. Oh, they couldn't get over your nine-leaf clover...' It was a miracle, incredible. He found his heart racing, his mind, sharper than it had ever seemed before. Perhaps they were right. He might have to practise, might need to get some help, find out how he might develope his gift- after all, he needed it now more than ever.

Miguel and Suzi sank back together into the impossible depths of their bed. Suzi ran her hands over Miguel's lips and along the line of his jaw.

'How can you be so sure Patrick Manee is one of the gifted? I was watching him all evening, but I never saw a sign of it. I didn't feel it. I know you are so much more attuned than I am, but, I don't know, I didn't feel it myself.'

Miguel kissed her gently on the forehead, nose and then slowly on the mouth.

'I'm afraid Monsieur Manee is not gifted, Suzi, but at

this moment in time, he thinks that he is and that has to be to our advantage. Do you not think so?'

Suzi pushed herself away from him as best she could. She looked into the dark eyes of the beautiful man before her. 'How could you lie like that? I'm... I don't know what to say.'

He pulled her back towards him and whispered into her ear.

'It was necessary, you will understand that later. You must know, I would never lie to you.' He held her tightly and she prayed to God that it were true.

SEVEN

Daniel checked to see if the road was empty. The street-lights illuminated everything with a warm and comforting glow. Tonight he cursed their brightness. Seeing no-one he walked around the periphery of the square. Once he had slid down a side alley behind the pub he would be relatively safe; his escape route was carefully planned, he had made this journey a hundred times before in his dreams. As he crept past the other doors in the street, his senses alive to any sound, he was amazed to find everything so incredibly quiet. There was not a soul moving about in this sleepy town save him. He felt privileged to be able to share this private moment with the town, he had become very familiar with its varied ramshackle charms. He glanced up at the castle. Illuminated by spotlights, it seemed Arthurian and ethereal. He would miss the view from the battlements, but tonight he had to escape from its gaze. Once across the street he could slide into the shadows, a quick run and jump and he was onto an old coalbunker and up and over a high wall. He scampered across this high-rise walkway, somewhat exposed, but in almost complete darkness. There was no moon and to an observer he would have been nothing but another inky smudge on the black face of the night. The whitewashed wall beneath his feet provided enough reflected luminance for him to find his way. He had to beware of the scrambling tentacles of Old-Man's beard and honeysuckle, which were festooned across his path. He descended from the wall and crossed a darkened allotment. With the people of Denbigh excluded from their homes, the neat rows of cabbage and carrots were neglected and overgrown with brambles. Skeleton

371

rows of bean poles and pea-sticks hid him as he slipped through long grass. Time and time again an unseen briar tripped him or whipped across his face. The tenacious grip of nature itself seemed to want him to stay in this open prison. Tonight he was leaving, nature's thorny hands would be left empty.

He had wanted to take others with him, but in quiet, whispered conversations he had been told to go alone. In groups they had far more chance of being caught; alone, via different and varied exits, they had more of a chance. The circumferential security around the town was quiet of late. For all their talk of wanting to protect the children from external attack and the GIOI, the show of security was concentrated almost exclusively at the main gates. There had been wandering guards with dogs, but the dogs seemed exquisitely sensitive to the gifted and, after showing their teeth once or twice to the children, they had all been withdrawn, their constant whimpering having become too upsetting for their handlers. In the last few weeks security had become even more lax, and even the wandering night staff that went from house to house had ceased to call. If he was to leave at any time it had to be now. Patrick Manee had as good as told him to go only a few nights before. 'There will be a new moon on Friday night.' was all he had said, but his eyes had spoken volumes. As he stumbled through the debris of abandoned conscientious gardening, Daniel wished he had a little moonlight to guide him. He had not been out of the camp for nearly six months now and as he strayed further from its core in the darkness, he almost felt a pang of fear. He had no idea if the external world had changed in his absence. He half expected to find a post-apocalyptic desert beyond the confines of the Northern hills. He carried a light rucksack, some high calorie food he had been able to sequester and a litre of water. He was not sure how far he could get without money, but in post-apocalyptic Britain perhaps there would be no need for such trivialities. They had of course received a continued barrage of television and film inside the enclosure, and there had been a steady stream of visitors, including his own mother on two occasions, but who was to know if such visits and images were controlled by the prison warders. There was a thin line between cynicism and paranoia and he had little idea which side of this he was on. His mother had told him not to worry, the 'accidents' and 'incidents' in France and America could not happen in Britain, of that she was sure. In the compound they had not heard any news of such events, though there had been quiet talk in the corridors that the gifted were being eliminated by stealth. There were many small groups hatching escape plans, and this had partly contributed to his own resolve to go immediately. He cursed himself that his own success might make things more difficult for those left behind. This was war, however, and there would be casualties on both sides.

In the last segment of his escape, he had to climb again. This section he had had to plan from afar, sitting with glasses on the highest points of the castle and church tower, scanning the view for suitably hidden escape routes. On one occasion he had even borrowed a high power pair from a guard under the pretence of birdwatching. He had tried to get several angles of viewpoint: errors of parallax could foil his plans and there were a few big leaps to perform. He scrambled up a pile of oil cans and onto a low garage, from this it was an easy climb onto the roof of an outbuilding, onto a window ledge and up onto the roof of one of the cottages. The slates were dry and his footing fairly secure, but his sudden height and exposure made his blood run cold. The air was warm and he could smell the roses clambering up the front of the cottage. He climbed the gable, treading softly in the hope that he would not wake the sleeping occupants. On the far side of the building the security fence was very close to the house. On the other side of that there was an old shed built into the structure of the quarry wall, When they had installed the fence the builders had lazily run its course between the two buildings. From the shed it would be an impossible leap up and over the fence onto the cottage roof, but it had seemed possible, at least from a distance, to leap over the barrier with the advantage of height. Now, staring into the darkness, Daniel was not so sure. He could just make out the line of the fence, but the shed was in total darkness. There was no telling if the structure would bear his weight when he landed on its roof, but it was worth an attempt. The fall was perhaps twelve feet from roof to roof, he had to stay high because of the barrier. It was a leap into nothingness. Daniel heard his heart thumping in his chest. From the castle he had imagined himself running down this slope of roof and making the leap, but now it was before him he realised that the incline was steeper than he had imagined. Once he had committed himself there was no going back, but it would be difficult to get the take off from the end. He had tried to dive once off the intermediate board at the swimming pool in Cardiff. He had gone with a friend as a child and he had sat on the edge whilst his friend, who was quite a confident diver, had encouraged him from the water below. His body would naturally form the right shape his friend had said, just relax and it would all naturally flow. He had sat, tucked up into a 'pike' edging slowly forward, buttock-cheek steps, heart pounding. He had dropped off the edge, silently, flown through space and had struck the water in exactly the same shape. The water had slapped into his chest like a sheet of plate glass; he could remember the incredible stinging pain even now. He tried to shake the thought from his head but it was firmly lodged. There was no plate glass water to break his fall, only a thin line of rusty razor-wire and the cold stone sides of a quarry.

He closed his eyes, breathed deeply and prepared to make the leap.

'Wait!' A hoarse forced whisper came from below. 'You'll never make it! Climb down and I'll cut a hole.' He saw no-one in the darkness below. For all he knew the voice could be that of his own common sense made incarnate. 'Come on, we haven't got much time! There is a perimeter guard on tonight and he is due in about ten minutes. Make your way along the top, there is a tree on the other side, you should be able to get down from there.' He was torn between making the leap anyway and following this unexpected advice. For all he knew it could be security preparing to surround and entrap him. If the latter case was true he was as good as trapped anyway. He told himself it would be better to be recaptured as an able-bodied prisoner than saving them the trouble of torturing him by smashing himself to pieces against the rocky cliff. He followed the apex of the roof and began to make his descent. The house appeared empty and he followed its wall to the foot of the fence. In the darkness he could hear the sound of wire snips. He could just about make out a shadowy form on the other side.

'Come on, we'll talk later.' A round hole of wire was pushed flat and he worked his way through, the stranger's hands guiding him through the clawing barbs. In a moment they were running along the side of the old quarry and up into the shelter of the tree line.

'My name's Brian, I've been watching you for a few weeks. You were right to make your escape now, things are hotting up.' He scampered up the hill into the darkness. Daniel kept close on his heals. Who was this lad who had been watching from the wings and why was he trying to help him, if indeed he was? Once clear of the glowing eyes of the town Brian stopped and turned to face him. 'I'm on a bit of a mission, perhaps you can help me. It might be dangerous, but we've got to try to help the others we have left behind'. He had called them the others, it seemed somehow misplaced and melodramatic. Daniel had never felt great solidarity with the gifted- they were, for the most part, just a group of people thrown together. He had never felt totally comfortable in their presence. Perhaps it was just because they were older, perhaps it was a side-effect of the gift. Now he was being asked to think of them as comrades. Perhaps the world had changed in his absence, perhaps these people would have to become his surrogate family. He wondered where his family were now. It had been a while since he had heard from his mother or Uncle Edward. Now he was free and standing in the middle of a

375

woodland clearing in the middle of the night with a complete stranger who had apparently been studying him from afar; it did not bode well. He did not know what was to be asked of him, but instinctively he knew he owed this lad something. He would offer his help in the first instance and then try to find his family. He and Brian shook hands and ran off into the night. The castle gazed after them, but apart from the clatter of pigeon wings and the dismissive cackle of a nightjar their flight went unnoticed.

EIGHT

Sergeant Phillip's hands were shaking as he primed the device. He was not fully briefed on how it worked, but of course it was not necessary for him to know the intricacies of the thing, only how to set it up, set it off and deactivate it. It was so small, just a thin metal cylinder, it weighed a hundred and fifty grams and looked for all the world like a slimline vibrator. (They called them Rumsfeld's Pleasure Members in the barracks.) It was not something he would want to find in his own bedside cabinet. He rotated the end of the cylinder, penile thin, silky smooth and rolled it in his hands. He took another slim device from his pocket, typed a few numbers into its small keyboard and waved it over the cylinder. It vibrated appropriately. His hands were still shaking as he placed it behind a radiator. He tried not to take one last look back into the room at the sleeping children. He was not sure he could deal with it. A small boy whined in his sleep and Phillips could not help himself but to glance across at him. The boy was not so different from his own son who was probably asleep at his grandmother's house at that very moment. He hoped his own boy's sleep was not disturbed with bad dreams. He himself was tired and perhaps even slightly unhinged from months of disturbed sleep. Strangely it was not the death of his wife itself that filled him with horror and self-loathing, it was the fact that he had not been there to prevent it happening that was the core of the problem. He had been away in southern Russia, guarding a pipeline from fundamentalist insurgents. He could have come home a week earlier, but he had been flirting with a local girl who worked behind the bar and had stayed a few extra days just in case the

377

promise of her eyes was matched by the rest of her. It had all come to nought, of course, such things invariably did. She was probably living it up with a navy boy now, fluttering those long eye-lashes to gain special favours or dispensation for a locked up relative. Everyone seemed to want something, nothing was given for free.

He had returned to an empty house; his timing could not have been worse. There was a note on the table, left by the police: a name and a number and that was all. The intruder had not broken in, there was no sign of a scuffle or violence. His son had been asleep upstairs and had not been woken. The police refused to confirm or deny his suspicion that the man had known his wife. He did not like to think too closely about that, but it was a possibility. Walking out of the hospital, having seen her cold, staring blue eyes (he had never realised until that moment quite how remarkable her eyes were) and hugging his son to him in the car park had been the worst moments of his life. The doctors said she was not dead: it was some kind of vegetative state. It was possible that someday she might completely recover, wake from her trance as if it were just a dream, but it was no dream. He had lived a nightmare and he had decided following those terrible initial moments of horror that someone would pay for that nightmare. It was shortly afterwards that he had been approached by special forces.

He had not wanted to return to work too soon; he said he needed to spend time with his son. They had approached him sidelong; he realised now that they had been testing him, delving into his mental state, assessing his anger. They said that the best way to get over his anguish was to be pro-active, to do something about it, to make a difference. He saw a significant increase in his pay- 'a little bit extra for his boy'- and they had started to tell him what they knew about the gifted. They told him there was a government paramilitary unit that had been set up to do something about them, to make a difference before it was too late. The gifted had infiltrated the highest levels of government and the military itself. They had been identified, and were being slowly moved aside, but it was not easy and the group were working under the most intense secrecy. He had never had to deal with special ops and the softly spoken words and the thoughtful discussion mixed with new and terrible knowledge was a heady mix.

The gifted were increasing in number, they were monsters who fed on the vulnerable. They had to be stopped and the best way to do that was to get them when they were young. He would not be killing innocent victims, they were all part of a separate breed, something non-human, something 'other'. His wife had been a victim and there were thousands more. The gifted were subtle, quick and persuasive. They looked like us, had lived among us for years, but they were not human. They would kill us in less time than it took us to draw a breath and all to satisfy some bizarre pleasure they obtained in the killing. A gifted child was a baby monster. It was a war of self-defence and survival and the human race could lose if it did not act immediately. He had heard all this before, of course, the papers had been full of such stuff, but he had not seen the pictures, watched the movies and seen the shimmering air and strange ecstasy of the gifted as they fed.

Van Helsing had steadied the faltering hands of his friends as they had knocked the stakes into the blood-filled heart of their transformed beloved. He did not know exactly how the virus would take hold on the children. It would be released in a droplet aerosol into the room, infecting everyone in the enclosed space. The capsule would then spontaneously combust, starting a small fire which would destroy all evidence of its existence. Unlike the vanquished vampire, these sleeping children would not see the face of the man who sealed their doom. He had been assured that death would come swiftly. The virus was short lived and non-replicative, each individual viral particle was carefully sculpted, primed and packaged, a tiny box of such exquisite intricacy that Fu Manchu himself could not have imagined it: molecular death wrapped up in a microscopic jewelled case. The molecular biologists were the craftsmen of the day; as a master watchmaker could fashion a timer for a bomb, so too a geneticist could design a bio-weapon.

He looked round the room a second time. The boy was still stirring, perhaps the gifted had dreams the same as our own. He walked close to the bed. The boy did look uncannily like his own son. Presumably though this boy still had a mother that recognised him. The boy twisted and rolled over, whimpered and was silent. Phillips resisted the urge to tuck him in. He took a deep breath and tiptoed to the exit. There was no rush, the device was primed for an hour.

As he slipped out of the compound he was unobserved. A carefully planned gap in the security protocol gave him a twenty minute window and strangely all cameras were busy scanning other exits from the enclosure.

An hour later a thin jet of moist air was injected into the rising convection current from behind the dormitory radiator. Thirty seconds later a control circuit became white hot igniting the aluminium cylinder containing it. Twenty minutes after that a young boy was woken from his sleep by a fit of uncontrollable coughing.

NINE

The pilot of the Cessna Skylane was not far out of Caernarfon airstrip. It had been an easy flight and visibility was surprisingly good. You could not always guarantee such conditions in this part of the world. As the hills rose up, the clouds seemed to reach down to touch them. Fields and farms, hills and valleys stretched out beneath them. If God took a hand in the design of the world he would have to observe his creation from a great height above.

On days like this, flying was a pleasure: the plane was behaving nicely and the aircraft powered along confidently as its shadow hugged the ground below. The pilot contacted the airstrip and gave an ETA and bearing. He then phoned his wife and gave her another ETA. He secretly hoped it would represent 'estimated tea-time arrival' but his wife's job was more demanding than his own and the tea arrival time would no doubt depend on his own culinary exertions.

He was thinking about what to cook when something caught his eye: a shimmer in the air, crackling blue on blue in the sky ahead. He tried to establish if it was truly a phenomenon outside the plane, or merely a trick of the light on the plane windows. There was definitely a tenuous vibration there, it most probably represented a change in the air density, a thermal boundary. He had no choice but to enter it- to avoid it would require aerobatic skills which he would have loved to possess, but sadly did not.

He braced himself for acceleration. A reduction in air density might send the plane into a stall, he would have to be careful. He was in it before he had even realised he was close.

He thought he heard a loud thud before he lost consciousness, but as he came to he realised it had been the sound of his own hand flying backwards and upwards to punch himself in the jaw. He was aware of incredible forces on him and the plane; he was in some kind of tight spin, the dials whirled around, compass, horizon and altimeter all in Dervish disarray. He was groggy and confused and suddenly incredibly cold. The plane tipped up and away and the reality of his situation sent his mind into free-fall, for there in front of the plane window was the curve of the Earth. The horizon span wildly away and left him in a silent nightmare of giddy confusion. He grabbed at the controls in blind panic, had he fallen asleep? Was it possible that his plane had climbed to some ridiculous altitude? No, it didn't make sense, it was impossible in a plane such as this; he could have never attained such a height. The engine had stalled and he was suddenly aware of the silence. He was spinning on the edge of space with no means to fly back in. He pulled at the rudder in mounting manic horror. This could not be happening, it simply did not make sense, it had to be some horrible dream. The horizon hove into view and was just as quickly gone again, a thin line of glorious blue, delineating the world of terrestrial life from the emptiness of space. He could clearly see the stars now as his eyes became accustomed to the light. The cold was becoming unbearable and he was also having difficulty breathing when suddenly he felt another thump. There was a flash of cerulean as if the line of the horizon had suddenly exploded across the dashboard and he found himself staring at the fast approaching ground. Every element of his being recoiled in horror. The sound of air rushing past burst into his awareness like a physical slap. As his fore-brain reeled in vertiginous panic his hind-brain reminded him that he had at least to try to fly the plane. He attempted to fire-up the engine as the world tumbled and spun, valley and sky, valley and sky, his two favourite things blurring into a terrible oneness. The engines coughed and then miraculously fired up, their throaty roar barely audible above the scream of the air around the fuselage.

He pulled in desperation at the controls and somehow converted his hurtling tumble into a tight barrel roll. His mind was spinning in a maelstrom of its own. Try as he might he could not pull the plane out of its dive. The harsh inevitability of this rolled over him like a wave and his thoughts suddenly became peaceful. He had seen the Earth from space, he had done something that few other humans had achieved. The whirling horizon, the spinning dials no longer worried him. Time dilated and slowed each breath, each heart-beat rising in crescendo and then fading away. It was the cycle of things, life and death, he was not afraid. He thought of his wife, his children and concentrated on the trajectory of his flight path . He would impact in an empty field behind a white farmhouse. As it roared towards him he could make out details. The farmhouse had a slate roof, a small garden, roses around the door, a washing line, an old tractor. The field where he would impact was bordered by stone walls. There were a few healthy trees (he could not make out what they were) and a few bleached, dead ones. It was into the arms of one of these that he was about to crash. Movement caught his eye from the path leading to the farmhouse (he was so much closer now). There was a child playing in the garden, a toddler on a painted tricycle. He could not make out the child's face, but it would be turned towards the plane now. He hoped the child would not be frightened. He worried for an instant that the child might be injured, by his imminent impact, but it was unlikely, there would be a fireball, black swirling smoke and an almighty crash, but the child would be sheltered by the building. In the instant before the end he saw several black rooks take flight from the tree. They must have let out a frightened cry before take off, but of course he could not hear it. It was unlikely that they would escape the blast. The ground rushed up.

TEN

'What exactly do you expect to find?' Daniel's voice was a low whisper in the darkness. They crouched behind a low wall on a hillside overlooking what appeared to be a large farm. The earth was musty with the smell of sheep and herbs, the stars were visible in the night sky all the way down to the curve of the hill.

'We think this is some kind of military headquarters. Apparently the farm has been deserted for a while. A few weeks ago I saw maybe a dozen Land Rovers here and some heavy equipment. I reckon it is all hidden in the barns. I want to get some photographic evidence for my contact. We think the army plans to attack Denbigh, to make it look like a terrorist attack. The GIOI people, you must have read about it.'

Daniel shook his head. 'We didn't get all the news on the inside. I guess our families didn't want to frighten us.'

'Or perhaps the authorities didn't want you to know so you could try to do something about it!' Brian hissed through his teeth. 'I should have been in there with you, I was lucky. They have been trying to find me for months apparently, but hardly anyone knows where I'm hiding out. I got here before they blocked all the roads. I was lucky.'

'But why did you come here? Why not escape, to Bermuda or something?' Daniel studied Brian's face in the darkness. 'I think I'd have wanted to get as far away as possible.'

'I wanted to see what was happening, and besides, I've got friends to hide me here. I thought I could help. You never know, perhaps we might. Shuuussh!'

A light appeared in the doorway of the farmhouse and several men stepped out. Lighters flickered, briefly illuminating their faces. The orange glow of their cigarette ends were visible in the darkness. Loud voices could be heard from within the building. The TV was on: they were watching something which involved a lot of shooting.

'We need to get into the barns to have a look but it all depends on the level of security. They don't seem too worried, there aren't many of them milling around, perhaps they don't expect any trouble. Wait!' From the edge of the barn they heard a low growl and then a bark. A gruff voice shouted and there was a tinkling of a chain. 'They are patrolling the ground with dogs! Shit.'

The new figure was illuminated by the weak light from the house. He approached the smokers and they all laughed. One of the men spoke to the dog and it barked loudly, they all laughed again. Another figure approached with another dog and what looked like a rifle slung across his shoulders.

'So there are at least two. This isn't going to be so easy.'

'Have you never freaked a dog?' Daniel whispered, 'It's easy, but it would help if we both did it together.'

'I don't know what you are talking about.' Brian looked back at him whilst ferreting through his rucksack. 'I've brought aniseed and stuff to leave a false scent trail. My girlfriend's father is a hunt protester, and I've got a crowbar to have a go at the windows, but that's about it.'

Daniel looked back pityingly. 'You have missed out not being on the inside. I learnt a fair bit whilst I was there and it wasn't all music theory. Come on, I'll show you, but we need to be closer. In fact, if we can get very close I might be able to weaken the guards. I'm not very good at it, but I'll try.' He was about to follow the line of the wall down the hill, but Brian grabbed his arm.

'Are you serious? Do you think you can actually screw them up, from a distance?'

'Yes of course I can, can't you? Has no one ever shown you how to focus the gift?'

Brian looked away, for some strange reason he felt

embarrassed and slightly afraid. 'I... er... I don't know how to do anything, to be honest I wasn't sure I believed any of that stuff. I'm not sure I have the powers.'

'This isn't the best place to talk about it.' Daniel felt somewhat embarrassed. How could he explain this to the older boy? It didn't seem right somehow that he should be the one to teach him. It was something you just learnt by watching others closely. The boys in the dorm had shown him a fair bit, but they were older and it was something you just had to learn about in private. 'You'll learn, it takes time and a bit of confidence, for some people it's really painful, and maybe it puts them off. We call them 'negs' in the camp. For others they get a kind of kick out of it, we call them 'pozies'. They are the ones you have to watch because they get addicted to it. They can't help it, and want to borrow time from everyone. The negs and the pozies didn't mix very well in the camp. We kinda have a problem with each other.'

'And what are you?' Brian was looking at him in a different light now, he was five years older than this boy, but he suddenly realised he did not know anything about himself. There was a world of which he was a part but of which he had not even the slightest idea about.

'I'm a neg. Its weird, the gift comes to me when I'm emotional; it's like a dull pain. I get it when I play the piano. I've always had it, but I can control it better now. Come on, I'll show you, let's get closer.' He turned and slid away down the hill. Brian followed close behind. He wished he had heard about this a bit sooner. Was he a pozie or a neg? He had to be a neg. He had never felt any particular highs or lows, but then he had not knowingly used the gift. It was all a bit confusing. He slid down the steep grass, suddenly incredibly self-aware. He felt good, he felt excited, but perhaps this was just the fear. He gripped the cold metal of the crowbar. He hoped he'd only need it for jemmying open a window.

ELEVEN

Margaret woke from a disturbed and wild sleep. In her dreams she had been floating with her beloved Michael. The sun had been hot on their bodies and they had been gently floating downstream. The water was warm, like it might have been on St Vincent, but Michael had never been there and the last time she had played in those waters she was a child herself. Michael's eyes were closed, and he floated on his back. Behind the serene expression were flashing eyes and a big smile. She knew that, he did not have to show her. She rolled over onto her own back, for some reason she found it harder to float this way. Perhaps it was because she was alive. The black thought sent a shudder through her body. Her poor Michael was dead and the waters that had taken him were the muddy, cold waters of the Thames. The sky had seemed to darken then, a big cloud taking the heat and the light. The waters had flowed faster and Michael had been carried away. She had tried to follow, to swim after him. In her fear she had called out to her husband, but had realised that he had gone years before. Her arms whipped the water into white spume, but Michael was gently sliding away. She felt hands from beneath, hands which slid up her ankles, calves and thighs; she wanted to scream, to waken Michael, to beg him for help, but Michael was dead. She found herself pulled beneath the water, the sunlight pooling to a distorted halo and then sliding away; she screamed but only swallowed water. Something told her not to look back, not to look down, but she could not help herself. In the darkness beneath her, climbing up her body, moving closer and closer was a grinning face, but it was

387

not the angular face of Kevin Masters that approached, it was Suzi, her own dear Suzi, eyes wide, mouth open to reveal hundreds of tiny, sharp teeth.

The curtains were drawn and daylight flooded in.

'Yo poor woman, I had to wake yo, you were workin' yoself into a terrible state in yo head, dear.' The nurse beamed down at Margaret, another ray of sunshine in the room. 'I've put yo tea on the cabinet and there's a paper, but don't go readin' it til you 'a waked up proper now.' Margaret thanked her and the ray of sunlight bustled from the room. The dreams had been coming thick and fast. But morning always brought clarity and calm. That terrible man had invaded her thoughts too many times, she had thought about what he had said time and time again. She was a victim, her kind were food for his own kind. She shook the thought away and took a sip of tea. Its warmth dissolved his grip on her heart. He was gone now but she still saw him in these recurring nightmares; but why should his place be taken by Suzi? It was nonsense. That girl was a blessing, her solace and consolation- why should her mind play such cruel tricks on her now?

Margaret wondered where Kevin Masters was now. He was probably looking for other victims, other vulnerable people like herself. She had spoken to the police, and they had told her he was being hunted. As Margaret thought of his cold eyes staring at her, his arrogant taunting, his slippery words, she wanted him to be stamped out like a poisonous snake. She wanted his kind to be burnt from the Earth. Then she caught a glimpse of the newspaper, a pile of children's bodies, boys and girls in pyjamas, faces turned away from the camera, dark stains, white coats and black masked police. She thought of Suzi and wept for them all.

TWELVE

The boys ducked down in the hollow behind a wall. To remain unseen they had had to struggle through the danker recesses of the farm. In the darkness they had stumbled through briars and nettles, cow muck caked their legs and Daniel could feel water and goodness knew what else penetrating his shoes and socks. The night was full of noises and their senses were electrified and acute. A fox screamed in the darkness and the two guard dogs lazily looked in its direction.

'Concentrate on the German shepherd; I'll try the Doberman.' Daniel whispered in the darkness.

'I don't know what to do!' Brian hissed back.

'Just reach out to him, with your mind. Try and touch him, with your thoughts... It'll all come naturally, you see. It doesn't hurt them, just upsets them, they do strange things.'

The animals were some two hundred yards away. There was little wind, but what there was was in their faces. Brian was not too keen on dogs. He was not sure he wanted to reach out to this one in any way. He was happy hiding behind the wall. He looked at its shaggy back, black and grey, muscles tense under sleek fur, ears alert to the slightest sound, nose quivering. It would be on them in an instant if the wind should change direction. He thought of it, teeth bared, its black maw, spittle flying, leaping over the wall. He thought of the dog next to it, angrily barking, snarling and pulling at its leash. He was filled with horror. What was he doing here? What was he thinking? He was not some kind of secret agent. He was just a kid hiding from the authorities. Maybe he should give himself up?

The thought flashed through his head, and as it did so the dog turned to look directly in his direction. The yellow eyes flashed in the light from the window, and the jaw dropped. Brian ducked out of sight, but as he did so he knew he was seen.

'Oh my God, oh my God, oh my God!' He started mumbling to himself. He felt Daniel's hand on his shoulder.

'Shhh. Don't worry, it will be alright. Trust me.'

Brian looked up at the younger boy and saw he was now looking directly at the big grey dog. His eyes were closing and he looked like he might be going into some kind of trance. Suddenly he shook, a sharp flinch as if wracked by a sudden and stabbing pain. It was accompanied by a sudden snarling and savage barking from beyond the wall. Fear flowed over Brian like a wave. The dogs would be on them in a second. He was about to make a run for it, when he felt Daniel's hand again, gripping him tighter.

'Don't run or the men will see you. It's all under control.' The snarling was deeper and angrier now and Brian slowly raised himself up to look over the ragged line of the wall. The German shepherd was straining at his leash, its eyes were closed and its hind limbs were scrambling wildly, but its forelimbs were supplicant and flat on the ground. Its big grey head was rubbing the ground from side to side, as if trying to rub something from its jaws. It growled and gurgled whilst its handler tried to drag it upright. The Doberman suddenly started jumping around it, excitedly, mimicking its postures and barking angrily. Its owner frantically tried to pull it away, but it was a powerful dog and it was as much as he could do to hold it. The air shimmered and Daniel's head whipped back as another surge of pain seemed to crash through him. Both dogs were now writhing on the floor, their hindlimbs upright, tails erect, but their forelimbs deflated and collapsed, their heads insensate, lips and tongues dragging through the dust. Brian slipped down beneath the wall and Daniel moved down towards him.

'They'll go crazy in a minute, they always do.' He whispered. 'If you don't like dogs, you might want to look away.

390

They can get a bit carried away.' The guards were shouting at their animals to get up, chains jangled, more voices were raised. The dogs foamed at the mouth, like cats who have tried to bite a toad, spittle flew. The taller man gave the animal's chain a vicious pull and bellowed at it to stand up. The dog turned and leapt at him, its spume-dripping maw clamped on his arm and the radius was pulled, like a great white lever from his forearm. He screamed and staggered back, the dog still gnawing the bone, trying to disentangle it from the gory mess which was his arm. The furore had disturbed those within the farmhouse and the door was flung open, the sound of Hollywood gunfire and screeching tires suddenly thrust out into the evening air. A young soldier took in the horrific scene but the other dog leapt at him before he could withdraw, knocking him off his feet and back into the building. The door banged shut and the sound of screaming from inside was muffled.

'Let's get a look at the barns whilst they are busy' Brian touched Daniel on the shoulder. 'Dangerous things, big dogs.'

They slipped down the last few metres of the grassy incline and scurried across the sticky concrete of the farmyard. Even though there had been no animals on the site for some time, the rank odour of cattle filled their nostrils. They slipped into the shadow of a milking shed. To their surprise the doors were ajar and they cautiously entered. The barn was in total darkness and they could not tell if it was full or empty. It was of metal construction, thin galvanised sheets hung on a skeletal frame. The structure buzzed with the slightest wind and distorted and amplified the sounds of groaning, shouting and sobbing which came from outside. Two gunshots in short succession suddenly rang out. Their retort echoed around the barn, shimmering into silence. Daniel felt Brian's hand on his shoulder. 'We should get a move on. I don't think they'd be too happy to see us in here.' A pool of light appeared at their feet as he fumbled with a torch, the light slid across the floor and caressed the surfaces of the numerous vehicles parked inside. The milking stalls had been dismantled and the barn appeared to be full of outsized military vehicles. They quietly investigated them, searching for clues as to their purpose. Several trucks were loaded with green metal boxes in various sizes.

'Do you know what you are looking for?' Daniel whispered as Brian struggled with a metal catch. 'I know nothing about weapons; they could be anything for all I know.'

'I've been swatting up on the Internet, I just want to get an idea of numbers of rockets and stuff and to find out who these people are.' The catch sprung open, the sound of metal on metal horribly amplified by the sides of the barn.

'Keep the noise down! I don't want to get shot this evening!'

The pool of light illuminated thin pale sticks of explosives and primers sitting like uncooked sausage meat in the padded case.

'There are no markings, nothing to identify anyone, on the equipment, on the lorries or on the weapons.' They cracked open several more cases. There were rifles, ammunition and canisters with only cryptic alpha-numerical codes for identification.

In one truck they found a cache of what looked like rocket-propelled grenades. Each blue plastic, snub-nosed cylinder still shrink-wrapped in a plastic bag. They looked like so many individually packed exotic fruit.

'Fuck me! They didn't come here for the scenery. You don't seriously think they would have used this lot on us do you?' Daniel's voice betrayed a hint of nervous horror. We are only kids for God's sake.' As the torch lit up box upon box of weapons he felt his pulse-rate rise and the blood rush to his face. It was true. This was all meant for them. Someone was going to kill them all, explosives to start, a cleansing fireball and a hail of bullets and bombs to pick up any escapees. The horror of it all threatened to crush him. How could they conceive of it, how could anyone be so cruel, so callous. He suddenly felt light headed, the yellow pool of light swam before his eyes and his legs slipped from under him.

Brian turned his torch on Daniel as he slipped from the

back of the truck. As he slumped clattering to the floor he feared Daniel had been shot, but as he crouched down beside him, it was apparent that he had just fainted. Brian lowered the boy's head gently onto his rucksack and raised his legs, propping them against the side of the truck. The sullen illumination from the torch caste shadows over his young face. He looked at that moment unbelievably vulnerable.

For a second Brian doubted that they should have come. He had put them both in the path of danger; perhaps he should have come alone. If he hadn't seen Daniel trying to escape he might well have had to have done that very thing. He had however wanted the moral support, wanted the companionship and secretly he had wanted to get close to one of the gifted, to feel the presence of his own kind at close hand, to feel like he was one of them.

Now the boy was unconscious and he thought for a moment he could hear the sound of footsteps outside. Daniel began to stir. 'I'm sorry, so sorry… I… don't know… what came over me…' He slowly raised himself to a sitting position, his face, pale and wane.

'It's alright, sit still for a minute. We'll get out of here when you are ready.' As Daniel nodded in relief they suddenly found themselves bathed in bright light. They recoiled from the glare; a voice from the doorway told them to stay where they were and not to try anything foolish. By the time they had become accustomed to the light they were surrounded. Three armed men in camouflage and combats stood over them and for the first time that evening they felt like two young boys. Strong hands pulled them to their feet and they were stripped of their belongings. When Brian tried to speak he was silenced by a slap that sent him reeling.

'Shut the fuck up and put your hands on your heads. Are you alone here? What did you think you were doing?' The man's voice was harsh and angry, but tinged with fear and self-doubt. Brian looked back into bright, nervous eyes. The soldier was not much older than he was. He looked at his feet. It would be better to say nothing. The soldiers looked at their commanding officer and at each other, clearly at a loss to know what to do with them.

'Tie them up and throw them in the back of the truck. We'll take them with us when we move out tomorrow.' The youngest of their number moved forward hesitantly. 'They are only kids, Sir, can't we just leave them here?'

'Shut up for fuck's sake! Just do what the fuck I told you. Do you think we are going on a picnic tomorrow soldier? These aren't kids, these are animals. I thought you understood that soldier, I thought you were with the program. This fucker is sucking your brains out as you are standing here. Aren't you, you little runt.' He pushed Brian ahead of him towards the back of the truck. Brian spun round to glare at him but was struck again and fell to his knees. Daniel moved to support him but the young soldier was too quick and pushed him roughly aside. The fear rose up in him again and he felt a sob rise in his throat. The air around him suddenly seemed thicker, time dilated and he felt the gift rising within him.

It was in this state that he saw the figure stepping out from behind the truck. He was heavily built, dark and with eyes that flashed black in black in his direction, a flash of concern, a slow nod.

The figure stepped into the circle; he moved with purpose, the air around him crackling blue. Guns were lifted, slowly, slowly, mouths dropped, eyebrows raised, comic surprise burst through the tight-set jaws. The first punch was a short left-hand jab, it uncoiled and twisted, found its mark on a slackening jaw, struck and followed through, flesh rippled away from the impact, bone resisted then splintered. The second punch was a cross, snapping out from his right hip, his upper body twisting, muscles tightening and relaxing in contra-rotating waves. The fist crashed into the young soldier's face, exploding his nose into a florid red splash. Brian saw the force of the impact move down the boy's spine, the head whipped back, the neck twisted, upper then lower back rippled, hips shot forward, lifting thighs and legs. He was knocked cleanly from his feet, arms and legs snapped forward as the universe imposed its laws where it could, his gun left his hands and was momentarily airborne. The twisting cyclone that was Miguel began to uncoil. His fist withdrew, the sinews unwound, eyes moved up and back. He pulled the gun from the air and grabbing the barrel swung it back and down into the chest of the remaining soldier. The man's ribs and the plastic butt of the gun splintered and cracked. The gun's magazine shattered and span off trailing silver and brass bullets behind it in an expanding Catherine wheel, a whirling form that mirrored the explosion of limbs and figures as they were thrown outwards by Miguel's fury.

As his anger dissipated, the booming clatter of bullets falling onto the concrete floor gently slid in pitch to become a ringing tinkling of metal. The crunch of flesh on stone yielded to silence. Two perfect punches. The motor memory felt so good, a surge of endorphins passed over him. Sweat leapt to his skin; his breath was drawn in as his heart stirred the coursing blood. Time re-imposed itself and with it the reality of three more devastated bodies.

Miguel looked down at them. They were all still, knocked unconscious perhaps, their minds possibly damaged by the temporal distortion. He did not have time to find out more.

The sound of a large diesel engine bursting into life dragged his thoughts together. 'Come on, we have to warn the others.' The boys looked at the man standing, panting before them. They felt the power coursing through him, felt him drawing on their own gift, his heart pulsing with theirs, his anger driven by their fear. They followed him in silence as they ran towards the truck. An attractive blonde was sitting at the wheel. A soldier lay unconscious by the driver's door, two halves of a broken pick-axe handle lay cross his motionless back. They jumped up beside her as she threw the vehicle into gear.

'I'm Suzi, this is Miguel'. The big Frenchman smiled shyly. 'We are here to help you. We really must get to Denbigh as soon as possible. I think things are going to get dangerous around here pretty soon. We'll drop you off as soon as we can, but first I think we need to get a little distance up the road.' Brian tried to speak, but he was silenced by a look from Miguel.

'You have done enough tonight. Your next mission must be to get as far away from here as possible.' He put his arm over Daniel's shoulder. 'Your uncle is not far up the road behind us. I'm afraid I don't know what the future is going to bring for us. But it might be best if you found him. Daniel looked back at their two unexpected saviours.

'I think we are probably in the safest place right here.' Suzi and Miguel exchanged glances and just hoped it was true.

THIRTEEN

Kevin Masters tried to raise his head but it felt as if it had been passed through a shredding machine and he slumped back, immobile. He could not remember how he had come to be there. He knew he had fed recently; his brain was still saturated with the endorphins of time dilation. He vaguely recalled meeting a family on the road, perhaps a child, he was not certain. The pleasure of the encounter persisted but the details were diffuse. An enfeebled reality was beginning to contrast more starkly with his own anabasis. He was getting progressively more powerful, but was beginning to care less and less about the consequences of such power. At this moment enrapt as he was with feelings of satisfaction he was only dimly aware of another feeling, another experience. It slowly burst through the fog of his thoughts: pain, yes, that was it. He had experienced considerable pain. He saw the image of a man in a ragged silver suit- it could be him, he was not certain- staggering from a group of slumped bodies, into the road, into the path of a vehicle: something big, something hard. It had knocked him through the air. He remembered it now; it had swatted him like a fly and had thrown him into a field. He remembered the noise of the thud, the flight, gloriously slow, hurtling through space, his very soul buoyed on the glory of his recently tasted manna. He was indestructible now, wasn't he? Wasn't he? A God among men; a man who could fly. He settled back into unconsciousness and once again forgot the pain.

FOURTEEN

There were thirty-six calls to make. Three to the newspapers telling them that there had been a threat issued by
GIOI against the children in Denbigh, three to the main
television stations telling them that an attack could be
launched at any moment, twenty-five to individual powerful family members of the children at the site in order to
spread the word and get some more vehicles on site for the
evacuation, three to the emergency services (privatisation
of the Ambulance and Fire services had resulted in a proliferation of emergency numbers), one to the head of security on the site so that should he be contacted he would not
immediately refute the suggestion and lastly one to his
friend in the medical site. This last call was most important of all as he wanted an independent witness to phone
in the terrorist threat. In the current climate of distrust
even fanatical terrorists had to have corroborating evidence before they were believed. There was no guarantee
that any of this would work. In all likelihood everyone on
the site would be killed. This realisation had settled on his
heart, a foreboding shadow that threatened to climb up
from his dark recesses and choke him. He had watched
from the church tower as Daniel had slipped away in the
night. In some ways he had wanted to follow him; to take
his chances crossing the fields and rivers. A lone fugitive
might slip through the net. He thought of the fifty murdered at Stalag Luft III and sighed. Only three of seventy-
six had made it back to safety. For this band of escapees
there would be no months of whispered planning, no
furtive cooperative dream of freedom. There was nowhere
to go. His was a civil war. For a moment he thought it

might be better just to give up and walk away, let the fire-bombs take the children in their sleep. He was certain then that this was the future that awaited them. He had watched the sleeping town beneath the old stone walls and in his mind the previously bulwark façade of the ruined castle had metamorphosed into a grinning and predatory skull. There would only be intolerance and death. There could be no other ending. The call from Suzi had only confirmed his greatest fears. He had been horrified that Brian had taken it upon himself to investigate the farmhouse; for a moment the fear had threatened to move from its place on his heart and complete his misery. He shook off this maudlin thought. If Brian could stand firm in the face of this danger, so could he. It appeared that Suzi, Miguel and the boys were not being followed directly, Miguel had seen to that, but they had not put all the soldiers beyond action. The army would doubtless attack anyway and their actions would only precipitate this sooner rather than later. They had taken the largest truck they could find, they would be at Denbigh within the hour. Manee screwed a scrambler into his mobile phone and prepared to make the last call on his list.

FIFTEEN

Chloe woke with a start from a disturbed sleep. She saw in the fading echo of her dream the walls of the castle, illuminated by an orange ball of flame. She wanted to cry and run to her mother, another echo, from a past now gone. She was a big girl now. She had lived away from home for nearly a year. She had no need to run to her mother. She would be safer here; her mother and father had said so. She would look after herself and any other little girl who was lost and lonely. In a while it would all be over and she could go home. The echo of her younger self dissipated with the echo of the dream. The streetlights filtered through the curtains, a warm orange, comforting, not the fearsome boiling heat of her dream. She looked around the dormitory for another child to comfort; but realised she was the only one awake. She rubbed her eyes gently, not wanting to emulate full wakefulness, for to do so would prevent her from slipping back to sleep when she returned from the kitchen. She was thirsty and wanted a glass of milk. Her mother had always brought her a glass of milk if she had a nightmare. Sometimes it would taste especially sweet, sometimes slightly bitter. Magic potions taught to mothers. One day she hoped she would be taught such potions. Tonight plain milk would have to do.

Pulling her cotton pyjamas about her shoulders she stepped off the bed and padded towards the kitchen. As she passed the sleeping bundles in the other beds she looked to see if any of her friends were asleep. It was strange, somehow naughty to look upon them sleeping, mouths open, eyes twitching. She looked away, suddenly shy. The kitchen had no curtain and although there was no moon to speak of the kitchen was bathed in a gentle glow from the streetlights and illuminated buildings. The town was silent and Chloe thought for a moment she might be the only person awake in the world. The fridge hummed menacingly and the door had to be wrestled opened. The light from within seemed horribly bright and she screwed her eyes up to avoid its glare waking her further. She took a bottle of milk from the door, placed it on the counter, found a tumbler and, two-handedly, poured herself a full glass. She studiously replaced the milk bottle top, placed the bottle (with both hands as she had been taught by her mother) on the shelf within and gently pushed the fridge door. The door sucked itself closed and there was only the most quiet of jangles from within. Its compressor hummed a slightly different key, but no child would have been disturbed.

She took a little sip of her milk, to prevent spillage and made her way carefully, holding her tumbler ahead of her (two hands), back along the line of beds. A child groaned in its sleep. Her friend Madelene smacked her lips and let out a long nasal whistle. Chloe saw her own bed come into view. She stopped, her feet and toes illuminated by a shaft of light form the bottom of the curtain. There was someone in her bed. It was impossible, silly, a dream, but this was definitely her bed. She ignored the figure with its rolling curly-black locks asleep with its back to her and instead concentrated on placing her glass of milk on the bedside table. Again she stopped. There, in the darkness was another, identical glass, filled to within half an inch of the top, just enough to prevent spillage. She placed her own glass next to this new one. Now she was sure she was dreaming. The child in the bed rolled over. She had a face Chloe knew well but had never seen like this before. It was her own. She slipped into the bed next to her identical twin. This was truly a ridiculous nightmare, but the dream figure seemed warm, like her mother and soon she was drifting back to sleep. This would all make sense, like it always did, in the morning.

SIXTEEN

George Norton-Smith looked at the thin piece of paper
lying on the table in front of him in a state somewhere
between shock and horror. His wife hovered at his shoulder. 'What is it darling? Not more genetic tests, it is getting
a bit ridiculous don't you think with the insurance people,
couldn't you pull a few strings with the department?'

Pull a few strings, the farce of it. He was the fucking
deputy prime-minister and they had dared, yes, DARED to
send him this abomination. The PM was slippery and far
too quick for his own good and far too bloody quick for
George's good. Norton-Smith had always seen himself as
the PM in waiting, but the bastard had hung on and hung
on. Was this his last slippery joke, had the bastard used
his wafer-thin advantage in the chain of command to play
this last sick joke on him? It was true he had been the
PM's major critic of late. The future was clear: they had to
stay in line. The Americans set the policy and they followed, that was the rule, it had been the rule for the last
fifty years if all were told. This problem was too big, to
'global' to be handled any differently. There would be tears,
there would be civil war, it was inevitable. Peace always
was part of the collateral damage in a war. The gifted were
a freak occurrence, a temporary abomination and they
would not be missed. As he thought those words the tears
leapt to his eyes. They would not be missed.

'Georgey, come on, what is it? What's the matter? It's not
your prostate again is it darling? You managed last time,
come on, tell me.' Norton-Smith rubbed his face with his
sleeve. He was not going to just roll over on this one. The
bastard would not get away with it.

402

'It's nothing, nothing.' He pushed past his wife and ran up the three flights of stairs to his office. He closed the door behind him, closed out the sounds of his family, his children fighting in the hall, the shipping forecast on the radio. He locked the door, sat at his desk, took a deep breath and phoned work.

'Michael, hello, this is George here. Could you put me through to the boss please?'

'I'm sorry George, but the PM isn't here at the moment. I'm afraid we are all off fairly soon.'

'Off, what do you mean? Off? Get Anthony on the phone now. He never misses his dispatch and he is not bloody well hiding out from me.'

'George, I'm genuinely really sorry. There is nothing I can do. You know the drill and we've got to move.' The line went dead for a few moments. 'George, we have always got on, I can't tell you how sorry I am. I really can't. I've got to go. Goodbye George.' The line clicked dead.

Norton-Smith placed the receiver in the cradle, his mouth was slack. This could not be happening to him. He picked up the receiver again. He would try the Chancellor's line.

Frantically he punched in the numbers, the codes, the departmental keys.

There was a long pause before the phone was answered. Then a voice he did not recognise came on.

'Hello?'

'This is George Norton-Smith. I want to speak to Billerbridge. Put me through to the Chancellor please, this is a matter of national security.'

'I'm sorry Sir, there is no Chancellor here. I am just the cleaner. We are packing Sir, sorry.' George smashed the receiver onto the cradle, sending the phone sliding across the smooth polished surface of his desk and onto the floor.

He sank back even more heavily than before. There had to be other options, there just had to be.

He opened his office draw and withdrew a mobile phone. He waited what seemed an eternity as the logos came and went and an icon appeared to indicate he had voicemail.

Remarkably it was a message from the Chancellor herself. Madelaine Billerbridge-Oakington had been an old friend at college. Their competition for the PMs affections and their own natural competitiveness had meant they had drifted apart, but she was basically a good-egg in George's eyes. He typed in the code and waited.

The voice message, though compressed and digitized was still remarkably familiar.

'George. I tried you at home, but they wouldn't let me make a connection. I'm afraid things have taken a bit of a bad turn. I wanted to warn you. I'm sure you will have got the message by now. You've been on the list for a while of course. We didn't all know, we haven't all been talking behind your back. I'm sorry it has come to this. I don't know if we'll ever see each other again. I just wanted you to know that at the last minute I was thinking of you and your family. I really am very, very sorry.' The message ended.

George fought back the tears and tried to return the call. The phone just hummed; there were no networks to be found.

SEVENTEEN

Kevin Masters awoke a second time. This time the pain in his limbs, the stiffness, the dehydration and the hunger were very much more real. He tried to move, to turn his head in the darkness, but his every effort met metallic resistance. As he moved something seemingly monstrous crashed and slid in the darkness, a great cacophony that reverberated in his head. He was wrapped in heavy chains from head to foot, his arms were fastened behind his back and chain passed across his throat, along his back and around his boots. Any extreme movements were met with a choking pressure across his throat. It was a miracle that he had not strangled himself in his heady ecstasy the previous evening. As his consciousness returned, he realised he did not know whether it was day or night. A sharp metal edge bit into the back of his neck and he felt his own breath, warm and acrid on his face and strange, unfamiliar painful pressure at his temples and on his cheeks. Initially he could not explain it but, slowly, he realised that his head was encased in some sort of metal box. As his horror mounted, his breathing became quicker, he struggled but the unyielding chain at his throat pulled tight and he found himself gasping for air. His lungs cried out as he sucked in his own warm spent breath. Panic threatened to overtake him again and he became limp as his energy was spent in a pitiful wail.

EIGHTEEN

The tape clicked off. Another night, another bedtime story. In her mind's eye she looked up at the suspended body of a young black man, foreshortened and looming, out from the shadows. The rope twisted, the tense squeal of rigging, his feet, marking out the directions of the compass, south, south-east, east. Two black minute hands sweeping time backwards and then forwards, marking time he would never experience. As Aldous Huxley's thoughts disentangled from her own, Lucy opened her eyes to see the pale face of the clock in the corner of the room. She felt the slightly restrictive soft warmth of the bedcovers, one layer too many in the sultry warmth of the home. Slowly, painfully, she withdrew her arms. It took most of her strength to push her top blanket away. As she sunk back into her pillow she thought of Patrick Manee. He would be with the children now. If anyone could offer them some sort of protection it was him. She would have loved to join him, to stand at his side as the planes flew over, to run again, even if it was from under a hail of bullets and flame. She would be left to die in this bed; she was no threat to anyone. The nurses had continued to come in, her favourite one had even slipped in extra rations, possibly at some personal risk to herself. She would die slowly, but she had known that such a fate awaited her for many years. Death would be a release, if not a happy one, there were still so many stories to hear.

She must have fallen asleep because the clock appeared to have suddenly leapt forwards; several hours had passed in a moment. Outside the window a blackbird was proclaiming a dawn chorus, but dawn was many hours away.

She had heard such enthusiastic singing before, in her youth, early mornings, after wild unbridled nights on the town, sneaking back in the hope that she could catch a few hours sleep before sunrise. She had wished the birds to silence then. Not wanting them to invite the dawn so soon. Tonight she just listened enraptured.

The swinging feet of 'Mr. Native' superimposed themselves on the familiar image of the clock; time screwing, twisting, forwards and then back. Unlike so many, Lucy knew she was not just a slave to this perpetual motion. She could hold back the irresistible tide. She was one of the most powerful creatures in the universe but death would take her as surely as it harvested the bird on the wire outside. She looked at the clock, heard the coruscating trills of the blackbird, and imagined the twisting rope suspending Huxley's immobile hero high in the darkness of the lighthouse. She suddenly experienced a sense of deja vu which rolled over her like a wave of nausea. It was only then that everything made sense. The realisation was subtle, yet so obvious she was amazed she had never thought of it before.

Just as the man swung in the darkness, first this way and then that, such was the fate of all men. There was no great arrow of time, no pendulum swinging in the darkness in the heart of a universal clock. She realised now that her own consciousness imposed the order, the direction. As she lay in the dark, trapped within the confines of too many sheets and a body degraded by the passage of too many years. How fast did time oscillate from its blinding beginnings to the present day? How many times had she lived her life? How many more times would she live it before the energy of the universe was ultimately expended? And when and where would that final and ultimate end come to pass? It was an impossible question to answer, but as she was elevated by these thoughts she knew she was having them, at that precise moment, in that bed between those four walls she had come to know so horribly well, for the very first time. Space collapsed and unfolded, blossoming and re-birthing in apparently endless, meaningless cycles. Only the mind of man imposed order on this oscillation. Only the mind of man gave direction to time's flight. She imagined herself living her life thousands of times in every blink of an eye, an eye that could not look back on the past, the past which receded at the speed of light. There was no present moment, no now in which she was living, only an endlessly repeating history and an uncoiling future. Perhaps the future had already occurred and she was travelling as a passenger in this wave of consciousness that had already lived a trillion times before. Lucy tried to see into the future, to push the clock round faster but it did not yield to her will. She smiled: it was a sad smile that only she would have understood. Perhaps there was no future for her. She settled back to dreamless sleep.

NINETEEN

Manee was tired, very tired. The strange fatigue seemed to penetrate deep into his very bones. He had hardly slept for days; his night-time vigil from the castle battlements, searching the woods and glades in infra-red for any potential army assassin had been a long and lonely experience. But it was not just his nocturnal habits that had left him drained and exhausted. It had been coming on slowly over the last few days. It was not totally unexpected, but he had begun to think himself immune. The gifted had been growing in strength; he could almost see the space around them humming with their building energy. He had stood for maybe half an hour watching a group of little girls playing in the street. Dream-like, their movements seemed painted to him, Degas-vision, drifting in and out of soft focus. The effect was serenely beautiful but he had had to tear his eyes away, partly because of the suspicion his interest would arouse and partly because he was feeling weaker and weaker in their presence. Miguel had stared into his eyes, those dark eyes, black pupils floating in a dark ocean and he had told him he was gifted too, he had known, there was no question of it. Manee was sure now that this could not be true, exposure to the gifted was killing him, destroying him, the days were sliding together, and his time was collapsing in on itself. He walked slowly through the sunny streets. In a few hours the full horror of the outside world would be thrust upon the gifted in Denbigh. Their incarceration had been a cruel invention of a frightened government, but in some respects their isolation had genuinely protected them from the worst excesses of the developing civil war. Strangely, the angry mobs had not

409

descended on Denbigh as they had at some of the other camps throughout the world. It was as if the fresh air and the mountains, the sensible farmland and the woods had imposed reason on them. Manee knew now that this peace was illusory and fragile, the army were coming in force and the gifted were not in any way prepared.

As he jimmied the lock on the gas-cylinder store he felt his army-phone vibrating. He answered it as he kicked away the remains of the catch and slipped amongst the propane-gas tanks.

'Hello?'

'Manee, is that you? What the fuck are you playing at?' It was the camp Governor, he had been gone a week now, it appeared he had at last found his escape route. Manee lay back against the cool white tanks and withdrew the plastic explosives from a canvas bag.

'Nice to hear from you, Mister Langerton. Most unexpected, what can I do for you?'

'Don't fuck with me Manee, just tell me what the fuck you think you can achieve with this stunt. I gave you a chance, I forewarned you. You know I did. Now you repay me by this piss-farce.' Manee pulled out a reel of duct-tape and holding the phone to his ear with his shoulder tore off a strip.

'Langerton, I've got no idea what you are talking about. Perhaps, if you really want to talk about it we could have a meeting in your old office, I understand it's been vacated by our military friends; I saw a Humvee leaving the site last night. It's a bit strange, don't you think, considering we have had a security warning?' Manee taped the explosives to the tank, pulled a slim fuse from an inside pocket and pushed it into the plastique. What on Earth did this odious man want? He had made good his escape, things were moving towards their unpleasant conclusion, surely that should have been an end to the man's involvement.

'You don't know who or what you are playing with, Manee. You are getting yourself into deeper water than you could possibly imagine. This is your last chance to get out of there with some semblance of a life. I've checked, you aren't on the list, what the fuck do you think you are doing there? You can't help them, you aren't one of them. You are going to be killed for nothing and there is no need for it. After this is all over the world will go back to normal, can't you see that?'

Now he knew for sure. The realisation washed over him and the fatigue reinstated itself with a vengeance. For a moment he felt his vision blur, was it a tear? He wiped it away. He was tired, very tired, and what did it matter anyway. Nothing had changed. 'Don't you hear me, Manee? You are not one of them. You are one of us and you have a chance. I'm giving you back your life.' Manee pulled a small electronic devise from his pocket and connected the exposed metallic ends of the fuse to it.

'What do you want Langerton?' Manee taped the electronic device to the surface of the plastic and admired his handiwork. Neat. The phone was quiet for a minute; when Langerton spoke again his voice was calmer, quiet.

'There is a girl; she is six, one of the youngest. We have had her in the camp under the pseudonym 'Jenny Williams' but her real name is 'Chloe Norton-Smith'. She is one of the daughters of the Deputy Prime Minister. He wants to get her out. He has asked me to pull the strings. There is money involved, Manee, lots of it.' So, that was it. Word had got around pretty quick and the vultures were already circling. Manee took one last glance back at his work and then slipped out of the gate.

'She is a little girl, Manee, she is six. God damn it, if you won't do it for the money do it for her sake. She has to be the youngest one there, if you get one out alive isn't that enough?' But the line had gone dead. He threw the phone down in disgust. His other line was flashing.

TWENTY

'I can't even see the bloody road block. We could be miles away from it. What the fuck is going on?' Edward slapped his hands down onto the steering wheel and let out a long, exhausted sigh.

'Come on, no point sitting here, let's go for a walk.' Agneta opened the door and was gone. Edward switched off the engine and frantically locked the car.

'Where are you going, what, what are you doing?' Agneta was knocking on the windows of the cars and lorries ahead of them. She nodded sympathetically at the occupants before smiling and moving down the line. By the time Edward had caught up with her she was in conversation with an elderly man driving a three tonne lorry.

'And that's all you know? You don't think we can push through? How many of them are there? I see. No, I'm not sure I want to face that either. We'll have to see. Yes, thank you.' She pushed the cab door closed and took Edward's hand.

I think we are too late. These people have all been contacted directly or indirectly by Manee, he has warned them there is a GIOI threat at Denbigh, they have come to pick up their children. The trouble is the government forces have apparently blocked all the roads leading into the town. We are still ten miles away.'

'Can't we just break the line, how large is the force blocking the road? They can't shoot us all.'

'There are tanks blocking all the main thoroughfares, about 20 soldiers at each roadblock. On this road there are armoured vehicles and an army helicopter. They aren't taking any chances.'

'Some of the parents must be gifted, probably quite a few of them. Perhaps they may do something. Perhaps we could mobilise them.' Agneta looked back up the line of traffic; tired, concerned faces, some quite elderly, stared back at her.

'No Edward, I don't think these people are going to break the barricades; perhaps, if the push comes to a shove, but not yet. They don't know what they are fighting against. I don't think they realise how far this has gone.

Edward looked back at the endless line of SUVs. 'Perhaps you are right. What do you propose we do?'

They drove their car to the edge of the roadside and began the long walk towards Denbigh.

'Ten miles you reckon? Do you know the way?' Edward was already wheezing as they rounded the top of the nearest hill. The day was clear, the air crisp but with a promise of warmth.

'No, I don't know the way, but I think it will become obvious.' As she said this the two of them were almost flung to the ground as a black shape roared overhead. It was almost immediately followed by another. 'Army choppers. I guess we'll just have to follow them.' Hugging the ground, the helicopters climbed away across the valley and were gone. From their vantage point on the brow of the hill, Agneta and Edward could see the line of cars stretching away into the distance. As the black choppers passed overhead they looked suddenly vulnerable. So many cattle all in a line, patient, docile, waiting for the next thwack on their thighs to send them a pace closer to the bolt gun. Edward's hand found Agneta's and they stopped and faced one another. The wind had caught her long blond hair and it framed her strong features in a writhing golden frame. For a moment they were king and queen of all they surveyed.

'I want to thank you.' Edward spoke softly to her. 'I could not have come this far without you.'

Agneta pulled him towards her and they kissed a long, deep kiss which spoke both of affection and emotion.

413

'You are a funny man, Edward. If we live through this I think we should really get to know each other. I need a nice man in my life.' She squeezed his hand affectionately and they began the slow walk across the fields.

TWENTY-ONE

Miguel clicked the radio off. The warning had been stark; the presenter obviously nervous and horrified. The government had declared a state of national emergency. All gifted individuals were to give themselves up for immediate confinement. Any actively trying to evade capture would be shot. To the last the government had tried to disguise their motives. The gifted were described as a reservoir of avian influenza, it had mutated, it was invariably fatal to the gifted; modifying their behaviour, making them dangerous before it finally killed them. Now apparently it was becoming lethal to non-gifted individuals; anyone aiding or abetting the gifted risked imprisonment or summary execution.

'I'm gonna drop you here guys. Best to stay off the main road but if you walk parallel to it, it'll take you to the outskirts of Chester, your mother and uncle can meet you there. Here...' Suzi handed Daniel a rucksack. 'There is food and water for three or four days, a map and GPS. We really don't know what is going to happen over the next few days, best just to keep as low a profile as possible. Hopefully we'll all meet up again after this is all over.'

'Do you think there is any chance they might, you know, change their minds?' Daniel looked into Suzi's eyes. 'Can't we do something to prove we aren't a danger? Can't we do something to help, make them want us?'

'I don't know, Daniel, I really don't. People change so quickly; they are afraid of us and fear has stopped them thinking properly. Maybe, in time, they won't be afraid any more and they'll be able to think again. Until that time we just have to hide.'

'We won't make it,' said Brian suddenly. His face was ashen; the blood had slowly drained from it as they listened in shocked silence to the radio. 'You heard them. They want us all dead and everyone in the country thinks we are infectious. We have no chance.' Miguel placed his hands on the boy's shoulders.

'No, we always have a chance. You must not dwell on what they have said. Just remember the risks and be careful. This is propaganda, my friend. They want you to give up hope, to give yourself in, to do their job for them. They are frightened of us. That gives us power. We are a minority, but we are not weak. You have seen yourself what we can do and we are not alone.'

As he said the words they heard the sound of a helicopter roaring low overhead. Brian looked out the window, his eyes wide with terror.

'They are coming for us!' Miguel restrained him.

'No, wait.' He followed the flight of the chopper, low over the fields. In a second it was gone. 'They are going to Denbigh. It wasn't a military machine. It must be the press. Manee has plans for them; he wants to make a bit of a show. Now hurry, you must get away from here. There will be a lot of military around. It could get nasty quite soon. This will have changed everything.' He opened the truck door and the boys jumped out. 'No time for long goodbyes. Go on, we'll see you soon.' The boys smiled back weakly, waved and then slowly made their way towards a copse of trees. Suzi put the truck into gear and they turned back onto the main road into Denbigh. Another helicopter passed overhead.

'How do you rate their chances?' Suzi looked back at Miguel, his tousled head sunk low on his shoulders, his jacket collar turned up, he looked older and more fragile than she would ever have imagined possible.

'About as good as ours.'

'What do you think is going to happen now the army has been fully mobilised?'

416

'I think they'll just hit Denbigh with air strikes. They might use gas, who knows? You saw the arms they had back at the farm. That's just the tip of an iceberg. They won't let anyone get out alive.' Suzi suddenly dropped anchor, the truck skidded and shuddered to a standstill.

'Do you really believe that? Because if you do; we might as well make a run for it ourselves. I've got petrol for perhaps a hundred miles.'

'Suzi.' Miguel took her hand. 'Running is no good. There is nowhere to hide anymore, not in this world. Not today. They will always find you. They can track us from space, their eyes are everywhere. The only reason we are not dead already is because we are not sufficiently important.'

'But the children, don't you believe we could get some of them out?'

'Perhaps before, but that was when the government was playing a different game. They have upped the odds, changed the rules. They want us all dead and they have laid their cards on the table.'

'So why go to Denbigh?'

'So we can look them in the eye as they drop the bombs.' Suzi looked away from him. It was going to be a beautiful day. There was a cloudless sky; they would be able to see the planes coming in from a long way away.

'And you really think there is no running away?'

'No, Suzi I'm sorry. We can try if you want; but it won't do any good.' Suzi sniffed back a tear. If things had been different she would have grown old with this man.

'Let's go to Denbigh. I've heard there is a nice castle there.' She shoved the truck into gear and they continued on apace. She felt Miguel's hand covering her own on the gearstick.

TWENTY-TWO

The children began to emerge into the crisp morning light. The youngest still dressed in pyjamas and slippers were held in the arms of the eldest. Some of the children had dressed in their best clothes, others were in army fatigues and boots, ready for action. The radio message had spread through the village like a suffocating gas. The children had all felt the need to walk into the sunshine and take a long breath of fresh air whilst they could. Manee watched them emerging, blinking into the light. Small groups huddled together and sobbed.

It was a village of children, a childish ideal that looked both naïve and fragile. A few of the older young men approached him en masse. He felt the intensity of their gaze, felt the pressure of their minds. He was weak now. The news of a potential imminent attack had accelerated his decline. It had wrought a change in the gifted and Manee felt this as wave after wave of crushing nausea. The young men surrounded him and their very presence made his legs collapse under him. As he slipped and fell the tallest among them caught him and gently lowered him to the ground. The remainder moved away, their eyes searching the horizon. The sky was clear and cloudless and the purple-green hills in the distance seemed so close you could have reached out and touched them. One of the boys turned to Manee and made as if to speak but words failed him and he followed the gaze of the others out into the hills beyond. Manee breathed slowly. The figures around him seemed blurred and indistinct. He saw a young girl running down the cobbled street and almost immediately saw the same image again, refracted as if in some strange prism. He was not sure if the images in his head were real or imagined, but the expressions on the distorted faces around him made him think he was not alone in this dreamlike state. In the distance he heard a cock crow, a half-strangled car-crash of a call which seemed to echo and echo as if it emanated from the bottom of a well. He felt a gentle breeze on is face but the trees seemed to sway independently of it and in a different time. A magpie flew past, it struck Manee as somehow incongruous but in his addled state he could not understand why. The bird was flying backwards and settled, in reverse on an exposed branch of a tree. In a second it had taken off again, this time forwards, retracing its previous flight path. Another wave of nausea threatened to overcome him.

'Here they come.' One of the boys pointed to the hills to the east. The sound of the rotors reached them a moment later; three black pin-pricks against the blue, approaching fast. On the road below appeared a convoy of trucks. From such a distance they appeared like so many Tonka toys, their scale inappropriate to the road. The helicopters left them behind and dispersed across the sky like a cluster bomb. They were met by three white helicopters which suddenly appeared from the south, civilian craft, which seemed effete next to the military equivalents; they circled and dived like mating dragonflies over a pond.

'It's the press,' said Manee, looking upward. 'I had hoped they would prevent this happening, but perhaps things have already gone too far.' As if in answer to this, the black choppers began to menace their smaller siblings. A loud-hailer blared out a warning that non-military vehicles should vacate the area. A stand-off ensued with the press chopper hovering nose to nose with an Apache bristling with weaponry. The children watched, fixated and fascinated, from the ground below. Some of the smaller ones started to cheer them on. Like a terrier standing up to a Doberman the chopper dipped, reversed and advanced. Camera equipment was visible inside the bubble of the cockpit and it was clear that frantic dialogue was ensuing. Suddenly the stand-off came to an abrupt end. The military vehicle dismissively peeled away from the balletic mid-air dialogue as another swooped in from the side. There was a flash as air-to-air rockets ignited and a woosh as they were deployed. The civilian chopper exploded in a brilliant orange fireball, which unfurled into a cloud of black smoke. Flaming debris began to rain down on the untended fields around the town. The children below let out a collective gasp; some turned away, but others looked on in anger.

TWENTY-THREE

The explosion and subsequent roar of approval from the
soldiers in the vehicle woke Kevin Masters from an uneasy
slumber. He was delirious with thirst and hunger and
another stronger desire threatened to overwhelm him. He
felt hands upon his body and the rough kick of a boot to his
back. He heard the crash of chains passing through metal
loops, the click of locks, felt the twists of cramp as blood
flooded into his limbs. All external noises were muffled
and surreal from inside his metal casing, but he still
detected something from outside. It was the sweet, narcotic, the echo of his own kind. He longed to be among them;
to draw from their strength, to lose himself in the blanket-
ing warmth of their shared gift.

'Get up sunshine, we are going for a walk.' He was
dragged backwards out of the truck and thrown heavily to
the floor, his hands and feet were shackled but linked with
long chains which reached up and fastened to his heavy,
metal mask. Hands dragged him to his feet, but his legs
refused to support his weight and he was half marched,
half dragged up the slope. He could almost feel the eyes of
the children as they scanned him from the castle above.

The helicopters roared overhead and orders were barked
to the children below. Children were shouting and crying
and he heard the clatter of weapons being passed from
hand to hand. More orders boomed down, all non-military
vehicles were to halt and wait to be searched. The warning
was repeated several times and then came a terrific roar
and Kevin found himself thrown to the floor, his legs
smashed from beneath him by a turbulent rush of air as a
military helicopter passed close-by overhead. In his metal
cage he thought he might go mad as the roar of the rotors

reverberated and screamed. He heard the chopper wheel around and away, and then heard it turning back, coming in for the kill. His breath was hot on his face and his heart beat pounded in bloodied eardrums. He tried to raise himself to run, but tripped and stumbled in his chains. An animal fear had replaced the calming influence of the gift. Then the crying of the children ceased and they became quiet. He felt a hundred pairs of eyes sweep across him like a laser. Their collective stare stunned him, he felt his own gift ignited by their gaze, but he knew he was not the intended target of their anger. He heard the terrifying whine of the rotors changing pitch, slowing, slowing, until he could hear the individual swishes of the blades as they sliced through the air. The other helicopters still screamed overhead but of the one now hurtling towards him there was almost silence. He heard only the air rushing over its fuselage as it plummeted through the air. His arms instinctively tried to cover his head as he heard the first of a series of crashes. There came a screech of tyres and a sickening crunch as two trucks collided into one another, then a tremendous explosion as the helicopter impacted into the upper stories of a nearby building. For a second there was stunned silence but then the shouting renewed. Kevin found himself grabbed again. He struggled against his bonds but to no avail. All around was confusion. There came the sharp retort of gunfire, close at hand. Through the metal mask it sounded artificial, the rat-a-tat of a child's toy. He heard the crunch of boots and bones, screams and cries of pain, the rattle of gunfire from all sides and then a shout.

'Miguel! No!'

TWENTY-FOUR

From his previous hideout in the disused quarry Brian watched the unfolding battle through Manee's binoculars. Daniel watched from the base of the tree below. Their commandeered motorcycle had had to be abandoned when they lost control and skidded into a ditch. The run to the top of the hill had left them both exhausted and gasping for air. The roar of the helicopters was muffled somewhat by the thick foliage above them and plunging into the depths of the woods had been a relief. They had seen the black cloud rising over the top of the quarry as they neared it, the Apaches had roared overhead but had taken no interest in them. By the time Brian had climbed the tree he could just make out Suzi bent over the body of Miguel, the bodies of forty wounded soldiers lay slumped around them.

From the shadows of the castle walls Manee saw Miguel spin and fall. The gunshots had come from a side-street and now the soldiers began to run towards Suzi. As they passed the gas depot they raised their guns to fire again. A black helicopter roared down from above them like a falcon diving for a kill. In a state between unconsciousness and delirium, Manee reached inside his jacket, withdrew his mobile phone, and dialled a short series of numbers. The explosion was enormous.

Manee watched in awe as the flames billowed out, orange and gold tracery rolled and roared, the fire seemed to bubble and boil, ever-expanding shells of flame rippling as the shockwaves rendered the air. The diving Apache was lifted and thrown through the roof of the nearby pres-

423

bytery by the force of the explosion.

Glass showered down from every window. He waited for the deafening retort but none came. The growing sphere of expanding flame and gas slowed and paused, shimmering between the blue sky and cold perpendicular of the war-memorial in the town square. There were no screams and no crying from the children. From behind the growing fire-ball Manee saw the sky darken and suddenly a strange peace came upon him. The world became still, the tinkling glass silenced, the rush of hot air and flame hushed. The air around him was blue and shimmering as if with the heat, but he felt neither heat nor pain. He looked about him, the weakness that had subdued him suddenly gone. He saw the children, shimmering in the blue haze, he followed their eyes. The explosion appeared frozen in space, debris and flame like an exquisite glass flower reaching upwards to the sky. Then he saw him. A man standing before the flames, His head appeared to be locked into a metal cage, his arms before him manacled and chained, arms raised as if in prayer. The first snaking tongues of flame had reached out and engulfed his arms and legs and they writhed amongst a blue fire that emanated over his body. Manee could hear screams from within the metal cage but he could not tell if they were those of agony or ecstasy.

The figure swayed and fell to his knees and Manee found himself drawn towards him. All around, the children were edging closer. A little girl ran forward from the crowd and stood a few feet away, transfixed by the spectacle of this human firework. Only Suzi remained still, slumped over Miguel's prone body. Manee looked at her, his mind suddenly awash with pity and sadness. In time they would have become friends. In time he might have gone to their wedding. In time he might have seen them bring up children. He looked away, but as he stepped towards the figure he felt his strength being drawn from him again. The weakness which had threatened to overcome him returned with a vengeance. The figures around him became a blur of shadows and light. Images began to flicker and repeat endlessly, the sky seemed suddenly dark, he was not certain but he thought he might have even seen the moon high above in the sky. As he stumbled and fell he felt the guiding hands of the children supporting him. He made the last few steps and slipped into unconsciousness as he placed his hands on the back of the kneeling figure.

Suzi looked up through a veil of tears. She held Miguel's still warm hand in her own. She saw the moments leading to his death replaying in her mind: the bullets frozen in space by her own gift as she fought to reach him, twisting through space from behind him as he struck out in all directions at his assailants. She saw them hitting home, saw them burst from his shoulders and chest, saw the final flash of his dark eyes towards her as the realisation of his death came to him. They had said goodbye in that split second. Now she felt her attention drawn from him and towards the glowing fireball which threatened to engulf her. In this moment, distraught with grief, she welcomed it, but its heat never came.

She saw a familiar figure, half obscured by a crowd of children. It was Patrick Manee crawling towards the flames. Their faces were illuminated by a strange, flickering glow, in turns both warm and cold. Then there was a flash of light. A circle of blue fire expanded out through the circle, it passed very slowly through the crowd, a rippling cool orb. As it passed each figure they recoiled from it, retracting momentarily. The figures appeared blurred now, shimmering behind the approaching wall of blue. They were walking backwards, retracing their steps, hand over hand, foot over foot. Manee staggered and rose up onto his feet. He turned to face her, his face full of pity and misery, but his eyes did not meet her own. He slowly retraced his steps, always walking backwards, and slowly turned away. As the blue wave passed over her Suzi held the image of Miguel in her mind, holding her hand in his uncle's garden in France, those dark eyes looking into hers; if this was to be her last thought, she wanted it to be of him.

TWENTY-FIVE

From their look out in the quarry, the boys watched the cold explosion unfolding and followed the approach of the shimmering wall of blue light. In its depths they saw the orange glow diminishing as the gas explosion recoiled. Debris that had been ejected from the blast leapt from its resting place and, twisting through the air, placed itself with incredible precision back to where it had originated. Splintered glass rained upwards from the floor and re-assembled itself into stained-glass windows. The Presbytery roof reformed, belching the black Apache into the sky. The fallen figure of Miguel rose from his resting place and up onto his legs, as those around him rose up to meet his flying fists.

Brian dropped to the ground next to Daniel. The wall of light was moving faster now, building up speed exponentially. There was nowhere to run. The two boys held each other tight as the wave passed over them.

TWENTY-SIX

In her quiet, warm bedroom, Lilly was woken from a pleasant dream. She had been a young woman again, twenty-four, on her first assignment in France. She had caught the eye of a visiting Ukrainian ambassador and had become very much attracted to him. They had talked, had a few drinks, and he had held her tightly as the band played old folk songs. Her reverie was interrupted by the clock. The clock, so familiar, was ticking, ticking. It was moving in reverse. Lilly stared at it crossly, concentrated, and watched it slow. She held it like this for several moments, then, with greater effort, she set it running forwards, then stopped it, and then let it run backwards again. She smiled, sank deeper amongst her warm sheets and allowed herself to dream that the good old days could come again.